Lorna Cook is the author of the Kindle #1 bestseller *The Forgotten Village*. It was her debut novel and the recipient of the Romantic Novelists' Association Joan Hessayon Award for New Writers. Lorna lives in coastal South East England with her husband, daughters and a Staffy named Socks. A former journalist and publicist, she owns more cookery books than one woman should, but barely gets time to cook.

Also by Lorna Cook

The Forgotten Village
(Published in Canada as *The Forgotten Wife*)

LORNA COOK

The Forbidden Promise

Published by AVON
A division of HarperCollins*Publishers* Ltd
1 London Bridge Street
London SE1 9GF

www.harpercollins.co.uk

A Paperback Original 2020
2

First published in Great Britain by HarperCollins*Publishers* 2020

A catalogue copy of this book is available from the British Library.

ISBN: 978-0-00-832188-8

Typeset in Minion 10.5/13.5 pt by Palimpsest Book Production Limited,
Falkirk, Stirlingshire

Printed and bound in UK by CPI Group (UK) Ltd, Croydon CR0 4YY

This book is produced from independently certified FSC™ paper
to ensure responsible forest management.

For more information visit: www.harpercollins.co.uk/green

For Mum, Dad & Luke
For being family. For being there. And just because.

CHAPTER 1

Invermoray House, Scotland, end of August 1940

Sometimes it's not the biggest lies, but the little white ones that bring about the most change. Although Constance couldn't possibly have known that by pretending she had a migraine in order to escape the house, there would be such lasting consequences.

Constance sat on the edge of the large rock that jutted out over the loch and hitched her evening dress up in what her mother would call an unladylike fashion. She removed her satin shoes and peeled off her stockings, dipping her legs into the cool water, soothing her dance-sore feet. She needn't be discreet; the edge of the loch was so far from the house that no one could possibly hear her, and given the strict blackout regime the housekeeper adhered to, no one could see her either.

Constance closed her eyes and then opened them almost immediately. Her migraine had been a fabrication, although the racket the band was making was exceedingly loud and growing louder the more enthusiastic both the players and the guests became. If she strained her ears now, she could hear them playing all the way from the loch. The need to escape her birthday party, to escape Henry, had engulfed her to the point she could think of no other way out but to lie.

Over the past few months she had found herself liking Henry. She had only known her brother Douglas's friend a short while, spending time with him when the two men journeyed to Invermoray on rare days of leave. He was older than her by only a few years, and she had looked up to Henry, idolised him and found herself following her parents' lead when they suggested he might be a good match. Henry had clearly liked her, or so she believed. Constance thought he would be different, not like the other suggestive and sometimes inappropriate men she'd met, of which there had not been that many, admittedly. But he had shocked her as they danced, as she nestled into him, enjoying the closeness. His hands had crept down her back until they were resting far too low, his fingertips grazing her bottom. She had become stiff, alert and then he had clutched her. It had taken all her courage to gently move his hands when she realised his behaviour was anything but romantic.

'Henry?' she had questioned, when he had pulled her closer again. He had smiled as if he'd done nothing wrong and she doubted herself. Was she being too prudish? The silver-grey silk ball gown clung to her skin as she danced, and she had caught Henry staring at her chest on more than one occasion. He had clearly found it a challenge to listen to her conversation, to drag his eyes up to meet hers. She had begun rambling, in order to cover her embarrassment, her growing sense of disappointment. When she had excused herself to powder her nose, uncertain as to what was happening and if she should allow it, he had cornered her, pulling her into the darkened orangery, which was unlit in case enemy aircraft should spot a light through the glass panes.

Constance knew men had needs and she wasn't unworldly. She knew what those needs were and what part she'd be expected to play. While she'd been told that a girl should save herself for her husband, there were many girls at her Swiss school who had bragged joyously that they'd been up to far more than they should with the opposite sex. But as much as she thought she might eventually want it with Henry she wasn't quite sure. Not yet. She didn't want him to go off her but whatever was happening between them needed to permeate. Just a little longer. Just until she was sure.

'You look beautiful tonight,' he had said, his eyes raking her body.

And then he had kissed her, his lips crashing against hers, his hands holding her shoulders. She had tried to put her arms around his waist, her eyes wide open, uncertain if she was responding correctly, unfamiliar with how far she should let this go. His eyes were closed and he was slowly ushering her further into the deserted orangery, until she was up against an oversized hothouse palm her mother had been cultivating for the best part of a decade.

His whisky-soaked breath had coated her tongue as he kissed her harder and faster and she wasn't sure if it was this, or the realisation her skirt was being lifted that made her suddenly rigid.

'Henry!' she chastised as she pushed free of his grasp. She attempted to laugh, to brush aside his behaviour.

'Come here.' Henry held out his hand. Tentatively she had taken it. Perhaps it was simply the party spirit and a little too much to drink that had motivated him into this small bout of madness. Maybe now he realised he had been pushing her a little too much and was relenting.

'Haven't you wanted this as long as I have?' he asked, nuzzling her neck.

Disappointment flooded her. Had he noticed her reaction to him and simply disregarded it? She didn't know what to say. Until this evening she had never seen this side of him and it had confused her.

'I don't know,' she said honestly. It was all happening too fast, and not at all like she'd ever imagined. 'I'm not sure . . . like this . . . here . . . ?'

'There's nobody about. We could find a dark corner; over there looks good. I'll lay my jacket down for you so you don't get cold on the tiles.' The suggestion of chivalry was misplaced.

'No, Henry, I don't . . .'

'If you don't know what to do, I'll show you. Now come on, lie down over here.'

'No, Henry.' She was firmer now. She finally knew what she wanted and it wasn't this. 'No.'

'If you loved me . . .' he said, incensed, letting his suggestion hang.

She knew in that very moment that she did not. Disappointment had engulfed her. How could it all end like this, so horribly?

Without another word she had turned and left Henry standing in the orangery, breaking into a run until she had found safety in numbers in the ballroom.

She needed to be as far away from Henry as possible, to think. And so she had lied. *A migraine so painful she thought her head would explode.* Her mother had baulked at the picture Constance had drawn in front of their guests and excused her daughter – it was almost midnight, and guests would be leaving soon. But instead of running to her bedroom Constance ran into the cool night air, past the fountain, skirting the ornamental garden and down towards the loch in the distance where she had always found her own haven of peace and calm. No guests would brave the dark journey down to the water's edge for fear they would trip to their deaths in the blackout and miss out on the Champagne her parents were doling out from their carefully hoarded supply in the cellars under the house. She was entirely alone.

Dangling her feet into the cool water, Constance looked back through the darkness to where she could just about make out the outline of the baronial mansion. Inside were fifty or so of her mother and father's closest friends, and barely any of her own, still celebrating Constance's birthday with little regard for her absence and even less for the war outside Invermoray House.

It was no longer the faint noise of the band playing, but rather another sound that suddenly caught her attention, causing her to look skyward. A smattering of low grey cloud hid something she sensed was looming closer in the dark night sky.

It took Constance a few seconds to understand she was listening to the sound of a Spitfire engine. But far from its usual smooth whir, it sputtered and whined as if gasping for breath. She saw its outline against the darkness of the sky above and the black mass of forest on the horizon as the plane dropped from the sky. Its engine went almost completely silent before it juddered to life and then died again, the propellers slowing to a complete stop. And Constance realised the pilot must still be inside, trying to restart the engine instead of doing the sensible thing and parachuting himself to safety. Perhaps in the blackout he had no idea how close to the ground he was.

As the plane sank even further, Constance knew it was going to crash and she scrambled to her feet, moving quickly over the jutting rock in case the plane should bank suddenly towards her. But it did not.

The Spitfire came level with her before hitting the water at such a horrific angle, Constance was sure one of its wings had been ripped clean away, sending spray high into the air. Instinctively she turned away to avoid the large splashes. After the loss of its wing the plane spun and tumbled on the water until Constance didn't know which way round it was. Where was the pilot? It took only a few seconds for the weight of water to fill the vessel before the plane gurgled and disappeared below the surface; the water smothering it entirely as if it had never been there at all. There was no sign of the pilot. No noise of him swimming to safety in the darkness. The false tide from the crash lapped strongly against the rock.

She stood shaking, her eyes wide, her breaths coming in quick succession, her hands still tightly clutching her shoes and stockings. Constance knew she had to do something, but her body refused her call to action. She was rooted to the spot, staring across the water at where the plane had been. She was torn. If she ran back to the house for help there would be no time. If she did not do something, he would be dead within minutes, if not already. She had to save the pilot.

Forcing herself to move, Constance clambered down the rock and into the water, cutting her leg on a sharp edge as she did so. She couldn't feel the pain, or the blood as it trickled down her ankle mixing with the water; so intense was her need to reach the stricken pilot, who she imagined hopelessly fighting with his safety belts and the hatch above. Her silk evening dress clung to her legs as she strode as quickly as she could through the water in the direction of where the plane had sunk from view.

Inside the house the grandfather clock in the entrance hall struck midnight, and the band played on to revellers unaware of the events outside. Congratulations were passed to Constance at the close of her twenty-first birthday. *Such a shame she had felt unwell. Perhaps too much Champagne had taken its toll. Her bed was the best place for her.* Shortly the band would finish, guests dispersing – their carefully saved petrol coupons taking them the distance to their homes and neighbouring estates – and then the housekeeper would begin the ritual of closing Invermoray House down for the night.

As the water reached Constance's waist she pushed her feet off from the pebbled loch-bed and let go of her shoes and stockings, so that they drifted away behind her as she swam further into the darkness.

CHAPTER 2

Scotland, August 2020

Kate should never have said no to the offer of a satnav for the hire car. There had even been a promotional discount at the car rental desk at the airport but she had, somewhat smugly, waved her mobile phone at the clerk and explained she had a free GPS app already installed.

But her signal had dropped out long ago and with the countryside becoming even wilder she reasoned her phone data wasn't about to return anytime soon. Kate pulled the little hatchback over by the side of the road and looked around for any sign of life. Any kind of sign at all would have been nice. She couldn't remember how far she'd gone down the long B road before she had glanced at her phone and found the app unresponsive. How long had it been like that? The last village she'd passed had been at least ten minutes ago and she couldn't even remember what it had been called.

As the sun dipped in the sky, she spread the map out across the bonnet and scanned it for something familiar. Thank God someone at the car rental office had placed one in the glove compartment. She would be arriving much later than she'd said she would. It would be the worst kind of first impression, turning up for her new live-in job as night was falling. There was no way

Kate was going to find her way in the dark so she was just going to have to keep heading down the road in the hope it would lead her to civilisation where she could get some sort of data reception on her phone. *You don't get this sort of nonsense in London,* she thought. Although London was the last place she wanted to be right then. She glanced up and down the desolate road. She'd wanted peace and quiet. But maybe not this quiet.

Kate folded the map up as best as she could, but it was a poor effort and she'd managed to fold creases where there hadn't been any a few seconds ago. She started the engine and drove, holding her phone in one hand, and somewhat dangerously glancing down, hitting refresh on the app every few minutes. There was still no joy. She needed to restart her phone in a last-ditch effort. She glanced down, holding the off button an interminably long amount of time until it gave the chance to swipe to confirm that yes, she really did want to turn the phone off.

As Kate glanced back up she screamed. A man was standing at the side of the road facing her, his mouth open with horror as she drove towards him. What was he doing in the road? He lifted his hands up to shield his face. At the very last second Kate dropped her phone, turned the wheel quickly to swerve away from him and stamped her foot down on the brake. The car skidded across the road into the path of oncoming traffic – or it would have done, if there had been any other vehicles on the stretch of inhospitable countryside road. Instead the rental car came to a stop at an angle that left the bonnet facing a row of tall pine trees at the side of the road.

She couldn't move. Her knuckles were white; her fingernails dug into her palms where she'd tightened her grip around the wheel. Kate forced herself to look in the rear-view mirror to see if the man was still alive. He wasn't there. She hadn't hit him. Or had she? She wasn't sure of anything.

'Oh my God. Where is he?' With shaking hands Kate unfurled her fingers from the wheel and unclicked the seatbelt. She went to open the door but the trouble was taken from her hands as the man yanked it open and stared angrily down at her.

She sat back in shock. His jaw was clenched and he appeared to be struggling to speak.

'Thank God, you're alive.' Her voice was shaky, her heart still thudding hard.

He stood back and gave her room to get out of the car. 'No thanks to you.'

'I'm sorry.' Kate climbed out and stood in front of him, her legs wobbly.

'You almost killed me.'

'I'm sorry. I'm really sorry. Are you hurt?'

'No,' he snapped. And then added as an afterthought: 'Are you?'

'No. I'm fine.'

The stranger looked past her and into the car at the crumpled map on the passenger seat. Kate watched him, hoping he was calming down. He looked about her age, late twenties with brown hair and brown eyes. He was dressed head to toe in running gear, with streaks of neon yellow banded around his wrists and legs. She should have seen him given this get-up, only she'd been distracted by—

'Were you on your phone?' He looked directly at her, unblinking. 'Were you texting while driving?'

'I . . . No . . . Of course not.'

He climbed into the car, knelt on the seat and bent to retrieve the phone.

'Hey, what are you doing?' she asked.

He stabbed at it a few times, but the phone was mercifully off.

'I could have sworn . . .' He trailed off and then reluctantly handed her the phone.

'You need to move your car. It's dangerous positioned like that.' He was glancing up and down the empty road.

Kate nodded but didn't move, concerned she'd just broken the law, almost killing someone at the same time.

'Can you do it or do you want me to?' He looked at her as if she was an idiot.

'I . . . you . . . I can do it. I don't mind.'

He raised an eyebrow and gave her a look that proved he was in no doubt she was a fool.

'You don't mind? Well that's just . . .' He shook his head in disbelief, stepping back and folding his arms. Kate was in no condition to drive but she got back in and managed to straighten the car and pull it slightly off the road, onto the gravel by the side. She switched her hazard lights on given that she was still on the wrong side of the road. And then she wasn't really sure what to do. The man was still standing there. Surely this was the point where both of them would leave and go about the rest of their evenings, but he seemed to be watching her expectantly.

Kate got back out of the car and stood awkwardly by the open door. She'd never been in a road accident before, not that this really *was* a road accident, but the look he was giving her made her think that if she drove on he'd have the police chasing her within minutes.

'So, what happens now?' she ventured.

'What do you mean?' He looked baffled.

'Do we . . . um . . . do we exchange details?'

He narrowed his eyes again. 'Why would we do that?'

Kate felt about two feet tall. 'I'm not sure,' was all she could say quietly. She was eager to be back in the car – so shaken she wasn't sure she could drive if she was really honest with herself but it was better than standing here with him.

'We don't need to do anything,' he said.

'OK,' Kate agreed.

His arms were still folded.

She started to apologise again but he cut her off. He glanced pointedly at his phone, strapped to a band on his wrist.

'Chalk it up to experience.' He put his headphones in his ears, fiddled with his phone, turned and continued jogging away.

Kate watched his retreating figure and when he rounded the bend she slumped against the car and exhaled loudly, relieved he was gone. *Chalk it up to experience?* How sanctimonious. What did he even mean by that? Regardless, she was thankful he wasn't pressing charges and that she'd never have to see him again. Kate looked back down the road to where he'd turned out of sight.

'What a bastard.'

She could have cried. What was she even doing here?

CHAPTER 3

Kate climbed back into the car and grabbed her handbag from where it had fallen into the passenger footwell. She took out her small bundle of good luck cards and reread her favourite, from her best friend Jenny. On the front was a picture of Kate holding an empty Champagne bottle upside down towards her mouth. She was pulling a stupid, but happy expression. It was only a few months old, but remembering the celebrations from the day she'd been promoted to senior PR manager still made her smile.

Inside the card wasn't the usual 'Good Luck' message. Instead it said, 'From drunken dare to worst nightmare. Knock 'em dead.'

Oh God, the dare. What had Kate been thinking, coming here on a whim and a dare? She couldn't lay all the blame at Jenny's door. It hadn't been Jenny's fault that Kate had quite simply had enough. If she had to turn up to promote any more bar openings with mediocre guest lists full of Z-list models and footballers' wives treating her like dirt she would have screamed. What was it about the almost famous that made them think they could talk to her and her colleagues like they were skivvies? And then when one had accused her of flirting with her husband. Well, the fallout from that had been unbearable. She knew why she was here if she really stopped to think about it. She needed to rebuild her reputation, away from the claustrophobic glare of London, her office, her colleagues, everyone who knew the awful situation she'd got herself in that night. The shame of the accusation was what had driven her here, as far away as she could possibly get. After the indignity and humiliation of the formal warning she'd received at work the next day, Jenny had drunkenly applied online for two jobs for her.

'You've always said you wanted to travel more,' Jenny had slurred, loading up a jobs website on her laptop. 'From Land's End to John o'Groats. I dare you. Where do you fancy?'

'Anywhere, anywhere, just fill the bloody forms in, attach my CV and hit send. It could be in Timbuktu for all I care. As long as I never have to deal with some reality TV contestant falling out of a bar drunk and into the lens of their own pre-organised waiting paparazzi, then it can be anywhere you like,' Kate had declared.

Jenny had hit send, they'd clinked glasses and Kate had forgotten all about it. Until a week later when a rejection email from a hotel in Cornwall had fallen into Kate's inbox. Apparently she didn't have enough experience promoting regional food and had not even made it through to the interview stage. She felt a slight pang of regret over the loss of a job she hadn't even known existed until that very moment. And it had set her thinking: maybe a change of scenery was the very thing she needed. No more awful bars. No celebrity hangouts. A chance to start afresh with her reputation intact.

And so when the second job application had proven fruitful and the owner of Invermoray House in Scotland interviewed Kate via an hour-long phone call and offered her the job at the end of it, she had jumped up and down for a full two minutes in joy.

'Not much in the way of visitors,' she had told Kate. 'Which we're hoping you can help with of course, dear. We're very out of the way up here.'

'Sounds perfect.' Kate had felt triumphant, knowing soon she'd be away from run-of-the-mill PR assignments. And it wasn't as if she had a relationship to tie her down. She'd been single for about a year and very happy about it. 'I accept.'

But now it was a different story. Lost and in the fading light, Kate had never felt so alone.

By the time she eventually found it, her satnav back up and running, Invermoray House was bathed in twilight. Kate drove down the long driveway and onto the large gravel sweep in front of the house. Her eyebrows rose involuntarily as she took in the grandeur of the building, marvelling at the way it was downplayed as a house when it was more a castle. As she pulled up, the car headlights gave the baronial building a warm yellow glow.

Kate barely had time to drag her suitcases from the boot before the large wooden front door was pulled open and a lady in her mid-sixties walked towards her.

'Can I help you?' She had kind, smiling eyes and bob-length straight brown hair.

Kate recognised her voice. 'I'm sorry I'm so late. You must be Mrs Langley-McLay?'

'Yes, my dear.' She gave Kate's suitcases the once-over. 'You aren't Kate, are you?'

Kate nodded and Mrs Langley-McLay's eyebrows knitted together.

'Then you aren't late at all, my dear. You're a day early.'

Kate's face fell. 'What? I can't be.'

The woman laughed. 'We said we'd start tomorrow, so I assumed you would *arrive* tomorrow.'

'Oh, I just thought . . .' Kate's voice trailed away.

'Well.' Mrs Langley-McLay moved forward to help Kate with her cases. 'There's nothing wrong with being keen. You take that other case and we'll see you inside. You must need a cup of tea and a sit-down after such a long journey. And then we'll see you to your room. Or perhaps you'd like a gin and tonic instead of tea? I was going to have one before dinner.'

'That would be lovely, Mrs Langley-Mc—'

'Oh, call me Liz, or else it's such a mouthful.' Liz placed Kate's suitcase by the bottom of the ornately carved mahogany stairs and indicated Kate should do the same with the other one.

Liz led her through the black and white tiled hallway, the roaring fire crackling away comfortingly in the large stone fireplace. Despite the fact it was mid-summer there was a nip in the air as dusk settled. Liz slowed down and peeked into the doorway of a room.

'Oh good, he's not here,' she mumbled to herself.

'Who isn't?' Kate asked as she followed Liz into the library. It was perhaps the grandest room Kate had ever seen. Rows and rows of leather-bound books lined tall shelves that stretched to the ceiling. A wooden ladder on wheels was positioned up against the shelves and for a moment she had a childish urge to leap onto it and slide around the room.

'Not to worry. Not for the moment. Now, let's fix ourselves a drink, shall we? Dutch courage and all that.'

Kate wondered why on earth Liz needed Dutch courage, but Liz changed the subject, asking about Kate's journey before launching into work matters.

'We've needed someone like you for quite some time.' Liz moved over to a drinks trolley and lifted the lid of the ice container. She plunked several pieces into two cut-glass tumblers. 'We're in a complete state, as I explained on the phone, so you'll be a bit of a jack of all trades while we get started.' She gestured for Kate to sit on one of two red velvet Knole sofas and she did so on the one nearest Liz, her back to the door. The sofas were worn, with horsehair sticking through, and the rope that bound the back together had once been gold but was now utterly frayed. It was a stark contrast to the leather volumes and the oversized wooden desk positioned near the French windows, which although old looked as good as new.

'Now there is a teensy issue with you arriving early. But it's nothing I can't factor in I'm sure. Only he might fly off the handle at first but his bark is far worse than his bite.'

Kate blinked as Liz handed her a drink. 'Your husband?'

'Heavens, no. My poor husband passed away a year ago. No, my son. But don't worry, because I'm sure he'll come round to it.'

'Your son?'

Liz nodded and sat on the opposite sofa. Suspecting Liz wasn't going to offer more information, Kate probed further.

'Come round to what?'

'To you, of course.'

'Me? What about me? Me being a day early?'

Liz chuckled, but it was a nervous laugh and her eyes darted to the hallway as they both heard the front door bang shut.

'To you being here at all.'

Kate stiffened as Liz continued. 'You see, I hadn't quite had a chance to tell him that I'd hired you. I was rather hoping to do it tonight, over dinner.' Footsteps sounded on the tiled hallway floor, getting closer to the library. Liz sped up. 'We were in desperate need of help and he flat-out refused to entertain thoughts of hiring someone. Says we can't afford it, which is piffle. You're an investment, of course. But he will rather blow a gasket at you being here. Terrible manners. Well . . . you'll see.'

Kate heard the footsteps stop.

'Thought I could hear voices,' a man's voice sounded from the doorway to the library.

Kate froze.

Liz spoke. 'James, I'd like to introduce you to Kate.'

Kate stood and turned slowly towards the newcomer. Before she'd even seen him, she just knew who he was. As Kate faced him, a polite but nervous smile on her face, she watched recognition pass over his expression before his smile slipped. His hand, outstretched to shake hers, dropped.

'Kate is here to—' Liz started.

'Finish me off?' James interrupted her.

Liz looked between the two of them, clearly confused. Kate wanted to die.

'We've met,' James continued. 'About an hour ago. I think it's fair to say Kate can't drive.'

'That's not fair,' Kate spluttered. 'You were on the wrong side of the road. You were *in* the road.'

'I bloody wasn't *in* the road. And pedestrians are *supposed* to face oncoming traffic.'

She was silenced.

'And you were texting,' James finished for good measure.

'I wasn't texting.' Kate was earnest.

'Oh Christ,' James flared up again. 'Is that why you're here? Did you follow me? To see where I live? Hoping to get some kind of payout, accusing me of . . . what . . . exactly? Well, I warn you we haven't got two pennies to rub together, so don't bother.'

'James.' His mother put her hand on his arm to silence him. 'Enough please. Kate is not here about that. Kate is here because we have employed her. *I* have employed her.'

James turned slowly and looked at his mother. 'You have done *what*?' His voice was dark, but Kate was relieved to find Liz maintaining her son's gaze, clearly used to holding her own in a standoff.

'I think this is best discussed outside, don't you?' The question was clearly rhetorical as Liz walked purposefully from the room. James looked at Kate and she smiled weakly with embarrassment. He shook his head in disbelief and followed his mother from the room, closing the door to the library behind him.

Kate's whole body was stiff. She couldn't believe it. She'd been hired, although not on a contract admittedly. She'd sub-let her flat to her brother, for Christ's sake. She couldn't go back to

London now, tail between her legs on day one of her new job. What if James overruled Liz and sent her packing, which he was clearly about to try? Where would she go at this time of night? There was a pub down the road. Maybe they had rooms, although out here in the middle of nowhere Kate doubted there was need for a pub with rooms to rent. She slumped back down awkwardly on the overstuffed sofa and tried not to listen to the muffled argument on the other side of the door.

The phrases she could pick out were in James's thunderous tones. '*No money . . . can't afford her . . . don't need any help . . . can do it on my own.*'

She exhaled loudly as she listened to James not handle the situation at all well. There was nothing she could do. She just had to await her fate. Kate looked around the walls at some surprisingly modern artwork and then spied a large book open on a table in front of one of the bookshelves. She wandered over, more for something to direct her nervous energy towards than out of any actual interest. It was an old Bible, the pages wafer thin beneath her fingers. She'd never been particularly religious and after reading the first few lines of the open page she gently closed the hefty book to look at its front cover. The title lettering had faded but she could tell it had once been gold. The black leather cover was crumbling in a few places, particularly the spine, its threads showing bare. She looked around – threadbare appeared to be a running theme in this room. Kate opened the cover slowly and carefully turned a few pages until she reached a page showing the *Family Record.* Trying to forget the argument outside, she became engrossed in what must be the Langley-McLay family Bible.

The names of the family members varied in colour, the ink of the earlier ones now faded sepia, the more recent names still black. The dates started in the early 1800s and the italic looped and swirled handwriting changed as each new family member's name was recorded with his or her birth date.

Kate thought of the generations of children who had come and gone, grown old, married and moved away, gone to war and died, lived and inherited before passing it on to the next in line. She glanced at the second page of the Bible, as the dates moved into the First World War. One child was born soon after the war: Constance Amelia Rose McLay, born August 1919.

But what struck her about this name over all the others was the black fountain pen mark that had been scored through her entire name. Whoever had crossed her entry through had done so with such forceful intention that the nib had gone through several of the sheets underneath.

Kate's first thought was that someone might have done this when Constance had died. But there was no date of death for anyone listed in the Bible – only births – and none of the other entries had been scored through.

Constance Amelia Rose McLay stood alone in having been deleted. Kate shuddered suddenly and looked around. She suddenly wished she was anywhere else but here. With Liz talking in clipped tones to her son outside the door Kate looked back down at the name.

She ran her finger slowly over the deep slice that the pen had made and wondered what kind of crime Constance McLay could possibly have committed that would see her name so meaningfully and forcefully removed from her family history.

CHAPTER 4

1940

The smacking sound the Spitfire had made as it crashed had been nothing compared to the dreadful gurgle that emanated from the water as it sucked the plane down into its inky depths. The whoosh had been sudden. And then there was nothing but the waves as they crashed around Constance, before the loch became eerily still.

Constance swam as fast as she could towards the middle of the loch, pausing to tread water and listen for a sound, any sound that might indicate the pilot was still alive. She pulled her dress up around her waist so she could kick her legs faster.

He was dead. He must be. He'd been under the water for far too long, surely. She wished the clouds would part, allowing the moon to cast some light on to the dark water.

She called out, even though it was hopeless. 'Where are you?'

Constance pushed her wet brown hair back from her face in order to see, although it was too dark to get her bearings. Her painstakingly pinned hairstyle was now loose and in soaked tendrils down her face.

'Where are you?' she called again. Foolishly, she believed if she shouted loud enough she might be able to summon him from the cold depths.

From the darkness to her left the silence was broken. A loud splash sounded as he surfaced, suddenly, violently. He'd emerged but he was flailing, splashing and gasping desperately for air.

Constance yelled that she was coming to help. The pilot was some distance from her and she didn't know if he could hear her. He appeared unable to reply, his gasps turning to coughs as he expelled water from his lungs.

She swam towards the noise, continuing to try to reassure him. As she swam into his view he swore, startled at her arrival. He appeared to be having a fight with himself.

'Are you all right?' Constance called. 'Can you swim?'

'Yes. No,' he said between gasps. 'Help. It's drowning me.' He was trying to undo his leather flight jacket and, in a panic, had his arms stuck in the wet material. Constance reached him and trod water as she wrestled the heavy flight jacket from him. As she held it in her arms the weight of it began to pull her down and she kicked with her legs to stay above the surface.

He started kicking off his waterlogged boots and saw her struggling with the jacket.

'Let go!' he shouted at her.

Constance hadn't known why she'd still been holding the jacket but she released the leaden weight. Like his plane, it disappeared into the water.

His panic seemed to rise as he struggled with his boots. Constance tried soothing him. 'Stay calm. The shoreline isn't far,' she said as she trod water. 'You must swim for it.'

The pilot followed her as she swam. She could hear his harsh breathing and sporadic coughing as he struggled to swim with boots full of water. Constance's love for swimming in the loch had worn off when she'd reached thirteen and Douglas had no longer been around as much to share in the fun. But she still knew the loch like the back of her hand. They were swimming away from the house, towards the far side of the wide loch where the wooden jetty jutted out. That shore was closer and after all the pilot had been through, Constance didn't think he could swim all the way back in the direction from which she had come.

She slowed to swim alongside the exhausted man, ready to drag him along if he should give up. But he continued. He asked only once how far away the edge was and after a few minutes Constance felt pebbles and sharp stones beneath her bare feet.

She turned to take his hand, to pull him from the lake. Weak from his ordeal, he grabbed her hand willingly, stumbled at the shoreline and then lowered himself down, crawling on his hands and knees out of the water. He lay on his front, facing away from her, and breathed deeply.

Exhausted, not from the swim but from panic, Constance fell down next to him. It was only as she sat still that she realised how cold she was and she began shivering. She hugged her bare arms but it was of little use whilst she was in wet clothes. The pilot turned to look at her, wide-eyed with shock, and then looked around at his surroundings. She could barely see his face in the darkness. His wet hair fell partly over his eyes, which were now trained on her face.

When he finally got his breath back he asked, 'Where in God's name did you spring from?'

Constance raised her hand and pointed across the water. 'The house. But I was already down by the loch.'

He nodded and looked to where she pointed. But Invermoray House, in blackout and so far away, was indiscernible. 'Were you on your own?'

'By the water, yes.' She shivered.

'You're cold,' he said as he forced himself onto his hands and knees again and then turned slowly into a sitting position.

'Yes,' she said simply. 'Aren't you?'

'I suppose I am.'

'We must get dry,' Constance said as she stood. The thin fabric of her dress clung to her wet skin. Goose bumps covered her.

'Where? To the house?' he asked. 'I'm not going back in that water to reach it.'

'It's too long to walk round,' she said between shivers. She thought as quickly as she could. 'There's an estate cottage that's empty. And it's closer. If you can walk for only a few minutes, it's just inside the tree line.' She pointed to where spruce trees loomed high.

'It's empty?' he asked, a flicker of something like relief on his face. 'No one lives there?'

Constance nodded.

'All right. If you're sure. But first . . . ' He wrestled each of his boots off and tipped out water before he stood and scooped the boots into his arms. His thick pilot's uniform clung to him and as they walked Constance wondered what on earth the pair of them must look like.

After a minute or two he asked, 'How much further is this cottage?'

'Not far.' Constance hoped she hadn't veered off course. She'd never been out to the unused ghillie's cottage in the dark before. There'd never been the need.

In the darkness of the forest the cottage appeared, looming suddenly. Constance tried the door but it was locked. 'Oh no,' she cried. 'I hadn't thought.'

The pilot leaned against the cottage wall and put his head back against it. His eyes were closed. 'Look under the mat.'

Constance stepped off the front mat and lifted it. 'Yes, of course,' she said as she retrieved the key. 'How did you know?'

'Honest people always put their keys under the mat.' His face was tipped up. Above them the clouds parted and the moon finally shone, bathing the pilot in light.

For the first time since she'd set eyes on him she was able to see fully what he looked like. He had a strong jawline and he was handsome. Not like a film star, although she'd not been to see too many films recently up here since the war started. They were miles from anything exciting like that. But he was handsome in the sense that if she'd spotted him walking through the village, she knew she'd have glanced at him more than once.

His eyes had opened and he was watching her. A small smile lifted the corners of his mouth. 'Are you going to open the door?'

Embarrassed, Constance fumbled with the lock and turned the handle. As they entered, a strong smell of damp hit them. The cottage had been shut up for about nine months, since the ghillie, like all the other male staff of fighting age, had joined the war effort. The ghillie's home, the only estate cottage not situated in the local village, had been closed up ever since and was awaiting his return.

Constance sought out a paraffin lamp on a low table and fiddled with it.

'Don't,' the pilot said sharply.

'Why ever not?'

'The blackout,' he replied. He was right. Constance realised the blackout blinds weren't in place and as the clouds moved aside, the moon filtered through the windows. 'Leave it,' he continued. 'For now. We need to get our wet things off before we freeze to death.'

He dropped his boots to the floor. They clunked heavily but Constance's eyes weren't drawn down. Instead she looked at him in horror as he pulled his blazer off and dropped that to the floor before starting on his wet shirt. He had undone at least two buttons, exposing his chest, before Constance pulled her gaze away.

'Hurry up,' he commanded. 'Take your dress off. Do you want to get ill?'

'You can't possibly expect me to remove my dress in front of you.' She couldn't keep the horror from her voice.

'I'll turn my back,' he offered. 'I've just crashed into a bloody great lake. I'm in absolutely no condition to think about *that* sort of thing.'

Constance blushed that he should even mention it. After

Henry's nightmarish behaviour in the orangery, she was petrified it might happen again, here, with this pilot. She was buttoned in so tight she was unable to free herself from her dress anyway. She was sure the silk was shrinking tight against her body thanks to the water. The buttons at the back were plentiful and started at the nape of her neck and ran down the dress until they reached the top of her bottom.

He had turned his back and must have been aware she wasn't moving as he said, 'Are you watching *me* undress?' in an amused voice.

'No! I need your help.'

He turned, rolled his shirt up and dropped it on the floor. She'd seen her brother Douglas's friends without their shirts plenty of times as they swam in the loch over the years but here, in this dark room with this man, it felt different. It was too private. He looked different to any of her brother's friends – stronger, taller . . . just different.

When she didn't speak he asked, 'What do you need help with?'

Constance had momentarily forgotten about the buttons. She turned and he began unbuttoning her wet dress, his hands moving gently down her skin until he finished. The room felt still and Constance was aware only of his hands as they moved.

As her unbuttoned dress gaped at the back he moved gallantly away and she became aware of the room again. The cottage had been left as if the ghillie had simply popped out for a few minutes. Other than the presence of damp and dust, items of furniture, ornaments and books had been left in the places that they had presumably sat for the past few years. From the back of a battered armchair the pilot pulled a tartan blanket and handed it to her.

Constance wriggled out of her dress as she wrapped the blanket around her. Her wet underwear was uncomfortable and she realised she was going to have to shake that off as well if she was going to warm up. Although it was August, the air was cold inside the stone cottage.

'I'll light a fire,' the pilot said. He moved around the room, fixing the stiff fabric wood-framed blackout blinds into place.

'You're still wearing your wet trousers,' Constance said. 'Look upstairs. The ghillie might have left some clothes behind.'

The pilot nodded and assembled the fire in the grate, forming a tripod out of a few logs of wood and balling up some newspaper from the basket, throwing it into the middle. He found matches in a pot on the mantel above, struck one against the wall and started a small fire in the grate.

'Warm yourself up while I find us some things,' he instructed.

Constance sat on the thinning rug by the fire and pulled the blanket tight around herself. The fire worked its magic and she stretched her bare legs out in front of her, wriggling her toes as the heat from the flames licked them gently. She marvelled at how she could be in the middle of her birthday party and then, only an hour later, soaked to the skin and alone in a cottage with an RAF officer whose plane had crashed into her loch. After a few minutes the pilot came downstairs wearing a pair of dry trousers and a thick blue woollen pullover.

'They smell of mothballs but they're dry,' he said as he stood next to her, offering her a pair of men's trousers and a thick white jumper that he'd found. He held out his hand and she grasped it as she stood. She said her thanks, took the clothes and went upstairs to put the trousers and shirt on. She rolled the waistband of the trousers over a few times but they were far too big and she kept her hand on them as she descended the staircase for fear they might drop to the floor.

Constance sat back down in front of the fire and tucked her wet hair behind her ears. The pilot sat next to her, the firelight casting him in an orange glow.

'What's your name?' he asked.

She told him. 'What's yours?'

'Matthew.'

'What happened?' she asked. 'I watched you crash; it was awful.

It must have been so frightening for you. I thought you must surely be dead.'

When he replied his voice was quiet. 'I thought I was going to die. I couldn't see a bloody thing. I kept trying to restart the engine but I knew it was no good. In hindsight I should have thrown open the hatch and bailed out much earlier on but I thought, one more turn of the engine should do it, she'll start up on one more turn. Goes against everything I was ever taught, given the old thing had been completely shot up. It's nothing short of a miracle she glided like she did. Full of bullet holes. I had no idea I was landing on water. If the moon had been out I'd have seen. Bit of a shock when I bounced and the cockpit started filling up.'

Constance exhaled. 'I can imagine.'

'Can you?' Matthew enquired, his eyebrows raised. 'Ever been shot at by the enemy, falling down to the ground with no idea where the ground actually is?'

She felt chastised. 'No.' She was quiet.

A log shifted in the grate sending sparks high up the chimney.

'Sorry,' he said quietly. 'I should be thanking you. Instead I'm being abominably rude.'

'It's all right,' Constance replied.

'No. No it's not. My mother would turn in her grave if she knew how easily my manners had failed me.'

Constance smiled. She wanted to say it was all right again. Why couldn't she think of anything else to say?

They sat in silence for a few minutes, both focused on the fire that lit the otherwise darkened room. She wondered if anyone would be missing her back at the house and whether the pilot was in any condition to trudge through the forest in the middle of the night. Perhaps, given his ordeal, it would be best to wait until morning before they set off so no one caught her in men's clothing.

'What will you do?' he asked, pulling her from her thoughts.

'Do? About what?' Constance turned to look at him.

'About me?' Matthew looked at her. In the light of the fire she could see his eyes were a pale green. She'd never seen eyes that shade before. They shone brightly and contrasted curiously against his dark brown hair.

'Well I rather thought, if you preferred, we should sit it out here and you could rest for a while and then in the morning—'

'Constance, can I trust you?' he interrupted her.

She swallowed as he said her name. 'Yes, I think so.'

Matthew laughed. 'Well if you don't know, then how do I?'

'Yes, yes you can trust me.'

'I need you to help me,' he said. 'I need you to . . . hide me. Just for a short while, I swear to you. Just long enough for them to think I'm dead. Will you do that?'

Constance's mouth dropped open. He had been so brave. He had been shot down and now, clearly, he was addled by his trauma.

'Who do you want to think you're dead?' she squeaked in disbelief.

'All of them. The whole bloody lot of them.'

'But . . .' she started. 'Your squadron? You don't want me to telephone someone, have them pick you up, have them look after you?'

'No, I do not,' he said. 'Tonight is the last night I participate in this god-awful war. And if I have to pretend I'm dead in order to achieve that then so be it.'

CHAPTER 5

He was mad. He had to be. Constance didn't know what to say. She stared at him. He looked back at her, a wary expression on his face. As if he half expected her to jump up, to begin scrambling away from him and back towards the house. She didn't think she needed to run from him but she half-wondered what would happen if she did. Would he spring up behind her and force her back to the cottage now that she knew his intentions to . . . what exactly? He looked far stronger than her and although he was clearly not handling the ordeal of his crash at all well, he looked as if he would be more than capable of stopping her if she bolted.

'Why?' she asked. 'Why don't you want to fight anymore?'

'That's the stupidest question I've ever heard,' he replied. 'Why do you think?'

She tried not to be offended but looked at him and waited.

'Only a madman actually enjoys it – the killing,' he replied.

Constance blinked. 'No one enjoys it. But it's war. It's your duty.'

His eyes widened. 'It's my duty to shoot other men out of the sky?' His voice was loud. 'To watch their planes fall away as I slam bullets into their engines?'

Constance thought about that for a moment. 'Well, yes. It is. I'm sorry but you must. My brother Douglas is a pilot,' she added.

'Good for him. Does he enjoy it? The killing?'

'I don't think he thinks of it like that.' Her brother had never talked about it. She wondered if she should ask Douglas. Constance wasn't at all sure she wanted to know. She thought of Henry with his wandering hands while on the ground and, up in the skies, his finger on a trigger. Something told her he probably enjoyed all of it.

Matthew picked nervously at a bit of fabric on the trousers he'd borrowed. 'I'm sorry,' he said again. 'I shouldn't have asked you to shelter me. It was wrong. I'm not your responsibility.'

'Can't you . . . can't you ask for a bit of leave, or something like that?' she asked. 'Time to think. You've just crashed. No wonder you feel like this now. But perhaps, tomorrow you might—'

He laughed bitterly but chose not to reply. The silence became uncomfortable.

'Could you become a conscientious objector?' she offered even though it seemed outrageous to her that this man had his chance to play his part in the war and was refusing to do so.

He shook his head. 'It's not that simple.'

'Really?' Constance's brow furrowed. 'Would you be court-martialled? Would it be desertion?' Her eyes widened in horror. 'Would you be shot?'

'Not here. They don't do that anymore.'

She breathed a sigh of relief. 'Prison then, perhaps?'

He pulled the thread clear of the trousers and discarded it. 'Most probably.'

'At least then you wouldn't have to fight anymore,' Constance placated.

'There is that.'

Constance watched the fire dance and sputter. If she returned to the house and told her father what had happened, what would he do? He would offer the man food and hand him a stiff drink.

Then he'd telephone the pilot's commanding officer and this man, visibly shaken and looking into the fire as if it held all the answers, would be carted off and pushed back into a plane in a matter of days, as was his duty. And then what? Would he just aim it towards the ground this time? A thought struck her.

'Did you do it on purpose?' she asked.

'Do what?'

'Crash?'

'No. Of course I didn't.' He looked at her sternly. 'I don't want to kill but I don't want to die either.'

Constance nodded.

He yawned. 'I must sleep.'

She looked at him as he stretched his legs out in front of him on the floor and rested his head back against the armchair. He closed his eyes. Constance chewed her lip, reluctant to move, reluctant for the night to end like this, with her dismissal.

Matthew opened one eye. 'Can you find your way back to your house in the dark?'

'Yes.'

He opened both eyes. 'Then you should go. The very last thing you want is to be found with me. Can you do something for me?'

She watched, waiting.

'Will you keep quiet? About me being here, I mean. Just to allow me to rest for the night.'

She nodded. 'All right. And then what will you do?' she asked as she climbed to her feet, clutching the loose waistband of her borrowed trousers.

'I'll go,' he said simply. 'I just need a few hours' rest. If you'll let me stay for the night, I'll leave in the morning. You'll never have to see me again.'

'Where will you go?' she asked.

He shrugged. 'I don't know yet. Regardless, it's not for you to worry about.'

'You need to hand yourself in. You can't run, if that's what you intend; it will only be worse the longer you leave it,' she pointed out. 'If you hand yourself in tomorrow, just walk back in as if you had just crashed and had some rest overnight, it wouldn't be a fib. Not really.'

He smiled. 'Thank you for your concern.'

He wasn't going to do that though. She knew he wasn't. What would he do? Where would he go?

He looked up at her from where he sat on the floor. His dark mood lightened. 'Thank you for swimming out to rescue me. It was very brave of you. Thank you for bringing me here too.'

She nodded. 'Of course.' As she reached the front door she turned to look at him. 'I won't tell anyone you're here,' she said.

It was his turn to nod. 'Thank you. I'll be gone in the morning.'

'Good luck,' she said.

'You too, Constance.'

Her hand was on the latch but she didn't lift it. His gaze was fixed on her and hers on him. She opened her mouth to say something, but she didn't know what. He watched, waiting.

'Wherever you end up going, please look after yourself.' She opened the door, slipped into the cold and closed the door gently behind her.

Constance moved quietly through the trees. The walk back would take her around fifteen minutes. The forest was cold, and her hair still damp around her neck. She looked through the trees to see the loch was now perfectly still. Somewhere in its depths was a Spitfire where only a matter of hours ago there hadn't been. She moved up the stone steps in the garden and slipped through the door to the library, which had been left unlocked. Presumably because her father, who was asleep on the settee in his dress suit, had still been using the room. A cigar smoked gently in a silver ashtray on the low table. Constance stubbed it out. Fearful of him waking and seeing her dressed in men's clothes, she crept into the dark corridor, climbed the stairs and padded her way silently to her bedroom.

She lay in bed. She couldn't sleep. She couldn't even think about sleep. Instead her mind wandered back to the cottage, back to the pilot. She wondered if he was sleeping. If not, what was he thinking about? He would be considering his options. Oh, the stupid, stupid man. What on earth would happen to him? She wished she hadn't left like that now. She wished she'd tried harder to talk him round, to make him see that running away, deserting, wasn't the answer. She also wished she had been more considerate. The man had just crashed his plane. How could she know what that felt like? She was playing no part in this war, as much as it irked her; as desperate as she was to break free of the confines of Invermoray and do something useful. But he was. He was fighting the enemy daily and had just crashed horrifically, almost drowning. How could she know what kind of state of mind was acceptable in that circumstance? He had just needed time to think and she had all but said she wouldn't help. She hated herself. She had no idea what it was like, this war, not really, stuck out here with nothing to do. She should have been more understanding.

As dawn rolled around Constance pulled aside the heavy velvet curtains that shrouded her bedroom windows. Light streamed into her room through the Splinternet tape that had crisscrossed the large windows ever since war had been declared the year earlier. The housekeeper had been diligent but Constance found it hard to believe German bombers would find Invermoray a worthwhile target. The base at Kinloss and the ships at Lossiemouth held far more interest, surely. She put her hand flat on the cold glass and looked across the loch, through the tree line, in the direction of the ghillie's cottage. But it was in vain. It could not be seen from the house. The sun rose gently above the mountains in the distance, heralding the morning, making the loch sparkle. He would be leaving soon. Maybe he had gone already.

Her stomach knotted as guilt gripped her. She couldn't believe what she had done. She couldn't face the fact she'd just abandoned this man. He had no one to help him. He'd asked her for help.

He hadn't eaten anything. Hadn't drunk anything. Had the water been shut off at the cottage? He might be in shock. He wasn't thinking straight. He was probably hoping she'd come back so she could offer to telephone his squadron and take him back. And even if not, he'd been fighting in the skies over England long enough for it to have affected him so badly he was considering deserting. He was clearly traumatised. She had to help him.

Constance brushed her matted hair, which smelled damp and of loch water, threw on any clothes she could find – yanking a blouse and skirt from her wardrobe and hopping her way into her brown lace-up shoes. She tried to pin her hair as she moved down the stairs, two at a time, but she was making a poor effort of it.

From the bottom of the stairs she heard her father's bedroom door open. She glanced upward in the direction of the sound. He must have taken himself to bed at some point and was now emerging for the day. The rest of the family and staff would be up and moving, if not already. Constance moved quicker, fearful of being seen. How would she explain where she was going, and why? At the side of the house she took the path that skirted the formal gardens. It would take her longer to reach the cottage but there was less chance of being seen. Constance avoided the loch shore, moving between the trees. When she was out of sight of the house she ran the rest of the way, bracken snapping under her feet as she sprinted through the wood.

He might already be gone. What time was it? She didn't have her watch. Five o'clock in the morning? When she reached the ghillie's cottage Constance almost slammed into the wooden door, she was running so fast. Breathless, she lifted the latch, pushed open the door and stumbled inside.

CHAPTER 6
August 2020

The door to the library flew open so suddenly it made Kate jump. She'd been gazing so absent-mindedly at the handwritten names in the family Bible that she'd almost forgotten the argument that had been taking place in the entrance hall between mother and son. James stood in the doorway and seethed. He appeared unable to speak, his lips forming a thin line. The pen mark that crossed through Constance McLay's name was forgotten as Kate closed the book gently – expecting her marching orders from the sullen James.

It was Liz who broke the silence, stepping round her son and across the threshold of the room. 'James will take you to your room, show you where things are, give you a bit of a tour. Perhaps you'd like to freshen up after a day's travel? And then we'll dine together, in about an hour or so. Just pop down to the kitchen. We only use the dining room for big occasions. Not that your arriving isn't a big occasion but . . . well . . . you know what I mean.' Liz blushed.

Kate found it hard to mask her surprise. She glanced at James. So, she was allowed to stay. The vein throbbing at the side of his temple indicated he was less than happy about being overruled by his mother and he now stood in a silence that spoke volumes.

'Thanks, Liz. That sounds lovely,' Kate replied, pointedly ignoring acknowledging the son in case the slightest thing she said sent him over the edge entirely. James merely stared at her, turned and walked into the hallway.

'Are you coming?' he called over his shoulder. 'Or am I showing myself to your room?'

Almost running after him, Kate found him about five stairs up, holding a suitcase in each hand, his chin pointed up as he ascended the staircase. Portraits lined the walls along the staircase but James moved at such a speed Kate wasn't able to get a very good look at them. Two of the paintings were faintly interesting: a young woman in a silver-grey evening dress, dark hair rolled and clipped near her ears and her brown eyes looking directly at Kate – or the artist, depending on how you thought about it.

The portrait by the side of it was of a very good-looking young man facing side-on in a sky blue RAF uniform. Both looked as if they'd been painted in the 1940s. Kate paused to take in the brushstrokes and the genial expression on the young man's face. The pictures had been moved about fairly recently. The paint surrounding these was a different colour, brighter than the rest of the slightly faded paint on the wall, indicating that the portraits that had hung there not long before had been covering a larger space.

Then Kate noticed she was alone. James had disappeared entirely and despite trying for an air of elegance, she scurried up the stairs to look for him. At the top of the staircase the corridor stretched both left and right. Kate turned left and stared down the lengthy hallway. Faded, almost threadbare red runner carpet ran down the centre of the corridor and pot plants on tall brass stands stood by the walls. Old framed pencil drawings hung between the numerous dark wooden doors that probably led to bedrooms. But there was no James. Kate turned back on herself and saw he was at the other end of the corridor past the stairs, watching her but making no sound. He'd let her turn completely the wrong way and had simply waited for her to realise. Kate smiled thinly despite the fact she was really starting to dislike James.

He opened a door and walked inside, taking her suitcases with him. Kate moved quickly down the corridor and then wondered why she was hurrying when he was behaving so childishly. She began ambling, looking at the pencil sketches of the estate that lined this side of the hallway. After about thirty seconds, James peered round the door to see where she was. She saw him out of the corner of her eye but made no move to acknowledge him. She didn't know why he brought out this side in her. James folded his arms and exhaled loudly. When she didn't move, he coughed to attract her attention.

'This,' he called as he moved back inside, 'is your room.'

Kate entered and stood at the threshold to the chintziest room she had ever seen. She was reminded of the old IKEA television advert that advised customers to chuck out their chintz. This was the 'before' picture. But while the room was overcrowded with floral eiderdowns and doilies on surfaces, the walls were devoid of any decoration at all. No pictures – nothing. The bare walls lessened the homeliness but Kate knew she couldn't actually feel homesick, because her empty little one-bed flat had never *truly* felt like home. She supposed it was because unhealthy working hours coupled with far too much socialising meant she never really spent much time in her flat. It had always been more of a crash pad. If she stopped to think about it, even when she lived at home with her parents she'd always been nomadic, catching last-minute cheapish weekends away with friends. Surrounded here by peaks and mountains, clean fresh air and a bedroom that was bigger than her entire flat, she might feel at home, might be able to settle even if it was only for six months. She glanced at James, his expression fixed. Perhaps not.

'The bathroom's through here.' James opened a connecting door and pointed. Kate followed him, walking past an ornate four-poster bed, housing an abundance of floral cushions. She looked inside the bathroom. It was white, mock Victoriana with brass taps, which was something at least. She was half expecting an avocado suite given the décor in the rest of the room.

'Very cosy,' she said truthfully.

But James was already at the bedroom door, one foot on the hallway carpet. 'I take it you don't want the grand tour now.' He couldn't meet her gaze.

'Well, not if you don't want to,' she conceded.

'I don't,' he replied.

Kate laughed, more out of shock than anything else. At least the man was honest.

'My mother tells me you're on a six-month contract – is that right?' James looked directly at her.

'Yes,' she offered tentatively. Though the job offer was on a six-month basis, she wasn't strictly *on* a contract. She didn't want to highlight that in case James clung on to that small detail and then tried to get rid of her again.

'We've got the next six months to cover the tour then, haven't we?' James turned and left.

Kate's mouth dropped open and she was left staring into the empty corridor where he had just been standing. 'Wow,' she breathed. How could anyone be that rude? This wasn't the way she'd been brought up, and given how charming and friendly Liz was, Kate suspected that wasn't the way James had been brought up either. Why was he like this then? She sat on the edge of the bed and put her head in her hands. A lesser person would have been scared off, of that she was sure. Perhaps James would warm to her, she hoped. Perhaps not. Either way, she couldn't make any rash decisions about leaving now. She would at least have to stick it out for a few weeks and see how the land lay; see how much involvement James had in the running of the estate and how closely she would be expected to work with him. Maybe it wouldn't be that bad.

*

Somewhere far below, a dinner gong sounded. Kate's eyes opened and she blinked at her chintz-clad bedroom, lit by the dim yellow glow from the lamp on the side table. She had only meant to rest her eyes for a few moments, but with horror she realised she must have fallen asleep. The nap hadn't been enough to recharge her empty batteries after a day of travel and she stretched and yawned in succession. While the flight up to Inverness had been mercifully short, the collective time spent travelling to and from and actually *at* the airport had been tiring.

Crossing to the window, she looked out to see it was growing dark. In the grounds, she could make out some kind of formal garden with a beautiful clipped-hedge parterre that sloped down towards a loch. The moon began its ascent over the mountains and darts of silver light shifted across the water as it lapped gently. The village, somewhere in the distance on the other side of the forest, from what she remembered from the drive, provided no light. The house was utterly remote.

The smell of something delicious cooking drifted into Kate's bedroom as she opened the door and hurried downstairs, realising she'd unwittingly ignored the dinner gong.

'Oh good,' Liz declared warmly as Kate entered the kitchen. 'You heard it. You should have seen the dust that flew as I rang it. We've not used it in years.'

Kate smiled and looked around the large, homely kitchen. It seemed like a relic from a prior decade. Wooden cupboards and Formica worktops were cluttered with cookbooks; some old, some very new. The new Ottolenghi cookbook was upright and propped open with a red wine bottle. Kate had that book in her flat, although she'd never actually cooked from it because she was out so much. She'd bought it because it had a drawing of a huge lemon on the front and went well with her pale yellow kitchen. Only now she supposed her brother was enjoying the use of it, along with her flat, while she was in Scotland. Kate wasn't sure how long she was actually going to be here given James's permafrosty reception. His back had been turned since she entered the room, as he flicked through a newspaper on the worktop.

'Did you get a bit of rest?' Liz asked.

'Mm, yes, thanks.'

'I'm glad. James has made lasagne. I hope that's OK?' Liz said.

'That sounds love—' But Kate was cut off mid-sentence as James swung round.

'You're not one of those bloody vegetarians are you?' he said accusingly.

'No.' Kate held his gaze wondering if he would have lost it completely if she had said she was.

He spun back round and nudged an old yellow Labrador out of the way with his foot as he opened the Aga door. 'That's something then, I suppose,' he muttered towards the oven. The mouth-watering smell was coming from the lasagne bubbling in the dish.

Kate bent down to the scratch the dog's ears as it ambled towards her and sat at her feet, investigating her silently. His tail thumped slowly against the flagstone floor and when it became clear Kate had no treats to give, he picked himself up and moved back to his bed on the other side of the kitchen. The scrubbed wooden table in the middle of the room had already been laid for dinner and Liz gestured for them to sit.

James placed the lasagne dish on a trivet and stared at it, as if he wasn't sure whom he should serve first. 'Help yourself,' he said eventually.

Kate hadn't realised how famished she was until now. The packet of pretzels on the flight up from London had been the last thing she'd eaten.

'Thanks, I will.'

'Do you drink?' James asked suddenly.

The serving spoon hovered between lasagne dish and Kate's plate as she stopped mid-serve. 'Er? What?' she asked.

'Wine? Do you drink wine? You work in PR in London so you must drink gallons of the stuff, but one doesn't like to assume.'

Kate couldn't tell if he was trying to be funny or rude, but a laugh escaped her lips regardless. 'Well, yes, I do actually. I mean, not lots—' she tried to save the situation '—but I do like wine. Are you . . . offering some?' God, he was hard to talk to.

He nodded. 'Red? Goes nicely with lasagne.' He looked toward the cookbook where the bottle of wine stood. 'I could open some if you want?'

Kate was about to say she would only have some if they were having some when Liz saved the situation from a politeness tipping point by hopping up and bringing the bottle to the table, turning back to fetch three wine glasses.

'Good to see your manners haven't failed you completely.' Liz told James as she opened the bottle. It made a satisfying plucking noise as the cork was withdrawn. He shrugged and started tucking into his plate of lasagne.

The clock on the wall ticked away, providing an awkward soundtrack for the dinner. Kate's PR training kicked in and she started on the small talk.

'This is wonderful,' she said truthfully.

'Thanks,' James mumbled.

Silence threatened to engulf the room again.

'James is really rather talented in the kitchen,' Liz enthused. 'I joke he'll make someone a lovely wife one day.'

He shrugged then shovelled another fork load of lasagne into his mouth.

As Liz and Kate continued small talk amongst themselves about the weather and the village nearby, James practically hoovered his food down. Kate stole small glances at him every now and again. He'd probably be quite good-looking, if only he'd smile. She glanced back at him a few minutes later and found him looking directly at her. 'Right. That's me done,' he said suddenly. 'I'm off to bed.'

He put his plate in the sink, took his wine glass with him and left the kitchen. He was avoiding her already; Kate was sure of it.

If Liz hadn't been sitting there Kate would have breathed a sigh of relief. Thank God he'd gone. He knew how to suck the atmosphere from a room.

'Oh, don't mind him,' Liz said, obviously spotting her expression. 'He's going to take a little while to get used to the idea of you being here. Between you, me and the gatepost,' Liz said quietly, 'he feels a bit undermined.'

'Undermined?' Kate helped herself to another portion of lasagne and Liz did the same.

'He's used to ruling the roost. Whole teams of people worked under him at the office. Before he left to come and help me. But of course you're now here, and you're an expert in a field James knows absolutely nothing about. So he's not really sure how he's going to manage you.'

'I see,' Kate said. But she didn't really see and wasn't sure how she was going to alleviate James's concern. 'Well,' Kate tried. 'I'm only here for six months so the plan is to sort of . . . get you started on the PR side of things – make sure my travel contacts in the media are onside over the next few months, make sure they visit and write glowing reviews, introduce you to all of them when they visit so you have an ongoing relationship with them. I plan to make decent headway and then I'll hand over the reins to you and James. Hopefully at the end of my time here, you'll be beating visitors off with sticks and might be able to hire someone locally just for a few days a week.'

'I know, I know, dear. We talked about this on the phone. All the other candidates droned on and on about how they'd need to move here permanently. How they'd be expecting a resettlement package and all that.'

Kate was pleased her honesty had paid off and she hadn't been as offensively demanding as some of the other applicants had obviously been.

'So don't worry about the nitty-gritty at this stage. For now,' Liz continued, looking conspiratorial, 'we need to work out how to get the visitors in and then we need to worry about the PR after that.'

'Well, that should be easy,' Kate said confidently. 'Good PR and a turnaround in visitors go hand in hand.' She knew her job inside out. It was a rare kind of travel journalist who said no to a free all-expenses-paid mini-break with their partner in exchange for a decent review. And with decent reviews, came an upsurge in tourism – unless there was something very wrong with a hospitality property. Kate could do this in her sleep. And the rest of it, planning out themed articles months in advance in line with what journalists were requesting for their features, that was just good relationships and diarising. 'You did mention on the phone you didn't have much in the way of visitors and I admit you are very out of the way. You weren't too sure about the events programme and we were going to take a look over the bedrooms to see what could improve but . . .' Kate cut to the chase. 'Liz, how many visitors does Invermoray House get?'

'None, dear.'

'None? Oh I don't just mean out of season,' Kate clarified, wondering why Liz was quoting the unimpressive out-of-season number. Although *none*, even for that time of year, was a worry.

'We don't get any visitors at all. Over any time period,' Liz explained. 'We don't have any kind of events programme. We have never opened the house to paying visitors. We've never offered overnight stays. I love the idea of turning us into some sort of boutique bed and breakfast but we wouldn't even know where to begin. I mean, do we need some kind of catering licence from the council to offer breakfasts or afternoon teas? But for now, what you see is what we are: a family home that needs to start paying its way. That's why you're here. We need you to help us do all of this. We need you to save Invermoray House.'

CHAPTER 7

What on earth had she got herself into? She'd done this job for years. But normally she turned up, following in the footsteps of a well-executed business plan, was pretty much thrust a strategy and then off she'd run and drum up interest with the glossy magazines, bloggers and the Sunday supplements. She'd take journalists out for lunch. She'd organise snazzy, all-expenses-paid press trips and then sit back and wait for the editorial coverage to roll in. She'd had it quite easy. She would be the first to admit to herself; although she'd never dared tell anyone else that, especially her clients.

But this was different. If Liz had outlined exactly how amateur this operation was, would she have come? God, no. She was a publicist, not a business strategist. She was the cherry on the cake, not the cake itself.

Kate looked at her watch as she lay in bed, unable to sleep. Ordinarily, it would be too late to text someone, but she knew Jenny would be awake and doing something slightly bonkers such as an all-night spin cycle class. '*Help*,' Kate messaged. '*They have no idea what they're doing*.' She paused before typing again. '*And neither do I*,' she finished with a flourish before sending a follow-up with a very brief summary of the situation.

Kate watched three dots appear on the screen, indicating Jenny was composing a reply.

'*You've handled worse than this, I'm sure,*' she replied. '*Remember that diabolical spa that thought they were good enough to get coverage in* Vogue? *You can do this blindfolded. Do you need more in the way of a pep talk or can I go to my trampoline disco class now?*'

Kate replied with a heart symbol and left Jenny to her latest late-night exercise fad.

She wasn't ready to sleep yet and was annoyed with herself that she'd forgotten to ask Liz what the Wi-Fi code was for the house. Kate actually rather suspected there wasn't one. After trying unsuccessfully to connect her laptop to her phone's 3G, she gave up and just scrolled through sites using the hazy 3G on her phone. She had one bar of signal and so had to wait an interminable amount of time for a page to load, but at least it was loading. She was looking up famous country houses, to see what they were doing to drum up business. She couldn't possibly be expected to formulate the entire business strategy, could she? If so, what the hell had James been doing until now, if not that very thing? Liz had said he was some hotshot who'd come home to Invermoray to run the house. Run it into the ground, clearly.

Kate thought of all the country houses she'd visited over the past few years, though there weren't that many. She googled Longleat, near Bath, remembering it thrived thanks mainly to a Safari Park. That was out of the question. She moved on to Chatsworth, Blenheim Palace and then looked more locally at Cawdor Castle before realising she was completely out of her depth.

This was a disaster. She'd been hired under false pretences. Although she suspected Liz had no idea of the difference between PR and business strategy and now they were all in this mess together.

She switched her phone off and put her head in her hands. She had two options. She could give in, explain to Liz that she'd been mistakenly hired for a job she wasn't qualified to do. Or she could breathe deeply and be pragmatic.

The sun streamed through a chink in the curtains and Kate blinked and looked at her watch. It was early, but not so early she could try to grab forty more winks before starting her first day at work. She'd had very little sleep, had been up all night formulating a rough kind of plan and had engaged in a stern chat with herself on more than one occasion to force herself to continue. She wasn't going to give in. For one thing, she could imagine the smug joy on James's face when she confessed she had no idea what she was doing and that it was probably best for all concerned that she drive back to the airport and not darken their door again. The image of his self-satisfied face riled her. But it was something else stopping her. Kate always made a point of giving clients the best service she could offer. She'd always told them that she treated their business as if it was her own. And she meant it. What would Kate try to do if Invermoray was *her* house?

And so, with careful, methodical planning, throughout the night she'd filled a notebook with short-term, and long-term ideas for raising cash. In short, she created something vaguely resembling a business plan. She'd made a point of not sleeping until she'd run out of ideas. And the ideas kept flowing, which meant she hadn't slept. So it was with an exhausted excitement that she stood zombie-like in the shower and tried not to fall asleep upright.

'I can do this,' Kate whispered as she stood in the kitchen and loaded the silver cafetière with coffee, 'I can do this.' In the morning light things weren't as bad as she thought. Often she'd make suggestions to clients about how to tweak their business. She understood getting people through doors. What they wanted. What they needed. With the hash they'd made of it at Invermoray so far, things could only get better. Kate had rallied her confidence and had chosen to wear skinny jeans tucked into ankle boots and her nicest shirt, which wasn't too crumpled from being packed away. She needed to find out where the iron was. Overall, she hoped the outfit conveyed seriousness to her role without being too staid.

'I can do this,' she repeated.

'It's not that complicated,' James said as he entered the kitchen, startling her so that she spilled coffee granules over the counter.

'Fill with boiling water, leave a few minutes and then push the plunger,' he continued.

'Right, yes.' She knew how to make coffee.

'Jolly good,' he said dryly. 'Enough in there for me?' His tone was lighter, not by a lot, but he certainly wasn't on as much of an offensive as he had been last night.

Kate made them both coffee as James scraped a kitchen chair out and sat down at the table. Maybe this wouldn't be as awkward as yesterday.

'So . . .' he started and then stopped.

'So . . . ?' Kate echoed. She was wrong. The awkwardness was seeping back into the room.

'So you're basically the cavalry,' James said with a thin smile. 'Come to rescue us because we've cocked it up?'

'Oh no,' Kate said quickly. 'No no no. I see us as more of a team . . .'

'Pfft,' James replied.

She wasn't sure how to respond to that. And it was hardly fair given she didn't know she was meant to be the cavalry.

'Do you know,' he started, looking out the kitchen window, 'I gave up my job to come back here. I don't know why now. I've been here all of five minutes, I *think* I've just about worked out where things are going wrong, I've sorted what I believe is a decent plan of attack and then without a chance to do anything about it I get . . .'

'You get . . . ?' Kate prompted.

'I get you . . . to be blunt . . . thrust upon me. Who's running who? Who's in charge? You or me? I've got no idea. But if you think you can just strut in here and throw orders around, you've got another—'

'That's really not why I'm here,' Kate cut in. And then she noted what he'd said. 'I'm sorry, you've only been here five minutes? What do you mean?'

'Three months,' James said. 'I've been back for all of three months. I wasn't going to. I came back after Dad died, got things sorted for Mum. But I had a job. A life. One I enjoyed, so I went back to that. And then Mum issued her call to arms and like a dutiful son I said I'd come and help. So I apologise for my hostility towards you yesterday, but I want you to see it from my point of view. I wasn't expecting . . . well . . . you know.' He gestured towards Kate and then sipped the coffee she handed him. But he clearly wasn't done and she watched him take a deep breath. 'In truth, I wasn't expecting to be told I was shit quite so soon, especially when I don't *really* want to be here.'

Kate nodded slowly. He'd been here for three months. Which meant that when she'd been hired a month ago and had worked her notice period, he'd only been here for two months when Liz had interviewed her. It sounded cut-throat but perhaps Liz just knew things needed to move at a quicker pace than they had been then.

'I'm sorry,' Kate said. 'I don't know what to say. Only, I think I'll be good at this and—'

James's eyebrows lifted. 'You *think* you'll be good at this?' he repeated. 'What the hell does that mean? Have you not done this before?'

Kate was spared answering as Liz arrived. 'Ah, good morning, all. Kate, shall we have the tour after breakfast and then we can talk plans as we go?'

Across the kitchen table, James's eyes narrowed.

CHAPTER 8

They moved through the house, Kate clutching her notebook and pen, writing things down as Liz and she discussed plans. Kate tried to keep the horrified expression from her face as they looked in some of the other guest bedrooms that were even chintzier than her own. Most had en suites, which would be a blessing when it came to offering bed and breakfast packages. No guest wants to traipse down a hall in the middle of the night in search of a loo. It doesn't exactly scream luxury and so Kate offered up a silent word of thanks to the McLay ancestors who'd seen fit to install additional bathrooms.

The polished ballroom and well-planted orangery were in good condition, although a pane of glass had smashed on the far side of the orangery and had been boarded up. Kate resisted asking how long it had been like that. A while, she suspected, and made a note in her pad to get it fixed. This was really a job James and Liz should have already tackled, but as she moved further through the house with Liz it was clear they were at sixes and sevens and Kate would have to take on a lot of everyday tasks if they were going to get Invermoray suitable for visiting journalists and paying guests.

By the time they finished the tour of the house, Kate's notebook was full of jobs that needed doing, the first of which was to organise the official paperwork to change Invermoray House from a residential property to a bed and breakfast.

'You can give that job to James,' Liz said. 'He's good at that sort of thing.'

Curiosity got the better of Kate. 'What did James do? Before he came back home?'

'Oh, something in computers,' Liz said dismissively. 'He's been in Hong Kong living the high life and, to be honest, I never *quite* understood what it was he did, tapping away all day on a keyboard. All sounded very dull, but like most dull things, it made him an awful lot of money.'

Did Liz have another reason for calling James back home other than helping run the house? Kate would try and work that one out later.

'Shall we look at the gardens?' Liz suggested.

Kate nodded. She had seen them, briefly, from her window last night and was rather excited to see them in daylight. As she walked, her mind whirred. Where was all this money James had made then? And why wasn't he ploughing it into the estate? Perhaps it was wrong of her to assume he would spend his hard-earned cash on his mother's house, even if it would be his one day, especially if he didn't want to be here – a fact he had made abundantly clear.

The ornamental gardens were a view to behold. Kate had been expecting another ramshackle sight but the gardens were lush and well maintained, the hedges clipped in linear fashion.

'This is my passion project,' Liz confessed. 'I do spend rather a lot of time gardening.'

'I can see. It's beautiful,' Kate said softly. The gardens, bordered by angular hedges, swept down towards the loch. At the centre was a statue of a globe held by three cherubs. Dahlias, hydrangeas and begonia beds held a stunning array of peach, pink and orange flowers.

'I'll confess I probably spend far too much time out here, and not enough in there.' Liz gestured back towards the house. 'I've probably spent too long with my head in the sand. Or the flowers. After my husband died, I'm not sure I was really up to it . . . saving the house, I mean. In fact, I'm not sure I understood the house needed saving until recently. It all became a bit topsy-turvy without me really noticing. By which point James had come back, and seemed better equipped to handle the day-to-day running of the house – quite willing too. And I think I rather left him to it.'

Liz brightened. 'But not anymore. I've placed too much pressure at his door and now it's time he had help. Not that he accepts it, of course. But in time he'll come round. Now, I wonder if I can leave you in James's capable hands for the remainder of the tour?'

At this, Kate's heart plummeted into her stomach. 'Of course.'

'Good, I want you to see the ghillie's cottage. I do think it would make rather a good holiday let but it's a bit of a journey round the far side of the loch so I think it's best James drives you.'

Kate's heart lifted itself back into place at this. A holiday cottage. She knew that would bring in much-needed revenue, although given the state the rest of the house was in, she dreaded seeing the condition of the cottage.

James was in the estate office, a low-level outbuilding made of the same grey stone as the main house and nestled between the house and the disused stables. Kate was distracted by the stables' distressed wooden doors hanging off their hinges. Through the open, wonky doors, she could see the stable was being used for storage. Furniture and all sorts of boxes stood piled up at odd angles. It may be worth a ransack later, to see if anything could be salvaged and used. There were clearly a lot of items and she was starting to see how easy it was to hoard. Generations of McLays had been adept at collecting.

The junk in the stables was nothing to the carnage that awaited her in the estate office. Liz led the way but it was a squeeze to get inside the room. Boxes of paperwork and filing cabinets jostled for space. There was barely an inch of floor. They picked their way across the room towards the set of two large mahogany desks where James sat facing them, watching warily as they approached. Kate was careful not to slip on pieces of paper that had obviously fallen to the floor from the piles of paperwork that needed a more permanent home.

James closed his laptop slowly and gave both Kate and his mother a look that indicated he was being ambushed. Why was this man always on the offensive? Why the near-open hostility? Kate knew he felt replaced, although if he gave her half a second to explain, and his mother too for that matter, he'd be able to understand that she wasn't there to bring the house down around his ears, but to work with him to save it. She would make a point of convincing him to like her later. Even if it killed her, Kate had to get him onside.

'James, darling,' Liz placated.

James lifted an eyebrow, making it clear he knew he was being buttered up.

'Would you be a dear and take Kate over to the ghillie's cottage? Explain what you've done and what you've been doing in general?'

James took a deep breath and exhaled slowly. 'Yeah. Sure. I'll take Kate over and explain myself to her.'

'Goodo,' Liz said as she left, entirely misunderstanding his tone.

'I don't need you to explain yourself,' Kate said once Liz had gone. 'Not to me. I just . . .' She paused and tried a less flustered approach. 'I think you and I have got off on the wrong foot.'

He put his arms behind his head. 'Do you, now?'

'Yes,' Kate said. 'You don't? You enjoy meeting new people and there being a permanent air of awkwardness?'

'Who says it's awkward?'

Kate looked at him wide-eyed.

'And who says it's permanent?' James continued. 'By all accounts you're only here for six months.'

It was Kate's turn to breathe deeply. 'Are you always like this?' she muttered under her breath.

'Pretty much,' he replied.

'Good to know. Listen,' she said, 'forget about the tour. Just hand me the keys to the cottage and I'll go on my own.'

'The key's under the mat but you'll never find the cottage on your own.'

'We'll see. Where is it exactly?'

'It's on the far side of the loch, through the trees. But there's no path from the loch anymore. The footpath that once was there has overgrown and the ferns and trees have grown up around it. The cottage is almost hidden now. I've been driving round from the woodland. I've cut a vehicle path through it and hacked my way through the rest to make a footpath to the front door. Take the Land Rover if you want. Just, try and drive a bit more carefully than you normally do.'

Kate ignored that last comment. 'I'm sure I'll find it on foot. I could do with the walk.'

'OK, so you're not listening,' he said, exasperation tingeing his voice. 'You won't see it. You'll miss it completely.'

'Key's under the mat you say?'

He rolled his eyes. 'Yeah, be my guest.'

Kate had never been so glad to get out of a place in her life. James was positively hostile, rude and unbelievably arrogant. And so . . . knowing. She breathed down the clean highland air and walked round towards the ornamental garden in order to find the path down to the loch.

'*You won't find it*,' Kate mimicked James as she slipped through the arched opening in the hedge towards the shore. Was the cottage invisible then? Stupid man. She walked along by the water's edge. The sun streamed down onto the expanse of still water. Kate paused to take in the view, feeling the warmth of the sun on her face and arms. Despite James's behaviour, her shoulders were unstiffening and she felt her body relax. A few moments standing in front of a peaceful loch were far more effective than the weekly yoga class she'd been taking back in London. A walk through the woods was just what the doctor ordered and she skirted the loch, feeling the comforting crunch of pebbles and shingle under her boots.

On the far side, Kate turned back by the tree line and faced the house. It really was a handsome building: imposing, baronial, stately – especially from here, where the view across the water and the ornamental garden gave the house an immaculate air, masking the near dilapidation inside. Kate smiled at her luck having landed a job here, then headed into the woods.

How long had she been walking? Half an hour? An hour? She really hadn't thought this through at all. The large pine trees loomed skinny and tall and their leaves rustled overhead as a hint of a breeze swept through before growing silent almost as fast as it had started. The ground was blanketed in green spindly ferns. It was a job to know where to place her feet, hoping they landed correctly on the ground, out of sight, beneath the deep greenery. Every few yards or so a clump of tall purple foxgloves grew, unexpectedly sturdy and tall between rocks and crevices. Further along, Kate smiled to see thistles, feeling like a tourist at having spotted Scotland's national flower. The purple flowers crowned them, completely juxtaposed with the rest of their oversized spiky appearance, transforming them into a thing of unexpected beauty. A large rock protruded by a series of trees, grouped together. She had passed this; she was sure she had. Was she going round in circles? What had first appeared striking woodland now appeared almost malevolent.

Kate stood still and listened. To her left she could hear the soft sound of running water, which couldn't be the loch. She was too far inside the forest. Other than the sound of moving water, there was silence. She walked in the direction of the sound to find a wide stream running through the woodland, its water tumbling over rocks, and its mossy banks dipped gently, easily accessible. Kate felt a bit like Bear Grylls all of a sudden and knelt, putting down her notebook and pen and dipping her hands into the cold water. There was Bear Grylls and then there was idiocy, so she sniffed the water dubiously. It smelt fine and, parched, she drank it. It didn't taste odd so she cupped her hands into the water again, feeling rather proud of herself at the same time.

'So you *can* take the city out of the girl,' James said from behind her. Still crouching, Kate whipped her head round. He smiled and there was a flicker of a handsome man hiding underneath his sullen exterior. And then the smile left his face and frown lines returned as if he'd just remembered he was waging his own private war against her. His Labrador bounded up to Kate, gave her a nudge with his nose and then turned his attentions to the river and began drinking.

'Sometimes,' Kate replied with a small smile, drying her hands on her jeans before retrieving her pad and pen as she stood. 'Where did you come from?' She glanced around. He'd not been following her haphazard route on foot; of that she was sure.

He gestured over his shoulder. 'I drove round. I just knew you'd get lost.'

'Not *that* lost,' Kate countered. 'You found me.'

'Not easily. I've been in these woods for about twenty minutes. And you're about ten minutes' walk from the cottage. In the wrong direction.'

'Oh,' she said quietly.

'I did try and tell you,' James said.

They stood and looked at each other. He was obviously a man who had to have the last word and Kate wasn't in the mood for a fight.

'What's your dog's name?' She changed the subject.

James smiled. 'Whisky. I didn't name him. He was my dad's dog. He's just sort of become mine since Dad died.'

'Good name,' Kate said. 'Appropriate, given we're probably surrounded by distilleries.'

'True. Although depending on the mood he was in, it was often difficult to tell if Dad was yelling for someone to bring him a stiff drink or if he was summoning the dog for a walk.' James looked wistful and as he smiled there was a hint of mellowness in his eyes. He was almost pleasant when he let his defensive barriers down.

'Shall we look at the cottage then?' Kate suggested.

'Don't get your hopes up,' James replied as he turned. She followed him. 'It's not been lived in since before the war. The house hasn't had a ghillie since then, so it's fallen into disrepair. I'm in the process of doing it up. I want to get it ready to let, then that's one thing ticked off the never-ending list of jobs. We'll get some incoming cash and it can help fund us while we sort the main house and whatever else we intend to do.'

Kate nodded. 'That actually sounds like a good idea,' she confessed.

'Actually?' James queried. 'You weren't expecting me to have come up with a decent plan myself?'

She sighed. It was disappointing how quickly he reverted back to defensive. 'Sorry. I didn't mean it like that.'

'Anyway,' he continued as they trampled through the thick undergrowth, snapping twigs and dodging nettles as they trod. 'As the main house started to fall away, so did the ghillie's cottage. After the war, there weren't as many staff, no ghillie, no real estate management – either land or financial from what I could gather. It was a case of trying to eke the coffers out as far as they'd stretch.

'Even my father, when he arrived some years later, with all good intentions, didn't have it in him to cast his eyes further than Invermoray House itself.'

'When he arrived?' Kate questioned. 'What do you mean?'

James looked at Kate as they walked. He was quite tall and she could feel herself almost jogging to keep up with his long strides.

'Has Mum not explained the family history to you?'

'No.'

He exhaled. 'God, where do I start?'

'At the beginning?' She smiled.

James raised an eyebrow and half-smiled in return as he launched into the story.

'The estate never used to be Dad's. He lived and grew up in a house in London,' James said. 'Dad was an artist . . .' This explained the modern artwork around the sitting room, Kate thought. 'Not the tortured kind, more the jovial kind,' he continued. 'But certainly the kind that never made any money. He and Mum lived happily in London with holes in the ceiling and the boiler forever going wrong. It's why Invermoray's fared the same in terms of maintenance. I think it's an attitude thing. Anyway, he inherited Invermoray in the 1980s, when relations of his passed away. Very distant relations from what I could work out. Either way, it was his. Dad quite fancied playing lord of the manor and so we sold the London house and decamped completely up here when I was a kid. In truth, I've never quite forgiven them.'

They stopped as they reached a clearing. 'I just assumed it had been in your family for generations,' Kate said.

'It has been, since it was built in the early Victorian era. But for the other branch of the family, the McLays. Our last name was . . . is . . . Langley but the will asked for the McLay family name to be carried on, bolted on to ours. You can't dictate that kind of thing from beyond the grave, the solicitor said, but Dad did it regardless; felt he owed it to them. So we became Langley-McLay, officially. Dad used it. Mum still does. But I don't.'

'Why not?' Kate asked.

'I suppose I felt like an idiot, changing my name, and a bit resentful at having moved up here. Invermoray never really felt like home. Never really felt like *me.*'

'So who were the McLays then?' Kate was curious now. 'Who asked you to adopt their name in exchange for the house, which by the way sounds like a really fair trade?'

'Fair trade? It's the worst kind of trade. This house is a bloody drain on us. Always has been.' James screwed up his face as he thought. 'It's some boring connection,' he told her. 'One of Dad's cousins or something like that. He and his wife were elderly. I think he died in the early Eighties and then she followed not long after. It's all a bit odd really if you think about it. They had two grown-up children, I believe. There's portraits of them in the house. Mum found the pictures buried in the attic a while back.'

Kate remembered the portraits on the stairs, the young man in RAF uniform, the girl in the silver-grey dress. She wondered if they were who James meant.

'They should have inherited, one or the other of them, according to Mum,' James continued. 'But for one reason or another they'd lost touch with their parents, or maybe died. I'm not sure. There was a family rumour they had been disinherited years and years earlier but Dad and his parents didn't take it seriously. So it was a complete shock when the line of inheritance missed out the McLays' direct descendants for whatever reason, skipped sideways and landed on us Langleys.'

Kate hadn't been paying too much attention to her surroundings. Instead she'd been entranced by James's strange tale. It was with some surprise that she found they had reached the cottage. James had been right. From the direction of the loch, the hedges had tangled into thicket and had built up to a high level, camouflaging it from view. It was unlikely she would have seen it had she been alone. Instead they had doubled round and approached the cottage from the direction of the road that ran to the front of the estate. James's battered Land Rover was parked some distance away on the track. It was a marvel he'd managed to locate her really.

'Thank you,' Kate said.

He frowned. 'What for?'

'Making the effort to find me, out there.' She gestured to what she had now decided was The Wilderness.

He shrugged. 'Don't worry about it. You might have found it eventually.' He raised his eyebrows theatrically. 'Then again . . . you might not.'

She couldn't help but laugh.

James bent down and pulled the brass key out from underneath the mat.

'That's a really brave place to keep it,' Kate said. 'Anyone could find it.'

'Out here?' He rolled his eyes as he unlocked the thick wooden door. '*You* couldn't.' He looked pleased with his own joke. 'Besides, it's not here permanently. I left it there so the roofer could finish and pick up his tools. At least it's watertight now. As I said—' he indicated the cottage '—it's not much.' James turned the handle and Whisky beat his tail as he caught up with them, impatient to be let inside. 'In fact some of the ghillie's stuff from before the war is still here. Dusty. Moth-eaten. The McLays couldn't be bothered to chuck it all out it seems, and neither could my dad. I did have half a mind that I could tosh the furniture up a bit instead of buying new. Holidaymakers love that reclaimed look, apparently. So don't be surprised if you think it looks like a museum. Because it does.'

He opened the door, pushed it open and they stepped inside

CHAPTER 9

August 1940

The cottage door slammed open, the metal catch clanging as it crashed against the stone wall inside. Constance was breathless; she'd been running so hard. In the woods she'd realised with every pounding step that, with a combination of duty and a longing to help him, she was desperate to see the pilot before he left as he'd sworn he would.

'*You'll never have to see me again*,' he had said. And for one awful moment as Constance stood at the threshold and looked in, she believed it was true. As she'd left the cottage last night he had been drifting to sleep by the armchair. But the space he'd inhabited was now empty. During the night he must have thrown a few more logs on the fire, their charred, smoking remains reduced to dim embers in the grate.

She ran upstairs to see if he had chosen to sleep in the bed, but the bedclothes remained unruffled and the scent of settled dust lingered in the room. With her heart full of disappointment, Constance descended the staircase.

He had gone.

The pilot, Matthew, had moved one of the spindle-backed dining chairs from its position by the kitchen table and over to the fireside. Over the back he had draped her dress. She imagined him picking it up from the floor after she had left, touching it, taking the effort to look around the room, to find something appropriate from which to hang it; putting it a suitable distance from the fire so it would dry easily but not shrink from the proximity to the heat. She touched the dress with her fingertips, wondering at the effort he had made for her; such a small act but it held meaning that Constance couldn't understand. He hadn't just left it crumpled on the floor as others might have done. She stood, not quite knowing what she should do next. Somehow, going back to the house, back to her daily life, didn't feel right. It was almost as if the events of last night, the aircraft disappearing into the water, swimming out to find the pilot, relief at finding him alive, sitting with him in this very room, held meaning, held an opportunity for . . . something? Not excitement. No. There had been plenty enough of that last night, heart pounding, frightening excitement. But something else nonetheless. The opportunity to be useful, to break free of the confines of the house and to embrace the war effort, even if it was only starting with keeping a stricken pilot safe while he recovered and came to his senses. It was a start. She looked around. All trace of him had gone.

It wasn't really for Constance to worry about, but she *was* worried for him. She couldn't help it. And now she would return home and see Henry, who had stayed the night, and her family at the breakfast table, other than Mother, who always took a tray in her room. Douglas would be talking non-stop about flying, about the 'Hun', about training or some such other nonsense. Henry, oh she didn't know what to do about him, but in all likelihood he would be shooting daggers at her for spurning his advances last night. Or would he remain as confident as ever, as if nothing had happened at all? The boys were due to return back to their base at Kinloss today. Henry had seemed pleased that he'd been posted there, but Douglas was livid. He wanted to be down in the south of England, down in what he called 'the real thick of it.' He was desperate for his squadron to be posted almost anywhere other than on his own doorstep.

Constance thought him rather lucky. He wasn't exactly out of harm's way up here what with all the docks and Royal Navy Fleets to protect. But he didn't seem to relish being a defender of his own patch of Scottish sky. She would have given anything to do something for the war. But until it became obligatory for women to join, if it ever became obligatory, Father had forbidden her. 'Work isn't for women like you,' he had said. But Constance was twenty-one now. Didn't that count for something? Was there really nothing she could do that would take her away from the incessant, stifling boredom of Invermoray? They were no longer travelling down to spend time at the London house each year and most of her friends had joined the war effort, travelling far and wide for whichever of the services they'd entered and sending letters about how they were wearing the 'most ghastly uniform', and 'eating the most frightful rations'. But their letters had been tinged with excitement, happiness, purpose. Father had closed up the London house the moment war was declared, deeming it foolhardy to decamp to a city where bombs may fall any minute. 'What kind of father would I be?' he had asked. 'If I took us into the eye of the storm?'

And so now they were shut up here for the foreseeable future. She felt as though her home was her prison. She would not go back to the house. Not yet. Constance often took herself off on long walks around the loch or the estate, for exercise and for something to do, and so they would not worry for her. She'd gone to bed with the story of her headache and had risen to walk it off. That's what they'd think. No one would care enough to ask. She folded the gossamer dress over her arm and reluctantly stepped out into the cool morning air. Perhaps the pilot was right. Perhaps running away was the answer?

What if she did as *he* had done, arrived somewhere in the middle of the night, no one at home any the wiser as to where she had gone? What if she packed a bag and made her way into a city where she might engage in some kind of war work? But what could she do? What were her skills? After her governess, there had been finishing school. That had instructed her how to be fashionable in polite society, what to say and what not to say in her native tongue and in French, which she had promptly forgotten the moment she'd set foot back on Scottish soil, although she had tried so hard to remember. In essence, it had primed her for marriage. But it had given her no useful skill in the middle of war. She thought of her brother and how men were given the gift of thorough education and the expectation that ran alongside it. Constance was expected to do very little and allowed to do even less.

Pinecones crunched underfoot as Constance walked. She knew the forest so well she paid scant attention to her direction. Before long she would find herself at the road that ran along the edge of the woodland. She didn't want to see a soul. Not that she would. Not since petrol went on the ration almost the very moment war was declared. Many of those living in Invermoray village didn't have cars anyway. That level of modernity had yet to stretch to her corner of Scotland and there was no danger of the bus passing at this time of day to and from Beauly.

After a while the rumble in her stomach alerted her that she should probably return home. She would sneak into the kitchen and see if she could snaffle a few treats left over from her unwanted birthday party. She would disappear into the pantry, as she often did, and Mrs Fraser – the cook – wouldn't bat an eyelid. Constance and Douglas were forever below stairs; had been ever since they were children. With hardly any other friends nearby, they had frequented the kitchens and spent time with the loud, laughing Highland staff. It had felt more familiar than above stairs.

With her father's nose perpetually in a book and her mother attending the plants in the hothouse, Constance had made herself scarce most days when her governess was not present. As a child, as long as she was neither seen nor heard she had elicited no strong words from either parent. And so, with very little else to entertain her, Constance had been taught to skin the rabbits she had caught when out with the ghillie. It had given her a huge sense of silent satisfaction at dinner when she looked at her parents elegantly eating from their plates, not knowing that their daughter had both caught and prepared their food. They would have been horrified and found her some other, proper yet awful way to express her energy or, heaven forbid, employed her governess for the vast majority of the time rather than just a few days of the week.

And then when Douglas had returned home from school at summer and Christmas, Constance's life had been complete again. He often joked that school had been his undoing and that if he'd stayed behind – like her – it would have made more of a man of him. He followed Constance and the ghillie about the estate, discovering patches of it he'd long since forgotten, helping to keep the deer populace down but closing his eyes at the last minute when he pulled the trigger, the bullets always missing their mark until he gave up one summer and decided, 'never again'. He'd never quite bought into the much-lauded idea that with no wolves in Scotland anymore it was the estate's responsibility to keep a check on its own numbers. Constance and the ghillie had admired his sense of decency but had often taken the gun from him and continued the job themselves while Douglas sighed resignedly behind them; happy to help wrap the venison into brown paper and string parcels but preferring to play no part in the animal's actual death.

It had always been Douglas who had been fussed over by the staff, his time with them precious, before he returned to a school he loathed. She hadn't minded a bit about that. She was just grateful for her brother's return – a bit of company for a few short weeks, a few times a year. But that was then, when they were younger, back when they'd had more staff. Now it was just Mrs Fraser and Mrs Campbell – the housekeeper – along with a couple of local daily girls who cleaned for them. But Mrs Fraser had mentioned there'd been rumblings the daily girls were intending to join the war effort. For one thing they thought they would be paid more, which was probably true. Constance didn't know, but at least then they'd meet people. Other people. Anyone. Whenever Constance mentioned work, she faced an onslaught of argument from her parents. No one married a girl who *worked*.

Her stomach rumbled again. She realised she hadn't eaten a morsel last night, what with so many guests to talk to and thoughts of escaping Henry, there simply hadn't been time.

After she'd eaten something she would sit in the window seat in the library and read or stare out at the loch, which now held a Spitfire within its murky clutches when yesterday, it hadn't. She wondered if she would ever reveal that to anyone. Perhaps to Douglas, one day. But not yet. She would give the troubled pilot time to move on. She would not be responsible for a search party assembling.

In the middle of the forest, she walked towards the trickle of the river, intending to scoop a few handfuls of water to drink. The ghillie had spent many an hour showing her how to tickle trout out of the river, before he had gone to war with the rest of the male staff, other than the gardener who was too old to fight and the gardener's boy, who was too young. Eventually Constance had got the hang of gently ushering trout from the stream of flowing water with nothing more than the tips of her fingers. She wondered what her mother and father would say if she did it now, returning casually to the house with tonight's dinner in her arms. She laughed out loud. She'd be condemned as a heathen.

The splashing of the stream was louder than usual and as she approached she realised that there was someone in there. The sound of blood swooshed in her ears as she realised it was him

– the pilot, Matthew. She was overjoyed. He was still here. She still had the chance to help him and to apologise for her appalling behaviour yesterday. He hadn't seen her but she had seen him. His clothes, or rather the ghillie's, were piled up on the mossy bank. He was standing facing the other direction and Constance could see he was completely undressed. He was splashing himself clean in the icy cold water.

He hadn't heard her approach over the rushing of the water so she took the opportunity to move. She would not hail him. His nakedness embarrassed her into moving quickly to stand behind the trunk of a tall tree. She hoped she was hidden. She turned and pushed her back against the trunk, her fingers splayed out behind her, her nails almost dug into the bark as she stared into the forest, full of joy that he was still here; that he hadn't yet left.

She moved, just a fraction, intending to peer round the trunk – just to see if he had got dressed yet, just to see if it was safe to come out from her impromptu hiding place, but then all thoughts of movement were interrupted.

'Is there someone there?' he shouted from the water.

Constance's chest tightened as she inhaled sharply.

He repeated himself and then, sounding nervous, added, 'Come out. Show yourself.'

She was trapped. She couldn't stay here all day hiding in a cowardly fashion but likewise couldn't just spring out. She stalled, thinking.

'I swear to God if there's someone there . . .' he called loudly, aiming for threatening, Constance was sure.

'I . . .' Constance called but further words failed her. 'Yes,' she said. 'Yes, it's me. I'm here.'

There was no reply. She couldn't move. She couldn't see him naked again, she just couldn't. The embarrassment of it. Her fingernails dug further into the trunk and she stared straight ahead into the forest. The pine trees swayed of their natural accord but she was almost unseeing of anything around her. What was he doing?

The answer became clear as the pilot appeared suddenly in front of her. He'd put his trousers back on but they clung damply and tightly to his skin.

'What are you doing here? Why have you come back? Are you on your own?' He looked around nervously, firing questions at her like bullets. His dark hair fell over his face; his eyelashes still held droplets of water, framing his light green eyes.

'Yes,' she almost stuttered, shocked that he had sprung at her so quickly. 'I'm alone.'

He was so close she could feel the heat from his body. He stepped back. 'I apologise,' he said. 'I was worried you'd brought someone.'

'Why would I?' Constance asked.

'To take me in, of course.'

'I wouldn't do that.'

The statement hung in the air between them.

He frowned, inching a fraction towards her. He pushed his brown hair back from his face and water ran down his neck. 'Why wouldn't you?' he asked.

'I don't know,' she said quietly. Although she did know. He'd seemed so fragile of mind, so bewildered, so shocked by his ordeal last night. He'd talked nonsense of running from his duties. Perhaps he just needed time. And if so, she could give him that. Time was something she had plenty of.

CHAPTER 10

Constance stood by the tree. She'd removed her splayed hands from the trunk but resisted the urge to pick the pieces of bark from underneath her nails for fear he would see how tightly she'd been gripping the tree; that she'd been so incredibly nervous she'd been clinging to it. Did he think she'd been watching him? She hadn't. She'd turned away *almost* the very moment she'd realised he was naked.

'Thank you for looking after me last night,' he said, bringing her back from her thoughts.

'It was a pleasure.' She had resorted to formality and tried to rescue herself.

'Why did you come back?' he questioned.

Constance thought. 'I wanted to check you were all right. I wanted to check you hadn't gone. I didn't want you to have gone,' she confessed and then could have bitten her own tongue off to stop herself from talking.

He narrowed his eyes. 'Why ever not?'

'Because, you're shocked, I think. A sort of shell shock from the crash. And you've not eaten anything. And you've got no money, I assume. Or papers. Where will you go? And although it's summer, it's terribly cold at night so you'll probably freeze to death.' She knew this last bit wasn't true but she pressed on regardless. 'And we're miles from anywhere—'

'Which will probably work in my favour,' he interrupted.

'Well, no,' Constance said. 'I don't think it would. There's Invermoray village a few miles down the road but that's it. What will you do? Hide out in a village for the remainder of the war? A stranger of fighting age suddenly turning up in a Highland village would be hard to overlook. Or were you hoping for a passing car to catch you on the road somewhere? I warn you, there are almost no cars at the moment, and anyone official passing will want to see your papers. Most of the Highlands have been cordoned off. We can't go anywhere without being stopped in our tracks by the army these days. There are so many houses being requisitioned up here and heaven knows what's happening, but it's all terribly hush-hush. So you won't get very far on foot. I could lend you my bicycle but the same problem applies. You'll be stopped. You could always wait for the bus,' she said, 'which is unpredictable in its timing at best. But for that you'll need money. Do you have any?'

The corners of his mouth twitched. 'Well, I must say, you've thought about this a great deal more than I have.'

'I've been thinking about you all night,' she said and then screamed at herself inside her own head.

'Have you now?' he asked. An eyebrow lifted and the smile deepened.

'Not like that,' she flustered and she faced the humiliation of watching him laugh at her.

'Well I should hope not,' he said, teasingly. 'A nice girl like you.'

She flushed. 'I felt horribly guilty,' she said quietly. 'That I'd just left you. That I'd abandoned you.'

He tilted his head to one side. 'I shouldn't have asked you to help me,' he said seriously. 'It was unfair. Perhaps you're right.' He raked his hand through his wet hair, sending droplets of water flying. 'Perhaps it was the shock. I wasn't thinking straight, asking a young woman to go out of her way to house a man who, well, who shouldn't really be here.'

'I don't mind, not now, not now that I've thought about it. And I have, a great deal. You should stay at the cottage. Stay as long as you like, as long as you need. There's plenty of clothes and I'll bring you food from the house.'

A snapping sound emanated from far behind him and Constance started. Matthew swung round. 'What was that?' he said quickly.

'I think just a doe or a stag perhaps. Since the ghillie left to fight they've been allowed to repopulate in droves. Father's done nothing about culling their numbers,' she babbled.

He continued staring into the depths of the forest as if he didn't trust her appraisal of the situation. When he turned back his jaw was set. He breathed deeply.

'If you mean what you say . . . if I *can* stay at the cottage, just for a while, then yes, I'm very grateful indeed that you're helping me. Completely indebted in fact.'

His smile disarmed her and she struggled to gather her thoughts, looking at the ground, as they walked back to the cottage.

'Stay,' she said softly, her eyes still cast down. 'I promise I won't tell anyone and I promise faithfully I'll keep you safe. Stay until you come to a decision. Until you feel ready to hand yourself in or return to your squadron or . . .'

'Do you really mean it? You promise not to tell a soul?'

Constance nodded.

'Thank you,' he said as they arrived at the cottage door. He held it open for her. 'It's not as simple as you think. It's not that I won't return to my squadron. It's that I can't.'

CHAPTER 11

August 2020

The interior of the cottage was in good condition. 'It's very . . . brown,' Kate offered as she looked at the solid wooden furniture and somewhat battered kitchen cupboards.

'Built to last,' James said. Illustrating his point, he gave the leg of the dining table a small kick as if it were a car tyre. The stone walls were their natural grey and Kate wondered whether painting them would be sacrilege. It would be tricky to put it back the way it was, should they not like the result. The sofa and armchair were so faded that she had no idea what colour they were originally. How long had it been since the war? Over seventy years of sunlight had faded the fabric, the dust probably ingrained within the fibres.

'There's one big bedroom upstairs but I thought I'd partition it and make it an en suite,' James said.

Kate nodded and asked, 'Where's the bathroom now then?'

'Outside.'

'What?' She was open-mouthed.

'The ghillie would have used a tin bath in front of the fire. The loo is in an outhouse attached to the cottage.'

'There goes the idea of toshing this place up quickly then,' Kate said with disappointment. 'Installing upstairs plumbing isn't going to be a five-minute job.'

James shrugged. 'Might be. For a plumber.'

'Hmmm.' She clicked her pen and made a note in her book.

'*Dear Diary*,' James quipped, '*James is such a nightmare*.'

Kate looked up and laughed, but he had turned and was examining the old cupboards. She moved over to the large fireplace, where an old whisky bottle of Macallan Glenlivet, marked 1926 but ten-year-aged, sat on the mantelpiece. Who had left it there? The ghillie, or someone else? And had it been there, on that mantel, ever since the war?

'I missed that when I cleaned the general rubbish out,' James said with a grimace. 'Although now I wonder if we could leave it as a piece of the cottage's history, among some other knick-knacks. Tourists like those, don't they? Although not too many, as we're the ones who'll have to dust them on changeover days.'

Kate nodded. 'Other than the plumbing and some new sofas, a lick of paint's all that's needed down here,' she said. 'Along with some mod cons such as a dishwasher, some pictures for the walls, maybe some moody landscapes of the Highlands, the loch, that kind of thing.'

'Repaint the dining chairs and table, make them . . . less brown?' James offered.

Kate agreed. 'Cream? Nice and neutral?'

James nodded and she realised she was slowly warming to him. Maybe they could work together after all.

They drove around the periphery of the estate in the rattling Land Rover. James seemed unfazed when, after a few minutes, a deer ambled its way across the road.

Kate inched forward in her seat. 'Wow, a real deer.'

Beside her James laughed. 'Not a fake one.'

'You know what I mean.'

He pulled the car to a complete stop so she could take a look, and Kate wound the stiff window down. The deer looked back at her and carried on chewing, obviously used to people. After a minute or so it decided they were friend, not foe, and bent its head confidently to continue foraging by the side of the road.

James's stomach growled and Kate gave him a look. 'Hungry?'

'I'm always hungry. Do you want . . .' He stopped, clearly debating if he should ask the next question.

'Do I want . . . ?'

'To go to the pub,' he finished. 'It's pretty good. Nice food. Decent wine. We don't have to. We can just head back to the house.'

Kate glanced round at Whisky, already asleep on the blanket spread over the back seat.

'It would be nice to see the pub and the village. I arrived in near darkness yesterday. It'll be good to get my bearings. And some lunch. Will they let Whisky in?'

James nodded and they set off towards the village, where he parked in the small market square. There was a coach parked on the far side and Kate looked at it curiously. So tourists *did* venture to this part of the Highlands. Perhaps they were on their way to or from a nearby tourist attraction. That was good to know.

Inside the pub, it was busy. James, taller than many of the other customers, waved over the top of their heads to the redheaded man pulling a pint behind the bar. He nodded in recognition.

She looked around. Many of the tourists were pensioners, probably just off the coach. When Kate looked back, James was scouting out a table in the corner of the low-beamed restaurant. He had to bend slightly to avoid hitting his head on the ceiling, before he threw himself into the high-backed bench. Whisky squeezed under the table and promptly resumed sleeping as Kate sat on the bench opposite. They had one of the last tables and it had only just gone midday.

'Angus, how are you?' James asked as the barman arrived with menus.

'Aye, not bad. Same day, different date. You know how it is,'

Angus replied. 'Don't need a menu, do ya, James? Already know what ya havin'?'

James looked embarrassed. 'We'll take menus. I might have something different today.'

Angus put menus in front of them, looked at Kate and then looked pointedly at James. After a moment he sighed, and stretched his hand out to shake hers. 'James has no manners,' he said. 'I'm Angus.'

Without looking up from his menu James said, 'Oh sorry, yeah, this is Kate. Kate sort of lives with us now.'

'O . . . K . . .' Angus said, clearly bemused.

'I'm working there, up at the house,' Kate explained as she leaned forward to shake Angus's hand. 'Helping to put the place on the map, so to speak. Turn it into a B & B and viable holiday business and then begin promoting it.'

'Great,' Angus enthused. 'Some extra rooms round here would take the pressure off us a wee bit. We're forever turning people away. Drinks?'

James ordered a large bottle of still mineral water for them. So, Kate reflected, this place had rooms and they were busy. It wasn't as out of the way as she had thought, clearly. She was just about to voice this when James inched forward conspiratorially.

'What's in that notebook of yours, then? Your master plan to take over?'

Kate sighed. *Here we go again.* She was just about to launch into her defence but James got there first.

'I'm joking,' he said, holding his hands up, 'I'm joking.'

But he wasn't smiling, and she knew this would be ground they'd cover again.

'Shall we order?' he suggested. 'The local steak and ale pie's good.'

Angus didn't look surprised when James ordered it. He showed Kate his notepad and said out of the corner of his mouth, 'Surprise surprise. I already wrote it down, look.'

Kate stifled a laugh and then sat back after ordering a sandwich. 'Are you that predictable?' she dared. 'Steak pie, every time you're here?'

'Not every time.' James shuffled on his bench. 'I'm traditional. I like what I like. I'm a man of routine, I suppose.'

Kate looked out the window towards the village square, watching the tourists as they got back on to the coach. Her mind whirred at opportunities to draw such a strong crowd to the house, but she resisted the urge to start scribbling in her notebook, lest James should comment.

'A man of routine?' she muttered absent-mindedly.

'Yeah,' he said. 'I eat in here once or twice a week. I cook a bit at home, or Mum does. Then I go running most evenings or I swim in the loch.'

She looked back from the window. 'You swim in the loch?'

'Sure. You should try it.'

'No thanks. Looks cold.'

He laughed. 'It's invigorating.'

'That's just another word for cold,' Kate countered with a smile.

They spoke about her background while they ate. Or rather Kate found she was speaking a lot, as it dawned on her she was being re-interviewed. She let him hurl question after question at her. He did it with an actual air of interest and so she tried to be as friendly as she could, while also feeling she was having to justify her position at the house.

'And so you left because . . . ?' James asked eventually.

'What do you mean?' she replied cautiously.

There was absolutely no way she was going to tell him she'd been accused of flirting with a bar-owner client, had received a formal warning that had gone onto her work record and, incensed, had thrown in the towel. After all these weeks, it still grated on her that she'd let her guard down quite that much that night; that she'd allowed herself to be led out the back door into the alley so her client wouldn't have been on his own while he'd had a cigarette, that she'd fallen into the trap of drinking too much and had found him dangerously close to her before she'd realised what he was up to and had put an immediate but polite stop to it.

But it had been too late. His wife had followed them, long suspecting her husband of playing away. He *had* been cheating on her, Kate was sure. But not with her. And as if that night hadn't been humiliating enough, the next day her account director said the bar owner and his wife had complained about *her* behaviour. Kate had been so upset she'd cried at work. And she never cried at work.

'If everything you worked on was so fantastic – if every project you touched turned to gold . . .' James said somewhat provocatively, 'why leave?'

'I just needed to get out of the rat race,' Kate deflected. As much as she could sense James almost coming round to her presence at Invermoray, it felt highly possible he'd use the truth against her in some way, presumably to kick her out. Right now, she didn't trust him enough to tell him.

CHAPTER 12

September 2020

Over the next few weeks, Kate had no time to worry about James and his suspicion of her – laced with what she assumed was mild dislike. He, Liz and Kate had sat down and worked out their various roles: who would apply for various licences, who would start renovation plans, and who would open discussions with tourism bodies to get Invermoray House noticed by the right people in their early days as a B & B. It was slow going and a million miles away from the fast-paced lifestyle Kate had just left behind, but it was actually quite fun, absorbing herself in the minutiae of filling in forms and trawling through holiday lettings websites to understand what they should be doing and when in terms of bookings.

This start-up side of a business was one she'd not experienced before and there was a real sense of satisfaction in watching a business begin from scratch, knowing that when they were ready to launch and she was going to put her PR hat back on, that she'd actually done a lot of the work getting them there. She had a real sense of ownership and with each passing day felt more and more immersed in Invermoray House. Kate suddenly understood why clients had been near devastated when she'd reported in with PR news that wasn't as positive as they'd liked. Telling a client about a bad review was never good, but she'd learnt over the years to forget about it an hour or so later, file it away as unfortunate, move on and organise the next glowing review; whereas clients seethed over it for months afterwards. She finally understood why. It wasn't just business. It was personal. Kate needed this to succeed; not just for herself, but for the house. Invermoray needed love, care and a new lease of life, even if all they could offer it for the time being was a lick of paint and a few new cushions. But the bare bones were there. The main furniture in all the bedrooms was solid oak or mahogany – imposing and Victorian in the main and therefore built to last. Invermoray House was an old dame in tatty clothes.

After James begrudgingly found Kate just enough space on the desk opposite him in the estate office, they worked together mostly in silence. Kate wasn't sure either of them noticed the quiet, their heads bowed over their laptops.

She'd grown used to working near him over the past few weeks, each of them buried in their respective work. Kate had finally finished compiling a list of online holiday letting agencies, commissions they charged, what was expected of each of them should they choose to work with them, and had narrowed it down to her top five. They'd need to sit and discuss it in detail when they next had an ad-hoc catch-up meeting. Liz trusted Kate just to get on with it and to loop her in at the end of each task. Whereas Kate couldn't tell whether James trusted her. He was enough of a control freak to ask pertinent questions about the work she was doing, but not enough of one to look over her shoulder or actually to take the work from her and do it himself, too engrossed was he with the legal minutiae of the business endeavour.

They wanted, ideally, to open as a B & B first and then, maybe, to fix the orangery and offer afternoon teas and guided tours of the house later on. Kate was busy working out how to get coach companies to consider Invermoray House as part of their upcoming tour schedules when James slammed his laptop lid and swore.

'Problem?' Kate dared. She felt as if she walked on eggshells around him, never knowing if he'd be reasonable in his reply or whether he'd shout.

'No.' He got up and thrust his hands in his pockets and stared out of the small window. 'I'm going for a run,' he murmured. He turned and looked at her; mock horror on his face. 'You aren't going to be out on the roads in that little rental car, are you?'

Kate gave him a confused look. 'No.' Although she'd managed to negotiate a decent long-term deal to rent the car on a six-month lease, she was barely using it.

'Good. I might survive this particular run then,' he said with a hint of a smile.

Kate gave a huge sigh of relief as he left her to her work. She wasn't expecting to be friends with him. Actually, she was lying to herself. She *was* rather hoping they'd have made friends by now. She missed her friends back home. She missed her colleagues. Most of them had become friends over the years, especially Jenny. She picked up her mobile phone, stood in the only spot in the office that allowed a semblance of signal and wrote a text message to Jenny. She asked her how she was, what she was working on and, if Kate popped back to London for a weekend to see her and a few other friends, if Jenny would put her up? She didn't think her brother and whoever he was calling his girlfriend that particular week would relish the idea of her rocking up to her flat that they now lived in, even if she gave them plenty of notice.

Kate looked at her watch. It was growing late and the sky was turning a beautiful shade of hazy yellow as the sun began its slow descent behind the tall mountain peaks in the distance. It wouldn't be fully dark until about 11 p.m. in the Highlands and Kate was growing used to the late sunsets and the startlingly early sunrises.

She closed her laptop and worried about what to cook for

dinner. They didn't have a formal rota but she'd established it had to be her turn by now. Liz would be out at a Women's Institute meeting and was grabbing dinner with a few friends afterwards. Kate was jealous. Perhaps she should have asked to go along, see what actually went on at a WI meeting, and make a few local friends. But James had said he'd be in for dinner and had looked at Kate with wide-eyed wonder when she suggested it must be her turn to cook. She didn't want to give him a reason to think any less of her, so she knew she had to offer.

She locked up the office, grabbed her car keys from the hall-stand inside the main house and drove towards Invermoray village. She realised she'd inadvertently fibbed to James. She would be on the road, wreaking havoc, after all.

Kate had been to the village only a few times over the past few weeks. She popped in more for something to do rather than anything else. The market square played host to an array of traditional shops that she thought were dying out almost everywhere else. A butcher, baker, fishmonger and greengrocer sat alongside each other and Kate had been pleasantly surprised to see a small library nestled into a corner of the square, near the convenience store. She made a mental note to join and perhaps see what, if any, classes they ran both there and at the little community centre. She was happy to investigate a watercolour class or a yoga session.

Next to her lights were being switched off in a hardware shop but her attention was drawn from the pale grey Victorian buildings to the pub opposite. Angus stepped out of the Invermoray Arms, his shift obviously over for the afternoon, examined the colourful hanging baskets overhead and then began swirling his car keys in his hand. He raised his other hand to Kate in greeting and she smiled in return as she walked across the square towards him.

'You goin' in for a drink?' he asked.

Kate shook her head. 'No, just hoping to grab some bits for dinner. I'm cooking for James.'

'Ah it didn't take him long to work his charm on you now did it?' He chuckled and Kate warmed to him.

She gave him a look. 'It's not like that. It's my turn, sort of. I need to impress him. I don't think he likes me very much.'

Angus's eyebrows went skyward and Kate wasn't sure exactly why she'd told him that.

'Get him a steak and ale pie and the man will love you forever.'

'Perhaps,' she agreed, keen to move on.

'The little shop over there's all right. Does a few bits and bobs. Or there's the butcher's, but I'm rather afraid you've left it a bit late to hunter-gather. Other than the little convenience shop and my pub, everyone closes at five. You can set yer watch by 'em. I need a few bits from the wee supermarket. I'll come over there with you.'

'What do you do for fun around here?' she asked as they walked to the shop.

'There's the pub,' he said proudly. 'And that's kinda it. But it's a real community pub so I don't see anyone moaning about being too bored. Why? You feeling the need to break free? Run wild?'

She laughed.

'My sister's in a book club,' he said. 'A bunch o' lasses who only knew each other in passing, so I doubt you'd be outta place. If you fancied joining, I could put in a word?'

Kate thought about that. 'Yes, actually, that sounds great. If you don't mind!'

They swapped phone numbers so he could pass Kate's details on to his sister.

'I don't think they do much talking about the book from what I gather. Mainly they drink a lotta wine.'

'That sounds even better.'

As they wandered around the shop Kate bought two thick pieces of local salmon and paired it with a pot of watercress sauce, various veg and a bottle of chilled Sancerre. Not exactly a banquet but, she hoped, not too try-hard either.

Angus looked disapproving as they stood at the checkout. 'I'm tellin' ya, steak and ale pie,' he joked.

Kate panicked he might be right. But it wasn't exactly the food part of dinner she was worried about. It was the conversation part. When James and Liz were both there, they cooked with happy ease and Kate loaded the dishwasher and cleared up. But there had, so far, always been the three of them sitting down together. Kate cursed Liz for going out. She was the glue that held their conversations together.

Kate returned to the house as the colour of the sky changed. She locked her car and stood in calming silence. The pinks and reds behind the bands of blue-grey cloud made it look as if the sky had been painted with tiger stripes in mind. It didn't happen very often, but when the clouds finally parted and the sun penetrated the wild Scottish scenery, it was a thing of wonder. The view changed immediately. Everything became clearer, greener and Kate could pick out the large patches of deep plum-coloured heather as it grew in swathes across the mountains towards the top where the forest had never quite managed to reach regardless of its thousands of years of clambering northwards. And then the clouds closed in on themselves and just as quickly, the view reverted back to one large and imposing shadow, each tree indiscernible from the next on the mountain range.

Kate stood in awe of the expanse of sky and listened to the distant sound of highland sheep *baa*ing to each other in conversation. She breathed deeply, feeling the clean Highland air enter her lungs. She told herself that if dinner went badly as it was bound to, she would come and sit out here, maybe by the loch, and just watch the world go by as the evening settled into night.

James had returned from his run and was freshly showered, his hair damp. He hadn't towel-dried himself properly and where he'd put his shirt on while wet, it clung to his skin. He was flicking through a newspaper on the kitchen counter, while holding a cup of coffee.

He turned as he heard Kate enter, the rustle of the shopping bag announcing her entrance. He gave her a wide smile, his eyes creasing at the sides, transforming his face completely and taking Kate by surprise. The action must have taken James by surprise, too, because it was almost as if it had suddenly dawned on him that he was supposed to be being unpleasant, and he wiped the smile from his face.

Kate clenched her teeth together. She hated the way he blew hot and cold; the way he masked rudeness by pretending he was joking. But his initial open smile had thrown her. He'd let his guard down until he'd reminded himself he wasn't supposed to like her – forcing himself to dislike her. As she thought about it, she found this interesting.

Kate said 'hi,' and then began unpacking the contents of the shopping bag on the counter. She could feel James watching her and when she unpacked the wine he was behind her reaching over for it. Kate turned to get the tin foil to cook the fish in, but as she did she was confronted with his chest. He was still behind her, preparing to move but not quick enough. 'Oh, I'm so sorry,' she said as she crashed into him.

'It's fine.' He moved away, allowing her to pass before he stepped back into position and rifled in a draw for the corkscrew. But a flicker of something bordering on physical attraction ignited within her and, horrified at herself, she quashed it immediately, glancing away.

Their dinner was laced with awkwardness. Contrary to Angus's warning James hoovered up his salmon and after a glass of wine seemed to relax, though not enough to actually speak to Kate. Did he feel as awkward as she? He put his knife and fork together and Kate panicked that she'd not bought enough food for a man who confessed he was always hungry.

'Thanks. That was lovely,' he said, probably more out of duty than truth.

'You're welcome.' Kate smiled.

He tapped his finger on the kitchen table and looked around, probably clawing desperately for something to say. And if so, then Kate silently congratulated him for trying. She decided to save him.

'I think I've found the perfect selection of websites for us to register with for holiday lettings. We should probably talk about cleaning agencies, get some quotes sorted for when—'

'Don't you ever take a minute off?' he asked, surprising her.

'Um . . .' Every minute Kate didn't think about work she thought she'd be chastised.

Whisky nudged her leg, hoping for the scraps of salmon. She gave the Labrador a scratch behind his ears and straightened up.

'I'm sorry,' James said quietly after a few seconds. 'I think about this estate all bloody day. I can't do it all night as well. I'll go mad.'

Kate nodded. 'It must be . . .' she grasped around for the right word '. . . complicated. Living where you work. Working where you live.'

He toyed with the stem of his empty wine glass. 'It is.' He sighed audibly. 'Do you fancy a drink? A proper one?'

Kate looked at her near-empty wine glass. She'd thought that was a proper drink.

'A brandy I mean. Or a whisky?' he clarified.

The dog's ears pricked at his name.

'Sure.'

They popped their plates in the dishwasher and Kate followed James through the hallway, past the ballroom with its doors open for airing – sheets cast over the settees that dotted the peripheries. They entered the sitting room that seemed to double as a study, its fire dimming in the hearth. James walked over and threw a log onto it. The scent of fresh pinewood emanated into the room as the flames curled around the wood.

While James opened doors to the drinks cabinet, looking for glasses, Kate stood at one of the tall windows and looked out. The last throes of evening sunlight cast a yellow gauze onto the ripples of the loch. This house, the beauty of it, despite its air of faded glamour; the loch, the village, the mountains that she hadn't yet climbed . . . she had all this yet to experience and only a few months in which to achieve it.

She turned to James, who had returned to a house he'd never considered home and seemed entirely ill at ease living in. It dawned on her he was, to all intents and purposes, trapped. The loyalty to saving his family home outweighed anything else he'd rather be doing. Kate viewed him with a new sympathy.

'I can see why you're not entirely happy,' she offered.

'Can you?' He paused midway through pouring a few fingers of whisky into a tumbler.

Kate recognised that tone. His hackles had risen and she wished she'd said nothing now, but her courage rose and she ploughed on. 'Yes,' she snapped. 'And don't be on the offensive all the time. Honestly, it's not attractive.'

His eyes widened. Then he laughed and continued pouring their drinks. 'Well,' he said as he walked towards her and handed her the drink. 'That's me told.'

Kate smiled, warily. She couldn't be quite sure if he'd disappear into a fog of contempt seconds later as he seemed wont to do.

'I'm here to help, you know. I'm not here to tread all over your efforts—'

'I know,' he said, still standing in front of her.

'I'm not here to show you up—' she continued.

'I know.'

'And I'm not here to be part of a team and then take all the credit for myself. This will work. We will make a success of this house.'

'I'm sure we will,' he said, an amused look on his face.

Kate frowned. 'So what's the problem then? Because, cards on the table, James, I'm not sure I can put up with your ever so slightly pissy attitude for much longer. You blow hot and cold and then sometimes you're just deadly silent.' Kate was becoming brave now. 'I've got to admit, it's thoroughly unnerving.'

He looked down at her, which unnerved her even more, and said nothing. He appeared to be having some kind of internal debate.

'You want to know what's wrong?' he piped up. 'What's really wrong? You want to know why I think you being here is a terrible idea?'

'Yes,' she said. Although given the ferocity of his tone, Kate wasn't sure she wanted to know any of it now.

He took her glass from her hand and placed it on the mahogany sideboard, littered with family photographs of recent McLays enjoying their schooldays and summer games on the tennis courts. It occurred to Kate to ask where those tennis courts were – overgrown, probably. He put his drink down next to hers.

'You want to know why I think you being here is a disaster?'

Kate nodded again, with less certainty than before.

'Fine,' he said as he grabbed her hand. 'Then come with me. There's something I need to show you.'

CHAPTER 13

1940

'What do you mean you *can't*?' Constance turned to Matthew. 'You *can't* hand yourself in? Why ever not?' They crossed the threshold of the cottage.

'I just can't. I just . . . can't. That's all.'

'What have you done? I don't understand.'

'You don't need to understand.'

How dare he? 'I'll admit the longer you leave it the harder it's going to be, but you can't live here forever. You can't run forever. Tell me.' She folded her arms. 'If you want my help, if you want me to keep my promise to house you here and tell no one, then you'll need to trust me. You'll need to tell me what you've done.' Constance sat on one of the settees and Matthew sat next to her.

He was silent.

Her mind ran wild. 'Have you . . . ?'

Matthew looked at her and waited, but Constance wasn't immediately able to voice her worst fear.

She swallowed. 'Have you murdered someone?' she asked eventually.

'Good God,' he cried. 'After my confession I can't go on shooting innocent men from the sky, you think I'm a cold-blooded killer?'

'No, of course not,' she said hurriedly. 'I just . . .'

'I've done something I shouldn't have done,' he said simply. 'Something that will land me in a lot of trouble when I'm caught. If I'm caught. But I rather intend not to be, if it's all the same to you.'

When he frowned and looked as if he wasn't going to continue, she prompted him. 'Such as?'

'I hit my commanding officer.'

'Good God,' she said, her eyebrows lifting. Douglas had spoken about the seriousness of military discipline but she had only a vague idea of what hitting a senior officer brought in terms of punishment. He would be court-martialled surely. And then prison? 'That was stupid. Why?'

'He was doing something he shouldn't have been doing, to a woman.'

Constance drew in a short, sharp intake of breath and her hand flew to her mouth. 'What happened?' she asked from behind her hand, although she sensed the answer would disgust her.

'We were at a dance, at the airbase. A few of the local girls had come along. One of them was getting progressively more drunk over the course of the evening, and my C.O. was actively encouraging it. She bumped into me, said she felt a little unwell so I offered to see her home safely. My C.O. told me my input was not required and then winked at me as if to tell me to simply go along with it, leave her to him, so to speak.'

Matthew looked at the floor. 'I'll admit, there was a part of me that knew what he was about to do and I'm ashamed to say I debated doing nothing, debated getting completely blotto myself. I'd just shot down a couple of enemy fighters and I don't think either of them parachuted out. Awful. Just awful. And then there's my C.O., the man who sends me out to kill, asking me to be complicit in something heinous.

'I wondered if this girl was worth the trouble I was about to land myself in. In the end, I knew I couldn't live with myself if I heard him bragging about how he'd . . . well . . . you know . . .

if she was passed out and I'd done nothing about it. So I went outside and found them round by one of the huts. She was barely able to stand; he had his hand over her mouth and her skirt hitched up to her waist. My C.O. hadn't yet got his trousers down. I pulled him off her, told her to find her friends and go home, and when he swung at me I swung back.'

Matthew paused, the pain of events etched on his face. 'I'm not the kind of man who goes around throwing fists but one punch was all it took. He was drunk and didn't have the wherewithal to come back for a second go. But the way he looked at me before he passed out . . . I could see the revenge he'd wreak written all over his face. I didn't stop to think any further. I panicked, ran, got in my plane and just pointed it anywhere. Didn't expect to get as far north as Scotland, or that I'd get shot down. Christ knows who by. So bloody cloudy out there I couldn't see a thing. But then if I hadn't been shot down, I might have ended up so far north I'd be in the sea.'

Constance listened and finally removed her hand from her mouth.

'For the first ten or so minutes, I was in complete fear that I'd be followed and taken back to base. Then as I bumped and bounced through the clouds and I began to calm down, I realised the whole event had actually done me a favour.' He looked bleakly at her. 'I can't do this anymore, Constance. This war, it brings out the very worst in some people. I can no longer be the worst version of myself. It causes us to hurt, willingly; to kill, willingly. It's driving me towards madness. I can't watch what war does to me and to others and I can't shoot men down whom I've never met but who are supposed to be my enemy. I just can't.'

He put his head in his hands but before he did, Constance could see the tears in his eyes. He needed rest and recovery, and now she understood why he needed to hide. 'I'm so sorry. I understand and I'm so sorry,' she whispered and put her hand on his knee. Beside her, he simply nodded.

CHAPTER 14

Matthew stood up eventually, walked over to the kitchen and placed his hands on the countertop, his back to Constance. She gave him a few minutes to steady himself.

'Are you hungry?' she asked gently.

'I am rather, yes.'

'I was going to go back to the house and fetch myself a bit of breakfast. I'll bring you something back.'

He moved over to kneel by the fireplace without looking at her. 'Thank you,' he said.

She bit her lip. 'I don't think you should light that.'

He tilted his head to one side. 'The fire? Why not?'

'The smoke will rise up the chimney of course. It's all right at night. No one can see the cottage from, well from anywhere, at night. But in the daylight, the smoke rising . . . I don't think it's a good idea. They'll see it up at the house.'

He looked at the fire as if it hadn't occurred to him. 'Yes, I suppose you're right.'

'You're lucky you crashed in August,' Constance said. 'Imagine if you'd crashed in the depths of midwinter.'

He stood from assembling the fire. 'In that case, I'll put another jumper on.' He moved towards the staircase before turning back. 'Constance?'

'Yes?'

'Thank you.'

She nodded and moved towards the cottage door. 'I'll come back as soon as I can.'

'Where have you been?' Her mother's accusing voice made Constance jump. It was rare her mother made the trip to visit the kitchens. Constance had been looking for food she could carry in her pockets or in linen napkins, trying not to draw too much attention to herself as Mrs Fraser prepared lunch.

'Your brother and Henry are departing. Do I need to remind you their leave's over? Finished all too soon, more's the pity. I do so like Henry,' her mother mused. 'I rather thought you did too?'

Constance was at the edge of the larder, her hand grasping a wedge of cold meat pie. It was too late to hide it. 'I did,' she said sadly, and offered no further explanation.

Her mother's gaze flicked to the pie. 'Are you feeling better now?' She said it in a way that made Constance think she didn't truly care.

Confusion clouded Constance's face. 'Pardon?'

'Your migraine?' her mother asked, folding her arms. 'The reason you left your own birthday party rather early.'

'Yes. Thank you.' Constance smiled and remained on the spot, waiting for her mother to leave. Try as she might, Constance had never pierced the formality her mother displayed towards her. She wanted to return to Matthew, to take him some form of breakfast. Even though meat pie was a strange choice she couldn't see anything else that would survive the journey to the cottage.

'Well, come to say goodbye then,' her mother commanded. Constance looked at the pie in her hand and without a word, put it back on the marble shelf and closed the larder door.

*

It was hours later when she was finally able to make it back into the kitchen to retrieve the pie. She had said a solemn and tense goodbye to Henry outside the house. He hadn't looked at all remorseful about his drunken molestations in the orangery. Constance was filled with anger now she saw him again and the last thing she wanted to do was engage in any physical contact with him but she stretched out her hand to shake his in order to ensure a tone of distant formality. Before Constance realised what he intended, though, Henry had brought her hand to his lips and kissed it instead.

He looked as if he wanted to say something but she cut him off. 'Goodbye, Henry. Stay safe.' She pulled her hand away. He looked displeased but Constance moved past him to bid her brother farewell. She wondered how her brother could be friends with a man like Henry. Douglas had always been too trusting of others, always the first to see the good in everyone. But then she also had thought Henry perfectly nice and charming, until her birthday party. What fools they could both be. As she moved toward Douglas she saw he was waiting for her, a smile on his face.

She thought of him, up in the skies. Was he as anxious as Matthew had been? Was her older brother simply wearing his smiling affability like a mask? Her eyes searched his for a clue as to his true feelings about the war.

Douglas grinned and then pulled her towards him, embracing her. 'Come here, Smidge,' he said into her hair.

'You've not called me that in ages,' Constance replied, standing back and looking at him.

'Perhaps because I've not been here in what feels like forever.' He held her at arm's length. 'You're not really a smidge of a thing anymore. You're all grown up now. I think that passed me by. Good party last night by the way. I didn't see you much towards the end.'

Constance mumbled a suitable reply and her eyes darted towards Henry, lounging carelessly by the motorcar where her mother fawned over him almost embarrassingly. She silently prayed that if Douglas did return soon, it would be without Henry in tow. 'Is it still as boring up there as ever?' she asked him.

He laughed. 'It's not so bad. But you'd think what with it all going on down in the south that we'd be shunted there quick sharp, but still nothing. I hate to think of them all down there, when there's some of us up here with very little to do in comparison. Things are really heating up,' he said. 'I feel it's my duty to do more.'

'Douglas,' Constance chastised. 'There's really very little more you could be doing. You hardly ever get leave.'

'I know,' he said. 'But still.'

'Are you sleeping all right?' she asked. She wasn't sure how to ask what she really wanted, about how it felt to be responsible for shooting men down, about how he was coping with that onerous responsibility.

'Yes, so dog-tired I can't do anything *but* sleep the moment my head hits the pillow.'

'Well, I suppose that's something,' she said, giving his hand a squeeze.

He rubbed his tired eyes and gave a yawn. 'Too many pink gins last night. Good job I'm not flying today. What with France falling and Germany having taken Denmark and Norway we aren't risking it up there anymore. So tomorrow I resume duties, circling about the North Sea, defending the Royal Navy from attack.'

'So no leave then?' Constance asked hopefully.

'I might make it back here for a night or two in a few weeks. Although,' he said quietly, 'word is we might be shipped off, not sure where yet. Could be Africa now Italy's bloody joined the war and we're battling hammer and tongs out there. So it may be a quick bout of pre-embarkation leave if any. Don't tell Mother and Father yet, will you? It's not all bad, being so close to home for now. Henry's people are down in Cornwall so there's no hope of him making it home very often.'

Frankly, Constance couldn't care where Henry's parents lived, but she did rather worry that Douglas might be shipped off somewhere frightening. And then there was Douglas's good-natured way of issuing invitations to all and sundry, meaning Henry would probably be invited if the two men were allowed a pass again.

'What about you, Smidge? What will you do?'

'I don't know,' Constance said truthfully.

'Well, for heaven's sake don't just sit around being bored, will you?' Douglas teased. 'Do something useful, if you like. And if you don't like . . . do something fun.'

Constance smiled. 'I'll try.'

'I'll see you before you know it,' Douglas said, pulling her in for another hug. He'd always said this to her. It was his parting shot when he'd left at the end of every school holiday. The last time he'd said it he'd been leaving to complete his training. 'And happy birthday, Constance.'

She wiped the beginnings of tears as she watched her beloved brother kiss their parents goodbye and climb into the driving seat. He was her only kindred spirit in the family. Her parents turned towards the house but Constance stayed and watched as the motorcar forged a trail of dust, snaking its way down the long drive and out of sight.

Constance climbed the few front steps and entered through the wide wooden ornate front door. She stood inside the hallway and held on to the back of one of the wingback leather armchairs, positioned in front of the fireplace. Nobody ever sat here. Despite the fire, it was often too cold in the hall. Her father preferred the confines of the study and her mother was often found in the orangery tending to the plants.

Constance steadied her breath for a few moments. The fire crackled in the grate, a fresh log beginning to char, presumably placed within the last few moments by the housekeeper, Mrs

Campbell, who was at the far side of the entrance hall, climbing the stairs. They were all busy about their days and no one knew. No one knew that on the other side of the loch, there was a pilot secreted in the cottage, waiting for her.

Constance's heart was heavy. As much as she loved Douglas, as much as they had always shared a strong bond, conspiring against their parents to run wild on the estate until they'd grown too old, she knew that if she couldn't tell him, she couldn't confide in anyone. If Douglas hadn't been a pilot himself, might she have done though? If only she had a better relationship with her parents, she might have been able to share her news in confidence, tell them of the pilot in the woods. She might have been able to ask her father for help, even ask him to visit the cottage, to talk to Matthew, man to man, and establish things that Constance may not have been able to. Her mother, even, might have been a consolatory ear, might have welcomed Matthew into their home for a few nights while they all worked together to sort things. Constance was jealous of many of her friends, whose parents were jovial and easy-going. Those friends seemed never to have hidden their hopes and dreams under the pretence of being happy, whilst waiting – just waiting. She could not betray Matthew to them. And so she knew she must keep her promise.

'Oh good Lord!' she cried as she suddenly remembered why she'd snuck back to the house. She turned in the direction of the kitchen.

'Constance,' her mother called from the end of the hallway. She was clutching a magazine. 'Do you have a spare moment?'

Ordinarily Constance was overridden with spare moments, each merging seamlessly into the next. But now she wanted to return to the cottage.

Without waiting for Constance to reply, her mother said: 'I'm rather getting it in the neck, somewhat.'

Constance frowned at her mother's sudden confidence. 'About what?'

Her mother waved her hand. 'Oh you know . . . not having been too involved in the war effort. Lady Amandale practically accused me of being a sympathiser. I had to explain that I've, so far, lain rather low because I didn't like to commit myself to something I didn't think I'd be able to be fully involved with. I did rather think joining some sort of association would scupper our plans to travel back and forth to London, but what with your father forbidding our journeying to and fro, I've decided we are going to *do* something for the local community.'

'Oh,' Constance said. She wondered what she'd be expected to do and then realised anything would be better than this meaningless existence. She nodded. 'All right then,' she agreed, without quite knowing what it was she was agreeing to.

'The truth is,' her mother went on, 'I was a bit ashamed last night. At the party,' she clarified. 'I was asked what you and I were *doing* and I didn't know how to respond. I was rather expecting that we'd take in some of those little evacuees but that lot from Guernsey have been scattered elsewhere over Scotland and we've not been called upon as yet to host any others. Regardless,' she pressed on, '*do* something we must. For the war.'

Constance nodded, excitement rising within her at the opportunity to help.

Her mother thrust her a copy of *Picture Post*. 'Your brother left this. Not my kind of read at all. No real fashion to speak of and it does rather harp on about the war a great deal but if you turn here . . .'

Constance raised an eyebrow while her mother found the page she was looking for.

'There's a piece on all the effort the Royal Family are making. They've chosen not to hotfoot it to safer climes, so far, and are firmly making their presence felt. And then—' her mother flicked to another page and jabbed at it with her diamond-ring-encrusted finger '—there's this lovely article about country houses being offered for the war effort, convalescent homes for soldiers, that kind of thing. We can help in so many ways. We too should be feeding buns to stricken officers or . . . something.'

Constance finally spoke. 'Would I be allowed to help? I did rather think you didn't like the idea of war work. Every time I've suggested it—'

'But, darling.' Her mother laughed. 'This isn't *work*. It's volunteering. It's completely different. It's completely *respectable*. *You* won't actually have to *do* anything.'

'But what if I should like to *do* something?' Constance tried again. 'It wouldn't involve me travelling. I'd still be at home.' *Where you can see me*, Constance added silently.

'I don't think so, Constance. What on earth is the point of polishing you up, knocking the wildness out of you at finishing school to have you do what . . . exactly . . . ? Donning a pinny and running around like . . . like . . .'

'Like a nurse?' Constance suggested suddenly, her eyes shining.

'Good God.' Mrs McLay shuddered. 'Unthinkable. No no,' she said as she strode off. 'Heavens, no.'

He must be so bored, Constance thought, picturing Matthew in the cottage. *And hungry*. She went into the library and searched for the beloved books she'd cherished in her formative years, and still did now. *What does he read? Does he even read? What kind of man is he?* She pulled three of her favourites from the shelves, confident he would appreciate the classics. Her father only allowed them in the library because they were bound in red leather, matching those of his fierce-looking legal and political tomes. She added them to the parcel she'd put together containing leftover pieces of her birthday fruitcake and a huge hunk of meat pie.

Tomatoes had been growing in the kitchen garden with wild abandon so she made a point to visit on her way to the cottage and scoop up as many as she could carry. How long would he hide here? How long would she risk getting caught stealing food? She could pretend it was for herself but she wondered if she'd be believed. Rationing hadn't seemed to dampen the enthusiasm of Mrs Fraser's efforts in the kitchen. In fact, it had hardly seemed to touch them at all, cosseted as they were out here in the wilds with as many fruits and vegetables as they could grow and plentiful venison from the estate. Last night's party had felt far too decadent. France had fallen; Norway and Denmark too. Soldiers had just been removed from the beaches at Dunkirk. She'd understood her father's reasoning for acquiescing to her mother's request for a party: that the world was a bleak place and that joy and laughter should be held on to at every opportunity. But it sat uneasily with Constance – all this excess. If it weren't for Douglas going off to fight, Constance could have been forgiven for imagining there wasn't a war on at all. Until she met Matthew.

She spied the decanters on the sideboard and the cupboards underneath housing sherry, port and whisky bottles with which the housekeeper topped up the crystal decanters. There were two half-empty whisky bottles of varying heritage and two near-full bottles of Macallan Glenlivet, 1926. She took the one at the very back.

She rarely drank. Wine with supper or a gin and tonic after a Saturday afternoon tennis match. Being Scottish, she'd grown up with a little whisky and water mixed together after dinner every now and again, much to her mother's horror and her father's pride.

The thought of Henry's meandering hands, the pressure of hiding a pilot in the woods, his reluctance to hand himself in . . . Constance opened the bottle and drank a stiff measure before replacing the cap tightly and putting it in her bag. After Matthew's ordeal, and his day inside the cold cottage, he'd probably need it also. Perhaps it would help soften the conversation between them and she could glean some further information about him.

She looked behind her as she stood at the French doors leading into the formal gardens, checking no one had entered the room to spot her leave. Glancing warily around her, she came upon the edge of the loch, meeting the safety of the forest and disappearing amongst the trees.

CHAPTER 15

'You came back,' Matthew said with a wide smile.

'Yes of course,' Constance replied, returning his smile as she closed the latch of the cottage door. 'I wouldn't have left you. I said I wouldn't.'

'I didn't like to presume,' he said with what Constance detected was a hint of shyness. He'd obviously leapt up from where he'd been dozing in the armchair at the sound of her entrance and Constance wondered if it was because he was frightened. Had he thought she might be the RAF, come to cart him off back to his squadron and face punishment?

They stood, awkwardly, neither of them quite knowing what to say to the other. She didn't want formality to creep back into her tone again.

'Are you hungry?' She gestured towards the knapsack she'd brought with her.

'Famished, yes. What's in there?'

'Pies, some vegetables from the kitchen garden and birthday cake.'

'Birthday cake?' Matthew questioned with raised eyebrows.

'Yesterday was my birthday,' Constance said simply.

'Many happy returns, Constance,' he said, looking at her.

'Thank you,' she replied. 'But there was plenty of cake so they won't miss it.'

It took him a moment to reply, clearly processing that she had risked her life to save his on her birthday. 'Where did you get the sugar for a whole cake?' he asked eventually.

Constance handed Matthew the bag. He took it from her with thanks and laid the items out on the wooden kitchen worktop.

'I don't like to ask,' she said with a sigh. 'My parents are happy to be kept in black market scent, stockings, Champagne and sugar.'

'And they can afford it?' he asked as he picked up the bottle of Glenlivet from the bag. 'Being kept well stocked in the middle of a war doesn't come cheap.'

'That's quite a brave question.' Constance laughed.

Matthew turned and smiled. 'It was you who started talking about your parents being willing recipients of black market goods.'

'Yes, I suppose you're right.'

'And . . .' he continued, 'I'm hardly one to judge, am I? The war has forced my hand in more ways than one. Perhaps it's done the same for your parents. People do things in times of war that they wouldn't do normally in peacetime.' He shrugged and turned his attention back to the bottle of whisky.

Constance looked at the back of his head, but she wasn't really seeing, more thinking about what he'd just said.

What would *she* be capable of doing? What would she be willing to do in war that she wouldn't at any other time? She had promised to hide a deserting RAF officer in a cottage. Would she have done that at any other time?

'The whisky is thoughtful,' he said, turning around and leaning against the worktop. 'Thank you.'

'My father won't miss it. He's got plenty.'

'Lucky him,' he said with a smile.

Matthew stood at the counter and almost inhaled a slice of pie as Constance sat on one of the kitchen chairs. She found herself watching his jaw move as he chewed.

'Would you like some?' He pointed to the pie.

She shook her head. 'Save it. I'll try to come back again tomorrow with more food. I'm not sure what I'll be able to scavenge but I'll do my best.'

'Thank you,' he said again.

She smiled at him. 'Matthew.' His name sounded strange as she said it. 'You don't have to keep saying thank you.'

'I know. But I am thankful; incredibly, unendingly thankful to you. I want you to know that. Whatever happens to me, I want you to know now, here in this moment of calm, in this strange little cottage in the middle of the Scottish Highlands, that I am sorry.'

'What are you sorry for?' she questioned. She had thought he was going to say thank you yet again. She hadn't been expecting him to apologise.

'I don't know yet. For the consequences of my being here, whatever they may be.'

She paused. What she was about to ask might elicit anxiety from him, but it needed asking. 'What do you think you'll do, in the end? Where do you think you'll go?'

Matthew looked down. It was a question he obviously had no answer to but Constance tried to push on. 'How long do you think you can stay here? It's just . . . it's not a permanent solution. I know you said you need time to think and of course, I'm doing the same. I did wonder if you might be able to present yourself at one of those emergency offices and pretend you've been bombed out, give them a false name and see if they can give you a fresh set of papers. And then from there . . .' Constance stopped. She hadn't honestly thought any further and was horrified to hear such dishonesty coming out of her mouth. 'Oh, I don't know,' she started up again. 'Or maybe go one above your C.O. and get your version of events in. Stealing the plane might not add to your defence but . . . there's such a risk of being discovered here that I think you should do *something*.'

'I'll certainly think about it,' he said and then smiled at her kindly. He pointed to the whisky bottle. 'I think you need this more than me.'

She chose not to tell him she'd already had a tot. 'Yes, all right,' she said, resigned, knowing he was deliberately avoiding the issue. 'If you're having some.'

He turned and looked in cupboards, retrieved two glasses and poured them both healthy measures of whisky.

'What's it like?' she asked quietly.

He paused the pouring of the whisky. 'What's what like?'

'Killing someone? Shooting someone down?' she asked. 'I can't imagine it, actually having to kill someone.'

Matthew was completely still.

'It must be horrid,' she volunteered and then felt entirely stupid at having said something so obvious.

'It is.' He handed her a glass and then sat down. 'Kill or be killed. My choice was unenviable, to say the least. That's why I can't do this anymore.'

Constance thought she saw tears in his eyes, but he blinked and then focused on drinking his whisky. She sipped hers slowly as a silence descended on the room.

'What would you be doing if you weren't a pilot?' she asked after a while.

A slow smile spread across his face and he looked into his glass, thinking. 'I don't know, not really. The war hasn't given me a chance to fathom it out. I left university early to join up but I'm twenty-one now and I doubt I'll go back to my studies after all this is over. Perhaps after the war you'll find me in a suit, catching a train to work each morning. Banking, insurance; don't most men of my ilk end up doing that? Funny,' he said with a short laugh, 'I used to think that sort of life sounded dull and safe. What I wouldn't give to be in a dull, safe job now. Instead I'm miles from home and utterly petrified of what each and every day will bring.'

'Where is home?' Constance asked, trying to bring his mind back to happier thoughts.

He smiled. 'Cambridge. But no one I know or love is there anymore. Still, I think I'll always be happiest amongst the fens and the countryside, the river and lazy days on Jesus Green.' He looked miles away. 'When my mother died, everything changed, and now I feel scattered to the wind.' He sat up straight and appeared to pull himself back from reminiscing as his tone changed. 'Home was no longer home. Father moved us around a lot. I rebelled, returned to Cambridge to study, but it didn't feel the same. And then of course, war broke out and here we all are.'

'Douglas was down at university there before the war. Did you know him?'

Matthew shook his head. 'No, I don't think so. So many different colleges. So many different people.' He sipped his whisky.

'I never got the chance to visit him there,' Constance continued. 'I've been to Oxford, but I don't suppose it's the same, is it?'

He laughed. 'Not to me. It's theatre and music and literature. It's punting on the Cam; it's lazy days picnicking at The Backs. It's . . . one of the most beautiful places I've ever been.'

'You were lucky to grow up there then.'

'Yes,' he said. 'I was.'

'But Jane Austen is surely a complete and utter fraud?' Matthew said, hours later.

'A fraud?' Constance was almost shouting. She moved forward and snatched *Sense and Sensibility* out of his hands. 'I'll take that back then, thank you very much. You don't deserve to even touch it.'

Matthew leaned forward and topped up Constance's whisky glass, refilled his own and laughed good-naturedly.

'Go on then.' He looked at her incensed face and began laughing. 'Defend her to me.'

'I shouldn't have to, but she's no fraud. She was a creative master.'

He rolled his eyes. 'Oh honestly. What did she know of any of this? The woman was playing make-believe, living through her characters, forging the kind of love lives for them she never had and then dropping down dead.'

This struck home for Constance, who had spent many an hour happily disappearing inside the pages of her beloved novels, living vicariously through her favourite heroines.

'Isn't that what all novelists do, play make-believe through their characters?' Constance suggested, clutching the book to her chest. 'And allow us, as readers, to do the same; to escape our environs and surround ourselves with ultimate joy?'

He paused for thought. 'Maybe, if that's what you're looking for from a novel.'

'Well what do you look for in a novel then?' she asked.

'Adventure. Danger.'

Constance reached towards the threadbare rug and picked up her copy of *Wuthering Heights.* With excitement in her voice she said, 'In that case you'll enjoy this.'

He looked at it. 'Don't even get me started on *her*.'

'Emily Brontë?' Constance questioned. 'She's my absolute favourite. Be very careful now.'

He took a sip of whisky and gave her a grin. 'She's your favourite? Well, I'm sorry to tell you she's the biggest fraud of the lot.'

Constance was no longer enjoying this conversation. She was trying not to throw her whisky glass at him.

'Why do you say that?' she asked through gritted teeth.

'Please,' he said. 'Gypsy lovers and ghosts at the window. I just can't take it seriously, any of it.'

Constance's mouth dropped open. 'Well, I don't know what to say.'

Matthew was enjoying this, she could see. He sat in the armchair opposite her, shaking with laughter.

He picked up the third book that Constance had taken from Invermoray House.

'If you call Dickens a fraud I'm taking back all the books, all the food and the rest of the whisky and I'll leave you here to rot.' Constance gave him a hard stare.

'Call Dickens a fraud?' he queried thoughtfully, turning the copy of *Great Expectations* over in his hands. 'I wouldn't dare.'

'Because he's a man?' Constance accused loudly.

'No, because he wrote the truth. He saw the horror in the world immediately around him and he wasn't afraid to tell those wealthy enough and literate enough all about it. He was nigh on a campaigner and—' Matthew held up Constance's copy of *Great Expectations* '—a bloody genius.'

There was something so deeply vulnerable about showing him her favourite novels. She'd been afraid he wouldn't like them, and whilst that fear had been well founded, he had opened up discussion, made her feel a passion for conversation that she hadn't felt in such a long time. She realised as she sipped her whisky and as he talked and asked her questions, that she hadn't had a proper discussion with anyone for ages. Constance felt almost alive, almost a whole person. Since she'd returned from finishing school she hadn't noticed herself drifting away, her sense of loss at . . . what exactly? Herself? She looked out towards the direction of the loch, hidden behind the tall pines, and it dawned on her. For as long as Constance could remember, she'd simply been treading water.

CHAPTER 16

2020

'What?' Kate asked as James's hand tightened around hers. He was pulling her, not painfully, but she felt his sense of urgency. 'What is it you need to show me?'

'You'll see.' He let go of her hand as they reached the entrance hall. The fire was dimming and Kate nervously tapped her foot on the large black and white square tiles. She watched him as he fumbled in the hallstand drawer, retrieving the set of keys to the estate office. 'Come with me,' he said.

Kate thought he didn't want to talk about the house, about business, after hours. So why was he dragging her back to the office? What was in there that she'd not noticed before? What could possibly be of interest at this time of night?

It was cold in the stable yard. Her nice-for-work, but not exactly warm T-shirt wasn't enough, and she wished she'd been wearing a jumper – in summer, for heaven's sake. She rubbed her arms as goose bumps formed.

James opened the estate office door and switched on the floor lamp instead of choosing the glare of the main light and they stepped their way through the paperwork littering the floor.

She aimed for light humour to defuse whatever anxiety he was clutching close to him. 'Time will soon come when I'll be able to work my way through all these piles of paper in pitch darkness,' she said.

'Time may soon come when you'll have to,' he muttered.

James wasn't in the mood, clearly.

He sat at his desk and Kate hovered opposite him, her hands resting against the back of her office chair. She watched as he opened his laptop, keyed in passwords and looked for something. At last he stood up, moving away from his desk.

'Here,' he said, 'sit.'

Kate raised her eyebrows at his tone. 'Please,' he added as an obvious afterthought.

There were a variety of windows open on his internet browser. This was nothing unusual. At any given point Kate usually had about ten or so windows open as she flicked back and forth, leaving some open for weeks on end as a reminder for a task she might get round to at some point. But the one James had left open for her to see was very clearly online banking.

Kate looked up at him and saw he was digging his top teeth into his lower lip, nervously.

'Go on,' he said, softer than before. 'I've got nothing to hide, take a look.'

Kate looked. There were a variety of accounts showing, savings accounts she assumed, all of which showed zero. But the main account had a huge number in it. Hundreds and hundreds of thousands. Or so she thought. She inched closer to the screen and her jaw dropped as she read the minus symbol that sat in front of the figure. A symbol of doom.

'Oh my God,' she exclaimed. 'It's . . . there's . . .'

'There's nothing in there,' James said. 'Or rather, there's less than nothing in there.'

Kate inhaled a large gulp of air, panicking on his behalf. She wasn't the world's best saver, but what little she earned had stretched just far enough to rent a nice little one-bed flat in an age when renting on your own at the edge of London was a near impossibility. She could afford food and nights out with friends – not many admittedly, one nice holiday per year and possibly a couple of mini-breaks if she sought out deals. Her bank account had gone into the red more times than she cared to remember. Her heart plummeted every time she opened her online banking app and discovered she'd overspent somewhere along the line. But this, *this*, was something else entirely. How had they done this? How had they got deeper and deeper into the red, by *this* much? Why had they waited until now to do something about saving the estate? And why on earth were they spending money – money they obviously didn't have – on hiring *her*?

'J-James,' Kate stuttered, dragging her eyes away from the screen and meeting his. 'How . . . ?' She didn't finish her sentence. There was no need.

He moved to her desk and sat down, resting his elbows on his knees and putting his head in his hands. 'Far too easily, I'm afraid.'

Kate looked at the top of his head as he worried his fingers through his dark brown hair. Slowly she closed the laptop lid.

Eventually he looked up at her. 'So now you know our dirty little secret.'

Kate remembered what he'd said earlier, that he knew her being here was a terrible idea. She wasn't a quitter but even she could see that he was right; that her being here was a drain on their non-existent resources and that, even sadder than that, it was in all probability too late to save the house. They couldn't spend any more money. They couldn't afford her to be there. He watched, waiting for her to say something.

'I should leave,' Kate offered eventually. She hadn't been paid yet – she'd only been there a matter of weeks and her first salary was due imminently. She was prepared to take it on the chin though. Almost. 'Yes,' she said with more confidence as she stood. 'I should leave.'

His hands dropped from his hair. He'd ruffled it into a mess and his forehead was riddled with frown lines. 'What?'

'You're right,' she said. 'I can't be here.'

'Are you quitting?' he asked. Kate thought he'd be happy but he just looked appalled.

She nodded and looked around the estate office. She wasn't sure why but she wanted to take it in, one last time: the chaos, the homeliness, all of it. Kate gave James a thin smile. 'I wish someone – you – had told me how bad it was when I arrived,' she said softly. 'You've just sat there, all this time, watching me get settled in. You can't afford to pay me. You can't afford to do anything. You need to sell, by the looks of things. You need to sell the house, the furniture, the lot.' For as long as Kate had been at Invermoray, James had made only thinly veiled remarks, never actually stating they were verging on bankruptcy. Showing her the accounts was brave, open, but what did he expect her to do now?

'Why did you show me this? You should have just told me when I arrived, "*You need to go home, Kate. We can't afford to pay you.*" You needed to tell me flat out. I'd have gone back to the airport and you'd never have seen me again.'

James opened his mouth to speak but Kate was on a roll and didn't allow him to cut in.

'Given I'd almost just run you over, I'm sure never seeing me again would have been just the ticket,' she remarked.

'I did tell you,' he said. 'I told you we didn't have any money. I did tell you, the night you arrived, that we couldn't afford you.'

Kate thought back, trying to recollect his words. 'You argued with your mother, actually. And . . .' she said, standing straighter. 'Where's she in all of this? What on earth has been going on here?' Kate sounded like a schoolmarm. She took a deep breath. She was far too close to throwing accusations of financial negligence at poor Liz, who had self-confessed to burying her head in the sand, choosing to tend to her garden instead of tending to the finances.

'It's too late tonight but tomorrow, I'll tidy up my reports for you, so if you do choose to carry on it will leave you in marginally less chaos than you're in right now. Then I'll book a flight home.'

James looked at her. 'Right. OK. Sure. That makes . . . sense.'

As she walked past him Kate paused and put her hand on his shoulder. He looked up at her, his expression like that of a lost child.

'God, what a mess,' Kate said as she left the estate office and closed the door gently behind her.

The next morning Kate woke up, absolutely hating herself. She'd barely slept but looking around at the floral bedspread tangled around her legs, she must have had a fitful night. She had been in a state last night when she'd got back to her bedroom. After she'd left James in the estate office, she'd collected her glass of whisky from the sideboard in the sitting room, had drunk all of it in two quick gulps as she climbed the stairs and had stared at the loch as it stretched out in the darkness of the night. The silver moon had reflected off its rippled surface, when the clouds parted.

Kate showered, scrubbing extra hard in the not quite hot water. She knew she was sloughing off her guilt. She had behaved appallingly, had spent the last few weeks believing James needed a wake-up call when it came to manners and there was she, emulating him and then going off the chart completely.

James was nowhere to be seen but Kate found Liz in the kitchen reading a copy of the *Daily Telegraph*. Liz smiled at her as she entered.

'Coffee?' Liz asked as if nothing had happened.

Kate smiled and then looked away, guiltily. Perhaps she didn't know. Perhaps James hadn't told her that Kate had resigned, that she'd seen the bank accounts and was leaving in order to do them a favour. Kate wasn't entirely selfless, she reasoned. She was, after all, leaving so she could find herself another job, one that could actually afford to pay her. She realised ruefully that it wouldn't be the first time she'd left gainful employment under a cloud of darkness. Although she sincerely hoped it would be the last time. It *had* to be the last time.

'You look awfully tired, my dear,' Liz said. 'I hope you don't mind me saying. You sit, and I'll make it.'

Kate agreed and sat at the scrubbed wooden table, glancing around at the kitchen. She rubbed her hand over her forehead and tried to halt the wave of sadness. She felt so awful for them: for poor Liz, who had tried to save the house far too late in the day, for James who had thrown in the towel at whatever job he had been doing in Asia and returned to this complete and utter downfall. Kate needed to speak to him before she packed and left. She'd not yet looked at the flight times from Inverness Airport but was vaguely aware there were quite a few flights each day back to London. She doubted the evening ones were all full.

She hadn't yet packed, and had said she'd get all her files in order before she left. There was a lot to do but she couldn't put her departure off. She really had to leave them to whatever it was they were going to do, but she couldn't leave without apologising to James for the way she had behaved last night.

It was as if Liz had read her mind. 'James has gone for a run,' she said. 'He'll be back soon.'

Kate nodded as she sipped her coffee. She needed to tell Liz she was leaving. She'd been the one to hire Kate, after all. But after last night, it was only fair Kate spoke to James first.

'I'd best get to it,' Kate said, taking her mug of coffee with her.

'Er,' Liz said.

Kate glanced back at her from the doorway. Whisky stood to follow her. He'd always followed James and Kate into the office each morning and set up home for the day in his bed in the corner. Kate waited for Liz to speak.

'Have you two had a falling-out?' Liz asked.

'What makes you ask that?'

'James looked awful this morning. You look awful this morning. Has something bad happened between you?'

Kate was unsure what to say. She opted for, 'No.'

Liz gave her a sly smile. 'Has something *good* happened between you?'

Kate's eyes widened. 'Christ, no!' How Liz could be so at home with the idea of her new employee having some kind of dalliance with her son was baffling. As Kate had discovered by accident, it was wise to keep away from even the appearance of a liaison.

'OK, OK, I was just . . . curious. That's all,' Liz said with a smile. 'He's not all bad you know. If you were thinking about . . .'

Kate's eyes widened even further.

Liz laughed. 'OK, I'll keep my nose out. Kate?'

'Yes?' Kate said nervously, turning back from the doorway. Who knew where this conversation was going?

'He's a good man. He's gruff sometimes, but his heart's in the right place. I'm really pleased to see the two of you working together to save the house. You know I'm here for any jobs you two can't handle but he's been trying so hard and I never expected him to manage by himself, it wouldn't have been fair. I think over the past couple of months he just assumed he'd be alone going forward. I am glad James has an extra pair of hands now.'

Kate felt the cold wave of guilt as it crashed into her. She nodded, gave Liz a half-hearted wave and went to wait for James in the office, Whisky trailing along behind her.

CHAPTER 17

The first thing Kate did when she opened up the estate office was check the flight times. She couldn't take her eye off the main goal, which was to leave by tonight. She had remembered correctly and there were a couple of flights out that evening. She reasoned she'd need to leave late in the afternoon in order to drive and check in on time.

Papers were strewn everywhere – even more so than usual. After she'd left James last night he'd clearly been hard at work. What time had he worked until? It can't have been too late if he'd summoned the energy to go for a run this morning.

Kate organised her files, which were already fairly organised, and printed out all the jobs she'd marked as urgent. She found a space on James's cluttered desk and left the list somewhere prominent so he wouldn't miss it.

Then she chewed her lip, took the note back and began working through it herself. It wouldn't take her long. She'd never been accused of being a control freak before, so taking charge of the entire list would be a mission. But she felt she owed it to James, despite the fact that they might not be able to pay her for the time she had spent working there. Kate knew it wasn't that simple: that Liz didn't intend not to pay her and that James, despite being a complete sod most of the time, probably wouldn't have allowed that to happen either. There was something honourable about him, she felt, that meant he would have found some money from somewhere. After all, he'd just paid for the roof at the main house and the ghillie's cottage. Regardless, she needed to do them a financial favour and remove the burden of having to find a salary for her at the end of every month, with no money coming in to cover it.

Two hours later Kate hadn't felt the time pass at all. It was only when her stomach rumbled – she hadn't been able to face breakfast – that she made an effort to go to the kitchen in search of food. She nibbled a piece of toast and looked out of the kitchen window. Whisky had followed her and sat at her feet, hoping for dropped crumbs of crusty doorstop loaf. Kate bent to scratch his ears. The dog had switched allegiance from James to Kate the moment he realised Kate ate more bread than his master. 'Do I drop more food than James?' Kate asked the silent dog. 'I'll miss *you* the most,' she said, pulling a buttery corner off and feeding it to him. She hadn't been here long enough, she felt, to truly miss any of them. But she knew it was the abruptness, the unexpected and hasty exit that made her anxious about leaving them all, leaving the house.

Like a ghost, she had unfinished business. She dusted crumbs from her fingers, put her plate in the dishwasher and went in search of James.

Kate searched the ground floor for James and drew a blank before heading upstairs and knocking on his bedroom door. There was no answer. Next to his room, a door was ajar. It creaked as she opened it, and she was surprised to see it wasn't a room at all, but a staircase leading upwards. She felt rather like Belle in *Beauty and the Beast* but as Kate wasn't a Disney heroine who had been instructed not to go looking around, she climbed the stairs. She didn't think James was up there but for some reason she carried on climbing regardless.

Upstairs were the poky attic rooms. Kate could see why Liz and James hadn't shown her them on the tour – they were far too small to be turned into accommodation. The eaves were low and each of the rooms along the narrow corridor would have just about fit a single bed and maybe a bedside table. There was no room for en suites on this level. No, she couldn't do anything useful with these rooms at the moment.

'Not my responsibility anymore,' Kate muttered as she began a half-hearted but nosy look in each of the attic rooms.

In the first room she came to there were old desks, coal scuttles, broken dolls and stacks of paintings turned to face the wrong way against the wall. She touched the painting closest to her and as she turned it over a scuttling noise made her drop the picture and swear. Was it a rat? Or a mouse? Either way, Kate backed out of the room and looked into the next. It was stashed with antique-looking trunks that would have fetched a decent price on eBay. Brides indulging in vintage-style weddings would lap these up for a fortune. She would make that suggestion to Liz and James and hopefully they could get some loose change for them. Smaller suitcases were also stacked haphazardly, as if someone had been playing a high-consequences game of Jenga.

On the far side there were two large leather-studded trunks and Kate blew the dust off the gold lettering of each. The first read Douglas McLay and the second Constance McLay.

Kate stopped dead. She'd forgotten all about Constance McLay, but she recognised her name immediately. Constance was the girl whose name had been scratched so energetically out of the family Bible. Kate was sure she'd seen Douglas's name near hers. She decided to go back to look at the Bible again. She only had a few hours before she had to leave and hadn't packed yet, so what on earth was she doing messing around in the attics, or going off to faff around with the pages of a Bible? She knew she was stalling for time. If she didn't find James then she didn't have to have an awkward conversation.

Kate descended the stairs two at a time. Whisky had given up following her long ago and Kate assumed he'd gone back to the kitchen to resume his much-loved position in front of the Aga.

In the library Kate opened the Bible and delicately turned the wafer-thin pages until she located the Family Record. She was right, there they both were: Douglas's name first followed by Constance's underneath.

She stood back and thought. James's story about the two children who had been disinherited, the parents who had left the Invermoray estate to Liz's husband . . . she wondered if the time-line fit.

Douglas had been born in 1914 and Constance, 1919. If the entry directly above their names, Alistair McLay, was their father *and* the man who handed the house to James's father, then these must be the two children who had lost Invermoray through fair means or foul. They were the last names in the Bible.

She closed the book carefully and turned to the window. It was then that she saw James. It was the flash of neon on his otherwise black running outfit that caught her attention. He was in the distance, on the other side of the loch, sitting on the jetty, legs swinging freely over the water. The action was childlike, vulnerable, Kate thought.

She turned the key in the long French doors and stepped out into the ornate formal garden. Liz had her back turned to Kate, clipping a yew hedge, and Kate moved past her quietly. Now she'd spotted James she didn't want to risk becoming embroiled in a long chat with Liz and give James time to move on elsewhere. Kate stopped at the foliage-covered archway that led to the path that ran down to the loch as it struck her that perhaps he had been avoiding her until she left. If so, then tough. It would be awkward but she needed to apologise for storming off. She could have handled it all so much better.

*

James watched her walk the whole way round the edge of the water, the pebbles crunching as she moved along the beach. As she got closer Kate saw he had the ghost of a smile on his lips.

She approached the jetty and he twisted his position to look at her, still smiling.

'Permission to come aboard?' Kate asked.

He laughed and looked back at the loch. 'That's for boats. This is just a jetty. But hop on.'

Kate walked the length of the jetty and sat next to him at the end, unsure how to start.

'You found me then,' he said.

'It didn't take me long. About two hours,' Kate said, glancing at her watch.

He laughed unexpectedly. 'Two hours? Where have you been looking?'

'Everywhere but here, it would seem.'

He nodded slowly. 'This is my thinking spot,' he said, by way of explanation. 'I come here when . . .' He looked down.

'When . . . ?' Kate prompted.

'When it's all just gone a little bit shit.'

Kate didn't know what to say so she tried the speech she'd been practising to herself as she'd ventured round the loch. 'I'm sorry. For last night. For being, quite frankly, a bit of a bitch. For telling you to sell the house, although I still think you probably should, and for leaving you to just get on with it on your own.'

'It's OK,' he volunteered. 'Nothing you said was untrue.'

'Thanks.' Kate crossed her legs underneath her. 'It's generous of you. But my delivery could have been better.'

'That's true. I was rather shocked.'

'I'm sorry,' Kate whispered. They sat with only the sound of the loch as it lapped gently against the wooden legs of the jetty.

'So what will you do?' Kate probed. 'After I've gone?'

'Ah yes, you're leaving us,' he said wryly.

'You can have a little party when I'm gone,' she teased.

'Celebrate having finally got rid of me. Took you less than a month. Quite good going.'

He looked meaningfully at her. 'I won't have a party. We can't afford one.'

Kate nudged him with her elbow and he laughed.

'Honestly, what will you do?' Kate was concerned, for him, the house, for Liz, for their ever-decreasing bank balance and the astronomical overdraft.

'Honestly,' he replied, 'I have no idea. We probably *should* sell the house.' He sighed. 'But it smacks of failure to me. Mum was knee-deep in debt when I arrived. I don't want to throw my poor old dad under the bus, so to speak, but when I arrived there was just so much to do. He really exacerbated the issue. I've paid for the roof to be fixed on the cottage because letting that to holiday-makers is probably the most immediate source of income. Then the main house roof almost collapsed. It was practically bowing and rain water poured in during the winter storm so I *had* to get that fixed too. That cost a few thousand to say the least. But looking at it through your eyes, it was all good money after bad.'

'No,' Kate said emphatically. 'No, don't say that. It needed doing.'

'I've spent almost all of my savings on the day-to-day running, food, bills . . .' He trailed off.

'Oh God,' Kate muttered. 'Your own money?'

'I've had to. I didn't really know what else to do.'

'Couldn't you have got a loan in addition to the overdraft?' she asked.

He looked at her, his eyebrows shooting up. 'Don't you think we've got one? We've got two. We've used them all up. They weren't huge, admittedly but even so, they're all gone. Dad spent a lot of them before he passed and what was left went on keeping the lights on, pretty much, before I started dipping into the money I'd saved over the last few years. And now of course, there's the interest on the loans to pay.'

'What a mess.'

'You know I was going to pay you, don't you? I was going to fund your salary, out of what little I've got left,' he said.

'Oh, James,' Kate sighed into her hands.

'But last night, I thought, what if we had carried on, you and I getting Invermoray *out there* – and Mum clipping hedges in the garden.' He laughed. 'What if we did? For six months? And what if we put it on the market at the same time? Hedge our bets, see which version of events we preferred and make a decision if we get any offers? I want to make this work.'

Kate looked at him, her eyes narrowed. 'I'm not sure.'

He looked up at the sky, at the grey clouds passing overhead. Kate did the same. In front of them came the *plunk* noise of something small surfacing briefly from the water and then disappearing back into the murkiness.

'What was that?' Kate asked, peering into the loch.

'A fish.' He laughed. 'Maybe a pike. Perhaps brown trout. We've got them in spades. I feel them nudge me when I swim, sometimes.'

Kate shuddered.

'They don't bite,' he said. 'I find it quite comforting, in a weird way, knowing I'm not totally alone in this vast expanse of water. Although often all I want is to be alone. Does that make sense?'

'I think so,' Kate replied. Until this move to the Highlands she had always thought herself a social person, happy seeking out the company of others. She'd never truly allowed herself much in the way of solitude, never quite enjoyed being in her own company. But then, she realised, she'd never allowed herself time in her own company. Sometimes being alone was actually a balm.

'I used to think this loch was a strange place, kind of eerie,' James said. 'When I was a boy I used to imagine all sorts lurking below the water.'

'Such as?'

'A monster,' James said with mock horror.

Kate rolled her eyes but she was smiling. 'A monster?'

'I was convinced, absolutely one hundred per cent convinced, that there was something in this loch,' he said. 'Something in there that wasn't supposed to be there. I don't know why but I just didn't feel alone.'

'And your natural conclusion was that it was a monster?' Kate folded her arms.

He nodded. 'I was a kid. I imagined there was some kind of creature in there, but I never felt it was malevolent. Never felt it wanted to hurt me. Just that it was here doing its thing. And I was here, doing my thing. I felt a bit lost, I suppose, and I reasoned that if there was a creature in there, it too was probably lost.'

Kate looked at James as if seeing him for the first time. A boy who had once swam with imaginary loch monsters had turned into a man completely overwhelmed with his family's debt. Poor James had spent the majority of his time at Invermoray keeping his head above water.

'I thought I saw it once, from the jetty. At the time I was embarrassingly excited. The Loch Invermoray Monster. It would have made us famous. I created a whole story about it in my head. This was back when I was a teenager, and all teenagers want is to be famous.'

But Kate's mind wandered from James's youth and towards the expanse of water stretching out in front of them. She stared into the loch. A monster. She knew there wasn't really a monster, but *what if*? What if they put out a little story that there was something hiding in the loch? This could be the fast injection of tourism Invermoray needed, and with it . . . income. They'd have sightseers coming from all over the country. Tourists were already in Scotland in droves and the ones that loved a good monster story were down at Loch Ness having the time of their lives. Why not entice them further up the Highlands with a good story? There was no concrete evidence there was a monster in the depths of Loch Ness and it had never made a difference to the tourism there. Kate had never met a single person who actually *believed* the Loch Ness Monster existed. But the myth lived on. Why? Because everyone loves a good story.

'Kate?' James asked and she realised she'd missed whatever it was he'd just said. 'I asked what time your flight is?'

'About seven o'clock,' Kate said automatically, lifting her eyes from the water to James but not really seeing him.

He sounded quiet, almost sorry. 'You'd better get going then, hadn't you?'

CHAPTER 18

She was going to stay. Only for a little while. James assured her he could pay her as promised and while she was riddled with guilt for taking his money when neither he nor Liz could afford it, Kate was going to work very hard for it. She'd long since given up on just being a publicist. She was going to do absolutely everything in her power to save this house.

The Loch Invermoray Monster. Admittedly it wasn't as catchy as the Loch Ness Monster but she rather felt it harnessed a proven formula and that it got the point across adequately.

James and Liz were none too sure of her plan.

'You want to put out a press release that we've got a monster in the loch?' Liz asked the next day, offering steaming mugs of tea from a tray as they sat in front of the fire in the sitting room.

'I do. It will mainly be subtle and will talk about the house as a new luxury bed and breakfast property but I know journalists who will be interested in the unusual angle and I'm sure once news spreads . . .'

'News?' James said with a sarcastic smile. 'News of what? There's no monster. We'll look like laughingstocks.'

'There's no concrete proof there's a monster in Loch Ness and that's done them no harm at all,' Kate said, pulling out some rough reports she'd hastily pulled together. After she agreed she would stay on, she had sprinted back to the office, quickly researched tourism numbers for Loch Ness and the amount of conspiracy theories surrounding sea creatures in Scottish lochs. Both numbers were surprisingly high.

'Some of the most recent data suggests the Loch Ness Monster is worth forty-one million pounds to the local economy,' Kate said confidently.

James's jaw dropped. 'You're joking.'

Liz raised an eyebrow. 'Never let the truth get in the way of a good story,' she said.

'That's the total spend in Scotland thanks to Nessie, right?' James asked. 'That's not just what they spend around the actual loch itself, is it? It can't be.'

'It is,' Kate said with a smile. 'It's what's spent at attractions around the water, boat tours trying to catch a glimpse of the monster, overnight accommodation, food and drink. They've estimated day-tripper numbers on top of this and believe forty-one million pounds a year is a conservative estimate.'

Kate could almost hear the cogs of thought turning inside James's and Liz's minds and felt she needed to bring them back down to earth somewhat.

'What I think *we* will make is far below that. Invermoray House isn't built up to cater for that number of visitors, and I doubt the Invermoray Arms will enjoy being completely overwhelmed more than they already are. Angus will kill me,' Kate said. 'And we're not going to get the equivalent rush of tourism that Loch Ness receives. But I think we will get tourism numbers we can handle. We'll be in control. And it won't change our plans in the slightest. We wanted to open a tearoom, bed and breakfast, and the holiday cottage. We can still do all of that. Only now . . .'

'We'll fill beds quicker,' Liz finished her sentence for her. 'And maybe not just in summer,' she said with hope rising in her voice. 'We'll sell more afternoon teas than we would have done. We'll be able to sell little picnic packs maybe, if tables are full in the tearoom.'

'Yes,' Kate enthused. 'That's a great idea.'

Liz and James looked at each other, smiling.

Kate sat back, wrapping her hands around her mug of tea. She was feeling quite pleased with herself. Although now she knew the hard work was really about to begin.

They sat for hours, drafting a faster version of their original plan. James went to the orangery and measured for the replacement glass panel. They decided this was the perfect place for the tearoom. It would be warm in winter and in summer when it might perhaps overheat, the formal gardens that swept down towards the loch were perfect for picnic tables.

And over the next few weeks, they prioritised. A glazier fitted new glass in the orangery and they cleaned it from top to bottom, working out where a cash register and desk might go; James received the longed-for catering licence and relevant paperwork to turn Invermoray into a bed and breakfast. He dealt with visits from the council telling them what they could and couldn't do and Liz and Kate set to work ordering catering supplies, tables and chairs, napkins, cutlery, fire extinguishers and all the small essentials they had previously had no clue about. They organised to rent elaborate coffee machines and Angus came to give a crash course in running a catering outlet. The outlay was incredible. But it would all be worth it.

In fact Kate didn't know what they'd have done without Angus. He appeared like a knight in shining armour. He knew they were out of their depths and offered to manage the tearoom for them when they got up and running.

'You can't do that *and* run the pub,' James baulked at his friend one evening as they propped up the bar in the Invermoray Arms, suppliers' paperwork and contracts laid out in front of them.

'Sure I can,' Angus said as he pulled a pint for James. 'My sister's back behind the bar now she's got my wee niece off to nursery in the daytime. I manage the Arms in the evenings now mostly, leaving me free to spread my wings a wee bit.'

James looked doubtful and Kate turned to him. 'We need someone,' she said. 'This isn't our area of expertise. But it is Angus's.'

Angus had looked pleased as punch. 'I'll need a hand though. One man alone can't run a tearoom and make sandwiches all day. I'll need help with serving and the like.'

'James and I can go on rotation?' Kate offered.

James agreed. 'It'll save some money, I suppose.'

'On that point,' Angus said, narrowing his eyes. 'What'ye gonna pay me?'

Kate left James and Angus to sort out the financial side of things; after all it was James's money, and when she returned from the ladies' room, she sighed with relief to find them shaking hands to seal a deal.

She sat at the bar and sipped her gin and tonic. Tomorrow would be the day she started drip-feeding information about the possibility of a monster having been sighted in the loch, as well as grand plans for the house. Kate was going to put the feelers out, inviting journalists to visit and hopefully give Invermoray House glowing reviews.

This was the part both James and Liz felt uncomfortable about and when Kate outlined her plans around the monster he muttered, 'This is lying.'

'We aren't telling people there *is* a monster in the lake. We're telling them there *could be one.*'

Angus laughed, overhearing them. 'Then that's not lying then,' he agreed with Kate. 'There used to be chat about locals seeing a monster in the loch.'

James and Kate both looked up at him, startled. 'Really?' Kate asked.

'We've got papers in the local museum that show early drawings of sea creatures in Loch Invermoray. And there's old newspaper articles,' he continued, 'from the turn of the century.'

'Go on,' Kate asked when Angus stopped. 'What do they say?'

'The usual, some local washing their clothes in the loch water saw some kind of creature, and then another local saw one carrying a Highland cow in its jaws and so on and so forth.'

'An elaborate way to disguise cattle rustling, I'll bet,' James scoffed.

Angus ignored him, continuing, 'They say the Loch Invermoray Monster appeared as a good omen. That she'd appear in order to bring a lifetime of happiness to those who spotted her. But that was back in the day and it's been a damned long time since anyone saw her. She's clearly not been feeling benevolent of late.'

James chuckled '*She?*' he queried.

Angus ignored him. 'Then in the 1930s some idiot takes that hoax picture up at Loch Ness and the rest, as they say, is history. All eyes on Nessie and the Loch Invermoray Monster just fades into memory. M'be a good thing. M'be not.'

Kate was captivated and she turned to James. 'See?' she said triumphantly. 'It's not a lie.'

James rolled his eyes and sipped his pint. 'I didn't know about any of this.'

'And those aren't the only sinister goings-on up at that loch o' yours?' Angus wiggled his eyebrows for effect.

'No?' James asked, a hint of exhaustion in his voice.

Angus leaned forward conspiratorially. 'Ha'ye heard about the drowning?'

'The drowning?' Kate asked, inching forward, the monster immediately forgotten.

'Aye,' Angus said. 'Not that long ago from wha' I was told. But you'd know all about it o' course,' he said, nodding to James.

'I haven't got a clue what you're on about.'

'You must do,' Angus said. 'I was told years ago. And you live up there.'

James shook his head.

'Back in the Forties, apparently. I don't know the exact details. But I do know that someone died in that loch.'

CHAPTER 19

1940

There were about twenty women present in the parish hall when Constance and her mother arrived for their first Women's Voluntary Service meeting. They had bicycled into the village, her mother taking her first wobbly moves on the 'contraption' with gusto. Constance had followed suit, although much more ably. There had been a lot of excitement when they entered and there were cries of 'Mrs McLay, how wonderful to see you here, and Constance too,' which shamed Constance. They should have been helping with the war effort long before now. Constance wanted to shout that she had tried so hard to be allowed to help in some small way.

'Oh you know how it is.' Mrs McLay had offered a pale excuse. 'We've just been so busy.' Constance moved away and took a proffered cup of tea from the butcher's wife, shamed even more as her mother explained that now the war was in full swing – the Battle of Britain raging in the skies over England – it was high time that she and Constance now chip in and 'do odd jobs to win the war.'

Constance wondered if her mother could hear her own words, the belittling tone she had adopted about the good work the WVS had been doing.

The postmistress moved over to Constance. 'Lovely of you to join us, dear.' Her warm smile reached her eyes, putting Constance at ease.

'Thank you,' she replied to the woman she'd come to know, in part, for the past few months. Since most of the male staff from the house had joined up Constance had taken to running her father's letters down to the post office herself and with very little else to do, the task of popping into the post office to send the odd telegram for her parents had often fallen to her too.

She had no idea why she was so nervous all of a sudden. She'd wanted to do something for the war effort for so long and was absolutely dying to get out of the house and do something useful. Very few of the women were near Constance's age, and those who were had husbands away at war, or children on the way.

The meeting started with talk about the new mobile canteen the WVS were to be provided with, who would staff it and at what times and the rota for visiting the men living and working at the lookout huts on the more remote aspects of the coast to provide them with tea, cigarettes, chocolate and other items they needed regular access to. The meeting moved on to discussions about helping the women who were visiting husbands stationed nearby and where to house them when they arrived, as they were unable to share in their husbands' billets. A 'honeymoon' house was suggested and Constance blushed as the women discussed, in hushed tones, conjugal relations and the need to keep up morale.

Constance wondered quietly what part she could play in all of this – perhaps drive the mobile canteen. She knew how to drive. Father had let her cause havoc on the estate in his motorcar, although the last time she had got behind the wheel of his Bentley Saloon it had been well over five years ago and that was only when her mother had been down in London shopping for the week. Perhaps she could have a little refresher drive before they handed her the responsibility of something so daunting.

'What do you think, Constance?' Her mother turned to her. 'Got to do our bit, haven't we? And the house is large enough.'

Constance had clearly missed something while she'd been miles away weighing up her suitability to staff a mobile canteen. She shrugged, embarrassed.

'Letting invalided airmen recuperate at the house,' Mrs McLay explained. 'We talked about this the other day? Remember?'

Constance's eyes widened. Was this really going to happen or was her mother paying lip service to the WVS? 'Yes. I think it's a wonderful idea. But what would Father—'

'Oh you leave him to me,' Mrs McLay said officiously. 'It's us women who make all the decisions, isn't that right, ladies?'

A chorus of knowing and sycophantic murmurs sounded around them. 'It will have to be officers though,' Mrs McLay clarified. 'And while we don't have that many bedrooms—'

Next to Constance, the postmistress smothered a laugh.

'We can house a few of the top dogs in the few bedrooms we do have available and perhaps the rest can bunk up in the ballroom and the orangery. Oh yes.' Mrs McLay was getting into the swing of it. 'This could work very well indeed. And we'll be doing our bit.'

Enthusiastic clapping began around them and Constance wondered what her mother had just done.

By the time the meeting closed, Constance's offer to volunteer to drive the mobile canteen had been turned down. Instead she had been given bags of old wool in order to help make 'comforts' for the troops. She had quite a good recollection of how to knit, having been subject to her nanny's frenetic needlework and knitting instruction at the nursery fireside.

But the thought of the house being opened up as a convalescent hospital worried Constance. The opportunity to work, if there was anything she could offer to do, sounded tempting. But there would be so many people, so many extra eyes on her, witnessing her comings and goings to and from the cottage when she had been of no consequence to anybody in such a long time.

At home in the study her parents were discussing her mother's rash suggestion. Constance stood by the door. She wanted to check Matthew had all he needed for the time being.

'Darling, you said yourself if we don't do something useful with the house, they'll simply take it from us and chuck us out. We *must* do something – those were your words, weren't they?'

'Well yes,' Constance's father blustered. 'But a hospital? Really?'

'This way,' her mother said as Constance entered the room, 'if we volunteer the house, we'll be able to make stipulations, about how it's used and we'll be able to remain here. We'll take a sitting room and the rest of the rooms we'll give over to officers' messes and whatever else they need. And it *will* be officers. We'll be able to ask specifically. They'll behave themselves if they're officers.'

After Matthew's horrific story about the actions of his commanding officer, Constance wasn't convinced by this point.

Her father's arms were folded. 'Yes, I suppose so.' He looked browbeaten. 'You clever thing, you,' he said half-heartedly.

'I thought we might be safe all the way up here but I heard on the grapevine the Erndale estate was requisitioned a fortnight ago,' Mrs McLay continued. 'The whole thing. They were given only four days' notice. Four days. Can you imagine? Very hush-hush. They weren't told what it would be used for but whatever department it is, they've got free run of the place. No word about when they can have it back. Lady Erndale had to take all the Gainsboroughs down and stash them in the cellar and Lord E's terribly worried about his wine.'

Constance stifled a smile.

'Really?' her father said, frowning as he moved over to the telephone on his desk. 'Right, if you think it's best, I'll put in some telephone calls. Volunteer our services before we have the whole house whipped out from under us. Where would we live if that happened?' he said, checking his watch. 'Bit late to sort. I'll do it first thing,' he mumbled, replacing the receiver and picking up his copy of *The Times*. 'We wouldn't return to London. Absolutely not. We'd have to rent somewhere a bit smaller for the duration, or bunk into the ghillie's cottage together. Could you imagine?' he said with a shudder.

Constance's head snapped up. The ghillie's cottage. Matthew.

'Everything all right?' her father asked.

She nodded. 'Fine, all fine.'

As she'd been making her way through the parterre towards the loch shore the elderly gardener had cornered her. Constance's heart had leapt into her throat. Her mother had been on the telephone and her father had been throwing himself into making sure all valuables were accounted for prior to turning the house into a convalescent hospital. As the gardener had politely doffed his cap, Constance had started and almost fallen into the flowerbeds. Secrecy wasn't her strong suit and she had stuttered while answering with a simple 'hello'. He had looked at her curiously as she made an about turn and wandered far too casually back towards the house, the handkerchief of food badly hidden under her arm.

Now, as she made her way back towards the cottage under the cloak of darkness she made a vow that she could only visit Matthew after her parents were safely tucked up in their beds and when what remained of the ageing staff weren't rambling around and able to see her. It was all far too nerve-racking.

'I'm not normally a nervous person,' she said to Matthew as he tucked into a leg of chicken. He looked at her thoughtfully while he chewed. 'It's just a strange situation,' she said, 'you, being here, when you're not meant to be. It's making me . . .'

'Nervous?' Matthew finished her sentence for her helpfully.

'Yes.' Constance laughed. She took a deep breath. 'I know you've only been here a few days but I do wonder if you've had time to think and, if so, what you've decided.'

'You do sound jumpy, you know.'

'I know,' she said. 'And believe it or not, I'm not normally like that either.'

He tilted his head to one side as he finished the supper Constance had brought him. He wrapped the remainder up in the linen napkin she had provided and opened the larder, placing it on the cold stone.

'Today I read one of the novels you brought,' he said.

'You're changing the subject.' Constance folded her arms and sat back into the settee.

He grinned. 'Oh, I'm getting there, in a roundabout kind of way.'

The fire was unlit as the day had been one of the hottest she could remember. Matthew opened a window and the night air added freshness to the room.

'Which one did you read?' she asked.

'*Wuthering Heights*.'

'The dreaded Emily Brontë,' she teased. 'You've read all of it? Today?'

'I started last night and I worked my way through most of it today at breakneck speed.'

Constance looked at him. 'I'm impressed.'

'Well,' he said with a sideways smile. 'I may have skipped a page or two here and there. She's very descriptive, is old Emily.'

Constance rolled her eyes in despair. 'And do you still feel the same as before? That Emily Brontë, along with Jane Austen, is a fraud?'

'Maybe not as much as I did yesterday. I was willing to be brought round.'

They looked at each other and Constance relaxed a little more.

'Do you still have any of that whisky left?' she asked.

'Of course. You think I've drunk the whole thing since you brought it?'

'Perhaps. Aren't all pilots drinkers?'

'That's a mighty unfair assumption.' He stood up to retrieve the bottle and two glasses. 'And I'm not sure it's fair to call me a pilot anymore, seeing as I've given up flying.'

She had almost forgotten that's what she had wanted to enquire about. He had put her off track but now she was going to be firm.

'So you've decided you're finished with it all?'

'I had already decided,' he said, handing her a tumbler of amber liquid. 'I told you that.'

Her fingers brushed his as she took the glass, instilling her with a nervous energy. 'But you aren't handing yourself in. Aren't going to ask for any help?'

He sighed and looked towards the ceiling. 'I'm not sure how I can.' He took a swig of his drink. 'Constance, may I ask a favour of you? In addition to housing me, I mean. In addition to bringing me food. May I ask that we don't talk about my leaving? Not yet. It makes me feel trapped, as if the world is collapsing in a heap on top of me. I am frightened. I may not show it but I jolly well am. But right now, here, with you, I feel safe. This is the first time I've felt safe in a very long time and, if it's all right with you, I'm not ready to let go of that just yet.'

Constance swallowed. 'All right then,' she said. 'If that's what you want.'

'You kindly promised you wouldn't tell anyone and I am hoping beyond hope that you still mean it.'

'Of course I still mean it,' she said softly. Although a flicker of guilt crawled across her mind that she had half-considered telling Douglas.

He smiled. Constance stood and walked towards the open window. The light from the lamp streaming out onto the overgrown garden should really have been shielded by the blackout blind but Constance made no move to put it in place.

'You don't feel cooped up here?' she asked as she ran her finger over the window ledge, picking up a layer of grime and wiping it on her clothes.

'A little,' he said ruefully. 'But it's for the best. I need time and I know I can't exactly sit in the pub and work it all out as a normal man should. Might attract some attention, a lone man of fighting age sitting in the pub in ill-fitting civilian clothing. So here it is.'

'Where's your uniform?' Constance asked suddenly.

'Its charred remains are in the fire,' he said. 'I never want to see it again.'

Constance opened and closed her mouth, aware she probably looked like a trout. 'Golly,' she said. 'I see.' Although she didn't, not really. In front of her a butterfly landed on the windowsill and Constance smiled. Gingerly she held out her hand and scooped it into her fingers.

'I haven't seen one this beautiful all summer,' she said.

'It's a peacock butterfly,' Matthew said as he moved to the window to take a look. 'See its bright eye-shaped markings on either side of its wings? Stunning.'

'How do you know what it's called?' Constance asked.

'You never had one of those strange frames with poor, deceased butterflies pinned by their wings, their names scribbled underneath in indiscernible Latin?'

Constance shook her head. 'We have an awful lot of taxidermy, mostly stags' heads from when the house was used more as a hunting lodge in my great-grandfather's time.'

The butterfly flicked its wings before stilling.

'We didn't have a large house in Cambridge,' Matthew whispered, eager not to disturb the butterfly. 'But on the walls we had a butterfly frame. Father was – is, I should say – a great lover of nature. He tried to instil that love in me but I'm rather afraid I was more into aircraft powered by Rolls-Royce engines than I was into things that flew under their own delicate steam. Birds and butterflies didn't really hold my attention. But I learnt their names all the same.' He smiled, his green eyes sparkling as he talked of home.

'Lucky thing, you,' he said to the butterfly. 'Able to come and go as you please. No holing up for you, trying to decide what to do next, where to run to, if anywhere.'

The butterfly flexed its wings and left the same way it had arrived. Constance watched it disappear into the inky night sky. 'I wish it were so easy for me to do the same,' she said quietly.

'Really?' Matthew asked, leaning back against the windowsill and regarding her keenly.

'I volunteered to drive a mobile canteen but was turned down,' Constance said. 'I feel useless, even though I'm clutching at any opportunity to help the war effort. In my spare time I'm supposed to be knitting socks for troops, would you believe? That's all I seem allowed to do. My parents will not hear of my working. My father flat-out refuses to let me go to London, or any other city for that matter. And so I'm here. I feel stuck, almost a prisoner.'

What would she have done if the war hadn't raged around them? The same sort of unexciting fate would have befallen her, only without the tantalising promise of adventure that her friends were enjoying.

Matthew regarded her. 'It could be worse,' he said.

'Oh I know,' Constance sighed. 'I have it so very lucky here, untouched by war – other than your rather dramatic arrival.' She smiled. 'And Douglas, who hardly ever gets leave. And I have an awful lot of spare time in which to appreciate my luck.'

'Are you really so desperate to leave?' he asked.

'I'm desperate to do something. I didn't think I was before, but now I am. The life I've been primed for is so entirely different from the one I want. Douglas thinks it's only a matter of time until girls are called up to do war work.'

'How very radical,' Matthew said with a hint of humour in his eyes. 'Your parents can't object then, can they?'

'No. But they will be very upset.'

'Have you never done anything that's truly upset your parents before?'

Constance thought for a moment. 'I don't think so. They never particularly liked me skipping about the woods with the ghillie, learning how to stalk deer, but that was when I was a child. As long as I was back in the schoolroom with my governess, practising my handwriting and my arithmetic at the allotted times then no more was really said.'

'Whatever would they think of you, out here, with me?'

'It will be a secret I carry with me to the grave, no doubt. Harbouring a man on the run.' He would remain her secret, even after he was gone. The only secret she had. 'If you need, I can find you some money,' she said suddenly. 'I have a little bit saved. Not much. But if you like, you can have it.'

'No,' Matthew said softly. 'I'm not taking your money. When the time is right . . .' He sighed and started again. 'When I am ready to go, back out there, back into the hell of the outside world, I will. But I won't take anything from you to enable that.' He took her hand and kissed it gently. She'd been unnerved when Henry had tried it but with Matthew it sent a shiver of delight through her. 'You have already done so much for me,' he finished.

'You will tell me?' she asked. 'You will tell me before you leave, won't you?' The thought of him leaving made her feel wretched. He was unlike any man she'd met before. He wasn't just wrapped up in his own, almighty issues. He seemed to genuinely care about her and how she felt.

'Of course I'll tell you,' he said after a moment's hesitation. His hand slipped away from hers.

'You never know,' he added. 'Perhaps you'll end up leaving before I do.'

Constance knew that wouldn't be the case but smiled anyway at his suggestion.

'If there's anything at all I can do to help,' he started, then laughed at his own suggestion. 'I know I'm of very little use to anyone at the moment.'

'You have helped. Just talking to you has been . . . truly wonderful.'

'If what your brother says is true,' Matthew said, 'if women will be called to work soon then at least all you need do is bide your time.'

'I do wonder what it would be like to spread my wings and fly,' she mused as she glanced out the window, towards the loch and into the distance where the butterfly had long gone.

'Flying's not all it's cracked up to be,' Matthew said quietly.

CHAPTER 20
2020

'A drowning? In our loch?' Liz asked. 'Nonsense. Absolute nonsense. Who told you that?'

'Angus seemed very sure,' Kate told her as they drank coffee at breakfast the next morning. 'Positive in fact.'

'Who drowned?' Liz put her cup on the kitchen table and cast Kate a curious look.

'Well I don't know,' Kate said. 'We were rather hoping you might.'

James watched their exchange silently as he sat back in his chair, arms folded, but Kate could tell curiosity had pulled him into the conversation; his toast remained untouched on his plate. Whisky thumped his tail hopefully under the table waiting for dropped crumbs that never came.

'No,' Liz said. 'No, I'm afraid I've no idea. What makes Angus so sure?'

'He was told when he was young.' James finally joined the conversation.

'Well,' Liz said, standing up and putting her breakfast dishes into the sink, 'if you two find out any more, do tell me. I'm intrigued.'

James made a non-committal noise and picked up his toast.

*

Kate looked at her watch and wondered if she could nip to the local library today and check out their archives. The odd death here or there probably wasn't newsworthy enough to make a history book, but perhaps newspapers from the 1940s, which is when Angus thought the drowning had occurred, would throw some light on the matter. Libraries had old newspapers, didn't they? Or were they held at the local records office? Kate would ring around later and see what she could find out.

She made a mental checklist of what she had to do today and knew there would be no time to go on the hunt for a drowning that may or may not have happened. Kate caught sight of James in the hallway as she collected the estate office keys. He was unwrapping a parcel containing a fully loaded toolbox along with a tool belt. He looked rather pleased with himself and started clipping the belt around his waist immediately. Kate tried not to laugh as she imagined him as some sort of Highland Batman.

Once at her desk in the office, she had lots of invitations to email out to travel journalists. They'd decided on a few tentative dates for the launch and she wanted to sound out some of her best contacts, to see if they would be free to come or if they might be able to send a freelancer. But before she worked out what she wanted to say on the invites, Kate put a quick search into Google: *Invermoray drowning*, but nothing useful appeared. She tried again with various versions of the phrase *Loch Invermoray Drowning* and *1940s Loch Invermoray Drowning*, but to no avail. This was all procrastination from the invitations but she knew that what she really wanted to research was the possibility of a monster in the loch. Kate didn't believe in things like that, but any and all 'evidence' would really help their cause if they were going to ham up the possibility of a monster.

Before she knew it she had wasted at least an hour falling down a fascinating rabbit hole of internet research. Although she preferred cold, hard facts, she wasn't immune to a good story and the 'sightings' people had uploaded of monsters, ghosts and other strange oddities had her totally enthralled. She noticed these stories had no accompanying photographs.

She read tales of ghostly pipers emerging from forests, of the ghost of a woman who stood at the door of a cottage in the centre of Invermoray, and screamed, foretelling the deaths of children. Kate shuddered and scrolled, hoping to find more interesting tales of monsters.

She was reading an intriguing tale of a mermaid-like creature, who would emerge totally naked from the water's edge of another loch nearby then find a lone fisherman, hold him by the hand and take him with her back into the water, luring him to a watery grave.

James's voice came from directly behind her. 'If the fisherman was on his own, how did anyone else see her?'

'Jesus Christ.' Kate jumped about a foot in the air, knocking her cold cup of coffee all over the table. James lunged forward to help, grabbing tissues from the box on Kate's desk and beginning to mop up the coffee that was seeping into the grain of the wood.

He laughed and Kate lifted her laptop so he could clean underneath.

'You scared the living hell out of me,' Kate chastised. If she hadn't been holding her laptop aloft with both hands, she would probably have thumped him. Her heart was still clattering in her chest. Ghost stories and people sneaking up behind her weren't a wonderful combination.

'Sorry.' He cast her an apologetic look. 'But that story's got to be complete boll—'

'Yes, OK,' Kate said with embarrassment as she replaced the laptop on the dried table.

'You don't believe any of that crap, do you? Ghosts and selkies and . . . whatever.' He gestured to the laptop screen and, feeling guilty, Kate clicked to close the browser window down. She would search in more detail for any mention of the potential Loch Invermoray Monster another time, when she was alone.

'No, of course not,' Kate bristled. 'But once I started searching . . .'

James sniggered and then put his hand on her shoulder and gave it a gentle squeeze. It was such an oddly personal thing for him to suddenly do that Kate stiffened. She didn't mean to. It wasn't that it was unpleasant. It was just surprising. She looked down at his hand and he must suddenly have felt as awkward as she did, because he removed it, flexed his fingers and then attempted to shove his hand in his pocket. The tool belt hanging on his waist prevented him and he ended up almost punching the hammer that was attached to the belt.

Was she interpreting this correctly? Was it just a friendly gesture? She didn't want to overreact, which she wondered now if she might have done. But likewise, she couldn't go through any unwanted complications with a client again and so she attempted to salvage the strange atmosphere that had entered the room as he rubbed his bruised knuckles.

'What have you been doing?' Kate asked, sure her voice was a bit high.

'Checking up on me?' he asked with a smile. 'Bit rich, isn't it? I find you surfing the net for monsters and sexy mermaids that kill fishermen and you want to know what *I've* been doing.'

Kate wanted to laughingly say 'oh bugger off,' but was very sure they weren't quite at the *colleagues who jokingly swear at each other* stage yet so she smiled back politely and wondered if he was actually evading her question.

'Come and see,' he said. 'I think you'll be pleasantly surprised.'

'What is it you've done?' Kate asked, glancing around. The words slipped out before she had a chance to run them through in her head.

James looked crestfallen. 'You can't tell?'

They were in one of the main bedrooms. Liz had been helping clear junk out from underneath beds and in doing so, rotten floorboards had been discovered in almost every room as furniture had been moved and rugs had been lifted.

'I've hauled out all the junk that Mum's been stacking up by each of the doors, taken it all up to the attics. I can sort that out another day. Anyway, all the mattresses look fine by the way so we can keep them . . .'

Kate wrinkled her nose. 'I think not,' she said in more of an officious tone than she meant. 'New mattresses, James. Crisp new bedding, soft towels, nice hand wash . . . If we're going to cut any corners it really can't be here.'

He sighed and sat down resignedly on an unmade bed. The springs creaked horrendously under his weight. 'You might be right,' he acquiesced, bouncing up and down on the bed just to be sure. 'So, I've tightened things up on all the four-posters,' he said, standing up again and tapping the floor with his foot. 'Replaced floorboards where they needed it and sanded others down so guests don't trip. The rotten windowpanes have been sorted too. I've been through most of this floor actually. Anything that needed doing, got done.' He twisted a hammer round in his tool belt in victory and his face held an unmistakable air of pride.

'I'm impressed,' Kate said as she moved over to the window to look at the fresh panes. All they needed now was a lick of paint.

'I've actually enjoyed it, all this getting my hands dirty,' he revealed. 'Never had too much call to wield a tool kit. Didn't realise what I was missing, sat at my desk, suited and booted, all these years.'

Kate gave him a knowing look. 'Having fun?' she asked.

'I am, in a strange kind of way. Whenever something broke in my apartment in Hong Kong it never occurred to me to try to fix it myself. Just rang the caretaker and up he came. But here, it's my family home. There's something comforting about rescuing it bit by bit, doing what I can myself. I might go and do some courses, tiling and plumbing and whatnot. Now I think about it, it's a shame I didn't know how to reroof or I could have saved myself a bloody fortune.'

Kate laughed. 'All this while I've been faffing around looking at mermaids and monsters. You kept that secret well hidden,' she said absent-mindedly while gazing around the room.

'Secret?' he asked.

'That you're good with your hands.'

'I've never had any complaints.'

His comment startled her. Was it her imagination that all the air had been sucked from the room?

'Right,' Kate blustered, tucking her hair behind her ear even though it was already securely tucked away. 'I can't stand around here all day admiring your woodwork.' God, she wasn't sure why she'd said it quite like that. It was an innocent enough remark but now she felt everything was a euphemism.

He laughed hard and Kate went to move past him. What on earth was happening? 'Got journalists to contact, don't you know?' She said it in such an unnecessarily singsong voice that she cringed, hating herself. She'd never been *this* hopeless around men. She could usually hold her own. But for some reason, James put her on edge. He made her jumpy whenever he was being a bit of a bastard, which thankfully seemed to have passed the more time they spent in each other's company. And now he was making her jumpy when he was being nice. Either he couldn't win, or Kate couldn't. She wasn't nervous around him. Or was she? How had this suddenly happened? After her most recent experience, Kate couldn't allow any miscommunication.

'I was thinking,' James said as Kate made it to the door. 'The walls of your room are bare. If you want to dress them up, there's pictures up in the attic. Quite a few, actually. Many of scenery, which I find quite boring but I know you like. Got a few of Dad's canvases up there too, I think. Bit bright. Not quite . . . er . . .

how do I say this without being disloyal . . . not quite to everyone's taste. There are also some family portraits and old photographs and I wonder if you think they might be nice to have out on coffee tables. You know, for guests to look at? We could go and see what you fancied for your room and I could help you bring them down?'

'Now?' Kate asked.

He shrugged. 'No time like the present.'

CHAPTER 21

The attic had been foreboding when Kate had been on her own but this time, with James, it had less of an eerie atmosphere for some reason. Perhaps it was his presence taking the edge off the strange energy. He moved around the attic with the confidence of a man totally at ease with himself. Kate watched him from the corner of her eye, unsure how she hadn't spotted that about him before.

Kate wandered over to take a look at the stacks of pictures that were facing the wall. She'd spied them before but hadn't looked fully. She crouched down and reached out. The dust under her fingers was grimy and she avoided the instinct to wipe her hands on her clean jeans. Regardless of whether they made use of them, Kate would make the effort to clean all of these pictures one day soon. It was such a shame they were up here in damp surroundings, becoming aged and forgotten.

In the corner of the room, James was picking paint from the walls with his fingers. Kate wondered what he was doing and he muttered something about 'still wet', and 'bloody roof'. She assumed the patches were from rainwater that had seeped in before James had spent an eye-watering amount of money having the house reroofed.

One of the pictures Kate turned round was of a long-forgotten McLay, she was sure. A dowdy, elderly female in a black dress whose eyes looked to pierce her soul. Kate shuddered and James took the frame from her and looked at it closely. The woman in the picture looked as if at one point she might have been quite attractive, but as old age had encroached she had turned bitter.

'Happy-looking woman. One for the charity shop, perhaps,' he said as he grimaced and put it back down on the floor.

It seemed a shame but Kate could imagine that a lot of items here wouldn't be worth much and may end up having a new lease of life if donated to a willing charity shop. Although she couldn't imagine anyone would want to buy this stern portrait. She turned another over. It was of a young man and woman. The frame had seen better days, like most things in the house, but the subjects were startlingly handsome.

James stood just behind Kate and looked at the double portrait over her shoulder. 'I recognise them,' he said.

Kate looked at the image more closely. 'In what way?' she asked.

James tutted. 'In a way that means I recognise them. It's the two on the stairs. But together, rather than separate. He's in uniform on the staircase. She's in some party dress. They're younger here.'

Kate looked closer. 'It is them, you're right. Much younger here. Her hair's different, more girly. I think that's what threw me. Let's rescue them and bring them downstairs,' Kate said. 'I'll take a few of the landscapes and put them up in the guest bedrooms which are devoid of portraits, and we can divide the rest up for the cottage and anywhere else that needs a few things on the walls. What do you think?'

James nodded as they walked back towards the staircase. Liz accosted them as they descended. 'Ah, you've found Constance and Douglas,' she said as she wiped muddy hands down her jeans. 'I knew I'd seem them together up there.'

Kate turned the portrait round to take a better look. 'So this is Constance,' she said, looking into the girl's dark eyes and finding them to be warm and friendly. Kate looked back at Liz. 'I found Constance's name, and that of Douglas, actually,' she said a little too excitedly, 'in the family Bible downstairs. Constance's name has been scrubbed out.'

James tilted his head to one side. 'Scrubbed out?' he questioned.

'Yes,' Kate said, looking down at the picture of the siblings in her hands. 'But Douglas's name is very much intact. How do you know it's them?' she asked Liz. There was no name plaque on the pictures.

'I took a closer look when I retrieved their individual portraits from the attic,' Liz said, 'and someone has scribbled their names and the year, 1940, on the fold of the canvases – perhaps the artist? The ones on the staircase are more formal than this,' she said, gesturing to the picture of the duo in Kate's hands. 'Maybe they're to commemorate an event such as a key birthday, or Douglas going off to war, or being made an officer, or something like that? I found it odd that they were all banished to the attic,' Liz continued. 'Did you find the picture of Augusta McLay, Constance and Douglas's mother? Dour-looking woman dressed in black, painted in the 1960s, I think. Hers was on the stairs when Constance and Douglas had been slung in the attic. I switched it round. Felt rather guilty actually.'

'Why?' James asked.

'It was Augusta and Alistair who bequeathed the house to your father. And then I go and take her image down. Not very gracious of me.'

'But she does rather have an expression about her,' Kate said. 'Not the friendliest-looking woman.'

They were still standing on the stairs; James and Kate covered in grime from the attic, Liz covered in mud. They were the very essence of a working estate being dragged back up from its knees.

'When we arrived,' Liz said, readjusting her hair in its side clip, 'the last of the McLays who had just passed away and given the house to your father were Constance and Douglas's parents. Considering the only pictures of their children were tumbling about in the attic upstairs, I would probably agree, Kate, not at all friendly. And of course they had disinherited their children in favour of your father.' She nodded to James. 'A man they'd never even met.'

'I can't imagine having children and then taking their pictures down and throwing them in a dusty attic,' James said.

'Precisely,' Liz agreed. 'And then of course,' she said, 'there was that awful rip in the picture of Constance.'

'Rip?' Kate asked.

'Yes,' Liz said as they moved to look at the picture of Constance hanging on the staircase. 'I've had the picture cleaned up quite a bit but also repaired. A friend of mine works as a conservationist for National Trust for Scotland and they took it in years ago as a favour to me; a conservation project for students to work on. When I found her in the attic—' Liz spoke about the image of Constance as though it was a person '—someone had had a go at her with a knife.'

Kate shivered. 'What?'

'Mmm,' Liz said. 'Started in the middle of her and sliced it all the way to the corner, here.' She pointed at the bottom left-hand of the picture.

Kate looked carefully. It had been mended so incredibly well that she could easily see why she hadn't noticed it before. 'They've done a fantastic job at mending it,' she murmured, her face close to Constance's portrait. The tear ran right from her stomach all the way down to the hem of her silver-grey dress. The slice had been huge, meaningful, and deliberate. Previously, Kate had thought that line in the brushstrokes had been a fold of her dress but she could see now with disbelief it had been from a knife.

Kate jumped as someone pulled the old-fashioned doorbell.

James dragged his eyes from the portrait. 'That'll be Angus,' he said. 'We're chatting through catering details. How are you getting on with the press invites?' he asked, bringing himself back to the here and now.

Kate gave him a look that said, *are you joking*? 'I've been up here with you, so not that well.'

'Best get to it,' he said with a grin. 'Chop-chop. And try not to get too engrossed in googling monsters and mermaids this time.'

Kate had drafted an initial press release but she was going to sit on it for the night before redrafting again tomorrow. She had tried not to go in too heavy with the myths and legends, instead merging tantalising details about 'historic sightings in the loch' with the information about the traditional Highland baronial house, a family home newly converted into beautiful accommodation, the setting, the glorious scenery. That reminded her, she still needed to work out a seasonal tariff structure for rooms and she added an urgent note to her lengthening to-do list to tackle this.

They also needed to make sure that they paired up with a local outdoor pursuits centre to take guests hunting and deer stalking. It wasn't something James or Liz were equipped to do and handing that responsibility over to a third party who specialised was just what they needed. They had enough going on without getting engrossed in shooting licences and the like. Fishing was different though. As the estate owned the loch, they could happily provide guests with the copious fishing equipment painstakingly gathered over the years by James's antecedents. Kate was starting to feel this was all coming together. Slowly, of course, but they were actually getting somewhere day by day.

She closed up the office and went into the house in search of some coffee. Instead she found Angus and James talking shop in the sitting room, paperwork and laptops scattered over the coffee table that sat between them. Angus turned and looked at Kate as she entered.

'Ah just the woman,' he said with a glint in his eye. 'What say you to a bit of yoga tonight?'

'Tonight?' Kate thought about it. She had been in dire need of something to do that wasn't sitting in the pub or the office. 'All right then.'

'Great, go and get changed and I'll drive ye.'

'Now?' She looked at her watch. 'It's only five o'clock.'

'Listen, lassie.' Angus laughed. 'I dunnae what time o' night you Londoners are used to going to yoga, but there's no twenty-four-hour gym classes up here. It's 5.30 p.m. once a week in the community centre and that's if our so-called instructor Brenda McCrea's managed to get her four teenagers fed their tea and parked in front of the TV without too much hassle.'

Kate laughed but stopped when she saw James's slightly put-out expression.

'It's all right if I nip off, isn't it? You didn't need me to work late?' she asked.

He shrugged. 'Do what you like.'

'Um, OK,' Kate said, unsure if he was annoyed he hadn't been invited.

'Do you want to join—'

'No I do not,' he replied quickly. 'I'm a runner. Not a yogi. Enjoy yourself.'

Kate was secretly pleased that Angus suggested a drink in the pub after the class. For all Angus had joked about the class being on the parochial side, Brenda McCrea had been a demon instructor. She'd also been incredibly attentive, correcting a posture Kate thought she'd perfected over the years but which, it turned out, she'd been doing incorrectly the entire time. The class she'd attended near her office in London had been relaxing enough, and she thought it had been spot-on but, along with so many other busy souls hammering their way through downward dog in between meetings, she was beginning to wonder if she'd been short-changed all those years. Her posture, as it turned out, was not good.

Angus had introduced her to the class and everyone had been so friendly. During the relaxation bit, where Brenda lit candles and dimmed the lights, Kate had fallen fast asleep. She had been woken by a laughing Angus, enquiring if James was such a slave driver that he'd had her burning the candle at both ends.

'Thanks for taking me,' Kate said as Angus brought two bottles of sparkling mineral water round from the fridge when they were sitting in the Invermoray Arms.

'You're very welcome. These are on the house,' he said as they sat at the bar and sipped. The fire roared away in the grate and Kate rolled her shoulders, continuing to unstiffen. The locals drifted in and out of the pub, stopping their conversations mid-flow to have a quick, friendly word with Angus. Kate noticed people stared at the pair of them and gave Angus a wink every now and again. It made her aware that when James and she had been in there, that hardly anyone said hello to James and in return, neither did he. Did he keep himself to himself so much? Or was it because his family owned the big house and that meant he couldn't really be considered one of them? Perhaps Kate was being too outdated.

'Does James actually have any friends round here?' she asked suddenly.

Angus choked on his water. 'What a strange question,' he replied. 'What makes you ask that?'

'I'm not sure. I think he might be a bit lonely.'

Angus smiled. 'Does he seem lonely?'

'Maybe. Maybe not,' Kate replied.

'All work and no play?' Angus queried. Kate nodded.

'He has me, I suppose,' Angus said thoughtfully. 'But he dunnae tell me much of consequence. When he comes in here we talk about sport and the news over a dram o' two of whisky or a pint. That's about it.'

Kate nodded. 'Has he ever had a girlfriend up here?' she found herself asking.

'He keeps himself to himself. A few of the single girls have had a go though,' Angus clarified.

'A go?' Kate asked naively.

Angus chuckled. 'Tried to get him to notice them. He's fastidious in avoiding their attention though. Dunnae why. If ye ask me, a quick roll in the hay'd do that man the world'a good. Uptight bastard that he is.'

Kate's eyes widened. That was perhaps more information than she needed. She took a giant gulp of her mineral water, trying to force the image from her mind.

'Can we have a proper drink now?' she asked.

'No you can't,' Angus said as Kate tried to grab the barmaid's attention. 'Water's good enough for you today after an hour of exercise. You cannae do a yoga class then hit the Hendrick's.'

'Ugh, fine.' Kate laughed and sipped again.

'Ye ask a lot of questions about James,' Angus said, folding his arms and looking knowing.

'No I don't. Just those ones.'

'Hmm, OK.' He continued looking at her.

Kate endeavoured to change the subject. 'What about you? Any girlfriends?'

'Nope,' he said, his arms still folded. 'I could also badly do wi' a roll in the hay but sadly no one's been forthcoming of late.'

It was Kate's turn to choke on her drink.

Angus dropped Kate back to the house at about half past eleven. They'd been in the pub ever since yoga had finished and Kate had been introduced to his sister. She'd extended an invitation for Kate to join her book club in a few days. Kate had written the title of their latest book on the back of her hand, making a point to go to the library and dig out a copy if they had one.

After, Angus had finally given in to Kate's relentless begging for a proper drink and they'd opened a bottle of wine. Angus had drunk just one glass as he heroically remembered he still had to drive her home, but his sister and Kate had hit it off immediately and had drunk the remainder of the bottle together. Kate noticed she also asked a lot of questions about James and was entirely entranced with the idea that Kate lived at Invermoray House with him.

As Kate walked into Invermoray House later that night she noticed all the lights were out, other than the one over the front door. It cast a glow into the entrance hall as she held the large front door open and pulled her key out of it. She wavered before closing the door, leaving herself in complete darkness as she fumbled around for the switch.

'What time do you call this?' James's deep voice came from somewhere inside the entrance hall. There was only the faintest flicker of light being cast from the now dim fire.

She sensed, rather than saw James get up from the staircase and walk towards her.

'Sorry, I grabbed dinner and drinks afterwards with Angus and—'

'I don't care if you grabbed dinner and drinks with Mary Queen of Scots,' he said as he flicked on the table lamp. 'You could have replied to my messages. I've been worried.'

Kate fumbled in her bag for her phone. 'Your messages?'

'I messaged you at 7 p.m. to check if you wanted me to keep any dinner back for you. And then I messaged about half an hour ago to see if you were actually coming back here tonight or whether I should lock up. It's really late and you didn't reply so . . .'

'Of course I was coming back,' Kate said. 'Where else would I go?'

'I thought you might end up staying the night with Angus.'

'What?' Kate said, the shock in her voice evident. 'Why would I stay with Angus?'

He shrugged. 'I don't like to assume. I mean, you're not a nun and Angus is a nice bloke.'

Kate's eyes were wide. 'It was just a yoga class,' she said as she finally found her phone.

'And dinner,' James responded. 'And drinks.' He spoke as if Kate sleeping with Angus was always on the cards, given she'd just had a meal and some wine.

'I don't sleep with men on the first date,' Kate said, utterly horrified.

James spoke in a more even voice. 'It was a date? I thought it was just yoga.'

'No, that's not what I meant.' Kate shook her head. 'It wasn't a date. I just meant . . . I don't know what I meant.'

She looked at her phone screen and remembered she'd turned her phone off during the yoga class and hadn't switched it back on. She did so now and watched as his messages materialised. She put her phone away. She'd look properly later.

'Well,' James said. 'I just wanted to see if you were coming home for the night. Now you're here . . . I'm off to bed. Throw the bolt on the door,' he shot at her.

James climbed the stairs and Kate returned to the front door and pushed the bolt into place for the night. She heard his bedroom door slam shut. After the fabulous night she'd had, she was now going to bed feeling utterly deflated. He was such a miserable sod. No wonder no one wanted to have roll in the hay with James.

CHAPTER 22

September 1940

The artist was taking an inordinate amount of time. Constance flicked her wrist in order to look at her watch before realising it was still on her dressing table. She'd been forced to discard it in favour of bare arms, which looked more ladylike according to her mother. She was sitting bolt upright on a stool, posing unnaturally in her silver-grey ball dress; the one she'd worn the night of her birthday. The daily girl, Daisy, had cleaned and pressed it and if she suspected it had been the victim of a dousing in loch water, she'd not said a word.

Constance rolled her head around, unstiffening her neck and listening to the terrible creaks and clicks as she shifted herself back into position. The elderly artist, Walter McAteer, was one of Scotland's finest portrait artists, according to her father. The artist smiled patiently as Constance resumed sitting perfectly still. He trotted over, placed a hand on her back and gently pushed her into a more upright position.

'There,' he said and moved back to his easel.

Her father stepped into the room. 'Beautiful,' he said, looking at the sketch and not at her. 'Just came to see,' he added, smiling at Mr McAteer. 'And to tell you, Constance, it's all go. Invermoray will be a convalescent home before long. Only too pleased to take the house off our hands, and as your mother suspected, they'll let us live here if we keep ourselves to ourselves in a handful of rooms only.' He looked around the ballroom. 'This'll be full of wounded servicemen dripping blood over the flooring within days by all accounts.'

'Days?' Constance asked.

'Things move quickly, when they want them to, despite there being a war on. Perhaps because there's a war on.'

With that, he turned and left, leaving Constance and the artist in silence, which she found welcome. She looked around the ballroom. The ornate white plasterwork and duck egg blue accents had been decided upon as the perfect complement to Constance's silver-grey dress in the portrait, and soon it would be the backdrop for the recovery of injured servicemen.

Daisy arrived with a tea tray and Constance wondered if she'd be allowed to move and actually drink any. She smiled a thank you to the daily girl and stared absent-mindedly through the large French doors and out towards the loch. Every now and again she could see the gardener as he moved a wheelbarrow to and fro in the parterre. While the house was changing, some things would always remain the same.

In front of her Mr McAteer wiped a brush on a piece of cloth and looked thoughtful.

'Do you think we might break for tea?' Constance nodded towards the tray.

The marvellous Mrs Fraser had rustled up some shortbread biscuits and Constance decided she would not eat her share but would hide a few inside a napkin and take them to the cottage when she could. She wondered if Matthew was waiting for her, amusing himself by continuing to work his way through the novels; if she should perhaps fetch more for him – a wider choice, maybe – or if she should let him persevere with her favourite novels until he learned to appreciate them. She smiled at this thought.

The artist helped himself to a biscuit. So far he had been a man of little conversation as he worked.

'Penny for them?' he asked.

Constance blinked and came to her senses.

'Oh, I was just thinking about literature.'

'Surely one of the best things in life,' he replied as he poured fresh creamy milk into their teacups. 'Along with art,' he said.

She climbed down from the stool and stretched her back.

'Yes,' she mused. 'I agree. But there's a war on and so surely we should be thinking of other things.'

The artist stirred his tea. 'If we thought of other things and ignored the beauty around us, I would have no work,' he said with a smile.

Constance sipped her tea. 'True,' she agreed. 'But this feels such a waste of time. For me, I mean,' she said hastily so as not to offend. 'There are so many things I could be doing, should be doing. I'm ready to live. But instead I'm sitting here in this dress replicating the night of my birthday, which has been and gone.' She looked down at her attire. 'I feel a bit silly.'

'The portrait is to commemorate your twenty-first birthday,' he said. 'I think no one can be expected to have fully lived by twenty-one. It will all come in time. Now shall we continue?'

As she did most days inside Invermoray House, Constance felt dismissed.

Constance arrived at the cottage with all the remaining biscuits as well as the end of a loaf and some tinned soup. It had been a long day and she was dog-tired from waiting for the portrait sitting to finish. She hadn't been allowed to look and found she didn't care. After she had said goodbye and thank you and listened while her mother chatted aimlessly with the artist, she had practically run up the stairs and changed in to some loose trousers and a beige Aran jumper. She'd waited until the coast was clear and in her rush to see Matthew had left her hair in the style in which she had painstakingly set it earlier with her mother and Daisy. While not a lady's maid, Daisy had a knack for setting hair that she'd taught herself from the pages of the latest women's magazines. Although now, hours later, the hairpins were starting to drop.

Constance threw the cottage door open and Matthew sprung up from the settee where he was reading.

'My God, woman,' he said as he tried to regulate his breathing. 'You're going to have to stop doing that. We need to develop a coded knock at the very least if I'm to keep my heart inside my chest.'

'I'm sorry, I wasn't thinking. I didn't quite mean to bound in like that. Only I thought you might be hungry and I've brought some things to eat.'

'Thank you,' he said, looking her over. 'I still have some food left over but top-ups are gratefully received. You look lovely by the way.'

Constance started to say a shy thank you but was cut off as Matthew coughed. He sat back down on the settee.

'Are you all right?'

'Yes, yes I think so,' he said dismissively. 'Just a cough. Tell me about your day.'

'No, let me look at you,' she said. She knelt next to him, placing a hand on his forehead. 'You're awfully warm. I'm going to open a window.'

'Don't you dare,' he said with a laugh that turned into a cough. 'It's freezing in here.'

'It really isn't,' she replied, still kneeling next to him. 'But if you insist, I won't.'

'So,' he said, 'your day . . . you didn't set your hair like that for me did you?'

Constance reddened as she gingerly sat on the arm of the settee. 'I did not. I had my portrait painted today.' The moment she said it she felt stupid.

'Whatever for?' Matthew asked, looking up at her.

'Mother and Father insisted. I suppose it was kind of them really. To commemorate my birthday. They commissioned one for Douglas when he got his wings and as I have nothing quite as impressive as that to recommend me, I'm having one simply because I'm *of age*.'

'And you've not enjoyed the process,' Matthew said, leaning back in the chair to get a better look at her.

'Not much, no. I feel rather useless and I want to feel useful.'

'You are useful,' he said. 'You've been keeping me well fed and at bay.'

She tutted. 'Be serious.'

'I am,' he said. 'I'm sure there's more you could be doing but what you are doing for me, now, don't think it's meaningless because it isn't. The war is truly in full swing – it's not ending anytime soon and if you cast your gaze about, you'll discover how you can play your part.'

Constance nodded. 'It's been a whole year since the war began. I don't think any of us have felt the war touch us until recently. Not really. And even Douglas was pleased to be gadding about in the air and not really heeding the fact he'd be firing enemy bombers out of the sky. I listened to father you see, when he said the war would be over by Christmas.'

Matthew scoffed. 'You didn't really believe that, did you?'

'I did, yes,' she said almost incensed. 'Didn't you?'

'No,' he replied simply. 'Herr Hitler is one determined fellow.'

'Yes, I suppose you're right. But I didn't know enough then and I still don't know enough now really.'

'Perhaps you should come out from under the protective layers your parents have provided. Unpeel those layers, slowly, and see what the world looks like with you in it. Listen to the wireless, read a newspaper and forge your own opinions rather than listening to your parents and taking their word as law. In fact, if you wouldn't mind, could you bring a newspaper with you the next time you come? I sorely want to know what on earth's going on in that war out there.'

'It does feel like it's out there, doesn't it,' Constance said absent-mindedly.

Matthew nodded as he cast his gaze around the cottage. 'Not in here. Not with us.'

Constance smiled slowly. He looked up at her and she worried she was being scrutinised. He coughed again.

'Would you like me to bring something for that cough, lozenges perhaps, next time?'

He nodded.

Outside the swaying pines provided a screen and the brambles threatened to usurp what remained of the garden. She felt completely hidden, safe in here with Matthew. Constance stared through the screen towards the loch. 'Preparations have started to turn the house into a convalescent home,' Constance informed him.

'A convalescent home?'

'For officers.'

'Well of course,' he said with a wry smile. He stood, slower than normal, and moved to unpack the food she had brought.

'I was wondering if I offered to help, if they'd let me. I haven't any training and I don't know how feasible it is that they'd let me jump in and assist, even in some small way.'

'You can ask,' he stated. 'Unless you choose to leave and help elsewhere?'

'Leave?' Constance asked, following him with her eyes. 'How would I do that? My parents would never let me.'

'How do I know?' Matthew laughed. 'Don't you want to leave?'

She shook her head. 'I did. Desperately. Until . . .'

'Until . . . ?' he questioned.

She felt silly saying it out loud, especially when until this very moment she hadn't even thought the next sentence inside her head. It had not dawned on her how she felt about him, had not occurred to her how much she had become attracted to him, how much she valued his company, his conversation and how much she valued *him*. It had been a little shy of a week but the intensity of the situation and the close confines the two of them were enjoying in the cottage was playing havoc with her heart 'Until you.'

'Until me . . . what?' he said with a look of genuine puzzlement.

'Until you arrived, until you needed my help. Just . . . until you.'

She felt completely foolish.

'Oh, Constance,' he said. He looked at the floor as if he didn't know where else to look.

She swallowed audibly, knowing she'd committed a faux pas with no idea how to redeem herself.

'I only meant—' she started.

'I think I know what you meant,' he said. He stopped and sighed. 'But how do I say this . . .'

She waited for the blow to come, the dismissal in whatever form it would arrive.

'I sit here all day, Constance, and I think about you.'

Her eyes widened. 'Really?'

He nodded. 'Yes, really. In amongst reading Austen and Dickens, of course. A beautiful, brave girl swims out into the loch and rescues me, houses me, feeds me, teaches me to value Jane Austen . . .' He looked at her and smiled. 'What else is a chap supposed to do if not think about a marvellous woman like that? I may be on the run, Constance, but I'm not blind. I can't stop thinking about you. I . . .' He paused. 'I'm not sure I have the right words to do you justice.'

She held her breath as he moved towards her. He appeared to be considering his next action. He reached out a hand and touched her face. It sent shivers through her entire body.

'But here's the sting in the tail,' he whispered. He was so close she could feel the warmth of his breath. But she wanted more.

'We shouldn't do anything about it,' he told her. 'We *can't* do anything about it.'

'Why not?' she breathed.

'Because one day very soon, this will all come to a crashing end. I will leave. Either that, or someone's going to bound through that door and they're going to force me away from you, and I'll have got you into the most tremendous trouble.'

'I know,' she whispered. 'I don't care.'

'I do. Constance, I cannot tell you how much I like you.'

'No?' she questioned, her heart thudding so hard it almost hurt. She hadn't thought it was possible that a man could fall from the skies and into her heart.

'I can't tell you because it's wrong of me.' He stepped back and she knew the moment for him to kiss her had passed.

He coughed louder now and took a wheezing breath.

He felt the same, but whatever they felt would not be acted upon. She wanted it to be enough, but deep down it wasn't. She opened her mouth but had no idea what to say. He gave her a pained look, as if he too wanted to say something that would forever change things between them.

Instead, Matthew took her hand in his and kissed it gently. 'I'm going to be in such trouble, Constance, if I'm found. After this long on the ground they'll never believe I was simply lost or injured. They'll know I've been hiding and my side of what happened that night will no longer be worth a bean. That's it for me. Court-martial all the way and then prison most probably. But when I'm gone, because I will eventually have to go, I want you to break free of whatever chains are keeping you here. See the world, do something useful, but most of all do something you believe in. Trust me, if you don't believe you're doing good it will be the undoing of you. As it was for me. My war has ended. But yours is just beginning.'

CHAPTER 23

Being with Matthew brought Constance excitement that she had never felt before in her short life. He made her feel so at ease the way no one else ever had; the way she'd never let anyone else. She had friends, mainly from pony club from her childhood and daughters of her mother's society friends in London, whom she kept in touch with. The odd letter here, a telegram announcing a visit there – but someone to talk to about the everyday? She'd not had that in so long, and she hadn't entirely noticed the loneliness creep in until now.

She sat at her dressing table, casting her gaze over her hairpins and jewellery. She never wore any usually and wondered why her mother had given her so much over the years. Her mother's hopes for Constance hadn't materialised into marriage, but quite how they would when she was buried up here in the middle of nowhere was beyond her. The frustratingly endless parties and incessant mingling in London had been too much for Constance and she knew her days of feigning headaches in order to escape dull parties had been numbered regardless. As the war intensified, her mother's writing table no longer held quite as many stiff card invitations anyway. The world was changing about them and had been for quite some time.

She'd been desperate to leave, to do something useful and Matthew had seen that and encouraged her to get on with it. But she didn't want to be away from the pilot in the woods who shouldn't be there. Matthew had admitted he thought about her all the time. And she felt the same. If she left now . . . all of that would end. And she didn't want it to end. But end it must. He wouldn't be here forever and they both knew that. But she dare not admit to herself how she felt about him, even after such a short amount of time. The heightened conditions of the past week had encouraged them to reveal so much to each other they would not have done in ordinary circumstances. She knew more about him than she had of any other man she'd met. She knew his reasons for doing what he'd done. She thought she understood him and, more than that, she was beginning to understand herself. The knowledge that he would leave one day very soon made her heart hurt.

The next few days brought immense change to Invermoray House. A representative for the Ministry of Health had deemed the estate appropriate and the conversion of the house from private residence to convalescent hospital was underway.

The Red Cross sent staff and medical supplies, beds, tables, chairs, games and books, which pleased Constance endlessly. Deckchairs and garden games were stacked under the portico and all of the furniture that would no longer be used by the family was moved into the stables and attics to make way for metal bedsteads. Every living area would soon be a small, makeshift ward with linoleum flooring rolled out to protect the boards and to enable easy cleaning. Some of the less expensive paintings, tapestries and the one suit of armour whose origins no one was quite sure of were left adorning the walls. The ornate ballroom doors were covered with protective hardboard to prevent damage by officers learning how to use wheelchairs and crutches. Items from Father's study were moved into the smaller of the two sitting rooms, which would be their only private living space.

'This clattering, I can't imagine how my nerves will cope with this,' her mother announced one morning. 'It's too much.'

Constance was secretly thrilled as she watched one of the many items of furniture from the guest bedrooms being removed by orderlies. It was happening.

'I had no idea, really, what this would entail,' Mrs McLay said, and the two women ducked as metal bedsteads and chairs were carried past them. 'Your father and I are relocating. Just until all this is over. There's a divine hotel near St Andrews where your father has been itching to play golf. We'll be there for the next week or so until all this passes. When the officers arrive, there will be none of this to and fro nonsense, I'm assured. They'll need calm. And so will we. I can't imagine why I suggested this.'

Constance put her hand on her mother's arm. 'Because it's a lovely thing to do. We're helping, in a way. And it means we get to stay, which is what you really wanted.'

Her mother issued a noise from the back of her throat. 'I don't know why we'd want to stay. Best to just let them have it, I think now. Our house isn't our own anymore.'

Constance could rally no sympathy. 'I know, Mother, but as you said at least we aren't being turfed out. We've chosen this and that must count for something.'

Mrs McLay looked at Constance. 'Yes, perhaps. You may come with us if you like, to St Andrews for the time being? Get away from the chaos?'

Constance's reply was almost too immediate. She could not leave. 'No. Thank you, Mother. I'll stay and . . . help supervise with Mrs Campbell. It's unfair to expect her to do everything alone. You go. We'll manage here.'

Her mother nodded and thankfully didn't force the point as her attention was occupied elsewhere. 'Where are you going with that, young man?' Mrs McLay strode forcefully towards a startled-looking porter who had accidentally turned in the wrong direction carrying a sculpture. 'Dear Lord, are we to be robbed?'

Constance threw the wide-eyed man an apologetic glance and moved towards the ballroom where a temporary desk had been set up and orders were being given to a range of uniformed staff. General service members were to either work as cleaners or to accompany Mrs Fraser into the kitchen where a schedule of meals for patients was to be administered. Mrs Fraser looked far from put out at the prospect of her kitchen being invaded by a workforce. She looked delighted as she scuttled away to proudly show off her spotless, well-equipped kitchen.

'High time we had some excitement around here,' she said joyfully.

Constance chuckled to herself and looked out of the French doors, in the direction of the ghillie's cottage. As eager as she had been for the hospital to arrive, this fresh barrage of excitement had brought with it so many people; so many who might see her as she crossed the grounds to visit Matthew and take him supplies. How would she manage it? How would she avoid quite so many people seeing her?

She had half imagined that each of the guest bedrooms would house just one officer, propped up delicately each day in one of Invermoray's Victorian four-posters. Her mother had clearly imagined the same situation. But Constance was listening quietly to the conversation happening around her. About six or so beds would be placed in each bedroom. She did some fast arithmetic: around forty beds upstairs in the bedrooms that the family weren't using. The downstairs rooms would mainly be for staff and relaxation, but the ballroom would house another twenty or so beds. Constance could see why her mother was overwhelmed. She was shocked there would be no doctors, only nurses, but Matron had explained to Constance's father that it was ad-hoc nursing required, not medical emergencies. The local doctor could come in when needed.

With medical staff given instructions about where to bed down and which duties to commence Constance lingered, not quite knowing what to do with herself. Her parents were departing and the house was being treated with the greatest respect, leaving Constance with very little to actually do.

Matron, a portly lady with a tight face, offered Constance a stern look. 'Can I help you?'

'Oh,' Constance replied uncertainly. 'No, I don't think so. I don't like to be in the way. But I did rather wonder . . . ?'

'Out with it, child,' she said.

' . . . if you required help?' Constance finished, gaining confidence, her fingers crossed behind her back for good luck. 'If, perhaps, I could be of any help?'

Constance soon found herself in the ballroom happily opening boxes of bandages and dressings, folding them and placing them into the new storage cabinets at the end of the room, behind the large baize curtain that had been assembled to separate the administration area from the makeshift ward. What should have been mind-numbing work was almost exhilarating. She was of use. A nurse came to tick off pills and glass bottles of dark liquid medicine. There wasn't much as all of the officers arriving would be recovering, rather than being treated for a medical emergency.

'What are these for?' Constance held up one of the tins of pills.

'Infections,' the nurse replied. 'On the off chance any of the patients come down with anything nasty. They shouldn't though. Matron looks like she runs a tight ship and we'll all be keeping the house spick and span.'

Around her beds had been assembled and side tables placed to the right of each bed. Orderlies swept and cleaned and when Constance had finished unloading medical supplies she offered to help make beds, learning how to ensure crisp corners were tucked in neatly. Constance smiled throughout; she was doing something, however menial, for the war effort. As she finished, the first of the patients arrived. The McLay family had been told it would all happen quickly but the wheels of war were more oiled than they had thought and ambulances were beginning their arrival at the front entrance of Invermoray House, a ramp now installed for those in wheelchairs.

One such patient arrived, pushed by an orderly. As he came past Constance, it was all she could do not to gasp in shock. She hadn't expected the patients to be so awfully disfigured. In truth, she wasn't sure what she expected. But not this. The man's left arm had gone, his blazer sleeve clipped up by his shoulder. The half of his face that she could see was slack, as if his muscles no longer worked, and the other half was hidden behind the thick, white bandage wrapped around his head. She checked herself and smiled at the man before glancing at the orderly, whose expression was blank, as if this was not the first such case he had seen.

What on earth had happened to that poor man? She had not noticed his uniform, so blinded was she by his obvious disfigurements. Had he been in the way of an explosion on the ground? Or was he a pilot who had suffered so horrifically in mid-air? The wounds did not look fresh and so she could only imagine what kind of treatment he had been through before being moved on here to convalesce. She shivered, although it was not cold, and thanked God that she was a woman. She wasn't brave enough to be sent into battle. She wasn't sure how any man could be, either. The reality of war, the war she was now beginning to see as more patients filtered through minutes later in various states of injury, was utterly sobering.

What good was this war doing to justify killing men and rendering them incomplete? While it was his duty, she now understood Matthew when he said he could no longer kill, no longer shoot men from the sky. Constance glanced over at the patient whose battle-scarred face was hidden behind his bandage. What glory was there for those men who fought bravely, if they would spend the remainder of their lives paying for it?

*

The house was noisy and full of people. Only a few beds in the upper rooms remained empty. But Matron informed Constance that they were expecting further patients to be transferred to Invermoray in the following days. It had taken all Constance's courage to leave the house in the end, putting on her shoes in the boot room and making her way into the cobbled courtyard. She fancied if anyone caught her, it would look less suspicious this way, avoiding the front of the house. At the back door a nurse who had been smoking started and stood up straight as Constance passed her. She muttered something about giving her a fright. Constance issued an apology and smiled, her heart thumping heavily. She hadn't imagined anyone would be in this part of the grounds and alongside gratitude that the house was making itself useful, and her with it, there was an overwhelming worry that things were now becoming more difficult.

She arrived at the cottage and knocked on the door, but there was no answer. Panic rose suddenly and thoughts of telling Matthew all the news from the house – all her news – diminished. The door creaked as she opened it and she looked towards the armchair, his usual spot. The books she'd brought him were piled up neatly; the kitchen was tidy and the cottage was silent. She put the bundle of food she'd brought with her onto the table and stood, listening.

'Matthew?' she called. Perhaps he was deeper in the forest by the stream, washing, as he had been the last time she suspected he had gone. Something didn't feel right, and she called his name again. Upstairs a creak sounded. She climbed the little wooden staircase that led into the sole bedroom and, with relief, watched him sleeping. The sheets and blankets were in a tangle and had revealed his sturdy sleeping form. He was in the clothes she'd left him in the day before, she was sure of it, which was strange when he had the run of the ghillie's remaining albeit limited, wardrobe. He'd been taking small bundles of clothes down to the stream, washing them during the day and drying them by the fire each night when it was safe for smoke to plume almost invisibly into the night sky.

His chest was rising and falling quicker than she thought normal and she watched as he coughed in his sleep, a groan emanating from him as he shifted slightly. Constance moved closer. The sheets were damp around him, his clothes sodden. Foolishly she looked towards the roof, but there had been no rainfall of late with which to leak through and onto the bed.

She exclaimed as she realised his perspiration was the cause of the sodden bed. She felt his brow, which was hot and clammy, his hair sticking to his skin. When she'd left him he'd not been like this. He'd been coughing, yes, and it had been worsening – the lozenges she'd brought him had done nothing. But now he was incapacitated.

'Matthew,' she called, panic rising in her voice. 'Matthew.'

A thick rasp came from his throat and she stared, helplessly. He was too hot. What should she do?

With great effort she pulled him into a sitting position, hugging him against her. His head lolled against her shoulder and with a great effort of will, she lifted the jumper over his head. His weight was almost dead against her and the jumper was heavy with sweat. She laid Matthew back down, cradling his head gently before rushing downstairs. She turned the tap on at the kitchen sink and ran the water, its pitiful supply fitting and starting as she looked around for a vessel. She filled two thick china teacups and carried them up the stairs, opened the wardrobe doors and found a shirt to dip in the cool water. Mopping his brow with the corner of a damp shirt would not do enough. She knew she had to do something else, but what? She took an armload of thinning towels from the shelves in the cupboard and threw them in the sink downstairs, letting the water soak into them. She wrung them out and ran back up the stairs, careful not to slip on the staircase as water dripped onto the floor.

She draped the larger towels across his chest and a smaller

one over his forehead, hoping to cool him down. Kneeling by the side of the bed, she held his hand. What was happening to him? Her stomach felt heavy with fear. 'Please don't die,' she whispered. 'Please don't die.' She removed the cloth from his head, which was already warm, and dipped it in the water before replacing it on his forehead.

Constance realised now she knew nothing about nursing, about what they were doing for the recovering officers up at the house. She watched Matthew struggle to breathe, and wondered if she should go to the house and beg for help. His eyes opened and he looked at her, although Constance had no idea if he actually saw her or whether he was looking absently through her.

'Please don't die, Matthew,' she repeated, rubbing his hand. 'Please don't die.'

He swallowed and his eyes slowly rolled back until she saw the whites and then he closed them again. She was torn. She began crying. She hated herself. Crying wouldn't help him. If she ran to the house to fetch help, it would take an age and she ran the risk of leaving him to die. She had promised to tell no one he was there. If she told and he was helped and then taken away because of her, she would never forgive herself. But if she didn't tell, he might die. She had no idea what was wrong with him. He needed medicine, but what? She'd been unpacking pills and tinctures and ticking them off a list all morning. They all had names she had never heard of before and if she ran to grab something for him, what if it was the wrong medicine? And what if she didn't give him the right amount – not enough or worse, too much and then she killed him! She shook with a mix of nerves and fear, telling herself this wasn't happening; that he wasn't really like this at all, that he was his usual strong self and that she was imagining this nightmare.

His breathing stopped and she stood up from her kneeling position and waited. When he didn't breathe she shook him, screaming, 'Matthew!' His breathing resumed and Constance fell to her knees as his eyes opened. He swallowed and looked at her, crouching beside him. He was almost white.

He tried speaking and she shushed him. 'Don't,' she said. 'Don't speak.'

'I . . .' he started, ignoring her. 'I . . . can't be here. You can't be here.'

His resumed his ragged breathing.

'Never mind that now,' she said. 'I'm going to the house. There's nurses, medicine. I'm going to get someone. I'm going to bring someone here to help.'

'No,' he whispered. 'Don't.'

'I have to,' she cried. 'You're sick. I'm afraid.'

He grabbed her wrist. It took an effort and she snatched her hand away from his weak grip as she prepared to leave.

'If I don't go, I'm afraid you'll die,' she told him, tears running down her face.

He closed his eyes and whispered, 'Let me.'

She would not. She left his bedside and took the stairs two at a time, threw the cottage door open, leaving it swinging on its hinges and ran back towards the house.

CHAPTER 24

2020

Kate's alarm beeped merrily for a long time before she realised what the noise was. As she turned it off she looked blearily at the messages James had sent last night. The first, friendly enough, asking if she was hungry, if he should cook something for her or if she was dining out. The second message housed overtones of mild concern. Would she be coming back for the night or did she need picking up? Kate cringed with guilt. He'd actually been quite sweet. But his reaction when she walked through the front door yesterday night had been a bit overbearing.

Another message pinged and she marvelled at how she'd become so popular all of a sudden. It was Jenny. Kate sat up with excitement. Jenny, her lifeline to the goings-on in the outside world. She asked Kate how things were going and reiterated her intention to come and stay for a few days, instead of Kate returning to London for a quick weekend. Kate had been all for this plan, only now she wondered where they'd put Jenny. The house was going to be ready for paying guests soon enough and prior to that they were arranging all the press visits. Bedrooms would be full, hopefully, if she didn't come and stay imminently.

Kate replied telling her as much and she hit reply instantly.

'I can share with you?' she offered. *'I'm due a bit of leave from work. How cold is it up there? Cold is a deal-breaker.'*

Kate smiled and replied, *'But sharing a bed isn't? And it's summer so it's warm. Sort of.'*

'That'll do. Shall I book a bit of time off work? I can help you out. You can dress it up as a bit of free labour. Might that keep the surly James off your back if I do come to stay?'

'Maybe. As long as we don't look like we're having too much fun in the process,' Kate typed.

Jenny sent Kate an eye-rolling emoji. *'Is fun banned? I'm not looking forward to meeting James. He sounds a barrel of laughs.'*

Kate was torn how to reply. Anything rude felt disloyal. But she wasn't sure he warranted her defence as things currently stood.

Before Kate had the chance to respond Jenny sent another message. *'Any fit men up there? Please say yes.'*

'Yes,' Kate replied.

Jenny's reply was immediate. *'Is this a lie?'*

'No comment. Please come anyway!' Kate typed as fast as she could. *'Please!'*

Jenny replied with a laughing face and told Kate she'd take a look at flights and see when she could take time off work. Kate put the phone down and almost skipped towards the shower.

One day merged seamlessly into the next at Invermoray and so when Saturday eventually rolled around Kate was actually surprised. And for once, she had made plans. She was going into the village and was going to try to pick up the novel for the book club. Then she was going to sit at the pretty little green on the edge of the village and while away the hours reading. She pictured an afternoon of uninterrupted relaxation.

Living on her own she wasn't used to giving her whereabouts to anyone. And Liz had made it very clear Kate wasn't expected to report in every second of the day, especially at the weekend, but she scribbled a note on the pad in the hallway next to the phone letting them know where she'd gone. Kate wondered if she could punctuate the note with a snide comment about keeping her phone firmly switched on for any urgent messages but then thought that might wind James up a little unnecessarily.

She parked the little rental car and headed for the library. Angus's sister Morven had told Kate she would pop in and sort a request for the novel for her, which Kate thought was kind of her. The librarian greeted Kate warmly and the moment she set foot through the door asked, 'You're not Kate, are you?'

Kate stopped. 'Well, yes. I am. How did you know?'

'I thought you must be,' she said in a lilting singsong voice. 'You're the only person round here I dunnae recognise.'

'This really is a small town,' Kate said.

'It is,' she agreed. 'I'm Kirsty. Morven told me to put this aside for you.' She waved a paperback copy of the book club novel as Kate approached the desk. 'We didn't have any in so this is the copy I've only just this moment finished. I hear you're joining us for book club.'

'Yes, if that's OK?'

'Of course it is. Fresh meat for the grinder.' She chuckled. 'Brenda McCrea's in charge. She's a taskmaster. If you've nae read the book she'll be for you. First time I turned up I was only really there for the chat and the wine but now I come armed with six or seven insightful questions.'

'Oh God, OK,' Kate said, realising Angus had no real clue what went on at this book club and that she'd been misled horribly.

'But if you go to her yoga class she looks on you a bit more favourably.'

'Oh phew,' Kate pretended to wipe her brow. 'I'm safe then.'

She filled in a form and showed some ID to obtain a library card and fielded questions from Kirsty as she ticked boxes.

'So how long are you staying then?' Kirsty asked.

'I'm not sure,' Kate said honestly as her pen worked through the form. 'I've been here for about two months. My contract's only for six in total and the weeks are whizzing by, so I'll be gone before I know it.'

Kate wasn't sure how she felt about that. She felt a bit flat at the prospect of it all coming to an end. But at the same time, she was eager to see all the hard work they'd all been putting in come to fruition over the next few months.

Morven arrived behind Kate as she handed the form in to Kirsty. 'How's your head been these past few days?' Morven asked, referring to their night in the pub after yoga.

'Fine,' Kate said. 'As James points out, I work in PR so I'm clearly a finalist for drinker of the year. Yours?' Kate asked.

Morven nodded. 'I'm a publican's sister. So I'm a gold medallist. You got the book then? I've just finished it. It's no' very good. Sorry about that. Brenda's choice this month I'm afraid. She does like to ram books down our throat that make us think. Kirsty and I are considering forming a breakaway faction and only reading books that've been turned into films.'

'Och, ssh,' Kirsty said. 'And me a librarian. Who'd have thought?'

Kate laughed, pleased to have finally found a few likeminded female souls. She remembered the other reason she'd wanted to visit the local library. 'Do you keep hard copies of old newspapers in here?' she asked.

'Aye, a few,' Kirsty said, pointing to the far corner of the single-storey building. 'All bound up properly. They're done by year. There's a local history section, which I'm quite proud of cultivating, over there. If you don't see what you want, come back and I'll dig around for you.'

'Thanks, back in a bit.' Kate left the two friends grimly comparing notes on the novel and went over to the local history section, which was minute in the already small library. The shelves held a few books about local folklore, which she pulled out and had a quick flick through. Then she looked on the lower bookshelves, where there were a few rows of oversized red leather books, spines faded in the sunshine that streamed through the high window.

Morven popped her head round the shelves. 'Right, I'm off. Gottae grab the kids from their Uncle Angus and drop them at their dad's for the weekend. Why he cannae come here to fetch 'em's beyond me but that's ex-husbands, eh?'

Kate gave her a sympathetic look.

'Ye after anything specific?' Morven asked, her body language suggesting she was itching to go.

'Yes, newspaper articles about a drowning. But it's OK, I'll have a dig around or I'll ask Kirsty for help. She looks keen.'

Morven spun round towards Kate, suddenly interested. 'She is. Verra keen. A drowning? When?'

'The 1940s, according to your brother.'

Morven looked thoughtful as Kate bent down to pull out the large red volume titled *Highlands and Islands Times, 1940*. 'Oh crikey, this will take me forever and it only covers the first few months of the year.'

'You'll have to get Kirsty to haul the rest from out back,' Morven said. 'She's cleared most of this section for books about loch monsters and selkies, which she's adamant exist.' Morven rolled her eyes and then after a few seconds she said thoughtfully, 'A pilot.'

'Sorry?' Kate asked, looking up at her.

'It was a pilot who drowned,' Morven said.

'How do you know?'

'My granddad told us, though I'm not sure how reliable his information would be. He used to tell me and Angus stories about how we shouldn't swim in the loch on our own, about how it would take a life and give nothing back. About how a pilot had gone into that water alive and come out dead.'

Kate shivered.

'But we ignored him o' course. We used to swim in that bit

where the loch curves round, slightly out of sight of the main house. Only when the weather was nice mind. And then they built that new leisure centre and Angus and I swiftly changed our minds about swimming in that loch. They put a wave machine in. At the leisure centre, not at the loch. It's broken most days now, but the kids love it. We never went near that loch again after that. I'd completely forgotten about that story. I give Angus ten points for remembering.'

Kate had been sitting in the sunshine on the green skim-reading the novel. She wasn't really taking it in. It was a little heavy going for her tastes but she was determined to make friends here and aside from yoga and the odd 'hello' to people in the pub, it was book club or bust. She hadn't noticed the weather changing. Dark clouds were gathering in the skies above and a cold breeze forced her to pull her cardigan tighter around her. She took her sunglasses off and looked towards the jutting mountains in the distance, watching as the grey-black clouds gathered, forming a shroud of darkness.

'Hello,' a voice sounded and Kate looked from the mountains to find James had arrived beside her. They'd barely exchanged a word since their run-in in the hallway a few nights before. He'd made a point of busying himself in the cottage, which he swore was almost ready to go, and Kate had been ensconced in the estate office. She'd not seen him at mealtimes and it only occurred to her now he might have been eating in the pub more often than usual.

'Hi,' Kate replied, wondering if he'd been avoiding her.

'I just walked up from the cottage,' he said. 'Finishing touches and . . .' He trailed off as he looked at the book she was holding. 'Enjoying it?' he asked, gesturing.

Kate looked at the front cover to remind herself what she was reading and then back at James. 'Not really, no, now I think about it.'

He laughed then looked awkward. 'I was just going to grab some early dinner,' he said.

Kate closed the book.

'Well, don't let me disturb you.' He started to turn away.

'You're not,' Kate said. She glanced at her watch. She hadn't noticed the time slipping away from her and she realised sadly that in all that time she'd barely made a dent in the book. 'I was going to grab dinner in the village for a change,' Kate said. 'You could join me.'

'Would you mind?' James narrowed his eyes.

'Of course I don't mind. Stop making every conversation we have awkward.' Kate laughed.

His eyes widened. 'What do you mean?'

'James, has it occurred to you that you make me feel really on edge, most of the time?'

He looked shocked. 'No.'

'Well it bloody should. Because you do.'

He sat down on the grass next to her. 'Why?'

'I don't know. You just . . . do.'

'I think that says more about you than it does about me.' He had a triumphant look about him as he said it.

Kate wasn't sure what to say to that.

'Anyway, dinner?' James skirted the issue. 'We could grab a few bits from the shop and have a picnic here?' he suggested. 'My treat.'

'Thank you,' Kate said. 'You don't have to pay though.'

'I know,' he said. 'Call it company expenses or whatever. Plus also I'm not paying you anymore, remember, so fair's fair.'

'What?' Kate exploded and then watched James laugh himself silly.

'I'm joking,' he said as a dark cloud formed in the sky. 'Actually, I think it might rain. Shall we grab fish and chips?' he suggested, pointing towards the shop across the square. 'We can take dinner home. I've a good bottle of Sancerre it would go well with.'

‘Sounds lovely. And while we’re on the subject of unpaid labour,’ Kate started, ‘my friend Jenny wants to come and stay. Would you mind? I thought she could coincide her visit with that of the journalists? She’s happy to help and won’t need one of the guest bedrooms because she’ll sleep in with me.’

James gave a knowing smile and raised an eyebrow at this. ‘Will she now?’

Kate shoved him on the arm and ignored his meaning. ‘I used to work with her so she said she’s happy to lend a hand. Perfect timing really. Take the pressure off you having to actually make polite conversation with all the travel journalists.’

‘Is she a publicist as well?’ He made a face.

‘Yes.’ Kate crossed her arms.

‘Ugh,’ he said. ‘Two of you to worry about.’

CHAPTER 25

The sky had quickly covered itself in a blanket of ink-black cloud. As James and Kate emerged from the fish and chip shop the heavens opened, throwing cold rain over them in piercing droves. They ran the few feet to the village square, where Kate's little runaround was parked.

'Good job you drove,' James said, clutching the bag of fish and chips to his chest. 'I walked up from the cottage and I'm glad I'm not walking back.' He yanked the door of the passenger-side open as the rain picked up its relentless beating pace. Kate slid into her seat, her hair sticking in wet tendrils to her face and neck. She wrang her hair out into the street and felt the cold water trickle even further down her neck and into the fabric of her now-soaked cardigan. She shivered and slammed the car door shut.

'That came out of nowhere,' Kate remarked. Around them the car steamed up, the scent of vinegary fish and chips making Kate hungry. James brushed his wet hair off his forehead and then opened the bag and offered Kate a chip before taking one himself. Kate put two in her mouth and chewed, the salt and vinegar sharp on her tongue.

After a few seconds she turned the key in the ignition. The hatchback was unresponsive, producing little but a repetitive clicking sound. She turned the key back, frowned, then tried again. The same disappointing noise emanated from the engine.

It was James's turn to frown and he stopped chewing, scrunched the bag up to keep the food warm and said, 'Try again.'

Kate did and the car started.

'I thought these rental companies were supposed to keep a healthy check on their cars,' James muttered as he fastened his seatbelt.

'It's been fine so far,' Kate said in uncertain defence of the car hire firm. But somewhere just off the edge of the winding estate road, the car betrayed her optimism and gave out entirely. The steering wheel locked up under her fingers and the engine became silent.

'Oh come on,' Kate said in despair. The rain was bucketing onto the windscreen, blurring her vision completely, its wipers now stilled.

'What on earth?' James asked. 'Give it another go.'

Kate tried, fruitlessly, to restart the engine before leaning over him and rifling in the glove compartment. She was sure she'd seen a leaflet in there about what to do in the event of a breakdown. But she must have moved it when she had been ransacking the car for the map, all those weeks ago when she'd arrived.

James undid his seatbelt. 'I'll take a look at the engine.'

Heroically he stepped out into the unyielding rain and stood at the front of the car before hurrying round to Kate's window and knocking on it. Given the electrics had given out Kate couldn't get the window down and so opened the door to find a soaked James glaring at her. 'You need to open the bonnet.'

Kate started to climb out of the car.

'No,' he said and Kate could just make out the fact that while laughing, he'd rolled his eyes. 'There's a catch, in there somewhere.' He gestured towards the footwell and when Kate couldn't find it he bent down, rummaging by her legs until he found the bonnet catch.

It sprung up and James disappeared round the front of the car. It felt rude just sitting there in the dry, so Kate stepped out and stood with him as he opened the bonnet. She was already soaked, so what did it matter if a little more rain hit her full in the face? Although as she looked up at the horrific black clouds still rolling in over the mountains, she could see the weather showed no signs of abating. She wondered if there was an umbrella in the car. If there was, it was rather too late for that now.

After bending over the engine and assessing it James turned towards her with a baffled expression.

'Do you know what's wrong?' Kate asked hopefully as she checked her phone. They were on the same stretch of road on which she'd initially almost run him over the day she'd arrived. She'd no signal then and she had none now.

'It's a dead zone out here,' James said and slammed the bonnet lid shut. 'I've got no clue what's wrong with this bloody car.'

'Maybe the battery?' Kate suggested. 'Nothing we can do about it, unless someone drives past who might have jump leads.'

They looked up and down the deserted road.

'Christ,' he said, rushing his hand through his hair to dispel water. 'We're too far from the village to go back; much closer to home. Actually, we're closer to the cottage, so we might as well just make a run for it. Get dry there and head over to the main house when the rain stops.'

'Fine,' Kate said. The downpour wasn't stopping anytime soon and she'd have agreed to anything just to get out of the rain. James gallantly ran round to the boot, picked out the hazard sign and jogged to place it a little way down the road.

'Let's go,' he said as he returned and reached inside the car for the bag of fish and chips.

By the time they arrived at the cottage they were drenched, their clothes sopping. James fumbled in his wet jeans for the cottage key and they almost collapsed inside.

'I hadn't thought it was possible to be even more wet than we were back there,' Kate said breathlessly as she pulled the lower part of her shirt away from her damp skin and wrang it out in the porch.

James dumped the fish and chip bag down on the wooden table in the kitchen.

'Ugh,' he muttered. 'This wet stuff is . . .' Kate looked over as he pulled off his shirt and threw it onto the floor where it landed in a wet heap. She blinked rapidly. James looked unsure of himself for a moment before he said, 'There are new blankets upstairs, I'll just go and . . .' He seemed to be having trouble finishing his sentences.

Kate wrung out her hair and stood in an upright starfish position. When James came back he'd taken off his jeans and was wearing a blanket like a towel, slung low around his hips. He brought over a tartan blanket and suggested Kate change upstairs.

It was heaven, taking off wet clothes and wrapping herself in something dry and warm. The central heating in the cottage was now installed and the new radiators were giving off a toastiness that was more than welcome.

Kate wrapped herself in the blanket and went downstairs. James had assembled logs in the fire and lit them. He'd obviously been busy these past few weeks because Kate noticed he'd installed a fender with a red leather bar for sitting on.

'This is nice,' Kate said as she perched on the edge and draped her clothes over it to dry.

'Thanks. Found it in the stables. Leather's worn but still looks the part. I'm afraid I don't know my way around a car engine but I can use a drill.'

Kate smiled and he held her gaze. For the first time in a long while she didn't feel awkward around James, which she recognised as strange given that they were both not wearing their full quota of clothes.

Kate tried not to look at his bare chest. He got up, clutching his blanket with one hand, and went to retrieve his clothes in order to dry them by the fire.

He presented the bag of fish and chips and they sat on the floor and ate, the sound of the fire crackling by their side as the logs caught and filled the room with a pleasant smoky smell. The food was cold, and the chips a little soggy under the weight of the vinegar, but Kate and James had grown ravenous and happily descended on them. After a while James disturbed their companionable silence by going to the cupboard and pulling out two bottles of red wine.

'I bought these,' he said, 'for those lonely nights when I was clearing out the cupboards and repainting them, giving them a new lease of life.'

He handed one to Kate and she opened it and drank thirstily. It tasted like nectar. 'Red wine's a bit strange with fish and chips, but it's delicious nonetheless.'

James laughed and opened the other bottle and they swigged like students.

'Angus introduced me to this particular grape,' James said. 'It's his favourite, or so he tells me. I'm surprised he hasn't had you drinking this by the barrel load.'

Kate looked at him, wondering what he meant.

He was doing a good job of looking nonchalant. 'So, when are you seeing him next?'

'I'm not sure,' Kate said honestly, popping another soggy chip in her mouth. She chewed. 'I guess at yoga.'

'And then dinner and drinks?' James suggested.

'Maybe. I think that might just have been a one-off. All that drinking will counteract the good work we do at yoga.' Kate gave him a smug look and swigged happily from her bottle as if to highlight her point.

James was quiet and she felt the need to say, 'There's nothing going on between Angus and me, you know.'

'No?' he challenged.

'No. Did you think there was?'

James shrugged.

Kate looked at him thoughtfully. 'You know . . .' she dared as the wine warmed her, 'a few people have suggested there's something going on between you and me.'

He raised an eyebrow. 'Who?'

'Angus. And his sister.'

'And what did you say?'

'I said no, of course. You're technically my boss.'

'There's no technically about it,' he said with a glint in his eye. 'I pay your wages, I *am* your boss.' He leaned forward and stole a chip from her bag.

'Hey,' Kate said and then worked her way through a few more mouthfuls of wine. It was going down beautifully.

She was growing uncomfortable on the floor and stretched her legs out in front of her. The blanket covered all the essentials but there was no mistaking James's gaze flicking up and down her bare legs before he looked away, towards the fire. He climbed to his feet and placed a couple of logs from the basket onto the grate. It took a few seconds and the fire flared to life as it licked at the new wood.

'So,' Kate attempted to change the subject, 'did you find anything of interest when you cleaned this place out?' She looked around. The cottage was pristine. The settees had been re-covered and draped with tartan blankets. He'd taken her advice and hammed up the Highland connection. Kate loved it and knew guests would too. In the kitchen, the table had been scrubbed and newly polished and the cupboards glistened with a lovely grey paint that looked like Farrow and Ball. Kate was impressed.

'I found some books – Austen, Dickens, Brontë. They must have been borrowed from the house as they fit in with the set of classics in our library. I found some old newspapers from around the time of the war as well,' he said.

'Anything interesting?'

'Not really. Just local news mostly. Air raid precautions, blackout times, that kind of thing. Some nice interesting pieces about sporting matches, and every single time a bomber plane – either one of theirs or one of ours – was spotted it was written about in great, mind-numbingly dull detail.'

It was then Kate remembered what Morven had told her about the drowned airman and she relayed the tale to James.

James sat back against one of the new sofas and sipped his wine. 'A pilot? Did he crash? Did he fall in from a boat while out fishing? Was he swimming and it all went wrong?' he questioned when Kate finished talking.

'I don't know,' Kate said.

'Hmm,' he said. 'I'd like to talk to Morven about it.'

'I'll ask Angus at yoga,' Kate volunteered.

James just nodded and looked at her.

She wondered what he was thinking. The more wine they drank, the braver she became. It didn't take a genius to see James was good-looking, especially when he let down his guard a bit. Feeling a bit drunk, Kate dared a question.

'Why are you still single?'

'What?' James stiffened. Kate's question had caught him by surprise. It had caught *her* by surprise. The wine was doing funny things to her and so she pressed on. 'I think Morven's got a crush on you. And Kirsty, the librarian, was very keen to ask questions about you.'

James looked stricken. 'Oh, that's . . . nice.'

'They're both very attractive women,' Kate suggested.

'Well, yeah.' James rubbed the back of his neck.

She was enjoying watching him squirm.

He raised his head. 'Why are you still single?' he challenged.

'Oh,' she said, stunned by this sudden turn of events. 'I just . . . am.'

'When was your last relationship?' he asked in quick-fire fashion.

'Jesus. Um . . . not that long ago.'

'Really?' He looked interested now. 'When?'

'About a year ago.'

'What happened?' he asked.

It had been one of those relationships that started easily and ended even more so. She and her ex had been so wrapped up in work and hectic schedules while they'd been trying to make their relationship work. It had probably been doomed to fail now she thought about it, which she didn't very often.

'It ended.'

James sat back and looked at the fire. Then he looked back at her. 'Badly?'

'Not really. Just fizzled out.' It was the truth. 'My ex and I are still friends,' Kate said proudly, 'in as much as exes can be friends. We send each other birthday texts and click "like" on each other's Facebook posts. That kind of thing.'

'That's very mature of you both,' he replied in wonder.

Kate wasn't sure if he was being sarcastic.

'My ex and I nearly killed each other,' he confessed.

Kate choked on her mouthful of wine. 'What?' She hadn't imagined he'd have been in a fiery relationship.

'She was a handful,' he said quietly. 'Liked drama.' He gazed back into the fire and Kate wondered if he was going to say any more.

'What happened?' she prompted, somewhat nosily.

'It ended badly,' he said with a wry smile. 'Lots of screaming and throwing things . . . her. Lots of storming off . . . me. But then when we'd calmed down hours later, apologetic, it would all go back to normal for a while. Until the next time.'

'Wow, I'm sorry.'

'And then,' he continued, 'everything changed. I wised up. We were renting an apartment in Hong Kong together. I told her I was leaving, not just her but Asia. I wasn't in love with either anymore. I hadn't been for ages; I just don't think I'd spotted it.

I needed to start afresh. I looked at job after job in London and decided I couldn't do it – leap from one rat race to the next. I came back to Invermoray. It was just supposed to be for a rest, a bit of a holiday. I felt as if coming home would be a solution, not the problem. I hadn't felt like that in years. And then, just when I thought I had it all sorted, it all went wrong.'

'What happened?' Kate whispered, completely engrossed.

'The day I was due to fly back here, my dad died.'

'Oh, James, I'm so sorry.'

He shrugged. 'It's OK.' He gave her a half-smile. 'Shittest plane journey of my life. Shittest year of my life, actually. Then everything moved at speed: Dad's funeral, me going back to Asia to tidy things up there and working my notice before relocating back here properly.'

Kate leaned forward and put her hand on his. A log in the fire sputtered and they were still for a moment.

'What with one thing and another,' he said quietly, 'Dad passing away and my relationship ending rather nastily, coming home to find the Invermoray finances in complete disarray, I've not really been able to take stock of what went wrong and why: whose fault it was. I'm sure we were both to blame.' He looked at Kate as if he half-expected her to tell him it was probably all his fault. But she was changing her opinion of James daily and could see that he was a good man underneath that slightly curt exterior.

'I don't always say what I feel,' he confessed. 'And then when I do . . .' He grasped for the right words.

Kate decided to help him. 'It comes out a bit aggressive?' she suggested with a smile.

He laughed and a flicker of the good-natured man he'd shown her every now and again surfaced. He stretched and Kate sensed he was keen to move on.

'So,' he said. 'Texting each other happy birthday messages and liking each other's Facebook posts? That's decent behaviour between two decent human beings.'

'I don't really do drama,' Kate said and then instantly regretted it. It sounded like a strange boast. But it was true. Life was too short for unnecessary rows and argumentative explosions. She'd always been the kind of girl who said what she thought, albeit politely; who could see a situation coming and could put a stop to it before it escalated entirely out of control. It's what made it all the more grating when she'd completely missed all the signs and come-ons from her bar client; the gentle hand on her back as he'd escorted her through the bar, the touching of her arm every now and again as they'd held strategy meetings over the unnecessary dinners he always suggested and always paid for. It had come as a complete shock when he'd tried to kiss her in the alleyway outside the bar. She didn't do drama, but Christ, she knew she could obviously be very thick sometimes.

'I can see that,' he replied.

He was looking at her with a soft expression but it was one she couldn't really interpret. To avoid his gaze, Kate drank again. She'd not eaten enough for the amount of wine she'd imbibed. It had gone to her head somewhat and she could feel her legs going to sleep. To avoid a complete onset of pins and needles she began to climb to her feet. She handed James her near-empty wine bottle as she did so and he looked at her with mild surprise.

'Do you need a hand?'

'No, I'm fine,' she said as she reached for the fender. 'Wow, this stuff's strong.'

'It is,' James chuckled.

Kate wasn't sure how it happened but she got the blanket caught underneath her foot as she stood. She managed to keep it in place by grabbing at it as it started to slip from her chest. She clutched it tightly. Her heart was racing and she wondered if it was a reaction to the wine or almost becoming completely naked in front of James. As she stumbled, James stood up so quickly it surprised her. He caught hold of her as she wobbled dangerously close to the fender.

'Jesus, you all right?' he asked.

'Yes, sorry,' she replied. 'I don't know what came over me.'

'I do,' he said, looking accusingly at the almost empty wine bottles he'd parked on the floor.

Kate found herself giggling. She was suddenly filled with the urge to touch his bare chest. It was the wine; she knew it was. It would be such an awful, terrible idea and she forced herself to look away.

He spoke softly. 'You all right?' he asked again. He was still holding her.

'Yes,' she whispered as she reluctantly met his gaze. She was drunk. And Kate could appreciate that without his usual frown he was dangerously good-looking. It was a deadly combination.

James swallowed.

It was a mix of so many things – the rain having drenched them and forcing them into these silly blankets, the wine that had affected them both, the fire crackling in the grate and, somewhat shamefully, a lust that had ignited in Kate from out of nowhere, a lust that she hadn't felt for anyone in such a long time. James looked down at her uncertainly. He must have been aware, too, that the atmosphere in the room had changed around them and that the pair of them were responsible for its change. Kate stopped analysing whether or not it was a good idea or a terrible one. All she knew was that deep down, she wanted to do it. Bravely, drunkenly, she stood up on her tiptoes and kissed him.

She had worried James might look surprised, push her away even, but he didn't. It was as if he'd been thinking the same thing and had been toying with the idea of kissing her, because he kissed her back, harder and faster than she had ever remembered being kissed before. She made a noise and he pulled away.

'God, I'm sorry, am I hurting you?' He touched her lips.

'No,' Kate said, in a complete frenzy of emotions. 'No.'

He put his mouth on hers again, softer this time, and then lifted her from the floor. She held on tightly to the blanket around her chest as he kissed her, although she didn't know why she was because in a matter of moments they both knew their blankets would be discarded on the floor. How had he done this to her? How had this infuriating man pulled this feeling of desire and need to the surface? He was her employer. What the hell was she doing? And yet, she couldn't stop. She was better than this, she was. Only she wasn't better than this right now.

'Oh God,' Kate groaned as he kissed her neck so sensually she thought she would melt. His hand cupped her face and she was desperate for him to pull her blanket off, for him to lose his.

She opened her eyes and the fire swam in and out of view, the flames appearing staggeringly high and then suddenly decreasing to their normal size. 'Oh Christ,' Kate said between kisses, although this time it wasn't the thought of sheer ecstasy of what was about to happen, it was something else that prompted her appeal to the heavens.

James held on to her hand and kissed it before he got up, staggering tipsily over to his wet jeans. 'I just need to get . . .' he looked sheepish.

Kate nodded. 'Be quick,' she said.

He cast her a surprised look and then laughed to himself.

'Oh, Kate,' he said as he returned and knelt over her, kissing her gently. 'I've wanted this for so long. Beautiful, maddening woman that you are.'

But Kate was no longer listening. Instead she pushed James from her. He cried out, startled, as he landed on the floor. But Kate wasn't there to hear it. Instead, clutching her blanket tightly she ran. She ran as fast as she could to the door of the cottage, yanked it open, bent over, and threw up.

The early morning glow brightened behind Kate's closed eyelids until she could bear it no longer and was forced to wake up. She couldn't work out immediately where she was and stared around at the interior of the cottage for a few seconds until she realised.

The fire was empty. Its logs, which had last night burned so brightly, were now reduced to desiccated flecks of grey ash. They looked how she felt – withered, less than half of what she should have been.

She coughed, her throat dry and for some reason sore. The blanket was still wrapped around her chest but at some point in the night she'd been covered even further with another new tartan blanket and James had placed a cushion underneath her head. Kate smiled. He could be very thoughtful sometimes.

He was asleep in the armchair, one of his arms tucked up underneath his head. He looked as if he was at an awkward angle and Kate wanted to reach out and touch him, stroke his face. Her own face flamed as she tried to quash the strong emotional attachment she'd somehow formed for him.

By the floor of the armchair was something she never wanted to see as long as she lived – empty bottles of red wine. She almost retched just looking at them. She cringed, as memories of last night returned to her ever so slowly. She was certain she had thrown up. She looked around the cottage. Not only did it look clean but, more importantly, it smelled clean. Had she thrown up and James had diligently mopped up after her, then cleaned her up as she'd passed out on the sofa? Surely not. If so, she couldn't face him after that. She would have to leave Invermoray now just to save face. Oh, the horror of it all.

And then something else struck her. Drinking heavily with James wasn't all they'd done together last night, was it? Had they . . . ?

Kate put her hand over her mouth as she clawed at memories that wouldn't quite rise to the surface of her mind: James and she barely wrapped in their blankets, James practically straddling her, his mouth on hers. She'd enjoyed it. She remembered that. The professional boundary had been breached and, mortified, she cried out inadvertently.

He stretched in the armchair at the noise, raised his arms

above his head and then he lowered them, opened his eyes and rubbed at the stubble that had formed on his jawline overnight. He made a pained noise as he rolled his head around and then looked at Kate uncertainly.

'Hi,' he said with a tired smile.

'Hi,' she said quietly from behind her hands.

'We drank quite a bit on not a lot of dinner.' He glanced down at the bottles and then back towards her.

'I'm so sorry,' she blurted.

'What for?'

She shook her head, reluctant to uncover her face from behind her hand. She wanted to hide forever. She wanted to leave Scotland and never have to see James again.

'Did we . . . ?' She left her question unfinished.

'No.' He swallowed. He gave her a half-smile. 'We got pretty close. But, no.'

'Oh thank God.' She sat back against the sofa.

'Charming.' He laughed.

'It's just . . . It would have been an awful idea.'

He nodded slowly. 'Yes, it would have been.'

'We have to work together,' Kate said by way of an explanation.

'We do.'

'And we have to look each other in the eye. And I couldn't do that if I'd slept with you. I just know I couldn't.'

He smiled. 'You're probably right. Definitely a terrible, terrible idea.'

Kate couldn't work out if he was joking or not.

'You're my boss and we . . . shouldn't.' Kate couldn't believe she had put herself in that situation again. The first time it had been a complete accident. This time she had wanted it, even though she'd known what the consequences would be. But consequences be damned. And now, waking up and facing him, she was so glad they hadn't slept together. She had allowed herself to fall into complete unprofessionalism at exactly this fragile time when she was successfully rebuilding her reputation. She hated herself for all of last night.

'Right,' he said but Kate wasn't sure if she detected a hint of disappointment.

An uncomfortable silence grew around them.

'So . . . we're fine,' Kate ventured after a few seconds. 'You and I . . . we're OK?'

'Yeah,' he said. 'Sure.'

She sat back, relief sweeping over her before the headache from hell took hold.

CHAPTER 26

1940

Constance's breath was ragged in her throat by the time she eventually reached the main house. Her lungs burnt and her mouth was dry but she barely noticed. She had to find Matron, or one of the nurses, anyone, anyone at all who would help her make Matthew better.

She recognised one of the women immediately from her mother's Women's Voluntary Service group and although brimming with desperation, Constance was roped in to help her push a young pilot officer in a wheelchair. He was missing the lower portion of his leg, one of his trouser legs pinned up over the knee.

He tried to make conversation with her and she smiled and nodded in appropriate places, desperately casting around for someone who might help. She pushed him into the ballroom where Matron stood to welcome the herd of invalids.

'Matron?' Constance started as she hopped from foot to foot. But Matron had engrossed herself with the young officer, soothing his concerns and finding him a suitable bed.

Looking around Constance could see four or five newly installed officers on deckchairs in the formal garden, reading books or enjoying the view of the loch. So many more pairs of eyes would be watching her on her journey to and from the loch. But it didn't matter. She would no longer be visiting Matthew in the cottage in secret after today. He would not be there. He would be taken in. She was about to expose his secret, reveal his location in order to save him. It was the only way.

Anything could have happened in the time between her departure from the cottage and her arrival at the main house. Constance chewed her nails, agitated. Matron must have sensed her desperation because she looked at her from where she was settling the young man and his possessions by a metal bed.

'Yes?' she said, impatiently. 'You seem to need something?'

'I . . . ' In all the time Constance had been standing there she hadn't thought of what to say. She couldn't do it. She couldn't say the words that would both save and condemn him. She panicked. Maybe she could craft a story, instead of telling the truth. But how would she explain this man of fighting age ensconced in the cottage? She could say he had been invalided out, but he would not be alone in a cottage if so, would he? He would be with his parents, or at a convalescent hospital. With his symptoms as they were, Matron would recommend his transfer to an emergency hospital, surely? And then they would wonder who he was, and would discover what he'd done and then there would have been no point in lying.

'Um,' Constance said, stalling for time; all the while knowing Matthew lay worsening.

'Young lady, are you quite sure I can't help?'

It was on the tip of her tongue to beg for help. But she shook her head. She couldn't tell a soul. She had sworn to Matthew she wouldn't.

She racked her brains, trying to remember the names of the pills she'd been unpacking and putting in the locked cabinets. Which one had been for infection? Or had they all been? The nurses had been kind, educating her as to what was what as she'd unpacked but Constance wasn't sure she would remember correctly now. Was Matthew even suffering from an infection?

Constance knew what she was going to have to do. It had to be worth a try.

She had been less careful than usual as she ran back towards the cottage. While she stayed on her normal route, out of sight, she had not turned back once to check if anyone had been watching her. Instead she had been intent on running, focusing on the forest floor in front of her, thick with ferns and prickly thistles, their purple flowers bursting forth and then being trampled underfoot as she made no effort to skirt round them. If anyone had followed her, it might just save Matthew. Then she would not have betrayed the promise she'd made. She would not have told anyone of his presence but anyone following her would know he wasn't supposed to be there, and would take him away and inadvertently save him.

At the cottage door, she paused and listened to the silent forest. The only sounds were of her own breath coming fast as she tried to calm herself from her lengthy run; and the delicate breeze as it shook the pine branches indiscriminately above. For a moment, her face fell. She was almost disappointed that no one had come. She had kept her promise even if Matthew died. She now doubted her actions and everything she was about to do because the task of saving Matthew now fell to her and her alone.

She ran upstairs. In the cottage bedroom, it was as she'd feared and Matthew was dripping with sweat and shivering. Constance opened the tin and tipped two pills into her shaking hand. She had no idea if this was the right amount but it felt like a good number to start with. Matthew's eyes were vacant but he obediently opened his mouth when she told him to and then swallowed the pills with a cup of water. Water ran out of his mouth and onto the pillow. She wiped it from his face with her hand. Kneeling down next to him, she watched him as he resumed his fitful sleeping.

Clasping her hands together she prayed with all her might. *Dear God, let him live. Let him live.*

As the night wore on, she watched over Matthew. Every time his breathing slowed Constance felt hers increase in panic. She wished she'd made a note about when she'd last given him the medicine. She was losing all sense of time. His brow was hot and she spent a great deal of the night soaking towels and cloths and placing them over him yet again.

In his sleep he licked his lips and turned slightly. Praying that she wasn't giving him too many, she crunched two more pills up and put the granules in his mouth. He coughed, sending some of the white mixture across his chest. She cried out in frustration. She was making a complete mess of this. She managed to coax him into washing down what remained of the pills with a fresh glass of water, all the while hoping she was doing the right thing.

She didn't know what hour it was. When she awoke, sitting upright against the wall next to the bed, it took her a few moments to remember where she was.

She blinked and looked up in the dim light towards Matthew. He was lying on his side looking down at her. She shifted, her back pained from the night spent on the bare floorboards, but she barely registered the pain. 'You're awake,' she breathed.

He nodded as she moved to touch his forehead. He was still hot but a much less worrying temperature. 'You're still dreadfully pale,' she said anxiously.

'I feel so much better than I did,' he said, looking around.

She offered him some water and helped him sit up and drink.

'Thank you,' he murmured. 'What happened?'

'I don't know,' Constance confessed. 'Pneumonia? Father had similar symptoms last year but not as bad as yours. I wish I'd paid more attention to how the doctor treated him. I had to guess what to do for you.'

He nodded slowly. 'Whatever it was, I think it's working.'

'Possibly,' Constance said self-deprecatingly. 'I stole some medicine and prayed fiercely.'

'You *stole* medicine?'

'Yes. From the hospital cabinets. I didn't know what else to do.'

'I'm sorry,' Matthew said. 'In amongst everything else I've made a criminal of you.'

She shook her head. 'It's there to help those who are sick,' she justified. 'I don't feel I did anything wrong. It meant I didn't have to tell anyone you were here.'

He bit his lip and looked away from her. 'Thank you,' he murmured. 'You shouldn't have had to do that for me.'

Constance stood stiffly and slowly pulled a blackout blind away in order to open a window and air the room. 'It's all right now,' she said. When she looked back, he had fallen asleep.

With Constance's help and at his insistence, Matthew managed to move himself out of the bed and down the stairs. As he slumped into one of the armchairs, Constance warmed a tin of soup on the stove and handed him some bread to chew while he waited. She hummed to herself and he watched her as she moved around the kitchen. When she looked over he had stopped chewing and was looking at her, smiling. She smiled back.

'I wish I could stay here like this forever,' he said. 'With you.'

Constance's heart beat faster and she could do nothing but nod.

'It's as if there's no war,' he said. 'Not inside this little cottage. It's as if it's just us. For the few moments each day you're here, it's as if there's nothing untoward happening in the outside world. There's just us, me half-dead,' he joked, 'and you, warming soup and being the best kind of nursemaid. I wish . . .' he started.

'Yes?'

'I wish things could be different,' he said quickly. She moved towards him with the soup and placed it on the little nest of tables by the armchair, kneeling down to him.

'You were wonderful,' he said. 'You *are* wonderful, Constance.'

She couldn't stop her heart from racing.

'Thank you,' he said, shuffling forward in his chair. 'So much, for last night, for looking after me. For being brave enough to steal medicine for me. You shouldn't have had to do that. Not for me. You are the very best kind of woman.'

No one had ever referred to her as a woman before. She still thought of herself as just a girl.

He inched forward on the armchair and held her face in his hands. Constance was sure he could hear the blood pumping fast through her body. It was like a siren in her ears. He was going to kiss her. He was going to kiss her and she had no idea what to do. The sense of longing overwhelmed her and she closed her eyes expectantly. But instead of kissing her, he placed his forehead against hers.

'God, Constance,' he said in a strained voice. 'It's the worst kind of punishment knowing you and I can never be.'

He pulled back suddenly and slumped against the armchair with exhaustion. She was bereft. She wanted his kiss. She wanted his touch on her and his denial of it forced her eyes to open and the reality of their situation to sink further in. He wouldn't be here forever. If she had his touch now it would only be for now but even so, giving herself to him would be worth it. He would be gentle; he would not use her the way she suspected Henry would have done. She dare not say aloud the feelings that overwhelmed her, but she'd never felt like this about anyone and she wanted to give herself to Matthew, completely. He was already being too much of a gentleman and it only made her ache for him more.

Matthew interrupted her thoughts with more practical matters.

'I think it might be time for me to have another one of those pills. What do you say?'

By the time Constance dragged herself back to the house for something to eat and some sleep she was beyond tired. The day was late and she was grateful her parents were away, unable to see her comings and goings. The housekeeper made a veiled remark about young ladies who stayed out at all hours.

'And now there are all these men in the house.' Mrs Campbell shook her head. 'I would like to see you being a bit more careful.'

'Of what, Mrs C? Of sick officers, doing what exactly?' she said wearily. She had never chided Mrs Campbell before but she felt the weight of the last twenty-four hours bearing down on her. 'I find,' Constance said, thinking of Henry and his actions in the orangery on her birthday, 'it's not the sick officers one should be afraid of. It's the perfectly healthy ones who pose the most risk to a young woman.'

Mrs Campbell raised her eyebrows. 'Well, I say,' she blustered as Constance made her way towards the staircase and her room. She needed a hot bath and just a little sleep before she returned to Matthew. She made a mental note to gather up some fresh bed linen to replace the sheets from Matthew's sickbed. In the age when they were all being encouraged to make do and mend, Constance was suddenly in no mood to wash Matthew's bed linen and wondered, guiltily, how wrong it would be if she simply threw it into the fireplace when they next lit the fire at night.

'Miss Constance, please come back. I have something important to tell you,' she heard Mrs Campbell say from the bottom of the stairs. 'And it's important.'

Constance sighed. 'Sorry, I was elsewhere.'

'I can see that,' the housekeeper said, folding her arms. 'I was asking where you'd been?'

'Oh,' Constance stalled for time. 'A walk,' she lied.

'Just a walk?'

Constance stiffened. 'Of course.'

'You missed the post.'

'I'm not normally here for the post,' Constance said, curious why it mattered today.

'There's a letter for you.'

'Oh?' She rarely received post.

Mrs Campbell looked nervous suddenly. 'And . . . and that's not all we've had.'

Constance descended the few steps she had taken and looked quizzically towards the silver salver that held the day's letters. 'There's something I think you should look at in lieu of your parents being here.'

Mrs Campbell's gaze lay on the silver salver. 'I think you should open it. Cook and I will find you shortly.'

'Golly, Mrs C, you do sound serious.'

Mrs Campbell put her hand on Constance's shoulder and then turned and left. It was possibly the most comforting the housekeeper had ever been towards her, including the time when Constance had fallen up the steps as a child and broken her arm.

The silver salver held a few items – business post awaiting her father's attention, an invitation to a wedding by the looks of the envelope, amongst other things. Not wanting to sort through it in the hallway with the quiet bustle of the medical staff moving around her, she took the post into the small sitting room that had remained for the family's use.

She put the stack on the walnut table and curled up on the Knole sofa to read the letter addressed to her. It was from Douglas. There was one underneath from him to her parents and she felt buoyed that he had thought to write her one just for herself. Her tiredness evaporated and she tore it open urgently. 'Oh Douglas,' she said happily as she read his letter, dated only a few days previously.

Dear Smidge,

Mother and Father tell me the house is now a convalescent hospital. What a turn-up. I suspect they sniffed the opportunity to remain and found a way out of losing the house entirely. Clever them. Found anything useful to do yet? I know you were eager. I had a bit of a near miss yesterday. Haven't told the parents. Know how our dear old mother worries. I hope they're proud. I hope you are too. We've all got to do our bit. Better to be up here soaring through the skies than down there, gun in hand and shaking in my boots. I think I'd have been no good at that.

I'm enjoying it for the most part. Meant to be coming home soon. Feels like only five minutes since I was last there but this reason's a tad different. Only a twenty-four-hour pass. Told you I thought that was on the cards. Can't say any more at present. I've said Henry can camp it out with me at Invermoray. He's not got time to make it down south and back to see his people in such a short amount of leave. Not long now, I think.

See you before you know it,

Douglas

She reread his short missive and then clutched it to her chest. She hadn't realised how much she missed Douglas. This wasn't like when he had returned to boarding school or university after his holidays. This was different. There he had been safe and at study. Now he was in the air, and at arm's length of the Luftwaffe. A near miss? Did that mean he had been shot at? Constance shuddered at that and at the thought that Henry would be spending his short leave with them. She hoped he behaved himself. If not, she would do far more than just turn and run this time. Where were they both being sent? She knew the skies in the south of England were inundated with enemy planes as the Battle of Britain raged on, although last time he was home he'd hinted at Africa. Were they being sent there?

She leaned forward to sort the rest of the neglected mail. The one underneath Douglas's letters was a telegram addressed to her parents. She would not normally be so presumptuous as to open mail for her parents in their absence, but a telegram smacked of urgency and the housekeeper had suggested she open it. She held the paper in her hand before turning it over and prising the envelope open.

From Air Ministry. We deeply regret to inform you that your son . . .

Her hands trembled as she read the two short lines of typed text. 'No,' she sobbed as tears filled her eyes. 'Not Douglas, not Douglas.'

Mrs Campbell and Mrs Fraser had been hovering outside the door. As Constance smothered a cry as her world collapsed, they rushed towards her.

'It's as we feared,' Mrs Fraser said.

Constance nodded, her eyes wide with shock.

'Oh dear, oh dear.' Mrs Campbell pulled Constance back onto the settee, while the other woman poured three measures of whisky from the decanter.

Constance couldn't touch her drink. 'He's been . . . Oh God,' she cried in despair. 'Douglas.' Her brother was missing but presumed dead, which surely meant she should hold out no hope. The Air Ministry wouldn't suggest he might be dead without believing it themselves would they? With shaking hands she passed them the telegram.

'*Regret to inform you*,' Mrs Campbell muttered as she read. '*Your son, Flying Officer Douglas Andrew David McLay, is missing presumed killed as a result of air operations Stop. Letter to follow Stop*. Oh the poor, poor boy.'

'But missing, presumed killed is *not* the same as killed,' Mrs Fraser chimed in. 'They just don't know where he is. Your father will be able to sort all this I'm sure.'

'Don't,' Constance said. 'Don't try. Just don't.'

The two older women looked at each other, neither of them sure what to say or do next. They stood mute as Constance stared blankly at the coffee table, looking through it, her mouth open but no words forming.

'I need to be alone,' she said, standing up. 'I can't think. I can't . . .' She looked around the room and at the two women as tears fell down her face. 'I can't . . .'

'I know, lassie, I know,' Mrs Campbell said. 'Come on, let's tuck you in to bed. It will all be much clearer in the morning.'

But it wouldn't. Douglas was gone. Her brother was gone. Her mind swam with misery and despite sheer tiredness, sleep evaded her that night. She thought of the last time she'd seen Douglas. The last time she'd hugged him goodbye. He'd been full of the joys of his duty, and his letter, which Constance now realised with horror was his last, was full of excitement at being sent off to see action. And now he was gone.

CHAPTER 27

The next day the house was full of the sounds of patients and staff going about their day. Constance moved as if in a dream, barely making the effort to move out of anyone's way. When she'd washed and dressed, slowly, laboriously – her mind unable to focus – she sat in the family's sitting room and waited, although she didn't know what for. She picked the telegram up, neatly replaced on the walnut table by either the cook or the housekeeper, and reread it.

It wasn't a dream. It was real. She thought she might vomit as the words swam in and out of view: *regret to inform you, regret to inform you . . .*

She put the telegram back on the table and closed her eyes to block out its existence.

She must have fallen asleep finally because when she opened her eyes some time later, it was to find her parents standing in front of her with fear and shock written on their faces. It had not occurred to her to go to the post office to telegram them at the hotel and summon them home. She had been too dazed to think of such a pragmatic move. Instead, one of the staff must have gone.

'Constance?' her mother asked tentatively, her eyes full of tears.

Constance sprang from the chair. Her father looked up slowly from the telegram and their eyes met.

'Missing,' he said in disbelief.

'Killed,' Constance said through fresh tears.

'You don't know that,' her father said. 'They don't know that. They're . . . hazarding guesses.'

Constance and her mother looked at him. Neither of them could bring themselves to remove the hope in his eyes.

In the cottage, Matthew would be sleeping, recovering or waiting for her arrival. Constance didn't know how it had happened or when, but she had fallen in love with Matthew. She knew it now. And she hated herself for it. Her brother had died while doing his duty. And she had fallen in love with a pilot who felt unable to do his.

They sat in silence for most of the day, none of them able to utter more than a few words at a time. Constance fell in and out of fretful sleep on the settee. Each time she startled herself awake it was with a sense of relief that she had woken from the middle of a nightmare in which her brother had died. And then the realisation that it wasn't a dream hit her and silently she felt tears run from her reddened eyes down her face.

Mrs Campbell entered the room, bringing a pot of tea and a plate of scones. She looked at Constance, who tried hard to return a smile, but grief enveloped her and she put her head in her hands and breathed deeply.

A knock at the door sounded and a nervous-looking orderly popped his head round the door, gazing around the sitting room and its plush furnishings.

'Yes?' her father snapped.

'Excuse me, sir, there's a young pilot by the door, looking for you.'

Her mother's eyes said it all.

Constance jumped up. 'Douglas?' she said, wiping her eyes.

The three of them ran from the sitting room as fast as they could, Constance leading. She ran along the hallway and into the entrance hall, almost pushing a young nurse out of the way.

'Douglas?' she called as she saw the young man in RAF uniform. He was standing rigid, holding a cane, his back to them.

As the man turned, Constance stopped dead. Behind her, her mother cried and sank to the floor, but Constance was only briefly aware of her.

'No. I'm sorry,' Henry said. 'I . . . I had to come. I knew you would have heard by now and . . .' His words drifted away.

Behind her, her father strode forward, his hand outstretched. 'Good of you to come, Henry. Considerate of you,' he said stiffly.

Constance wondered how her father could summon politeness whereas she wanted to shout at Henry, to ask how he dared come here, *why* he dared come here. She turned to her mother, crying in desperation on the floor. 'I'll put Mother to bed,' she said.

'Come through,' Alistair said. 'Fresh pot of tea ready. Or perhaps something stronger?'

'Tea would be fine,' Henry said. 'Thank you.'

Henry gave her what Constance supposed was an attempt at a comforting smile as he passed her. She was too upset to do any more than return it as she and her mother ascended the staircase. She resumed her position in the sitting room a short while later, after tucking her mother into bed and watching over her as she fell asleep. She had not held her mother's hand. She wished they had the kind of relationship where that would be a welcome gesture, but Constance knew it would not. Douglas, always the favourite, would have held their mother's hand. Although ironically, were he still alive he would not have needed to.

Henry sat awkwardly on the edge of the sofa, his cane propped next to him. He drank tea while her father paced the room.

'What happened to you?' Constance asked as she sipped the now-cold tea from her china cup and looked towards Henry's cane.

'I landed badly,' he said. 'Had to parachute out. I didn't do it very well. It's not broken—' he gestured to his leg '—but it hurts to walk on it.'

'Oh,' Constance said. And then, 'I'm pleased you're alive. Were you shot down?' she asked as she looked out towards the window where officers had set up a small game of cricket, driving a wicket into the neatly clipped lawn. Ordinarily she would have been worried about how late they would play, how many of them would be out on the lawns in such fine weather, prohibiting her pass down through the grounds and into the forest. Behind his desk, her father slumped and looked blankly at Henry.

'Yes. Three days ago. The same time as . . . It's why I came, actually. I wanted to tell you what happened.'

'To you?' Her father spoke in a disbelieving voice.

'No,' Henry clarified. 'To Douglas.'

Her father stiffened and Constance almost dropped her teacup. 'You were with him?' she asked. 'You were with Douglas?'

'At the end, yes.'

'Don't say that,' she warned. 'Don't say the end as if it *is* the end. We don't know what's happened to him.'

'He was shot down,' Henry said. 'Quite a while before I was. He wasn't the first and I wasn't the last. A few of us took a hit.'

'Where?' her father asked.

'Over the Cairngorms,' Henry said and then shifted uncomfortably. 'Sorry, this damned leg.'

'What happened?' Constance asked. 'To Douglas.'

'I wanted you to know,' he said. 'He wouldn't have felt a thing. I think it's important you know that.'

Constance held her breath and very slowly placed her teacup on a side table. 'Henry? Are you saying Douglas is dead?'

'Yes,' he said tentatively, looking between Constance and her father. 'I thought you'd have had a telegram by now. Doesn't it say that?'

'It says missing presumed . . .' Constance said and an uncomfortable silence descended on the room.

'He . . . I mean . . . he . . .' Henry began.

'Just say it,' her father said quietly from behind his desk.

'His plane was an inferno. He disappeared far below me. And then the plane . . . it . . .'

Constance put her hand over her mouth. 'What?' she whispered. 'What?'

'It crashed,' Henry said in a quiet voice.

Her father rubbed his jaw and looked anywhere but at Henry.

'I'm sorry,' Henry ploughed on. 'I am. But I think it's important that you know he wouldn't have suffered.'

'But . . . he was on fire?' Constance questioned slowly. 'Of course he suffered.'

'No,' Henry said emphatically. 'I'm very sure it was all over before . . . you know.'

Constance gulped down bile as she thought of flames engulfing her brother as his aeroplane plummeted towards the ground. She hated Henry more than ever for coming. They would have been better off not knowing.

The sound of the grandfather clock in the hallway broke the silence as it chimed the hour. It brought them all to their senses.

'Thank you,' her father said stiffly. 'For coming. For telling us. We know now not to hold out any hope.'

Henry missed her father's meaning and replied, 'You're very welcome, sir. It's the least I could do. I'm of very little use in the skies with this blasted leg,' he said.

'Are you on leave?' Constance asked, wondering torturously if this would have been when Douglas would have come home for his pre-embarkation leave.

'Medical leave, yes. I can't fly. Can just about walk. I thought to travel home to recover but I think the train journey south might just finish me off.'

'Well you must stay here,' she heard her father say unconvincingly.

'As long as you need. If you think the journey might be too much. We're overrun with limping officers. Another one won't break us, I'm sure.'

It was unlike her father to make decisions without her mother to guide him, or to make them for him. Constance lifted her eyebrows in surprise.

'That's very kind of you, sir,' Henry said. 'In truth, I was rather hoping my recovering here would be a possibility.' He looked towards Constance and smiled.

'Constance, could you . . . ?' Her father waved his hands dismissively, indicating she would sort accommodation for Henry. 'Now, excuse me,' he said, shuffling a stack of papers.

Constance walked Henry to Douglas's room, carrying his small suitcase for him while he limped a few paces behind her. The other bedrooms were occupied with nurses and invalids. The idea had been for Henry to bunk in with Douglas, when he stayed, not for him to occupy Douglas's room on his own. Constance's heart sank as she opened the bedroom door. While neat and tidy, thanks to Mrs Campbell, Douglas's room was exactly as he'd left it. His favourite model aircraft hung from his ceiling on fishing wire, biplanes from the first war when it seemed preposterous another war would follow only twenty or so years later. Relics, those model aircraft now. Douglas had never wanted to remove them, update them with the Hurricanes and Spitfires he now flew. Or rather, used to fly, Constance realised with fresh shock.

'Awfully kind of you,' he said, looking around the room. 'Poor Douglas.'

'Yes,' Constance replied, feeling numb. 'How long will you be staying?' she asked directly.

'I . . . well . . .' He pointed at his cane. 'I've a few weeks away from the controls at least.'

'And you'll be staying here, all that time?' she asked.

'I think, perhaps a week and then I should be able to make

the journey down to the South West to see Mother and Father for my final week before I resume duties. I believe it's rarer than hen's teeth to get a seat on a train these days and I can't possibly stand all the way yet.' He reached out his hand and touched her on the arm. Constance withdrew. She couldn't bear him touching her.

'Listen here, Constance,' Henry started. 'I want to apologise for the other week. For kissing you. And the manner in which I did it, more to the point. I realise now it was foolish of me. Abominable behaviour. I wonder now if I gave you a fright and . . . well . . . I apologise.'

'Oh,' Constance said, her voice laced with shock. 'Thank you.' She realised that was the wrong thing to say and finished with, 'Apology accepted, Henry.' She was in no frame of mind to relive that night in her mind, let alone discuss it with him. She could only think of her beloved brother. Henry no longer seemed important enough to think about.

He held out his hand to shake hers and clasped it a little too tightly. 'Start again?' he offered. 'I realise that night in the orangery didn't help my chances with you one bit.'

'Chances?' she said with horror.

'Yes,' he said slowly. 'Constance, you must know how I feel about you? You must know why I'm here?'

'I . . .' She began to withdraw her hand but he clutched it.

'And I'm unsure how you feel but if I did come on a bit strong then I don't want you to hold it against me. I'd like to wipe the slate clean and see if I can't make you like me.'

She wanted to tell him that, once, she had liked him. She had liked him a lot and had wondered what it would be like to step out with him properly and then further down the line, even marry him. But that was before. She couldn't be with someone like him now. She had seen his true colours and compared him to Matthew – the man she knew she loved, who was kind, generous, loving and undemanding. Matthew was holding Constance at arm's length, forcing himself to keep her at a distance. He respected her, whereas Henry had behaved abominably and heaven knows how far he would have gone in the orangery with her that night if she'd let him. 'Make me *like* you?' she said disbelievingly. 'I do like you,' she fibbed. She just wanted to leave his presence now. 'But as Douglas's friend.'

'And nothing more? No chance of anything more now?'

'Henry,' she said and then took in a slow breath. She lowered the tone of her voice to placate him, gently prising her hand from within his. 'My brother has just died. You have come here to tell us the horrific manner in which he left this earth.' She struggled to keep the emotion from her voice. 'And, if it's all the same to you, I think we should be friends, and that is all.'

He looked crestfallen and for a mere moment her heart went out to him. She'd never been in a position of letting a lovesick man down before, gently or otherwise, and she hoped that he wouldn't take it too badly. 'I'm sorry,' she said soothingly but firmly ending the discussion.

Henry turned his back on her and walked further into the bedroom. He said nothing but instead, merely nodded and sat on Douglas's bed. Constance couldn't bear to watch him make himself comfortable in her brother's room.

'I'll let you settle in. I'm unsure when supper is,' she said. 'I've been eating at all sorts of times now to accommodate the medical staff and the patients and now Mother and Father are back—'

'Fine,' Henry cut in. He sounded lost and looked dejected. 'Fine.'

Constance closed the door and stood for a few moments before moving off. She'd never been in this position before and felt so awfully sorry for Henry. But somewhere between grief for Douglas, and pity for Henry was the glaring memory that played out in her mind of Henry in the orangery, unrepentant until it had been far too late.

*

It was too late to visit Matthew that night. The pain of losing Douglas and the strained and lengthy dinner she had been subject to with her parents attempting conversation with a subdued Henry was too much. Light small talk was killing her. It was as if they were playing a charade. Her mother had emerged from her room and had actually dressed for dinner as usual. She looked so formal, so out of place in her elegant dress and pearls. Constance had not dressed properly and was in her wide culottes and blouse that she'd been in all day. She had assumed with the house now at sixes and sevens that formality would have been discarded; that the telegram about Douglas would have changed everything and they would rub along in shared grief together.

Her father had cornered her before dinner and instructed her not to talk of what Henry had told them, not to tell her mother that Douglas's plane had become an 'inferno', as he put it. She tried not to be sick just thinking about it. Similar instructions had been issued to Henry, who sat through dinner, attempting to make small talk to an audience whose hearts weren't in it. She nursed her one glass of wine, while Henry drank at least three throughout their ridiculous three-course dinner. The food tasted leaden, as if all the flavour in the world had been removed now her brother had died. She poked her steamed pudding with her fork, knowing it was wasteful not to eat it, but even through the guilt of rationing, she was still unable to put a single morsel in her mouth.

Constance struggled to imagine the feelings she'd previously felt for Henry as she watched him over dinner. If he hadn't done what he'd done in the orangery, everything would be different. She'd never have run, never have seen Matthew's Spitfire crash, never have known him, never have fallen in love with him. Henry had tried in a ham-fisted fashion to apologise but it wasn't enough. She vowed to keep her distance and to hope that this week, his recovery here, would pass quickly.

And then hopefully he would be gone.

CHAPTER 28

October 2020

For the most part Kate tried to avoid James in the weeks following the mortifying events in the cottage. The kissing, the fire crackling, the vomiting. She cringed and mouthed 'Oh God,' every time she thought about it.

James seemed to find excuses to spend the time leading up to the launch sorting last-minute bits and pieces in the cottage and Kate spent her time in the house with Liz, sorting final items for guest bedrooms, and with Angus arranging the tearoom in the orangery, although they hadn't quite sorted advertising and marketing for it yet.

Kate was on the floor in the hall packing up local whiskies and some of the most mouthwateringly crumbly shortbread biscuits she'd ever tasted into gift boxes. She'd been putting them together for the assortment of journalists that were about to descend on them. When she looked up, James was standing in front of her.

It was all she could do not to blush. Every time she saw him, which was hardly often at all at the moment, she just wanted to die.

He rubbed his hand across his mouth. 'Hi.'

'Hi,' Kate said, looking anywhere but at him. She carried on boxing up parcels, looking around for the scissors and the reel of tartan ribbon she'd bought in the post office in order to finish the look entirely.

James knelt down and handed her the scissors from the sideboard. 'Here.'

She made a point of avoiding touching him as she took them from him. How she wished they could go back to that night. How she wished none of it had ever happened. She was starting to think throwing up was the thing that had saved her. Imagine what it would be like now if they *had* slept together. They could barely look at each other as it was, and all they'd done was kiss, with hardly any clothes on, drunk in front of a roaring fire.

'Oh God,' she said quietly and felt her cheeks flame.

'Pardon?' James said, looking at her. He was still kneeling in front of her and she wished he'd just go away.

'Nothing,' she muttered.

'What time is your friend arriving? It's today, isn't it?'

'Oh, crikey, Jenny.' Kate had completely forgotten.

She flicked her wrist to look at her watch. 'In about an hour. I'll never make it in time. I'm supposed to be picking her up.' Although Kate now severely doubted that the hire car, which had been repaired promptly after she'd called the rental agency and moaned loudly, would actually make it to Inverness Airport and back, despite having been fixed. She sprung up from the floor and James stood with her.

'I'll get her,' he offered.

Kate looked down at the floor, littered with ribbon, gifts and boxes and at Whisky, who was thumping his tail next to her, knocking most of her careful arrangements.

'Would you?' she said, putting a gift box back into place and gently pushing Whisky away. Kate still had to print all the press releases and information packs, put them in their specially printed folders and put them in the editors' bedrooms. Then she had to run through the schedule of events with Liz, who had agreed to take the guests on a guided tour of the house after the journalists had settled in from their journey the following day. They would also be taking them to the village and giving them a slap-up dinner at the Invermoray Arms. Angus was particularly delighted that his pub might get a mention in the glowing travel pieces they hoped the editors would write.

'Of course.' He pulled his Land Rover keys from the hallstand drawer. 'Send me her phone number so I can ring her at the airport if I can't find her. What does she look like?'

Kate fumbled for her phone and found a picture of her and Jenny at Kate's leaving party. They both looked a bit drunk but you could at least tell it was them. James opened his eyes in surprise as he looked at the phone. 'She's . . .'

Kate stiffened. 'Yeah?'

'She's really pretty. Right,' he said quickly and headed towards the door. 'See you soon.'

Kate sat back down on the floor and wrestled with the ribbon. As she heard James's Land Rover pull away a huge part of her wished she hadn't agreed to let James pick up Jenny.

Kate fell into the settee and closed her eyes as Liz offered her a glass of wine. Kate felt ill just thinking about it. 'No thanks,' she said. 'I'll grab a water in a sec.'

Liz looked at her curiously and then asked, 'Remind me, how many journalists we have coming.'

'Six. Plus partners.'

'Oh golly.' Liz took a large mouthful of wine.

'There's nothing to worry about,' Kate reassured her. 'I've done this numerous times and we have a very busy schedule of events for them.'

'We've sorted the bed and breakfast rates?' Liz asked hopefully. 'In case they ask?'

Kate nodded. 'We have. All sorted. All printed out and in the press kits. But if there's any information missing, which there isn't,' she said quickly, 'then I'll send it on to them after their visit.'

'And we've got Champagne for an evening drink before we take the guests out for supper at the pub?'

Kate laughed. 'Yes, Angus has sorted it all at a good rate. And he's devised a special tasting menu to show off his culinary skills.'

'He's a brick,' Liz said.

Kate had to agree. 'And he's coming back to cook breakfast for the guests in the morning before they go either deer stalking or fishing on the loch with the outdoor pursuits company. Then after that they can lounge here and relax on the lawn with a drink, or James has volunteered to take those that want to go out for a tour of the local area,' Kate said as she watched her employer mentally process it. 'Invermoray House is beautiful. The estate is beautiful. The rooms look fantastic. There are only six journalists—'

'Twelve,' Liz cut in. 'With their partners, that makes twelve people to worry about.'

'OK, so there's twelve of them and there's four of us if you include Angus who is handling the hardest bit, the food. Actually, there's five, if you count Jenny, who is marvellous at picking up any slack and running with it. You're in very safe hands.'

She nodded. 'We are. I know we are. You've been wonderful. We just need to get through the next twenty four hours and then we can relax.'

Kate wasn't so sure about that. She wondered if Liz had forgotten that after the journalists came the real paying guests, with any luck.

James had been logging into the booking system over the past few days and had been leaving excitable Post-it Notes on Kate's computer with updates of how many booking enquiries they'd been receiving. It was the only communication the two of them had really had since the awful night in the cottage.

They heard the front door bang and chatter sounded in the hallway.

Liz smiled. 'That'll be them.'

Kate rushed towards the sound of James and Jenny.

Jenny gave her a huge grin and threw her arms around Kate.

'You're here,' Kate said into her long brown hair as they hugged. 'How was your flight?'

'Fine.'

'And your drive? You found each other all right?'

Jenny threw James an appreciative glance. 'Perfectly.'

'I'm so glad.'

Kate introduced Jenny and Liz and they went through to the sitting room, where Liz offered Jenny a glass of wine and a tumbler of water, which Jenny gulped.

'Was it bumpy over the mountains?' Kate asked.

'No. All fine and I spent more time queuing at the airport than I did in the actual air. Such a short trip,' she said as she sat down. 'This house . . .' she said as she took a sip of her wine. 'It's from a fairy tale.'

James smiled as he sat down next to Liz on the sofa opposite.

'So, where are you guys at with the press visits and what can I do?' Jenny asked.

Kate filled James and Jenny in and was secretly happy to see the impressed looks on both their faces. 'So,' Kate said, 'they're all coming in on the same flight and I've got a minibus picking them up from the airport just after lunch. We've got a few light snacks here in case they didn't eat much on the plane . . .' She told them the details as three pairs of eyes watched her keenly.

Kate had been so busy it hadn't even occurred to her to eat and it was only as Liz ushered them all into the kitchen that they discovered Angus was whipping up a delicious dinner.

'Angus.' James strode over and the two men greeted each other warmly. 'Didn't realise you'd be here.'

'Volunteered. Morven's running the show over at the Arms tonight and so I thought we deserved a celebratory dinner. I brought a bottle of Champagne over from the pub and I've cooked "Angus's next-level chilli con carne". I'm just warming it up and adding the final flourishes.'

'Next-level?' Jenny asked as Angus stirred what looked like peanut butter and coffee powder into the dish.

'Secret ingredients,' Angus said, tapping his nose with his free hand. 'Hi, I'm Angus, I don't think we've . . .'

'This is Jenny,' Kate introduced them. Angus smiled at Jenny in a way Kate had not seen him smile before and a little part of her wondered if there'd be time to play matchmaker before Jenny returned home.

Jenny and Kate dragged their tired bodies up the stairs to bed after they'd helped tidy the kitchen and said goodnight to everyone. James had taken Jenny's case ahead of them and said an awkward goodnight at their door. He seemed unsure whether or not to air-kiss Kate as Jenny had done to him. In the end he decided against it.

'Night, James,' Kate said as she slowly pushed her bedroom door closed.

'Um, night. Good work, Kate. See you in the morning,' he said stiffly.

Kate gave him a half wave and muttered something even she wasn't sure of as the door closed.

She moved into the room and was about to start telling Jenny which drawers she'd put aside for her when she looked over to find her friend with her arms folded and one eyebrow up towards her hairline.

'What?' Kate asked when it was clear Jenny expected Kate to speak first.

'Well,' Jenny said with a huge grin on her face. 'You're welcome.'

'Sorry?' Kate asked in confusion.

Jenny unfolded her arms and pointed her thumb towards the door. 'Lord of the manor out there.'

'James?' Kate queried looking towards the closed door. Kate hadn't told her about their night that never was and so she wondered if and how Jenny knew.

'I apply for this job for you, throw you in the direction of eligible men and I don't even get so much as a thank you?'

Jenny folded her arms again and resumed smiling, her eyes boring into Kate's. 'And Angus?' she continued with a low whistle when it was clear Kate wasn't going to reply. 'Well, no wonder you didn't turn and run back to London the moment you arrived. You've been surrounded by fit men and you've not said a word. How is it . . .' she said in a wondrous tone, 'that I'm in a city of about nine million people and can't meet a single attractive, normal man, and you're in this little village with . . . how many people?'

Kate knew where she was going with this and returned her smile. 'About three hundred maybe?'

Jenny rolled her eyes. 'Three hundred people and there's gorgeous men everywhere.'

Kate wasn't sure how to answer this.

Jenny ploughed on. 'Which one are you dating?'

'Neither of them,' Kate said with horror.

'Are you dating someone else? Are there *more*?' Jenny was astonished.

Kate laughed. 'No. Well, there may be more but I've not really noticed. I'm just not dating either of them.'

'Why not?' Jenny sat on the edge of Kate's four-poster bed. 'Are they gay? Oh damn, are they a couple? For Christ's sake.'

'No.' Kate laughed. 'No, they aren't gay. James definitely isn't. I don't *think* Angus is.'

'How do you know James isn't?' Jenny asked, quick as a flash.

Kate flushed.

'Oh . . . are you . . . have you . . . ?'

'Jesus, no, Jenny,' Kate fibbed. 'He's my boss.'

Jenny looked towards the door thoughtfully. 'Well, he's not *mine*,' she said with a smile.

As they started unpacking Jenny's cases, it dawned on Kate that her lovely friend was suddenly making her nervous.

The journalists' visit passed in a blur. Kate felt as if she was on high alert the entire twenty-four hours. She'd organised press launches more times than she could remember, but there was always something exhilarating and new about each one.

She'd chosen her press contacts well for this trip and they were fun and enthusiastic. A few of them had even invested in sets of tweeds so they could go deer stalking and look the part. Thankfully the outdoor pursuits company they used to organise this weren't the gun-toting kind and the activity was following the herd of deer in 4x4s, taking photographs of the animals and the scenery.

James had dusted off his father's sets of waders and fishing rods and had taken a few of them fishing for trout in the stream in the woods.

Angus had done them all proud with a fine feast in the pub and had prepared a draft tearoom menu, which he'd asked Kate to put into the press kits.

Liz's history tour had gone down well and she'd remembered to include stories about the Loch Invermoray Monster, which she was completely making up but which Kate could see the journalists taking in without question. At one point Kate had to cough to catch her attention when she became quite elaborately gory reeling off a story of a drowned airman whose dripping-wet ghost haunted the ballroom.

'What the hell is she doing?' James asked Kate out of the side of his mouth as they caught her telling the story halfway up the staircase, the journalists open-mouthed but entranced.

'Thank you so much for coming,' Kate said as she closed the minibus door and stood with Liz, Angus, James and Jenny to wave the journalists off.

She'd managed to get decent time with each of them to find

out what they thought, when their articles were likely to run, how much page space they thought they could dedicate to Invermoray House and what further information they needed. They'd loved it. They'd loved Liz's slightly bonkers family history stories. It turned out she'd got in full swing when they'd been in the garden and James and Kate had taken their eyes off her. She had given a dramatic retelling of how Constance and Douglas had been callously thwarted of their inheritance, which the journalists lapped up.

They'd loved that the ghillie's cottage had been transformed after eighty years' abandonment into a private getaway, although for diplomacy's sake Kate and James had agreed they wouldn't let any of the journalists stay in it in case the ones who didn't felt hard done by. But they'd loved the house. They'd loved its history and its faded glamour. They'd loved the orangery and being surrounded by oversized plants when they'd had breakfast in the morning. They'd loved the ornate plasterwork in the dining room and the flumpy sofas in the sitting room.

They had seen what Kate had seen and she realised in turn that she was becoming very attached to Invermoray. The thought of returning to her tiny little flat in London and seeking out a job amongst the hubbub of a big city did not enthral her. She had found it far too easy to settle in here. She usually adored the differing challenges that came when working for a PR agency: having five or six big clients on the go at the same time, different projects, the joys and the stresses. But here, at Invermoray she was challenged and she hated to admit this to herself, she was settled. She didn't miss her old job at all. She didn't miss her flat. She didn't miss the city. Kate did miss her friends and parents but as Jenny had proved, they were only a short flight away.

Anyway, her contract would be over in a little under three months, her time here ticking away. It was probably for the best that Kate was leaving. Regardless, it wasn't her decision to stay or go. It was James's and Liz's and she wasn't sure James would be front of the queue to keep her. Even after all these weeks later she couldn't stop cringing every time she thought about what James and she had very nearly let happen between them and the awkwardness that had ensued as a result. Even so, the thought of leaving was depressing. But if she was being pragmatic, then over the next couple of months she should probably start thinking about her next career move. Perhaps something similar, a project just like Invermoray.

'We're going to the pub,' Jenny said as she caught Kate at her desk about an hour after the editors had gone. Dusk was descending and Kate was dog-tired but she had to commission a photographer to take professional shots now the house was complete. And the website needed updating.

'I can't,' Kate said.

'Oh come on, hon,' Jenny encouraged. 'If anyone deserves a drink you do. I came to help but you had it all so completely covered I felt like a spare part.'

Kate swung on her chair to look at her properly. 'Nonsense, you were fantastic. I saw you dashing off to fetch waders and I know you were serving at breakfast this morning with Angus.'

'He coped marvellously but I'm a spare pair of hands so I made myself useful. I'll stay with you if you're not going to the pub,' Jenny offered.

'No. You should go. Please go. You deserve it. Enjoy what's left of your sort-of holiday.'

James stood by the door. 'You two ready?'

Jenny looked at James and then leaned in close to Kate. 'I'm already enjoying my holiday,' she said conspiratorially.

Kate swallowed nervously and when she spoke, her voice strained in her throat. 'You guys have a good night. Catch you later.' Kate waved them off and then settled in to catch up. But after ten minutes she'd still just been staring blankly at her computer screen and was unable to focus.

She slammed the lid of her laptop more forcefully than she'd intended and sat back in her chair. 'Oh forget this,' she muttered to herself as she locked the estate office and pocketed the key. A walk to clear her head was the best thing.

Decompressing. It's a phrase she'd read in a women's magazine and it applied in spades to her right now. She'd been flat out for so long she hadn't spotted she was getting a bit burnt out. A walk would be more beneficial than a drink in the pub. Maybe.

Kate sucked down the clean Highland air as she walked purposefully in no direction whatsoever. She was desperate just to keep moving, to blow the cobwebs away after having been so confined for so long. She needed to taste freedom of sorts and began running. In her skinny jeans, T-shirt and ankle boots, she felt like an idiot. She wasn't a runner. Running was James's thing. Thoughts of James flashed through Kate's head. What was wrong with her? Why, suddenly, couldn't she stop thinking about him?

'Come on,' she said to herself as she reached the small church that bordered the edge of the estate and the very outskirts of the village. She was in sore need of a rest and she leaned against the Church of Scotland sign that read 'Invermoray Kirk'. Nearby was a stone crypt, ivy creeping its way over and she moved towards it, resting her back against the stone as she sat, breathing deeply, until her ragged breath eventually regulated.

The kirk was made of the same grey stone as the rest of the village and it looked gothic, its grey stone blackening through age. Kate reasoned the church must have been built around the same time as the village – late Georgian? Early Victorian? There were relatively new graves in the furthest corner but one nearby was from the mid-1900s.

Kate ran her fingers over the soft grass as the clouds closed in above the mountains. When it rained here, it rained hard and fast and without a care as to whether people like her were out for an early evening jog. But she wanted to sit. Just for a moment while she cleared her mind. There weren't many tombs like the one she was practically leaning against. It was more ornate than some of the other headstones and the three or four other prominent tombs.

Kate absent-mindedly ran her fingertip around the letters and dates that had been carved into the stone, memorialising someone who had died so long ago. She thought of the many Scottish rainfalls that had landed on this tomb, softening its hard edges; the snow that piled up in the harsh winters and then cleared in spring; the ivy creeping around the tomb and over it, further and further year by year only to be cut back by a gardener once every now and again. It was at that overgrown stage now and most of the inscription had been covered, leaving only a few letters showing.

After Kate had finished being morbid, imagining herself being buried somewhere this peaceful when she eventually passed away, she looked properly at the stone, at the name she'd been absent-mindedly tracing and not paying close attention to. She read the name McLay, faint through age, drawing in a sharp breath as she read on. The birth year was 1919 perhaps? She couldn't tell. Nineteen-something certainly. The month of death September 1940, although the exact date was unreadable. Hastily, she tugged at the piles of ivy, ripping away strand after strand, ivy catching underneath her fingernails as she fought to see whose first name had been inscribed. But the lettering underneath the weed had long since weathered away through eighty years of rainfall and creeping ivy. As much as she squinted to make sense of it all she could only see a few letters. There was an 's' in the first name and if she squinted harder she thought one of the two middle names started with an 'A'.

CHAPTER 29

1940

'You look so much better,' Constance told Matthew. She smiled at him and her heart beat just that little bit faster. She had considered herself quite covert, creeping out of the house with so many people present. She didn't want any of the officers to see her. They were mostly tucked up in bed, blackout blinds firmly pushed into place around the windows in the various bedrooms and in the ballroom. But it wasn't them she worried about, not really. Now her mother and father were firmly ensconced back in the house, and with Henry visiting, she needed to keep a watchful eye on the darkened windows as she moved discreetly from the house and around the loch.

And so, tonight, the first night in two that she'd managed to creep out since they had been informed of Douglas's death, she had been especially careful. If anyone caught her, she would be done for. She gulped, realising that actually, it would be Matthew who would be done for – rounded up, court-martialled and imprisoned. Or with the Battle of Britain raging in the skies in the south of England and pilots in short supply according to Henry's dinner table talk, Matthew might even be forced back up in the air. She wondered which was worse, which punishment he'd actually prefer if it came to it. He would rather be imprisoned she imagined. No more fighting, no more killing. He was hiding from the war and now, in a way, so was she. Let them hide together, she thought, even if it was only for now.

He was stoking the fire. Constance issued her special knock, three short raps and two long ones, and then entered. He looked up, his dark hair falling over his forehead, and he swept a hand up and pushed it back. 'Thought you were never coming,' he said with a grin.

'I'm finding it hard to get out of the house,' she said. 'I worried about you so much.'

'I'm so much better,' he said. 'Those pills,' he said in wonder. 'Even managed to wash some shirts and bedding. Found an old tin tub in the outhouse and boiled some water up. Damned near burned myself to death carrying it, but the sheets are like new now.' He looked pleased with himself and Constance smiled.

'I had planned to bring you fresh bedding,' she said, 'but I didn't know how I was going to make it out with all of it under my arm. It would probably have lain scattered in the woods as I went, like Hansel and Gretel but with a trail of blankets.'

'No need,' he said as he stretched. 'I could get used to this way of life. I'm very self-sufficient out here.'

'Really,' she asked as she laid down a bundle of tins and food on the kitchen table. 'Don't need all this then?' she teased. 'I'll take it all back, shall I?'

'Don't you dare,' he said darkly. 'I'd waste away if it wasn't for you.' His tone became quiet. 'I'd have died if it wasn't for you.'

'Let's not talk about it,' she said with a shake of her head. She'd had enough talk of death. She opened her mouth to tell him about Douglas. But as she looked around the cottage, at the sheets drying over chairs and blankets laid out to dry over the old laundry rack, pulled down from the ceiling, she changed her mind.

It was different here. It was a piece of tranquillity. Homely. Matthew made it feel . . . Constance didn't know what she felt but it was a different, lovely feeling to what she felt inside Invermoray House. During the day when the noise of the house, the unwanted attentions of Henry and the pain of Douglas's death became too much, she counted down the hours before she could go to the cottage. It was her escape, her secret.

Earlier that day, Henry had asked Constance to play cards with such a hopeful expression on his face and they had sat on the lawn. A couple of officers had joined them before the gong had sounded for their lunch. Every so often she'd been aware she was glancing across the parterre, over the large expanse of still water towards the cottage. Henry had squinted through the bright sunshine and enquired what she was looking at. She felt so heart-thumpingly close to accidentally giving Matthew away.

'Nothing of course. Just looking at the loch,' she had said far too defensively after the officers left.

'Your brother and I swam across it last summer,' he'd said. Inside, Constance had crumbled.

'Please,' she said quietly. 'Please stop mentioning Douglas.'

He was solemn and then he put his hand on her knee. 'I am sorry,' he said. 'Truly, I am.'

She nodded and looked at her cards through blurred tears, but couldn't for the life of her remember which card game they were playing and which hand she had been trying to cobble together. Henry had not removed his hand from her knee and so she looked at it in confusion. Eventually he had taken the point and removed it, but the whole incident had left her feeling vindicated in her repulsed feelings towards him. He had apologised for his behaviour on her birthday. But the apology would never outweigh what he had done that night.

Constance didn't want to tell Matthew any of it. She didn't want to tell him about Henry, about his wandering hands and the fact, if she actually thought about it, Henry had quite scared her. She didn't want to tell him about Douglas; about his plane going down in flames and the last letter she'd received moments before she read the telegram that was not even meant for her. If she spoke it out loud she would have to talk about it and then it would be real; it would devastate her anew and infiltrate the life she was pretending to have in the cottage with Matthew.

She knew this way of life would have to end for both of them, and soon. How it would all come to a head was beyond her comprehension, but she loved Matthew. What they had now was precious in wartime, regardless of how it had started and how it would end. She didn't want to corrupt what they had here, such as it was. She didn't want to shroud the walls of the cottage in the despair and death that followed her around Invermoray House. The wounded officers in the house were only another reminder of the grim reaper's firm touch on those around her. And Matthew had almost died. There was too much death. She'd thought herself immune from the horrors of war but now it had struck.

What she wouldn't give for Douglas to return, missing as presumed, and safe after all. Matthew had lived, had survived his illness and on the same day, she had found out Douglas had perished. Life was too fleeting. Matthew deemed himself cowardly but Constance no longer thought of him that way. He had escaped the clutches of death by swimming free of his wreckage. Had survived his illness but what if it happened again?

'Are you all right?' Matthew asked.

She looked at him blankly. 'Yes,' she said, nodding slowly. 'I'm sorry.'

'Are you sure?' he prompted. 'You disappeared for a moment there.' He was watching her closely, a kind but expectant look on his face.

'Yes, of course,' she said.

'I'm sorry,' he said. 'I didn't mean to—'

'You scared me,' she interjected.

'What do you mean?' he asked in confusion.

'I thought you were going to die.'

'No,' he said softly. He stepped forward to touch Constance's face but she turned her head away, despite longing for his touch. This, whatever this was between them, was cruel. But it remained unspoken.

'I think you should hand yourself in,' she said.

'What?' It was clear he couldn't believe she was suggesting this after all they had discussed.

'I couldn't help you,' she cried. 'I didn't know what to do. I didn't know where to turn. I was within a hair's breadth of telling someone about you, begging them to come here and save you.'

He turned white and looked at the floor.

'They'd have known immediately you weren't supposed to be here,' she said. 'They'd have asked questions; questions I wouldn't have been able to answer because I promised I wouldn't. I didn't know how to save you,' she told him. 'I wanted desperately for the pills to work but if they hadn't, then I'd have killed you. It would have been so stupid of me, not to have fetched help.'

'I'm pleased you didn't,' he said.

'What if you'd died?' she shouted, anger and a well of emotions getting the better of her.

'I didn't.'

'That's not the point.' Her voice rose again. 'I was frightened.'

He stepped towards her.

'If you'd handed yourself in earlier then we wouldn't be in this predicament,' she accused.

'We? *You're* not in any predicament,' he shouted back, completely stunning her. 'It's not you who has . . .' He looked as if he was choosing his words carefully. '*You're* free to go whenever you like,' he said more calmly. 'You don't have to be here, looking after me, bringing me medicine, bringing me food, checking on me. You don't owe me anything. Quite the reverse in fact. I owe *you* everything. I owe you my life. Twice now. I'm racking up quite a tally.'

Tears fell down her face and she wiped them away.

‘Don’t cry. Oh, Constance, please don’t cry,’ he begged.

‘I’m not,’ Constance fibbed. ‘I should have just left you to drown,’ she murmured.

‘Not very sporting,’ he said with a smile. ‘And I wouldn’t have drowned,’ he said confidently.

‘You would. You were engaged in battle with your flying jacket as I seem to remember.’

He laughed. ‘True enough.’

‘And then there was all that fuss with your boots. What a palaver.’

‘I was a bit caught up, as I recall; fighting a losing battle.’

‘Well, I was trying to rescue you while fighting my *own* battle with a stupid floor-length dress but did you hear me shouting and hollering about it? No you didn’t, because I wasn’t moaning half as much as you, I wasn’t grumbling at all actually—’

She was silenced as he strode purposefully towards her, stopped and before she had time to realise what he was doing, he had looped an arm around her waist, pulled her towards him and kissed her.

CHAPTER 30

She had never been kissed like that before. There had been moments outside tea dances when her mother had been elsewhere and boys had found her pretty enough, or perhaps willing enough, to want to steal rather chaste kisses. She had never enjoyed the clumsiness of it. And then, buried up here in the Highlands there had been nothing for years. Not until Henry, of course, but his had been an unwanted attention, forced and clumsy. Despite the dearth of eligible men in these parts, now she thought about it, she had never really wanted to be kissed by Henry. Not like that. But this, this kiss with Matthew was different; her body pressed against his chest, his hand on her back holding her gently but firmly as his mouth explored hers. The thought of being kissed and enjoying it confused Constance. It had never been like that for her. And the thought of other things delighted and perplexed in equal measure. Her entire body tingled with delight and the pleasure of his touch gave way to the maddening desire that rose within her. A feeling she had never felt before. Slowly they broke apart.

His eyes searched hers. As he moved back she wanted nothing more than to pull him back to her, to feel his mouth on hers, but she couldn't speak, couldn't think.

Matthew smiled uncertainly. 'Was that . . . was that all right?'

Constance nodded as she looked into his eyes. 'Yes.' She rested her hands on his chest and waited, although she didn't know what for.

'Oh, Constance,' he whispered. 'I thought my luck had run out when I crashed but I didn't realise it had only just begun. I never want to be without you. But I know, very soon, this . . . charade . . .' he looked around the cottage '. . . this false hope I've given myself, will come to a very abrupt end. I can't stay here forever, much as I'd love to. You'll get caught coming here or your parents will soon start wondering where you're sneaking off to and to avoid that happening, to avoid you getting wrapped up in my mess . . .' He stroked her cheek. 'Constance, as much as I hate this idea, I'm going to have to leave soon.'

Somewhere, at the back of her mind, she had known this was coming and she closed her eyes. The people she loved the most were leaving her. She knew he was right but she wasn't panicked about getting caught with him, but worried that she would accidentally lead someone into his path, and then he would be in horrific trouble. In keeping him safe here she had been putting him at risk.

'I know,' she said resignedly. 'The threat of you being found increases with every passing day. Every time I leave the house I look over my shoulder. Every time I enter the cottage I wonder if you'll still be here. I understand you must go somewhere safer. You can't spend your life like this. Life is too short as it is.' She blinked away all thoughts of Douglas's passing and focused solely on Matthew's face. 'It's fleeting. You're standing up for what you believe in, not fighting when you feel you can't. I haven't found my place in this world. But I've found you and your kindness and your goodness and . . .' She didn't want to say *vulnerability*, but she felt his vulnerability in spades. 'I've fallen in love with you,' she dared. 'I love you and I don't want you to push me away because one day soon you'll have to leave me. I want us to love each other, here, now, because this might be all we ever get.'

He hesitated, running his hand through his hair but saying

nothing. Constance felt his pause of only a few seconds as if it were a day, that she had exposed too much of herself and she waited nervously for his reaction. And then he lowered his head and kissed her. In the dim light of the cottage with the fire crackling and warming the room, Constance wanted him. She wanted him the way she'd never wanted anything in her entire life.

Matthew said her name questioningly as she began unbuttoning his shirt. She felt brave in doing so but not brave enough to meet his gaze. His arms hung limply and his breathing grew heavy before he shrugged off his shirt. She placed her hands on his chest, warm beneath her fingers.

His face was uncertain. 'Constance, we can't. I don't want you to regret this.'

'I won't regret it. I promise you, I won't.' She pulled him towards her, kissing him passionately before he groaned. Giving in and clearly fighting his instincts, he picked her up and carried her to the settee.

Her body tingled as his fingers brushed over her skin. His gaze left hers only to locate her blouse buttons in the dimly lit room. One by one he undid them, removing her clothing gently, peeling her skirt from her until she was in her underclothes.

Constance watched him intently, expectantly as he kicked off his trousers and moved back towards her, love and tenderness in his eyes. Shaking, nervous all of a sudden, she started to lift her slip over her head and she felt his hands gently touch her, his fingers gliding over her arms as he lifted it from her body. He dropped it on the floor and unclipped her stockings. He began kissing her neck, her chest, her shoulders before finding her mouth, whispering to her, reassuring her he would try not to hurt her, that he would love her forever. Their naked bodies entwined, she wrapped her legs around him, letting herself love and be loved, forgetting about the world around her, about the war as it raged and about Douglas's death. As dawn broke, she closed her eyes and shut out the dire panic she felt knowing that Matthew, too, would soon leave her.

CHAPTER 31

They slept on the settee, their bodies still entangled, his head on her chest. Constance was the first to wake and she blinked slowly, looking towards the fire as the last of the logs glowed red, giving out little heat as they crumbled slowly to ash. The warm weight of Matthew's sleeping form made her feel safe. One of her hands was within his and she moved her free hand up to his dark hair, stroking it back where it had fallen over his sleeping face. 'I love you,' she whispered and then laughed at the madness of the last few hours.

Matthew woke, groaned in tiredness and sleepily lifted himself onto an elbow. He blinked and looked down at her before his face broke out into a sleepy smile.

She smiled back and bit her lip to prevent herself from laughing again. Lunacy was spreading through her, she knew it.

'I thought I'd dreamt it,' he said. 'You, me, the cottage, all of it. When I opened my eyes, I thought for one horrid moment none of it was real and that I was back at the base, waiting for the next bout of hell.'

He kissed her softly and then climbed off her to his feet. She sat up and watched as he picked his trousers off the floor and climbed into them. Constance yawned and stretched. She wondered what time it was. Had they been asleep a few hours, or all night?

Slowly, the awful memory of Douglas's death seeped into her mind and threatened to destroy her. 'Oh God,' she whispered as her memory caught up with her.

'What did you just say?' he questioned. And then as he watched tears stream from her eyes, 'What's wrong? Why are you crying?'

He rushed to her, sat down and pulled her towards him, kissing the top of her head. 'What's the matter, Constance? Is it me? Oh God, are you regretting—'

'No,' she protested, looking up into his face. 'No. I don't regret that at all. It's just, I had some dreadful news and I don't think . . .' She sobbed and he stroked her hair.

'You don't have to tell me if you don't want to, but I've been told I'm a good listener.'

She cried into his chest and then when she'd recovered herself marginally, told him about Douglas, about the way in which she'd found out he'd died. He held her close. She told him about Henry telling her that Douglas had fallen from the sky. Without knowing why, Constance told him what Henry had done to her in the orangery the night she had watched Matthew's plane crash into the loch. She felt Matthew stiffen as she spoke about how Henry had lifted her dress.

'He did *what*?' Matthew exploded.

'But it's fine,' she said hurriedly. 'It's . . . he's not going to do it again. I won't let him. But it was galling to sit and play cards with him on the lawn earlier when all I want is to be with you.'

'He's still here?' Matthew said, his eyebrows rising. 'Henry is still at the house?'

'Yes,' she said with a sigh. 'My father invited him to stay while he recovers. He's staying in Douglas's room and he's . . . oh I don't know . . . something about not being able to travel so far south with his leg being the way it is.'

Matthew's face was a mixture of horror and disgust. 'If he touches you again, Constance, I will beat the life out of the man.'

Constance laughed. 'It's very gallant of you but he won't touch me again. And there's nothing he can do that will hurt me now. I think he's remorseful but the damage has been done and there's nothing he can do that will make me like him the way I used to.'

'You liked him?' Matthew asked. 'A lot?'

'I liked him enough,' she replied. 'But not anymore.'

They held each other and Constance nestled against Matthew's torso, soothed by the rise and fall of his chest and his heartbeat.

'I'm so sorry,' he said quietly. 'About your brother. You didn't say.'

'I didn't want to. I didn't want to say it out loud.'

Matthew was quiet. 'I feel . . .'

Constance shifted back on the settee to look at him. She narrowed her eyes. 'Yes?'

'I feel awful. I feel as if I've taken advantage of you. Your brother has just died and you came to me and I made love to you . . .' He looked agonised. 'But . . . Oh Christ, Constance, I'm so sorry. I have no self-control. You were upset. I should have known something was wrong, truly wrong. I hate myself.'

'No,' she said. 'No. Don't. Don't say it like that. Don't say it as if I didn't want to. I did. And my brother's death had nothing to do with it. I have wanted you to make love to me for . . . I don't know how long, it's all blurring. Please don't make me sound as if I don't know my own mind.'

He blew out a breath of air from his cheeks and nodded. But she could see uncertainty etched over his face.

'Please know,' he said emphatically, 'that I would never do anything to hurt you.'

'I know,' she said, planting a kiss on his mouth to silence him.

They held each other for a few silent minutes before Constance reluctantly moved away from Matthew's warm embrace to the window, where she lifted the blackout blind. 'Oh good Lord,' she cried as the sun's rays fell on her face. 'It's morning. I've been here too long. I'll be missed.'

Matthew began gathering the rest of her clothes, helping her hurriedly into them.

'When will you come back?' he asked.

'Whenever I can. Have you still got enough food?'

'Plenty.'

She started to turn but he grabbed her hand. 'I love you,' he said and a frown clouded his features. 'I love you, Constance. And I worry about you. In that house with that man. I hate that I can't do anything to help you from here,' he said. 'But if Henry tries anything . . . if you need me to come to the house . . .'

'No!' she exclaimed. 'No, you mustn't do that. Please, promise me you won't come to the house.'

'All right,' he said reluctantly. 'But one word from you is all I need.'

She moved into his arms and kissed him in the doorway. 'You don't need to worry. I wish I'd not told you now. Please, put it from your mind.'

She heard his stomach grumble and she laughed. 'Eat something,' she teased. 'I'll be back before you know it.'

She turned and left, running through the woodland. Every time she thought of Matthew, making love to her, holding her, kissing her, she smiled to herself. She knew she should feel shameful but she felt overjoyed.

The thought of Henry in the house worried her anew. Matthew was right, of course; she really did need to watch out for him. A leopard didn't change its spots. The fact Matthew had threatened to be her saviour if Henry tried anything like it again made her shiver with excitement. Not at the thought of him actually hitting Henry, but at the thought he loved her enough to fight someone for her. She wondered if it was wrong that thrilled her? But of course, if Henry did try anything stupid, there was nothing Matthew could really do, stuck out in the cottage.

CHAPTER 32

2020

Kate returned to the house, walking slowly through the churchyard and over the heathland, its hues of greens and deep yellow grasses melting in with the plum heather.

The scenery was completely lost on her. The grave she had been sitting next to had thrown her. It made the story about the disinheritance a rather confusing one. Both Constance and Douglas had been born in nineteen-something as the family Bible stated and then disinherited. But something told Kate that it was one of them in the ground at Invermoray Kirk. She just felt it.

And if she was right, why was one of them buried, here, only minutes from the estate? Had they been disinherited but then stayed here? That was odd. The date of death was September 1940 and one of the McLay children was dead and buried. What had happened to the other one? As Kate entered the house, it was quiet. They must all still be at the pub. She thought back to the Bible inside the study; Constance's name scrubbed out. Kate stood in front of the picture of the girl in the silver-grey dress, the repaired rip only evident if Kate looked close enough.

Kate suddenly wanted to talk to James. She wanted his take on it. But after the longest two days they'd had here, he was enjoying himself in the pub with Jenny, Liz and Angus. Kate smiled. He deserved to enjoy himself for a change. Like her, he had worked so hard of late.

Kate put the tomb to the back of her mind and returned to the estate office feeling refreshed. She wanted to check on the status of their bookings. They'd had an enquiry from a woman in Canada who was keen to hire the cottage with her disabled husband in a few weeks. She wasn't sure he would be able to make the many stairs in the main house and she'd wanted to see further pictures of the cottage before she committed. Kate had some rudimentary pictures she'd taken on her phone – because James had made great effort to paint the staircase white and attach rope handles on the wall, along with some photographic prints of stags, Kate had thought it pretty enough to photograph. She counted the steps in the picture and emailed the photo to the lady enquiring.

Kate began uploading the shots she had on her phone to the Invermoray House website and the various booking agency websites they were using. It was a temporary measure until she sorted the elusive professional photographer. While she was uploading, a reply pinged in from the Canadian confirming that the stairs would be fine for her husband and she would book the cottage. Kate jumped for joy. The cottage's first booking. Now she really wanted to talk to James. Kate picked up her phone to message him and then put it down again. Let him enjoy his night out without her disturbing him about work. It could wait until morning.

Kate climbed into bed buzzing with a strange frenetic energy. Her body was aching, her eyes stinging with tiredness, but her mind was full of the excitement of the past few days. She didn't know what she was more excited about, the wonderful press articles she was expecting to start appearing in the Sunday supplements and online versions of the newspapers over coming weeks; or their very first cottage booking. Kate heard Liz return, muttering something to Whisky about having accidentally locked James and Jenny out. She clunked noisily down the stairs, taking them at whippet-speed before Kate heard her begin the journey back to her bedroom. After Liz's door closed, Kate listened out for the other two, remembering she was sharing her bed with Jenny and waiting for her to come up.

Kate must have fallen asleep after a while even though she'd told herself she was never going to be able to drift off after all that was running through her mind. She heard laughter on the stairs and looked at her phone in the darkness to see what time it was. Two o'clock in the morning. Perhaps Angus had decided to have a lock-in and that's why they were back so late. Kate was a bit jealous, although after what had happened the last time she drank, it was probably wise to have stayed behind and avoided gin and tonics for a bit longer.

In the hallway Kate heard James's deep voice say something that Jenny obviously found hilarious. He whispered theatrically to her to be quiet and they both drunkenly chuckled. Kate sat up, smiling at all this going on out of sight, and watched the back of her bedroom door, waiting for Jenny to amble into the room drunk and her usual humorous self.

But no. It had become quiet in the corridor. What were the two of them doing out there that required no talking? Kate's mind ran wild.

Oh God, she thought, starting to feel sick. *Why are they so quiet? Why aren't they speaking? Are they kissing?*

She felt her face go cold as she realised Jenny wasn't coming back to her room to sleep that night. Along the corridor, James's door banged shut behind them.

CHAPTER 33
1940

'Where have you *been*?' Henry asked.

Constance stopped dead as she entered the house, fear trickling through her. The grandfather clocked chimed ten o'clock. How would she justify her absence for most of the morning?

'Oh, Henry,' she said. 'Good morning. How are you today?'

The entrance hall glowed as the fire flickered, but fear at having been caught creeping into the house made her feel cold.

Henry looked around nervously. 'I've been looking everywhere for you. You weren't in your room.'

Constance folded her arms across her chest. 'You went into my room?'

'Of course,' he said. 'I knocked first. Your bed was not slept in.'

'My bed was indeed slept in,' she said as if Henry was mistaken. 'I remade it this morning. Mrs Campbell has enough to do without tidying up after me. Did you make your bed this morning?'

'I . . . no . . .' he said as if she was mad and then his tone changed to one of anger. 'It's not boarding school for Christ's sake and you didn't answer my question.'

'No,' she sighed. 'I did not. Nor should I have to.'

When Henry spoke next he was more kind. 'You aren't letting me speak,' he bumbled.

Constance did not reply, but simply waited expectantly. She wanted to fall into a hot bath and then see if any of the orderlies wanted an extra pair of hands today. Although she knew she'd have to keep out of her parents' way if so. She was growing exasperated that everything she did was in secret. And then tonight, she would return to Matthew and fall into his arms. She smiled to herself at this and it was only when Henry called her name again she noticed he was still standing there and she hadn't listened to a word he'd said.

'Sorry, Henry,' she snapped, running out of patience. 'What is it you need?'

'Come with me,' he said sternly. 'You've been wanted for the best part of an hour.'

'Why?' she said, her eyes narrowing. But she allowed herself to be led. He placed his hand on her arm and it was all she could do not to snatch it away.

He opened the door to the family's sitting room and entered in front of her. 'I found her, eventually,' he said self-importantly. He was blocking her view of the room.

'Henry,' Constance said behind him, her eyes involuntarily rolling. 'What on earth is the fuss about?'

Henry moved out of the way, his leg suddenly dragging behind him when she was sure it hadn't been a moment ago. She realised he wasn't using his new cane and that it was propped up next to the furthest settee. Next to the cane, on the settee, was her father, tears in his eyes; something she had never seen before. Her mother, yes – tears far more often than were strictly necessary. But her father? No. Mrs Campbell and Mrs Fraser were standing by the French windows. Constance was surprised to see them in the room. Her parents preferred to keep the staff at arm's length.

'What's wrong?' Constance asked.

And then she thought she knew, as she looked at the document her father was holding with shaking hands. 'The letter,' she said quietly. 'It's the letter we were expecting, isn't it? About Douglas.'

Her father nodded and then smiled at her before wiping tears with the back of his hand.

'Where's Mother?' Constance asked. 'Have you read it?' she asked. 'Mother should be here.'

'She was looking for you,' her father replied. 'Where have you been?'

'I—' she faltered.

'No matter,' her father said. 'You're here now. In fact,' he said smiling, 'nothing matters now. Nothing at all. Herr Hitler could bomb us all to dust and it wouldn't matter.'

'Father?' Constance asked, entirely confused. 'What are you talking about?'

Her father looked past Constance, over her shoulder.

She whipped her head round and then gasped. Her hands flew to her mouth, and try as she might, she could not speak, could not move towards the man who was coming through the door, resting against her mother, an arm bound up in a sling, a huge cut down one side of his face, held together with thick stitches.

Through a voice strained with pain, Constance heard him say, 'Hello, Smidge.'

'Douglas? Douglas!' Constance closed the distance between them and blinked as her vision blurred with tears. 'Douglas,' she said between sobs, 'you're alive. You're alive!'

He pulled her towards him with his good arm. 'Just about,' he said as she pulled back and looked into his face. He was here. He was really here.

'It was touch and go for a moment, I can tell you,' he said as he held her shoulder. He leant against her and then straightened. 'Still a bit wobbly.'

'Let your brother sit, Constance,' Henry suggested.

'Of course,' she said, leading Douglas to a space on the settee. 'Why are you up and about? You should be resting.'

'I was looking for you. I'd been waiting about an hour after I arrived, dozing on and off on the settee. No one could find you so I decided I'd look for you myself.' He smiled. 'Ah – hurts when I smile. Hurts when I do anything much at the moment. But a few weeks at home should help.'

'But how . . . ?' Constance started. Her tears had subsided but confusion had taken hold. 'How are you alive? Henry said . . .'

Henry smiled at his friend. 'I was wrong,' he said. 'Happily, fantastically wrong.'

'I pulled my 'chute,' Douglas said. 'Bloody kite was a mess, engine on fire, I wasn't long for it and so out I went, but I was, alas—' he looked embarrassed '—a bit too close to the ground.' He gestured to his arm.

'We were told you were missing, presumed killed,' she said in disbelief.

He smiled and then winced at the pain that pulled at his cut. 'I was only missing for a few days. Lovely farmer's wife took me in. I was rather dazed and she bandaged me up. She heard the Spit' go into the mountain. Mighty sound it made apparently, and then she saw me float down in a dangerous tangle of parachute silk and rope and came out to get me. She saved me when I'd surely have died out there at the bottom of the mountain. She got me into the house, and got a few drams of whisky in me to ease the pain before I passed out. And not from the drink either. I was in absolute agony. She said I was rambling, in some kind of shock, so letting sleep take me was the easiest way. She splinted my arm for me while I was asleep and looked after me for days until I was compos mentis enough to be left alone. No telephone to ring my unit for miles so yesterday morning she rode her little cart horse to the post office to summon help. Took her half the day. She didn't have to do any of it, really. Didn't know me. But sheltered me regardless. A good woman. Her husband's away fighting,' he said quietly, apropos to nothing. 'I'd like to go back,' he said, 'say thanks properly and all that.'

'No telephone?' Henry asked. 'Bit odd.'

'Not really,' Douglas replied. 'Not everyone can afford one, you know. And out in the middle of nowhere, not rigged up either.'

'Poor you, being laid up there,' Henry said.

'Lucky me, more like,' Douglas said. 'Thank God for the kindness of strangers.'

'My God, Douglas, you're lucky to be alive,' Mrs McLay said.

'I am,' he said, 'I owe that wonderful woman my life.' A trace of a smile lit his face and Constance wondered if he had fallen for the farmer's wife. Douglas had never spoken before about any woman, although there must have been some over the years, surely.

Douglas and Matthew had been in similar situations all this time and the way the RAF were being shot from the sky with alarming regularity these days, Constance was sure this need to shelter injured men temporarily was going on all over the British Isles. Both men had been injured, Douglas physically but Matthew mentally. And Douglas had chosen to return to his unit, whereas Matthew couldn't. Thank God for the kindness of strangers, Douglas had said. She had to keep Matthew safe, the way the farmer's wife had kept Douglas safe. Constance felt deep gratitude to the woman she would never meet for saving Douglas and nursing him back to health until he had felt ready to move on. And until Matthew was ready to move on, she must do the same. As much as he said otherwise, Matthew was her responsibility now.

CHAPTER 34

2020

Kate couldn't eat anything at breakfast. She was morose and knew exactly why. Jenny and James. It had annoyed her. It had upset her. But more than that, she was disgusted with herself because of how she felt. It shouldn't bother her that they had spent the night together. But it did. It really did. Jenny had crept back into Kate's room at some point in the early hours of the morning, presumably to avoid a walk of shame when Liz and Kate rose. But Kate was wide awake, facing away from the door and had felt the bed sag as Jenny climbed in and fell promptly asleep. Kate had felt tears prick the backs of her eyes and she'd blinked them away before eventually closing her eyes. But sleep hadn't been her friend last night.

Jenny; her best friend. And James. Kate hadn't really known how she felt about James before, but she did now. She liked him. She liked him so much and he and Jenny had [illegible] Kate couldn't think about it. She wanted to cry. It was her fault. Jenny had asked Kate how she felt about James. And she had said she didn't like him. Why had she done that? Kate had attempted to throw her off the scent but instead all she'd done was throw the two of them together. Kate should have been honest with her from the start. This is where fibbing led. She had been so happy here, with

James, with Liz, Angus . . . all of them. And James had got under her skin as much as the house had.

Despite that night in the cottage that almost led somewhere dangerous, James obviously didn't feel anything for her, or else why would he have slept so readily with Jenny? Any idiot could see Jenny was stunning but . . . still.

As the wee hours turned into a social hour, Kate sipped coffee and stared out the kitchen window, now completely glad her time here was coming to an end in a few short months. She was practically wishing it away and made a vow that wherever she went next categorically could not have a male within a hundred yards. Far too much trouble. How was she supposed to focus on her work now?

'What shall we do today?' Jenny asked as she entered the kitchen.

'Oh,' Kate said, putting her coffee cup in the dishwasher. 'I thought . . . work. There's so much to do. I've still got to sort this photographer. I've a mind to look for another one today as the first is being so flaky.'

Jenny never masked her feelings. 'Let James do that. I'm going home tomorrow morning. Come on,' she drawled.

'I can't. Really. Sorry.'

Whisky ambled in, followed by James, who looked sleepy, his hair dishevelled. Kate felt her stomach tighten as he gave her a slow, lazy smile. She had to turn away in case her face betrayed her.

'Morning,' he said.

'Hi,' Kate said. She didn't know what kind of longing looks they were giving each other behind her and she didn't want to know. 'Right,' she said officiously. 'Work to do. Have a good day, Jenny.'

Kate left the kitchen and turned down the hallway. She felt tears behind her eyes and clenched her fists in a vain attempt to calm herself but of course it didn't work. She could hear the pair of them, in the kitchen, their tone muffled.

'So she's just left you to fend for yourself?' James said.

'It's OK,' Jenny said loyally and Kate heard the cupboard door open and close as someone retrieved cups. 'She's had a lot on.'

'You need someone to show you around a bit today?' James volunteered.

Kate could have screamed. She couldn't listen to the rest of this, so she pushed herself away from the wall and went to the estate office. As she reached the office door she realised she'd forgotten to retrieve the keys from the hallstand drawer. 'Fuck's sake, Kate,' she chastised.

She stood against the door, not finding it within herself to get a grip on her chaotic mind. Across the cobbled yard the stable door banged shut, making her jump.

Kate went over and opened it.

'Hello?' she called into the large space. The stable was rammed with boxes and old-fashioned furniture. She was about to head back to the house to get the office key when she heard scuffling.

Liz's head popped out from one of the stalls at the far end of the building. 'Good morning,' she said. 'If it isn't our star PR.' She laughed at her rhyme. 'Fantastic two days, Kate. Well done you.'

'Thanks,' Kate said, and felt just a little bit better about herself. 'What are you doing?'

Liz gestured around the disused stall. 'I've been up for hours. After my little historical chat to those lovely editors, I've got the bug for it. I knew I'd seen some things out here, props and the like.'

'Props?' Kate queried.

'Mmm,' she said, looking around. 'For future guests. For my talk.'

'Oh right.' Kate hadn't envisaged Liz having to do a talk to every set of guests that stayed at Invermoray. It would be a lot of work and she told her as much.

'But they loved it yesterday,' Liz said proudly.

'That's true,' Kate replied.

'And I enjoyed it,' Liz said, giving Kate a curious look.

'Well, then,' Kate replied. 'You should carry on. What are you looking for?'

'A stethoscope.'

Kate swallowed. She'd not had enough coffee for this. 'Sorry?'

'The house used to be a hospital, during the war. Bits and bobs got left behind – gas masks, empty medicine tins and the like – and I knew I'd seen a stethoscope out here in a box. My husband's family really were a bunch of hoarders. Heaven knows why they didn't think to bin a ratty old stethoscope.' She dug into another box and retrieved it with, 'Ah ha. But thankfully, for me, they didn't. Now what else can I use? Oh look at these lovely pictures.'

They clambered further into the stable, tripping over a cracked plastic box containing all sorts of bric-a-brac. 'A hospital?' Kate asked. She struggled to imagine the house as anything other than a cosy if somewhat ramshackle, sprawling home.

'Mmm. We didn't know for ages. That lovely Kirsty in the library told me. She's a bit of a history buff. No records here about it, but then I don't suppose there would have been. The Red Cross or whoever was in charge of it would have all the records I suppose. Anyway, I'm not interested in boring old documents when I've got this stethoscope and these pictures.'

Liz and Kate bent over a box file with old black and white photographs. Most were tatty and ragged at the corners and the smell coming from the box was damp and mouldy. There were some lovely images of nurses and merry-looking officers, lounging on deckchairs on the lawn. One very handsome man was looking laughingly up at a young woman. The date scribbled in pencil on the back of the photograph read September 1940.

Liz looked down. 'Ah, there's something about a man in uniform, isn't there?'

Kate smiled and then looking closer said, 'Oh, it's Constance, isn't it?'

'Constance McLay?' Liz said, peering down. 'Yes, yes it is.'

'An actual photograph of her,' Kate said, smiling. So far Kate had just seen the portraits and while she was certainly stunning, the artists hadn't done her justice at all. 'She's a beauty.'

Kate peered at the man in the photograph next to her. Although the photograph was black and white she could see he had a large cut down one of his cheeks and some ugly-looking stitches.

Kate peered closer at the man. There was something familiar about him. 'Oh, this is Douglas,' Kate said happily. 'He's been bashed up a bit by the looks of things.'

'Mmm, so he has. How lovely to have something real, of them both together, I mean.'

Kate nodded and then remembered something. 'Liz, were there any other McLays living round here during the war?'

Liz shrugged. 'I don't think so. I think it was just the four of them. Hence how my husband inherited the estate. The only candidate left in the family, although admittedly that was in the Eighties. Why do you ask?'

Kate frowned and then asked, 'Do you know what happened to Constance and Douglas?'

'Disinherited,' Liz said as she turned to flick through the pile of photos of officers and orderlies, nurses and other staff.

'Yes, but I mean *after* they left Invermoray?'

Liz looked thoughtful. 'No. Assume they moved away. Disagreement with their parents, finding out you'd been disinherited, wouldn't you move away and never come back?'

'Yes, I would, I think.'

Liz carried on rummaging in the stables but Kate's mind was running wild. Both Constance and Douglas had been alive in September 1940, according to this photograph. So why was one of them dead and buried in Invermoray churchyard that same month? And which of them was it?

CHAPTER 35

Kate stood on the stairs later that day and looked at the portraits of the siblings. Douglas really was rather good-looking. She looked this way and that, wondering if it was him or if it was the uniform that was working its charm. The portrait here was obviously painted before he'd acquired the huge gash on his face evident in the photograph. Or if it had happened before, perhaps the artist had decided against including it in the portrait. There was something about Douglas that reminded Kate of James; there was a family trait about the eyes when smiling. Kate pictured James in an RAF officer's outfit and then blinked the image away guiltily.

Her heart sank when she thought about James and Jenny. Kate had, to all intents and purposes, driven the two of them together. It was completely her fault. What if James and Kate *had* slept together that night in the cottage? Would it have just been a one-night stand, something intense in front of the flickering fire because they knew it could never have been repeated or would it have led to something else, something that would have started with delicate fragility and turned more substantial with time, the beginnings of a relationship that they would have explored tentatively together? She would never know. As much as it hurt that she knew it would never happen now, she resolved to move on, to forget about it. If he and Jenny chose to conduct a new, long-distance relationship, then Kate supposed it was something she would just have to get used to, as much as she hated the idea. She loved her friend. Jenny deserved to be happy. And so did James. And if Kate had allowed herself to get hurt in the process then it was her own stupid fault and no one else's.

A cough sounded behind her and she turned on the stairs to find Angus in the hall.

'They not back yet?' he asked. 'Jenny and James, I mean.' The way he said it made it sound as if they were already a couple and the comment stabbed Kate as if it was a knife.

'Back? No. Not yet. Where have they been?' she said light-heartedly, hoping her voice didn't betray how she really felt.

'We,' Angus said. 'Where have *we* been. I drove m'self and met them down there. They must have come back a funny route. The three of us think you'll be proud. We've been to Loch Ness. We took notepads,' he said proudly.

Kate smiled. 'Why?'

'We have plans. For the monster.'

Kate raised an eyebrow. 'Our fictional monster you mean?'

'Pft, you'll nae make any money wi' that attitude.'

Kate laughed but a headache was taking hold and she wasn't sure she could listen to plans, no matter how lucrative they sounded.

'I'll get James to tell me in the morning,' Kate said. 'I think I need to have a little nap. I didn't get much sleep last night.'

'You were missed, you know. We had a great time but it wasn't the same wi'out you drinking the bar dry wi' us. We all said it.'

Kate squeezed his arm. 'Thanks, Angus,' she said and went to bed feeling just a little bit better.

'Kate, open your eyes,' Jenny said gently, waking Kate up. 'You all right? You've been out for the count.'

Kate sat up with a jolt and rubbed sleep from her eyes. She nodded blankly at her. 'Mmm, fine,' she managed to say, although she felt unbelievably groggy and in desperate need of a glass of water.

'I've got to go, sweetie. My flight's soon.'

'What? What time is it?'

'Seven a.m.'

Kate gasped. She'd slept all afternoon and all night.

'I'm so sorry, I . . .'

'Ssh,' Jenny said soothingly. 'It's fine. I didn't want to wake you. James said you should rest.'

'Oh my God, I'm so . . .' Kate started to apologise again.

'Hey, listen,' Jenny said with a naughty glint in her eye. 'I was kept *very* well entertained. And, I don't like to jump the gun, but I suspect I will be back up here soon enough, if you don't mind.'

'Really?' Kate asked more sharply than she intended. 'Why?'

Jenny looked coy and flicked her wrist to look at her watch. 'I have to go but I'll text you all the salacious details.'

'Do you need me to drive you?' Kate was still in her clothes from yesterday. 'Do I have time to shower?'

Jenny shook her head. 'No need. All taken care of.' Kate hugged her and nestled into her shoulder.

'Safe flight. Love you.'

'Love you too, darling.' Jenny blew Kate a kiss as she left the room.

She was gone. But she said herself, she'd be back. Kate tried to be happy for her. She deserved something lovely. And James was actually quite lovely. Kate heard his Land Rover pull out of the gravel drive. She wondered if he'd carry her bag for her, if they'd have a heartfelt goodbye at the terminal, make plans for her return. She wondered if they'd kiss. Of course they would. She got out of bed and walked groggily towards the bathroom.

'So,' James said as he found Kate in the estate office that afternoon, 'I've not seen you since yesterday afternoon. Have you been playing a really elaborate game of hide-and-seek with me?'

It hurt just hearing his voice. Kate shrugged and carried on typing on her keyboard. She was having an email rally with another photographer, desperately trying to book him for tomorrow after the first had been very cagey about when he'd be free to visit. The weather was supposed to be nice and the estate looked better bathed in sunlight.

'No,' she replied. 'I've not been playing hide-and-seek with you. I've been here, working.'

'You OK?' he asked.

'Sure. Why wouldn't I be?'

'I don't know . . . I just . . .'

Kate stopped typing, her fingers hovering over the keys, waiting for him to continue, but he changed tack.

'Jenny's nice, isn't she?'

'Yes,' Kate said as her heart sank.

'I'm glad you invited her in the end.'

'Uh-huh.' She continued tapping out her email.

'I'm shattered,' he said slyly. 'I've not had much sleep these past few days.'

Kate stopped typing again and visibly stiffened.

'Jenny and I . . .' he started.

But Kate cut him off by pushing her chair out and almost ramming it into him. He sprang out of the way and gave a startled cry.

'I need coffee,' Kate said and left the office.

'Has James told you his exciting news?' Liz asked Kate over dinner the next day. James was out. Kate suspected he was mooning over Jenny's absence and had taken himself to the pub for a pie and a pint. Kate had cooked what she hoped were gourmet chicken burgers but what actually looked like anaemic rocks. Liz still nibbled at them though and Kate thanked her for her valiant effort.

'What news?' Kate said as she presented a little bowl of homemade garlic mayonnaise that didn't look too shabby.

'We have visitors coming,' Liz said triumphantly. 'A TV crew, to be specific.'

Kate paused, halfway through uncorking a bottle of white wine, and stared at Liz. 'A TV crew?' she asked.

Liz nodded and helped herself to some salad. Kate noticed she'd put her chicken burger down.

'This is great news. But how did James organise that?' Kate was a little put out that James had steamed ahead of her, booked a visiting media crew and then hadn't thought to even tell her.

'One of James's old school friends is in the area, filming a documentary about Scottish myths and legends. They're doing something at Loch Ness and James got in touch and mentioned we might have a monster. They're keen to take a look around and do some filming in the loch perhaps.'

'*In* the loch?' Kate asked.

'Apparently.' Liz nodded. 'They talked about getting hold of one of those underwater camera things.'

'Well that's . . .' She wasn't sure what it was. Was it great? They wouldn't find anything and then they might look like laughing-stocks. But then they'd never found any concrete evidence the Loch Ness Monster existed and that had never hurt the loch's tourism, and if it was about myths and legends rather than monster hunting it could actually be quite a coup to have them film here. 'This is great,' Kate decided. 'This could really put us on the map.'

'I thought you'd be pleased,' Liz said. 'They arrive tomorrow. James thought it best to get them here before our first proper guests arrive and his TV presenter friend is in the area filming anyway.'

'Tomorrow? Right, well that's . . . soon, but wonderful,' Kate said. She wondered what on earth they would find, if anything, in the water. And for a reason she couldn't pinpoint, she was suddenly apprehensive.

*

When she found James in the estate office the next morning, looking calm but busy, Kate was torn between berating him for booking a TV crew in without telling her and congratulating him for such an audacious move.

'Hi,' he greeted her as she entered the room, carrying two mugs of coffee. Kate was slowly coming to terms with the fact that James and she would be nothing more than employer and employee, and as she put his mug of coffee on top of some messy-looking paperwork, she felt newly benevolent.

'You're up bright and early,' he said as he took his coffee gratefully.

'Well, busy day. Film crew.' Kate looked at him pointedly.

'Yes, I know. Can't believe it myself.'

'Didn't think to tell me?' Kate asked.

'You're not happy?' he asked as his face fell. 'Thought you'd be over the moon. What a win!'

'You left your mum to tell me,' Kate said. 'Why didn't you tell me you were organising it?'

'Do you mind?' he asked.

'No, not really but a heads-up would have been useful.'

He sat back in his office chair and looked at her. 'Is this about the TV crew or is this about something else?'

Kate reddened. 'What do you mean?'

'You've been really strange with me since the press trip, since Jenny went home. What's going on?'

'Nothing,' Kate said as she sat in her chair and opened her laptop.

'I took a job off your hands,' he said, folding his arms across his chest and looking directly at her. 'I saw on social media that an old friend was filming a TV show in the area. I just dropped him a quick line and told him about us and about the legend of our monster and asked if he wanted to take a quick look if he had time. I wasn't expecting a reply at all, but he said he'd love to meet up, have a drink, take a look around and maybe do some filming. If he includes the footage, it'll be in the documentary on BBC early next year. Did I do something wrong? I thought this is what we wanted, as much exposure as possible. What's the problem?'

Kate sighed and then summoned a smile. 'No problem at all, honestly. I just wish you hadn't told me the night before. Or rather, I wish you'd told me when you knew about it and not left your mum to tell me the night before.'

'I'm sorry, Kate. It was all very sudden. And you've been uncommunicative for a few days and I thought you needed time to wind down after the press visits, so I just took the initiative. If you want to fight about this any further can you book in a time with me later this afternoon, because we've got bookings enquiries coming out of our ears and I need to keep an eye on this inbox.' He looked back down at his laptop screen, signalling the end of the discussion.

Liz, James and Kate stood on the front steps to greet the crew when they heard the van approach on the gravel drive. James was smiling, ready to greet his friend of old. Kate was waiting curiously and fully expecting the crew to decide they didn't want to film after all. TV could be so fickle.

When the TV crew climbed out of the van, she was surprised at how small a team they were. Only a handful of men and women accompanied James's friend. She had no idea what any of them did and let them take the lead, deciding for themselves what they wanted to look at and film.

James and his friend greeted each other warmly, wrapping their arms around each other in a bear hug, talking to each other about how long it had been. 'Five years, at least,' James said as they walked towards Kate and Liz. 'Whose wedding was it? Dan's? Can't remember,' he finished. His friend barely got a word in to reply before James sprung towards them to make introductions.

'Mum? Don't know if you remember him; and Kate, I'd like

to introduce you to my very old but very clever friend Guy Cameron.'

'Hi,' Kate said, laughing at James's overenthusiastic introduction.

'Hi,' Guy said, shaking her hand and smiling warmly. 'Nice to meet you. Hello, Liz.' He embraced James's mother. 'Remember me?'

'Of course I remember you,' Liz said, warmly. 'Always the one to take home the history cup at prize-giving each year, as I recall.'

Guy grinned, introduced his team and they waved as they pulled various bits of equipment out of their Transit van. Kate wondered what half of it was as fluffy mics on long sticks were assembled. The crew stayed put while they went inside to talk. Kate couldn't quite catch what Guy and James were saying but she saw Guy beam at a question as he replied, 'She's due any day now. I'm getting it in the neck being up here.' He laughed. 'Two days, then back home to Dorset and then I'll be a father. Can't quite believe it.'

'Enjoy the peace and quiet while it lasts then,' James replied as they sat down on the settees.

Liz went to make drinks and Kate sat and watched the two men interact. Every now and again, one of them clarified something for her about a long-lost friend or a school antic that had got one or both of them in trouble. She got particularly confused about a story involving toilet roll, a waste paper bin and a fencing mask but she didn't mind that she had no clue what they were talking about. James was animated, smiling, and Kate couldn't help but smile as she watched him. She didn't think she'd ever seen him this genuinely happy in the months she'd been here.

'So I thought,' Guy said and Kate realised she'd been miles away, 'that we'd do a bit of filming here. I'll do some general chitchat, not related to Invermoray but about legends, monsters and selkies. Invermoray's a great backdrop for that, with the loch and the house and the mountains. Then after that, we'll get the sonar out and have a play around. We've got a dinghy we use to launch it from. It's a bit small but you can come out alongside us if you've got a boat?'

James shook his head. 'Rotten, like most things in this house. Used it for firewood months ago, I'm afraid.'

Guy shook his head and laughed. 'You used a boat for firewood? Crying out loud, James. That's an absolute sin. Anyway. We'll take the sonar out and see what's what down there.'

'And what are you looking for? On the sonar?' Kate asked. 'I mean, how can you tell what's a monster and what's not?'

'Well we just thought we'd have a play around really. Some great techy scenes to punctuate me droning on and on at the camera.' He turned to Kate. 'If we find anything then wonderful, but honestly we never expect to find anything exciting. It's more for atmosphere and it'll show us a rough map of the loch-bed.'

'How much filming will you do?' Kate asked.

'We'll see how we go. If we get anything remotely interesting such as shoals of fish, it always looks good on camera so we'll play it by ear. Usually a ten-second shot with a voiceover makes good TV.'

'Ten seconds?' Kate queried. 'Is that it?'

'Probably all we'll need in the water,' Guy said kindly. 'James told me all about the house and your hopes for it, so doing a bit of filming with the house in the background will hopefully help in some small way as well. If it doesn't get edited out,' he said. 'Not up to me what goes on the cutting-room floor, I'm afraid.'

James and Kate had both inched forward, listening as Guy spoke about the stories he'd been documenting so far about monsters and legends around other lochs.

Liz appeared with drinks and Kate excused herself as the two men caught up. She went to the orangery, working her way through the tables that Angus had set up for the journalists and watching through the windows as the cameraman set up his equipment.

Guy galloped down the steps and Kate watched him join his team.

James had come to find Kate. 'This is a bit different, isn't it?' he asked with boyish excitement.

Kate nodded.

'Ever dealt with anything like this before?' he continued.

'Not like this, no. I guess we just leave them to it?' Kate said.

'The dinghy has the sonar operator, a cameraman and Guy, so it's a bit full and for boring insurance reasons Guy says we can't go on the boat. But he says we can go and watch from the shore when they start the sonar,' James said. 'It'll transmit to a screen on the dinghy and to one set up on the shore.'

'Exciting. I don't think I know what sonar images really look like,' she said.

James gestured out of the window as Guy caught their eye and waved to them to follow him. James looked down at Kate, his eyes shining. 'I guess we're about to find out.'

CHAPTER 36

1940

When Constance eventually returned to Matthew, he was deep in the forest, standing in the river and wearing nothing but a pair of trousers.

She had managed to get away as the sun was starting to set. She had barely touched her supper. Douglas was napping on the settee downstairs and her father and mother had been reading the newspaper and answering correspondence respectively. She'd said she would go for a walk and return shortly. Neither parent had so much as looked up from their tasks when she'd voiced her plans. She hadn't seen Henry all afternoon.

The sound of rushing water deafened Matthew to Constance's cry. She raised her hand in greeting from the riverbank, the afternoon sun dappling her vision every few seconds as the tall pines swayed back and forth gently. He raised his arm and waved silently to her. It didn't feel real, as if she was living a second life out in the forest. For the brief moments she could visit Matthew she felt torn between two worlds. She wasn't entirely sure what she was doing but she never wanted this to end. *Let him stay out of harm's way. Let him live,* she thought. *It's not cowardly, it's not. He's mending, healing.*

'What are you doing?' she called as he dipped his hands into the water.

'Trout tickling,' he shouted. 'Or rather, I'm trying but I'm no good. They come to me but I can't get them to stay put long enough to slow them.'

Constance laughed and then sat on the bank, removing her shoes and unpeeling her stockings. She tried to pick her way over the small rocks, smoothed by many years of exposure to the rushing water. She hitched her skirt up to avoid it getting wet.

'Oh thank God,' he said loudly. 'Save me. I don't know what I'm doing.'

'I'm not coming in,' she called back with a laugh. 'I'm going to watch as you tickle our dinner into submission.'

'They don't like me. They won't lie still, not even for a moment.'

'You don't want it to lie still, you want to entrance it,' Constance said.

'Tell me what to do,' he pleaded.

'You must wait,' she said. 'You must be patient. Let it swim into your hands, work your fingers from the tail upwards, gently. Then you must use the tips of your fingers to rub its underside. It should slow its movements.'

Matthew stood in the water, his arms lowered. 'I feel stupid,' he said with a smile.

'You will,' she said, adjusting the position of her feet on the rock as the cold water flowed over them. 'But be patient.'

They waited and Constance turned around, wondering if she'd heard a sound behind her. They were so deep in the forest that no one would be passing; the officers mostly too injured to wander this far. Given the strict security that had engulfed the Highlands over recent months, no one else should be passing.

'I've got one!' he shouted and she spun back round. 'Now what?'

'Don't shout for a start. Do as I told you, slowly, gently. Then when your fingers reach its head, grip hard and lift it from the water.'

She watched for a few seconds, smiling, holding her breath.

And then, 'You've done it!' as he lifted a still trout from the stream.

He was laughing. 'I can't believe it. I've done it. I've bloody well done it.'

'Throw it onto the riverbank,' she commanded, picking her way back to where she'd left her shoes and stockings.

The fish landed next to her and she did what the ghillie had told her to do long before he'd gone to fight, back when she was a child and had run amok on the estate. She picked the fish up and hit it against a rock. She turned back to Matthew and called for him to keep going but his face was aghast.

'You hit it,' he called.

'Yes, it's the most humane thing to do,' she replied. 'Or they die slowly, gasping for breath. It's not fair.'

She watched him shake his head in disbelief as he carried on. When they returned to the cottage a short while later, they were clutching enough trout to eat for dinner.

Constance remained bare-legged, tucking her feet under her as they lit the fire, cooking the fish skewered on bits of wood that they had soaked in water to stop them catching light over the fire. She told him about Douglas returning injured but very much alive.

'Oh, Constance, I don't believe it. I'm so happy for you. And for your brother. What an unbelievably lucky man he is.' They embraced and she could hardly keep the smile from her face.

'How utterly wonderful,' he mused as they cooked their supper. 'How is he?'

'In good spirits, I think,' she said. 'But he needs to recover. His arm's broken and his skin is burnt on his torso from the fire so he won't be allowed to fly for a while.'

'I can't imagine crashing while being on fire. Awful. Now he can rest, recuperate.'

They each held a stick and picked flecks of cooked fish off, eating with their hands.

'You're a puzzle to me,' he said between mouthfuls.

'Am I?' she said, confused. 'Why?'

'You're the bravest girl I've ever met. You swim out to save me, you know how to tickle trout. I've never met a girl like you.'

'I shall take that as a compliment,' she replied as she picked another flake of fish from the stick and ate it, the crisped skin crunching as she chewed.

'Do.' He grinned at her before planting a kiss on her mouth. 'How is Henry behaving?' he asked, his expression changing. 'I do worry about you, you know. I feel so helpless here. I don't know what I'd do if he did anything to you.'

'You don't have to worry about Henry,' she said, not wanting him to be anxious. 'He's harmless, I think, deep down.' Although as she said the words she wasn't sure she entirely meant them.

'I hope you're right,' Matthew replied.

They were silent while they finished eating, listening to the sound of the fire and the wind as it started up in the pines outside and whistled around the thin windowpanes.

'Take my pullover when you go back,' he said. 'You'll be cold in that thin blouse.'

'I don't want to go,' she said. 'I want to stay here, with you, forever.'

He smiled ruefully and the two of them nestled in to each other. 'If only that were possible,' he said.

'Hello, Squidge,' Douglas said sleepily as Constance entered his room the following afternoon with a cup of tea and his freshly laundered uniform. He attempted to sit up in bed but with one of his arms bound up in a sling he was finding it trying.

'Here, let me help,' Constance said, putting the tea on his dressing table and placing the pile of clothes on the end of his bed. She helped him sit up then plumped his pillows for him.

He laughed. 'Not you too?'

'What do you mean?'

'Fussing. Has Mother sent you up to check on me? This is the third cup of tea in as many hours.'

'Is it? No, I came of my own volition. But Mrs Campbell had cleaned and aired your clothes and so I thought I'd lend a hand and see if you needed nursing back to life with a cup of tea.'

Douglas looked at his watch. 'I'd much prefer a brandy.'

'Well, you can't. I've brought tea and I'm not going back downstairs yet,' she said with a smile.

'Some nurse you are,' Douglas said and took the teacup and saucer from her. They sat in amiable silence as Douglas sipped his drink and then rested his head against the pillows.

'What was it like?' she asked. 'Falling from the sky?'

He shrugged. 'They tell you what to expect. And it all sounds jolly straightforward, especially when you practise how to pull your 'chute. And then it happens and you have to overcome the shock of being hit and realising that no, it's not going to be all right and that you can't get the plane down. Then comes the blind panic and the sense of relief at getting out alive and remembering your training all in the blink of an eye. And really, it's awful. An experience not to be repeated, one hopes. But it will probably happen again. At least now I know what to expect. Others aren't lucky enough to get a second run at it. I've seen so many shot down and afterwards we've gone into the mess, drunk like idiots and sung songs in their honour, scrubbed their names from the chalkboard when they don't return. Not really understanding, not really *wanting* to understand or to think about it for more than a few minutes soberly. Then we move on, or at least we try to. I nearly became one of those whose name gets wiped off the board, who has songs sung drunkenly for a few hours in their name and then . . . nothing. Absolutely nothing. Gone. Forgotten.' He took a deep breath. 'While I sat in that little croft with . . . her, I realised I've done nothing. I've been nothing. I've made no impact.'

'Oh, Douglas, of course you have—'

'Not really, Smidge.'

'Are you frightened, to go back inside a plane, I mean?'

He thought about it. 'No, I don't think so. I wonder if it's a bit like falling off a horse. If I just need to get back inside a cockpit and hope for the best.'

They sat for a while and Douglas sipped his tea.

'Henry said he watched your plane go down in a ball of flames. I can't imagine anything more horrifying,' Constance said.

He looked at her and gave a wry smile. 'Not as horrifying as it could have been,' he said sombrely. 'I lived, after all. Thanks to her, mostly.'

'What was she like?' Constance asked.

'Lovely,' he said simply.

'Do you think you'll go and see her, when you're better? Or after the war is over?'

'How can I? She's married. I may write a letter to thank her and then I'll leave it at that. Even then I wonder if it will do more harm than good.'

'But you love her?' Constance probed. She was so desperate to tell him about Matthew; so desperate to tell him how much she was in love, the secret threatened to burst from within her. But she mustn't.

Douglas nodded. 'Yes, I think I do love her. How perceptive of you. I didn't realise it until I was too far gone. But it was clear she only had eyes for her husband and missed him terribly. She showed me a picture of him all kitted out in his uniform. He's gone off to sea, surprising given he's a farmer and could have chosen to stay here in a reserved occupation. Noble sod went and enlisted. Good-looking chap too. Sounded decent. I hated him immediately obviously. Only there a few days but she was the most wonderful woman I've ever met. Kind, humble, caring, interesting. And she was beautiful, a natural beauty. And that smile. I just . . .' He rested his head against the headboard and stared up disconsolately at the ceiling. 'Oh, Constance. Never fall in love with someone you're not supposed to. It causes all kinds of problems.'

'Yes, it does,' she said quietly.

It was dark when Constance arrived at the cottage that evening. Matthew was heating a pan of water by the fire when she returned with fresh supplies. He had taken off his shirt, thrown it over the back of a kitchen chair and was examining a blade. He looked up when she entered and smiled.

'Mother and Father are fussing over Douglas and I've managed to sneak away sooner than I thought.' She walked towards him and allowed him to envelop her in his arms. 'I'm so happy,' she said as she closed her eyes and nestled against his chest.

Matthew kissed the top of her head. 'So am I,' he said. Unspoken between them lay the fact that this could only ever be temporary.

'What are you doing?' she asked.

'Attempting to have another shave. I've only been doing it every few days and I haven't managed to find a mirror. So far I've made such a hash job of it.'

Constance reached up and felt the stubble forming over his chin. 'It makes you look as if you belong here, in the woodland. I quite like it.'

'I don't,' he said, kissing her hair again and moving to reach for the pan of hot water. 'It's time for it to go. Watch as I lacerate myself?' he teased.

'I'll do it,' Constance offered, 'if you like?'

They sat at the kitchen table, the pan of water and a cake of soap that Constance had brought in the supplies earlier in the week between them. She watched as he soaped his face and rinsed his hands in the pan of water.

He looked at her with mock panic and then moved back slightly. 'Ever done this before?' he asked.

She shook her head. 'How hard can it be?'

He grabbed her wrist as she moved towards his face with the blade. 'Now hang on a second.' He laughed. 'There's a method to this.'

She rolled her eyes. 'Oh, I've watched Father and Douglas do this over the years. Up, down, up, down, yes?'

'No,' he said in horror. 'It's just one direction. Just down. I'm regretting this now,' he mumbled, letting go of her wrist.

'Oh be quiet,' she said as they inched their wooden chairs closer towards each other. Her legs were in between his as she leant in.

'And slowly,' he said, retreating a little.

'Good God, man, do you want this done or not?' Constance asked in exasperation.

He mumbled something she didn't catch but the twinkle in his eye told her he was enjoying this. She started shaving him gently and slowly his breathing regulated. Constance felt a sense of calm and closeness with him and every time she caught his eye he smiled before he resumed a serious expression and allowed her to continue.

'Stop it,' she teased, 'you're putting me off.'

'I'm doing nothing of the kind,' he said and then closed his mouth as she leant in to shave the final few patches of stubble. He put his hands on her legs and slowly, gently, traced a finger on her thighs, running it up and down over her stockings. She batted his hands away and laughed as she attempted to finish. 'Do you want scars all over your face? If so, carry on doing that.'

'I can wait a few minutes,' he said, desire flickering in his eyes.

'There.' She leaned back to admire her handiwork as he reached for the towel and wiped the remaining soap from his face. He ran his hand over his jawline. 'Smooth. Does it look it?'

'Yes, a rather fine job even if I do say so myself,' Constance boasted. She sat back against the hard wooden chair, her legs still in between his. He folded the towel and placed it on the table and looked at her, his face completely still.

She swallowed and her breathing, which had been so controlled while she shaved him, was now picking up pace. He leaned forward and kissed her, gently and tenderly. They were at an awkward angle on the hard chairs and Constance felt his arms around her, picking her up. She laughed with delight, hooking her legs around his waist as they moved towards the fireplace. He laid her on the floor and she pulled him on top of her, reluctant for his lips to leave hers. He lifted himself up and looked at her, drinking her in. Slowly he ran his hands along her stockinged leg, his fingers finding the clasp high up by her thigh. She heard the snap as the clasp released and he started to peel the nylon from one leg before doing the same to the next.

Frenziedly she sat up, fumbling with his trousers as he kicked them loose. As he made love to her in front of the fire she thought of how difficult they would find the rest of the war, when the inevitable happened and he was gone; she wondered if she'd ever see him again after all of this, if he'd ever be able to make his presence known to her after the war was over. She thought of how much she loved him; she thought of that fateful night she had watched him crash in the loch, and then as he whispered to her how much he loved her, she stopped thinking entirely.

Later, when they had both dressed he placed another log on the fire, looking pensive. Constance was immersed in the contentment that loving Matthew and being loved in return brought her. But at the very peripheries was the shadow of war that loomed large. The war had not affected her very much so far, even with the house having been turned into an officers' hospital. Douglas had returned alive and so the grasping fingers of Hitler had not brought lasting despair in their clutches. Not to her. Not yet, at least.

Matthew sat behind her, as she nestled against him, feeling his warmth through his shirt and through hers. Behind her, she felt his body shake very gently and she spun around to look at him.

'What's wrong?' she asked as she scrambled into a better position once she had realised he was wiping tears from his eyes.

'I'm sorry,' he said. 'Not very manly is it, sitting here like this . . .' He didn't finish his sentence with the word 'crying', but that's exactly what he was doing.

She held his hands as she knelt in front of him, her eyes searching his. 'What's wrong?' she asked again. 'Tell me, please.'

'Oh God, Constance,' he said. 'If I tell you, I don't think you'll ever want to see me again. It will change how you look at me and, even if I'm not picked up, then all of this ends anyway.'

She waited and then when he didn't speak she asked, 'Why does this end?' Tears filled her eyes as cold dread ran through her.

'Don't you cry,' he said gently, turning to look into her eyes. 'Please don't cry. I love you, you know and . . . oh God, this war,' he said, putting his head in his hands. 'It forces us to do things we don't want to do. To be things we don't want to be, to fight when we don't want to fight, when we don't believe we should.' He looked at her. 'I'm frightened and I'm a coward. Isn't that enough?'

'Giving up is your mind's way of protecting you,' she said soothingly. 'It's not normal to show no fear at all, I'm sure.'

'I was forced, you know, to join up,' he said darkly. 'I'd been in the Air Cadets at Cambridge.' He went quiet and looked towards the fire.

'And so you joined the Air Force,' she prompted.

'Yes. Had to, really. Had to do something. Didn't want to be a foot soldier. I enjoyed flying. I knew how. I knew I was good at it. I suppose it's cowardly really, being a fighter pilot. Long-range killing, never having to look your enemy in the eye, shielded as you are in the cockpit. And if I'm honest, I thought it was all rather good fun at first. Couldn't wait to get in a plane each day. Didn't really think of the repercussions, didn't think about what I was fighting for. Didn't really think I was fighting for anything.

It didn't apply to me. I was just doing my duty, and actually, for a while having a jolly good time to boot. But then I started shooting men out of the sky. I was good at it. Pinpoint precision. And down they fell, one by one by one. Funny, really,' he said, looking at her briefly before glancing back to the fire. 'I didn't think of them as men. I thought of them as planes. I was just shooting planes down. I mean, I knew there were men inside of course, but they were no one, faceless, not real. None of them had stories, wives, mothers, children.' He threw a piece of kindling into the fire and they watched it catch.

She held his hand. 'It's all right,' she said. 'You had to do terrible things in order to stop Hitler from doing even more terrible things.'

He paused before speaking and then replied, 'None of it's all right. I shouldn't be here. You shouldn't be here. I've asked the worst thing of you. I've asked you to help me and—'

'And I've fallen in love with you,' she said.

'Don't you think there's a part of me that hates it? That I've done that to you?'

'You haven't done anything to me,' she said desperately. 'Don't you think I know my own mind? I want to be with you, now, here and then afterwards.'

'Constance,' he said in a pained voice. 'There won't be an afterwards.'

'What do you mean?' she said, panicked.

'I'm going to prison for a very, very long time. By the time this war's over, if it ever ends, if I ever get out of prison, you'll have fallen in love with someone better than me, someone more deserving of you—'

'Don't say that,' she interrupted. 'You can't tell me you love me and then dismiss me.'

'I'm not dismissing you, Constance. But I know I need to let you go. If not today, then tomorrow, or the next day. But this can't go on. I can't hide forever. I can't run either. I've been thinking about this and I can't imagine what will happen to me when I hand myself in, but I know I need to do it. I'm not sure it will cleanse me of what I've done – the men I've shot down. But to begin making amends for it all, I must start somewhere.'

Constance felt a tide of devastation smother her. 'You're giving up? You're going to hand yourself in?'

He had tears in his eyes and Constance leant forward and brushed them away. Was love supposed to bring such equal measures of happiness and pain?

'I don't want to lose you but if you wanted to hand yourself in, if you felt ready, I'll come with you. We'll do it together.'

'No,' he said emphatically. 'You can't be anywhere near me when it happens. You can't even be seen with me.'

'Why?'

Matthew started to speak but was cut off by a sound outside. The two turned around and stared in horror as the cottage door flew open and Henry stepped inside.

CHAPTER 37

2020

'OK, are we ready for this?' Guy said on his walkie-talkie from the dinghy. 'Let's see what's down there.'

At the shore, the production team looked faintly bored, as if they'd done this a few times during the course of filming and had had enough of standing at the edges of lochs looking for imaginary monsters. Huddled round a laptop screen that had been set up on a small trestle table, Liz, James and Kate vied for space to watch. The screen was dark for a few moments, nothing out of the ordinary, and Kate's gaze drifted towards Guy Cameron. He was talking animatedly to the cameraman as the small orange dinghy sat still on the calm loch. Kate shivered. The season was changing around them, the greens of the scenery slowly shifting to a burnt orange and she wondered how she'd missed the arrival of autumn.

As the robot was lowered into the loch and the technician steered it into the water, Kate had expected a blipping noise, as if it was sonar on a submarine. But the director, Martin, explained it was a different system. No one expected anything to appear so soon and they couldn't hear what Guy was saying to the camera, but Martin was listening to Guy through a headset and every now and again, he'd send him a quick message via walkie-talkie that made very little sense to Kate.

She looked around, a little bored, wondering what she needed to do for the guests from Canada who were arriving in a couple of days. Kate disappeared into a mental checklist involving ordering a lovely welcome pack full of local supplies and milk. Angus was going to make them a pie and provide some greens for their first night welcome meal and all they had to do was warm it when they arrived.

'What the hell was that?' James grabbed Kate's arm and she jumped and looked at the sonar screen.

'What?' she asked.

'How did you miss that?' he said in horror. 'It was huge.'

'What was? What was?' she asked desperately.

'I don't know. What was that?' James turned to the director who was already communicating with Guy to go back round.

'We saw it,' his disjointed voice replied over the walkie-talkie.

'Oh my God,' said Liz. 'It was massive.'

Kate looked at both of their shocked faces. What had they just seen?

'It was still,' she heard Guy say. 'It wasn't moving.'

'What do you mean?' James said to Guy and then, realising Guy couldn't hear him, he turned to Martin and asked quickly, 'What does he mean?'

The man shrugged. 'Let's find out.'

'James, are you sure you've never lost a boat down there?' Guy asked over the radio.

James shook his head and Martin told Guy as much.

The robot had turned, making its way back to the object in the water, where it appeared as an oddly shaped, blackish blob on screen.

There was silence. James slowly took hold of Kate's hand, the intense silence unnerving both of them. Kate wasn't sure if James even realised what he was doing. Liz gave them both a quick glance and then resumed looking at the screen.

'It really isn't moving,' they heard Guy say.

'We know,' James said impatiently and then turned to Martin. 'Tell him we know. Ask him what it means.'

The director looked faintly offended at James barking orders at him, but did as he was told.

'I'm not sure. The technician's not sure either. It's such a strange shape,' Guy said. 'We're going to watch it for a while and then maybe we'll move on and scan the rest of the loch.'

'No, don't do that,' James almost shouted. 'Stay with it. What if it moves and you miss it?'

Martin gave James a pointed look and James fell silent, his hand still around Kate's. Twenty minutes later, the dinghy returned to the shore and Guy made his way over.

'Well that was very interesting,' he said, rubbing his hands together.

'Now what?' James asked Guy. James looked down and finally noticing he was holding Kate's hand, let go and mumbled, 'Sorry.'

'It's OK,' Kate said, feeling oddly bereft as his warm hand left hers.

'I'm not sure. One second.' Guy walked over to his director and they talked between themselves, gesturing to the loch and then their watches every now and again.

'OK, we've got a plan,' Guy said. 'We're scheduled to film at Eilean Donan Castle tomorrow. But we can carve out an hour or two the day after that and come back.'

'Come back and do what?' Kate asked.

'We've hired an underwater robotic camera and an operator for the day. We've a couple of other things to film that day but if you don't mind, we'll come back and send it under.'

'Wow,' Liz muttered.

'I know.' Guy gave them all an encouraging look. 'Then we'll be able to see exactly what that is.'

Kate sat on the jetty, looking back at the house as the sun began its descent behind the mountains. She'd brought a mug of coffee out with her, wrapping her fingers around it for warmth, but by the time she'd reached the jetty her drink was practically cold. She sipped it regardless and took her shoes and socks off, dangling her legs over the side, although the chill water was far below her feet.

She smiled as she saw James heading towards her, clutching a bottle of wine and two glasses. He raised the bottle in greeting as he worked his way around the shoreline and she shuffled up to make room next to her.

He sat down and handed her a glass before twisting the cap off the wine bottle and pouring. 'It's just a cheap and cheerful Pinot from the supermarket.'

Kate put her mug down on the wood behind her. She was grateful the wine was white and not red. She still didn't think she could drink red after that night in the cottage.

They both sipped their wine and stared across the water towards the house. Neither of them really knew what to say and the silence was comfortable as the water lapped around the wooden jetty posts.

'What did you think when you saw that image on the sonar?' Kate asked after a while.

James shrugged. 'I've been thinking about it since Guy and his team left. And I just . . . well . . . I don't know what to think.' He sipped his wine.

'Me neither,' she said, truthfully. After Guy left, Kate hadn't had a chance to speak to either Liz or James about it, although she was sure they'd been talking non-stop amongst themselves all afternoon. Kate had been in the cottage, preparing it for their first guests and placing the order for the welcome hamper with Morven at the pub.

'There's a big part of me that's actually quite worried,' James revealed.

'Worried? Why?'

'Don't laugh at me. But what if we're responsible for disturbing something that's been down there for hundreds of years? I wasn't expecting them to find anything, but seeing that . . . thing . . . on the monitor? There's actually something down there. And now I feel like this might have got a bit out of hand.'

Kate blew air out of her cheeks. He had a point, however ludicrous it all sounded.

'It won't be a monster,' Kate said, somewhat half-heartedly.

James nodded but looked unconvinced. 'Angus, Jenny and I did the Loch Ness boat tour. The chap who ran it said that the loch was so deep it was entirely feasible that there were things down there that would never be found. That if there was a monster, it would have to have bred to have existed for so long. They reckon they'd found at least three things on the sonar that were larger than a great white shark,' James said. 'I mean, our loch's not that deep, so it might all be entirely different here but . . .' His sentence remained half finished.

'What's your point?' Kate asked gently.

'This chap runs boat tours "in search" of the monster,' James said. 'But he said that whatever is down there, there's more than one and in his heart he prayed to God no one ever really found them. They deserved to be left alone. I think he had a point.'

He ran his hand over his jaw. 'I've never been responsible for anyone other than myself,' he confessed. 'I mean, outside the realms of a work environment. I've been so angry with Mum without realising it, for hiring you behind my back. And angry with you for being here, although I knew it wasn't your fault. But Mum told me today that she never wanted me to have to save the house, especially not by myself. After Dad died she wanted me here, as much for me as for her.' He frowned. 'I strongly suspect she wanted me away from my ex as well now I think about it. Anyway, it's taken me my entire adult life to care about this house, to want to keep it standing for future generations. This house, this loch, I feel as if I've got some kind of responsibility now when this time last year, even six months ago, I couldn't really have cared less. And so, as mad as it sounds, if we don't protect whatever's down there, who will?'

Kate thought as they sipped their wine and she stared up at the mountains, where the dark rocks loomed large. She was softening towards James, or rather, she already had softened towards him; she just hadn't felt it creep up on her. Jenny was a lucky girl.

'Guy seems like a good man,' Kate said eventually. 'What if we ask him, if we see something on the camera, not to tell anyone?'

'Are you mad? The man works in TV. This'll be the find of his life. We'd be asking him to keep the secret of the century. Not to mention all his crew. I think it's too late,' James said. 'He's booked this camera and the operator and he's rearranged his schedule to film here. I can't just tell him to forget about it now, can I?'

'It's bad form,' she said, putting her PR hat on for a moment. 'But, James, if you don't want to . . .'

James sighed. 'Let's just hope whatever that thing was in the loch, that it's decided to make itself scarce before the camera goes down.'

Kate could see he was uncomfortable with the idea. They sat for a while longer, discussing the house and investigating licences to host weddings. She and James made plans to pretend to be newly engaged and to do some reconnaissance to find out how other estates were pricing their wedding packages; what kind of extras they laid on top. They jokingly made plans to design their own individual dream weddings and find out how much it would cost.

James laughed at this. 'I'm a man. I don't have a dream wedding.'

'But surely you have some idea of how you'd like to be married?'

'Well . . .' He looked sheepish and Kate was instantly curious. When he spoke it was slower, thoughtful. 'I guess it's a feeling more than anything. I want that feeling of being in love and of being loved, knowing that we're two people who are completely right for each other; that the moment is right. I don't think it matters where we are.' He shifted uncomfortably as if he'd just let her inside his soul and was instantly regretting it.

It was such a beautifully succinct way of putting it. 'That's lovely,' she said quietly.

'Do you have a dream wedding?' he asked, looking at her.

'Not really,' she said thoughtfully. What could she say now that wouldn't sound shallow after that? 'I mean, maybe. Don't most women have a vague idea of how they'd like to be married?'

'Tell me,' he said, topping up their wine glasses.

She thought and said jokingly, 'I suppose somewhere like this isn't too shabby. But not inside the house. And not in a marquee either. I've never really seen the point of hiring a beautiful house and then confining everyone to a marquee.'

'So not inside the house and not outside the house, little Miss Picky. Where then?'

She looked around the loch. 'Here, actually. Here's perfect. If we could offer guests the option to marry at the shore, or on this jetty, as well as inside the house, I bet we'd make a killing.'

'Is that what *you'd* like?' he asked softly.

'For you to make a fortune? Definitely. That's why I'm here,' Kate said, purposefully evading his question.

He looked at her through narrowed eyes as if he wasn't sure of what to make of her deliberately evasive answer.

Kate suddenly felt nervous. 'I don't think it's going to happen for me,' she said more honestly.

'Christ, why ever not?'

How was she ever going to meet a man and settle down if she was focused on re-establishing her career and quite possibly jumping nomadically from one location to the next at least for the foreseeable future? 'Because, Mr Nosy, it hasn't so far,' she said, reverting far too easily to being deflective.

'You haven't found the right man,' he said, holding her gaze. It wasn't a question.

He leaned towards her and she held her breath before retreating a little. Why was he trying to kiss her after he'd been with Jenny? But he wasn't. James simply grabbed her coffee mug and sat up straight, looking faintly awkward. It was too much for Kate and she looked away.

'Kate—' James started, but was cut off by the sound of Kate's mobile ringing in her pocket.

'It's Jenny,' Kate said, pulling it out and swiping to answer. The signal, as always, was hazy but Kate could hear that it wasn't Jenny at the other end of the phone but Jenny's mum, Christina.

'Hi, how are you?' Kate asked, knowing immediately that something was wrong. Why else would Jenny's mum ring Kate from her daughter's phone? 'What's wrong—?'

Christina cut her off.

'No,' Kate said as she listened. '*No.* When?'

Next to Kate, James mouthed, 'What's happened?'

Jenny had been hit by a car while out on a Boris Bike. Tears coursed down Kate's face. Her lovely friend was fighting for her life in a London hospital.

'I'm coming down,' Kate said, scrambling to her feet. 'I can be there tonight.'

Kate ran from the jetty, still cradling the phone against her ear. Behind her she could hear James's feet thudding on the shingle and pebbles that surrounded the loch as he ran to catch up with her.

Kate wasn't sure if Jenny's mum had rung because she wanted Kate to travel back to be with Jenny, or because she knew Kate would want to know something awful had happened to her best friend. Kate realised in that moment that she'd been a terrible friend. She didn't know what had happened between Jenny and James, but she knew that she had to find it in her heart to be happy for them if Jenny made it through this. As Kate remembered James, she stopped running. If he liked Jenny then he had to know. 'Jenny's been hit by a car,' she told him.

'Shit,' James said, looking horrified.

'I need to go to her,' she said. 'Can I go?' He was her employer after all but she prayed he would let her take impromptu time off. And if he didn't, she was going anyway.

'Yes, of course,' he said immediately. 'I'll drive you to the airport. Where's your passport?'

Kate raced to her room, stuffed clothes into an overnight bag and hurriedly grabbed her passport before meeting James outside where he was already in his car and ready to go. They bounded along the winding roads, passing mountains and ruined castles in James's Land Rover, but she took in none of the dramatic scenery. Kate was blind to the lush green grass and the deep purples of the heather and the winding rivers as the evening sun cast its long shadows, dipping behind the mountain. She could only think of Jenny.

At Inverness airport James took charge, booking her flight for her and making sure she was all right, which she wasn't – not really.

They moved through the painfully slow rigmarole of air travel in relative silence. Kate was so wrapped up in her worry she didn't notice that instead of saying goodbye, James came through passport control with her and sat at the gate. She wished she wasn't so far away from home, although now she had no idea where home really was. She felt stranded, halfway between the life she knew and the life she'd very nearly carved for herself.

It was only as the flight to Gatwick showed *boarding* on the screen that Kate glanced at James. He was holding a small overnight bag and looked as worried as her.

Kate did a double take. 'Are you coming with me?'

'Of course I am.'

'To London. To see Jenny?' Kate was dumbfounded.

'Yes.'

'Do you have your passport?' she asked stupidly.

'How do you think I got through security?'

'Oh,' Kate said, unsure quite what to make of this. He was coming to see Jenny. He liked her. He *really* liked her.

'That's lovely,' Kate said, although every single part of her wanted to cry. She roused strength from out of nowhere and boarded the plane.

At a time when Kate had completely fallen apart, James was magnificent. He steered them both through passport control at Gatwick, and he'd booked a taxi to pick them up. Kate was surprised to see a suited driver clutching a placard with *James Langley* written in bold letters.

The driver took them both to St Thomas's Hospital in Westminster. They got out into a road brightly lit by London streetlamps and the glare from the hospital windows. Kate had grown so used to the lack of light pollution in the Highlands that London at night seemed far too dazzling now. How quickly she had forgotten. She took a deep breath.

'Jenny will be fine,' James said, taking her hand and giving it a squeeze as they walked through the doors. 'I'm sure she'll be fine.'

Kate wasn't sure who he was trying to convince.

James stepped forward to the information desk and asked about Jenny's location, turning to prompt Kate to supply Jenny's surname.

Jenny had been moved from A & E and was now in the acute medical ward. They moved at speed through the hospital's clinical surroundings until they found the ward and the nurse in charge informed them that Jenny was already accompanied by two visitors and that they'd have to wait.

Finally, Kate came into her own. 'But we've just flown down from Inverness. I'm her best friend,' she said. 'And this is her . . . boyfriend. Please,' Kate pleaded. 'Is her mum one of the two? If so, can you fetch her for me?'

'Yes. But visiting hours are coming to an end soon . . .' the nurse said, petering off, clearly sensing it wasn't worth the fight. 'I'll go get her mum for you.'

James's hand was still wrapped around Kate's. Feeling disloyal to Jenny, she slowly took her hand away.

Jenny's mum, Christina, a small woman with a mass of curly hair and the same bouncy attitude as her daughter came out to them. 'Oh, Kate, you came all this way.'

'Is she awake?' James asked. 'Is she all right?'

'She's been in and out of sleep all afternoon but the doctors think that's the fault of the painkillers rather than anything *too* serious. She hasn't bumped her head, thankfully. And with a few days' rest, they think she should be right as rain. She's been very lucky. She's very shaken and has a lot of bumps and scratches and she's broken her leg in two places. She's waiting for her cast.'

Kate was so relieved she cried.

James put his hand on her shoulder and gave it a slight squeeze. 'Can we see her?' he asked.

Christina nodded. 'Only two visitors at a time I'm afraid and there's already two of us in there so I'll stop out here for a bit and one of you can pop in. Last bed on the right.'

'Kate, you go,' James said. 'I'll wait here.'

'Who are you by the way?' Christina asked James.

As Kate moved into the ward she heard James introduce himself and Christina reply warmly, 'Oh yes, she's mentioned you.'

Kate buried the feeling of remorse that Jenny and James had been thrown together and instead she focused on the deep gratitude that beautiful, funny, clever Jenny, her wonderful friend, was going to be all right.

Jenny was dozing against her pillow, her skin paler than Kate had ever seen it. Her hair was clipped up on top of her head in a messy bun. She looked gorgeous even through all of that. With James having travelled all this way to see Jenny, Kate knew at some point she'd have to nip out of the ward for a few minutes to let him in, but for now she sat in one of the two plastic chairs next to Jenny's bed. A blue curtain hid them from the ward.

Jenny groaned and opened her eyes briefly. 'Oh, Kate,' she said groggily. 'You came.'

Kate leaned forward and held Jenny's hand that was lying limply on the blanket. 'Of course I came,' Kate said with tears in her eyes. 'I was so worried. When your mum said you'd been hit by a car . . . Jenny, I thought you might die.'

'Drama queen,' Jenny said softly and then closed her eyes again, but she wasn't sleeping.

'I'm so glad you're OK.' Kate clutched her hand.

'Me too,' Jenny said and licked her lips, casting her gaze around for a cup of water. Kate took it from the little tray next to her bed and held it out to her and Jenny sipped through the paper straw.

'Are you in a lot of pain?' Kate asked.

'A bit,' she said and laid her head back on the pillow. 'Even with all the painkillers.' It took a few seconds before she could speak again. 'But there's nothing quite like seeing a lovely man to take the edge off the pain.' She glanced over Kate's shoulder and Kate turned, expecting to see James.

'Angus!' Kate cried.

'Hey, Kate.' He gave her a slow smile. 'How're ya?'

'I'm fine.' Kate looked back at Jenny in confusion.

'I know,' Jenny said as a blush crept up her pale skin.

'But . . . ?' Kate could barely speak.

Angus saved Jenny from exerting herself by explaining. 'I really like your friend.'

Jenny smiled and it was Angus's turn to blush, his face turning the same red colour as his hair for just a moment.

'What are you doing here? How did you get here so fast?' Kate asked.

'I was already here,' he said. 'I flew down a few hours after Jenny left Invermoray.'

'No,' Kate said slowly. 'You didn't.'

'I did. Impetuous, wasn't it?' he said with a shy glance at Jenny. 'Jenny and I hit it off in the pub, celebrating. I said I'd never been to London and she invited me to come back wi' her. We've become . . . um . . .' Angus looked at Jenny for help.

'We're seeing each other,' Jenny said, equally shyly.

Kate was wide-eyed. 'That's marvellous.'

'It is, isn't it?' Jenny smiled, even though her eyes were now closed.

'But – James?' Kate questioned.

Jenny's eyes remained closed. 'What about him?'

Kate didn't dare say anything in front of Angus about Jenny and James disappearing inside James's bedroom; about Jenny not returning to Kate's room to sleep until the early hours of the morning.

'He's here,' is all Kate could think to say that sounded suitable.

'Is he?' Angus said. 'He came wi' ye. Tha's lovely. Is he out there? I'll go out and say hi.'

Kate nodded and then panicked for both men. She was sure it was all about to get very awkward in the corridor with two men vying for Jenny's affection. Angus moved forward and dipped his head to give Jenny a kiss on the mouth. Jenny reached up with some effort and touched his face, before she dropped her arm back on the blanket and Angus disappeared around the curtain.

Kate spoke quickly before anyone returned to hear them. 'What do I do about James?'

'What do you mean?' Jenny looked confused.

'He came here for you,' Kate said.

'What?'

'He travelled down here to see you.'

'Why would he do that?' Jenny had a look of total confusion on her face.

'Because he likes you.'

Jenny shook her head. 'No. He likes you.'

It was Kate's turn to ask a clipped, 'What? But you were in his room? Did you sleep together?' She asked the question she really hadn't wanted to know the answer to. But she needed to know right now.

'No! Of course not. We were in his room because we were getting a bit pissed and he's quite good fun when he takes that stick out of his backside. James and I had a couple of nightcaps and I snuggled up with his dog. We chatted and I swear, all he wanted to do was talk about you.'

Kate's mouth dropped open and she simply said, 'What?' again.

'I indulged him,' Jenny said and adjusted herself on the pillow, her face contorted into a grimace for a few seconds.

'Don't speak,' Kate encouraged. 'Just rest.'

'No,' Jenny said and continued, 'it's fine. He asked all sorts of questions when he finally got me on my own, questions I don't think he could ask in front of Angus and Liz for fear of them catching on; questions I don't think he'd have asked if he'd been sober. We'd had quite a bit to drink and so I'm not sure he was as subtle as he thought.'

'Questions? What questions?' Kate asked.

'The usual. When was your last relationship, what kind of man did you usually go for, where did you see yourself settling down eventually. It was sweet, really but then it got a bit boring. I mean, I love you but once I'd established the man was totally head over heels for you I did rather wonder why he wasn't asking you these things himself. I was trying to grill him about Angus and he wasn't having any of it. Then I tried to steer him onto another subject by picking up the book on his bedside table, some thriller. I told him what I was reading and he said, "*Oh Kate's just read that one.*" And before you know it, we were back onto you again.'

Kate let out the breath she'd been holding. She smiled.

'I knew it,' Jenny said. She looked thoroughly exhausted from Kate's fast line of questioning. 'That look on your face says everything. You like him.' It wasn't a question.

Kate groaned and put her head in her hands.

'Why did you tell me that you didn't?' Jenny enquired.

'I was worried. We work together,' Kate said from behind her hands.

'So?' Jenny asked, a look of confusion on her face when Kate looked up at her.

'Oh, Jenny, I left my job at the agency under a cloud because there was all that mess with the bar client. It wasn't even my fault. I hadn't even registered what he was doing until it was far too late and his hands were on me but I learned there and then that getting involved with your boss is just far too dangerous. As much as I want to, if I got involved with James . . . oh God, it's just too unthinkable.'

'You're right,' Jenny deadpanned as she sat back and closed her eyes. 'You should just die alone.'

'Having a relationship with my boss . . . it's inappropriate,' Kate said.

'Kate, I don't think he cares about that.'

'What do you mean?' she asked.

'I didn't know how you felt about him,' Jenny said, opening her eyes again, 'or else I'd never have told him.'

'Told him what?' Kate asked darkly but she was sure she knew what Jenny was about to say.

'He asked whether you were happy in Scotland and I said he should ask you himself. But he also asked about how this job compared to your last one and I think I said something like "*no gross clients trying to grope her in a back alley*," or something to that effect and then when he looked confused I told him what had happened to you.'

'For Christ's sake, Jenny!' Kate didn't mean to be so loud.

'He was outraged for you,' Jenny clarified. 'I told him it wasn't your fault; that you'd done nothing to encourage this idiot and he agreed. He said something very feminist about how easily a sex-starved man can ruin a woman's career.'

Kate instantly began overanalysing. What did he mean by that? Did he mean him and that night in the cottage? Or did he really mean her bar client? What did he mean about career-ending? Was she about to be sacked? She wasn't normally plagued with insecurity but now she was panicked. Was James now even further away from her than she'd thought he was? Her head swam.

Jenny looked stricken as James appeared around the curtain.

He gave Jenny a warm smile and put his hand on Kate's shoulder. Kate flinched. 'Just seen Angus,' James said, shaking his head. 'You sly devils. I didn't see that coming. You all right, Jenny?' he asked her.

Jenny looked from Kate to James and nodded meekly before giving Kate an apologetic look.

James and Kate stayed in a budget chain hotel fairly near the hospital and as it was far too late for dinner by the time they turned in, they said goodnight and went their separate ways. Kate was awake all night, tossing and turning, wondering about James, marvelling about Jenny and Angus. Angus had felt horribly guilty. While going out on the Boris Bikes had been Jenny's idea it was only so she could show Angus the key London landmarks. And then she'd been hit by a car and had, unbelievably, lived to tell the tale. Kate was so utterly grateful all round but still she couldn't sleep. Jenny had told James why Kate had left her last job. What if James secretly thought Kate had encouraged her last client? What if he thought she went around making a habit of inappropriate behaviour with all her male bosses? That night in the cottage . . . Kate could have screamed.

Kate went to see Jenny at home the next afternoon. She'd been discharged and Angus was staying with her in her flat. He seemed happy to run around fetching and carrying for Jenny. She wasn't able to move much and her leg was now in a thick cast. He made them all tea and had baked a batch of shortbread biscuits. The way he smiled at Jenny, the first flushes of something, perhaps love, shone from them. Kate couldn't have been happier for them.

James and Kate boarded the plane that night and fell asleep the moment their heads hit the orange easyJet headrest. When she awoke on touchdown it was to find she'd slumped into James, her head on his shoulder, his arm around her protectively. Kate felt warm and safe. And something else, something she dared not admit to herself. She checked herself and moved away from him.

He swallowed and opened his eyes as the pilot welcomed them to Inverness. Kate refused to make eye contact. She was too embarrassed.

'Sorry,' he said as he rubbed his eyes and sat upright. He removed his arm from around her and undid his seatbelt.

Was Jenny right? Did he like her the way she liked him? And was it right to do anything about it? They lived together and worked together. For now. If her contract wasn't going to be renewed at Invermoray she would inevitably have to leave to wherever she found her next role and she would probably not see James again. That thought made her feel sick. But if she was going to be able to stay, especially now there were bookings coming in and they might actually be able to afford her if they wanted her, then surely having a relationship with her boss was the very worst thing to do.

And then there was the elephant in the room. He knew why she'd left her last job and she wanted to hear from him what he thought, wanted to tell him herself what had happened. She glanced at him as he drove them back to Invermoray. He was as silent as she, his jaw clenched, his eyebrows furrowed. What was he thinking about? As they wound through heather-strewn pastures they studiously avoided talking about their relationship, about the surprise appearance of Angus in London, and especially about the camera the TV crew was about to send into the loch.

CHAPTER 38

1940

Henry's eyes darted wildly as he looked from Constance to Matthew sitting on the floor by the fire. They, in turn, stared back at him in wide-eyed horror.

Matthew scrambled to his feet, knocking over the whisky bottle, its amber liquid running between the gaps in the floorboards and out of sight. Constance climbed to her feet and got caught in her dress, stumbling forward.

'Henry!' she cried.

Henry said nothing. He merely looked at Constance and then at Matthew, clearly desperately trying to work out the situation in the cottage.

'Henry,' Matthew said, his teeth gritted. Constance knew Matthew was restraining himself, having finally set eyes on the man who had frightened her so much on her birthday.

'Who is this?' Henry pointed at Matthew, although he was looking only at Constance.

'This is . . .' She looked desperately at the man she loved, pleading silently for him to come up with an answer with which Henry would be satisfied.

Matthew strode forward, a fixed expression on his face. 'Matthew. Pleased to meet you.'

Reluctantly Henry shook hands, etiquette taking precedence.

Constance licked her suddenly dry lips and tried to quell the panic rising within her.

The two men moved apart and Henry looked around the cottage, at the upturned whisky bottle now empty. Constance bent and picked up the sticky bottle before placing it on the uneven stone mantel above the fire. She wiped her fingers on her dress.

The cottage door still hung open and Henry placed his hand on it as if to shut it, but seemed to change his mind at the last minute.

'I'm sorry,' he said with a frown. 'Who are you?'

'Matthew,' he said, his voice darker than before. 'I just told you.' His posture was tense and alert.

Henry appraised Matthew, nodding slowly. 'Matthew *who*?'

'I'm a friend of Constance's,' was his vague reply.

'I would say, judging by the manner in which I found you, looking very cosy by the fire, you are a little more than just friends. Am I wrong?'

Constance found her voice and tried to make herself heard above the sound of blood pumping in her ears. 'You're wrong,' she said, a little too loudly.

'Is this where you've been sneaking off to?' Henry accused.

Neither Matthew nor Constance responded as they looked at each other uncertainly.

'Constance, you're very quiet. Cat got your tongue?' Henry tilted his head to one side expectantly.

'I've been teaching him to read,' Constance said, finding inspiration at last as her gaze fell on the books piled on the nest of tables.

'You can't read?' Henry looked suspicious.

Matthew said 'no' in a flat tone as Henry moved towards the books and picked them up, one by one, reading the gold-embossed titles on the spines. He nodded and held one up.

'You're starting with some heavy literature then. *Great Expectations*? A novel where almost none of the characters are *quite* what they seem.' He let his statement hang in mid-air.

'I think perhaps some of the characters are simply misunderstood: Magwitch in particular, more a victim of circumstance than a deep-rooted criminal,' Matthew said.

Henry nodded slowly. 'An insightful conclusion for a man who can't read.'

Constance was desperate to reach for Matthew's hand, but was determined not to add fuel to whichever fire Henry was already burning in his mind.

'Whereabouts are you from, Matthew with no last name? You're not from round here, that's for sure. You sound like one of us and yet . . . you say you can't read, something I don't believe for a minute. So, shall I tell you what I think is going on?'

Matthew and Constance looked at Henry, waiting. 'I rather think our little Constance here is up to all kinds of unsavoury acts with you. I think she's been sneaking out under cover of darkness to be with you, a man who lies about himself. I now know exactly the kind of woman Constance is,' he said with disdain. 'But who are *you*? How long have you been here? Not five minutes, that's for sure. It's far too cosy in here for that. Who are you *really*?'

Neither of them replied. The wind whistled into the cottage through the open door, blowing the fire so sparks sputtered out, landing on the rough wood floor before they dimmed and left black tracer marks behind. Constance moved to shut the door.

'Leave it,' Henry commanded. 'I'm not staying.'

'Where are you going?' Constance asked.

'Back to the house,' Henry said meaningfully as he moved towards the door.

Matthew blocked his path. He was a head-height above Henry but it didn't seem to faze the smaller man.

'Stand aside, there's a good man,' Henry said.

'No,' Matthew said.

Henry laughed. 'What *do* you think you're doing?'

'What are you going to do?' Matthew asked, ignoring Henry's question. 'When you get to the house?'

'I think it's time your parents discovered the kind of girl they've raised, don't you?' he said in Constance's direction. 'Sneaking around at night to be with the wrong sort of man.'

'No,' Matthew said. 'This has nothing to do with her. None of this is her fault. Leave her out of this.'

'Why?' Henry asked, his eyes narrowing. He folded his arms. 'All right, I'll play along for a moment or two. Suppose I don't tell the McLays what their darling daughter has been getting up to. What do I tell them? I'm going to have to tell them something, after all. It's my duty. I'm a guest in their house and I suspect, you aren't supposed to be here at all.'

Matthew looked down at Constance and she back at him with a mix of horror and fear. He shook his head at her. 'It's over.'

'No,' she insisted, stepping towards Henry. 'He's one of you,' she said. 'He's a pilot and he crashed, in the loch, weeks ago. He's been injured and frightened and I hid him. I'd have done the same if it was you. Hell, someone did the very same thing for Douglas. He's been . . . disoriented but it's all right, now he's going to hand himself in. And so, you see, you don't *have* to tell anyone anything,' she came to a rushed conclusion.

Henry's expression conveyed deep suspicion. His teeth caught over his bottom lip.

'When?' he asked, looking at Matthew.

'When what?'

'When did you crash?'

'I've lost track of the days,' Matthew said.

'But you know what night you were flying, what sortie you were on?'

'I don't remember and it's not important even if I did.'

Henry nodded but didn't look convinced. 'Come with me then.'

'Why?' Matthew asked.

'If you want to return to your squadron, come with me and we'll telephone from the house. You'll be back up in the skies tomorrow.'

Constance and Matthew looked at each other. 'He can't,' Constance said.

Henry raised an eyebrow. 'Why not?'

'He's frightened. He needs more time.' It sounded weak even to Constance.

Matthew closed his eyes and hung his head.

'More time?' Henry questioned disbelievingly. '*Are* you frightened?' His lip curled in disgust. 'What kind of man are you? Never mind. So you've absented yourself, without permission. And you expect me to overlook this cowardice. I've just been shot down. I almost broke my leg—'

'Where *is* your cane?' Constance queried.

'At the house.'

'If you walked all through the forest without it I'd say you were ready to fly also, wouldn't you?' she questioned.

'This isn't about me,' Henry shouted at her. 'This is about him. And why you're defending a man you've known for such little time. Nothing about this adds up, Constance. You've put yourself at risk. He could be anyone. And your family deserves to know the kind of man you've been hiding. You just wait,' he said to Matthew. 'You'll be in prison in no time. Refusing to fly. I've never heard anything so cowardly. Now let me past.'

Matthew lowered his arm from the doorframe and with despair and a resigned expression, let Henry go.

'Why are you letting him leave?' she cried as she sped towards the door to chase after Henry. 'He's going to tell.'

'I can't keep him hostage,' Matthew said, pulling Constance back and holding her close. 'Let him go. It's over, Constance. It's really over. I don't know whether to feel fear or relief.'

'No,' she said, pulling back from him. 'You must run, you

must . . . I don't know what you must do but don't let them cart you off to be court-martialled. I love you. You're a good man. I know you are.'

'No,' he said, looking her in the eye. 'I'm not. Before . . . before Henry, there was something I was trying to tell you.'

'What?' she asked in bewilderment.

'Constance.' He took her hands in his. 'I'm so sorry for what I'm about to tell you. I'm so sorry I hid it for so long. I should have told you the very moment I could. And now I've left it too late. But I love you. I will always love you and I want you to know everything. And then, I won't stop you if you want to join Henry in reporting me.'

'Reporting you?'

Matthew nodded. 'They will work out who I am, sooner rather than later, and then they'll telephone the police.'

'But I thought they would inform your squadron first,' she said in confusion.

He took a deep breath, looked into her eyes as tears formed in his own, and told her the very worst thing Constance thought she would ever hear.

CHAPTER 39

2020

Kate sat on the damp shingle at the edge of the loch, some distance from the camera crew. She was sure the damp was penetrating her jeans and wished she'd brought a blanket. She could see Guy was busy readying himself for filming, looking over his notes and practising a few lines to an imaginary camera while the real one was being set up. The producer was setting up a makeshift area at the loch side.

James sat down next to Kate, realising the shingle was damp too late. He stayed put.

'What did you decide?' Kate asked him.

'I couldn't ask him not to send the camera down. I couldn't tell him I'd changed my mind. I felt like an idiot.' He picked up a flat stone and gently threw it towards the water where it skimmed once, twice and then disappeared below the surface.

'Don't you want to know?' Kate asked quietly. Grey clouds were gathering overhead. 'Whatever it is . . .' She shrugged. She couldn't possibly comprehend what could be down there.

'All right,' Guy called. 'We're ready. Come and watch the screen. Let's see what's down there.'

Liz arrived from the house carrying a tray of tea for all the crew.

Kate thought she'd be excited now it was all happening but was so nervous her fingers were shaking. Her line of thinking was now where James's was, that if there was something down there, she really didn't want to know. And she didn't want anyone else to know.

'Let it be gone,' she whispered as Guy's dinghy moved across the water, its engine whirring away until it was almost out of earshot. 'Let it be gone.'

James looked down at her, his face tense. Kate reached and held his hand, the way he'd held hers in this same spot, only days earlier.

As Guy's boat reached the middle of the loch, he radioed in that the camera operative was sending the tethered drone camera under. They watched it lowered into the water until it was submerged in the darkness and far out of sight to those standing on the shore. The operator fed the tether out slowly once the dinghy engine had been killed.

'We'll film a run-up scene and see if it's still there,' Guy said. 'It'll make it a bit more interesting for viewers to have it appear at the end of a few seconds of filming. If it's still there, of course.'

'He's talking like he thinks it's actually real,' Kate said with a strange, false laugh.

'If that thing on the sonar the other day was a monster, then it'll be long gone by now I reckon,' the director said. 'No monsters have ever really been found, have they? Has anyone ever grabbed hold of the Loch Ness Monster, dragged it to shore and said, "*Here we are then*"?' He turned back to the screen and gave it his full attention. James stifled a laugh and gave Kate a look. She felt a bit lighter at Martin's grounding comment.

Kate's heart raced in direct contrast to the camera's painfully slow movements through the dark water. She could see on the screen that it was deeper than she'd expected, skimming along about twenty feet above the sand and shingle of the loch-bed.

'You know,' Martin started up again, 'they sent a sonar drone down to map Loch Ness and they found a film prop of the monster. I reckon they thought they'd had the find of the century. It was shaped like Nessie, long neck, the lot.'

'Oh,' Kate said absent-mindedly.

James ignored him, watching the camera feed intensely.

Suddenly something lurched into view – or rather, the camera came across a huge, motionless object.

'Oh yes,' Guy's director said excitedly. 'That's it.' He radioed to Guy. 'Send the camera down lower. Skirt around it.'

'What on earth is that?' Kate said.

But Guy had obviously turned his radio off and was speaking to the camera rather animatedly. Then the radio clicked and they heard Guy say in wondrous tones, 'It's an aeroplane.'

Kate almost threw up in relief. 'What?'

The camera moved, approaching the plane from the back. One of its wings was missing and so she could see how it had been easy to mistake it for an oddly shaped monster from the sonar images.

The plane was covered in all sorts of marine life; schools of little fish swam in and out. The controls were rusted to near oblivion. The hatch that should have been above the pilot's seat was long gone.

Guy was talking at great speed and Kate was struggling to catch what he was saying. 'It's from the war,' he said, sounding like a schoolboy who'd had too much sugar. 'I can't believe it, this is so exciting.' He clicked the radio off and began speaking to the camera again.

Martin turned to them, wide-eyed, as he listened via his earpiece to Guy speaking to the camera. 'Jesus Christ,' he muttered.

'What?' James asked impatiently.

'What?' Kate echoed.

The director smiled. 'This is too good to be true,' he said, any thoughts of a monster forgotten all round.

'What?' James, Liz and Kate said in unison.

'No, no,' Martin said with a smile. 'I'm going to let Guy do the honours.'

Kate thought she would explode with impatience as they waited for Guy to finish chatting to the camera, for the underwater camera to finish filming, for it to be lifted into the boat and then for the boat to return to shore. They made their way down to the water's edge, the director wearing a wide smile on his face.

'Well done,' Martin called over to Guy. 'That was great.'

Guy was so excited he didn't wait for the boat to come to a complete stop. Instead he jumped down, into the water, drenching his trainers and his jeans up to his ankles.

'Did you see that?' he called to them as he bounded over.

'Yes, but we don't know what it is,' Kate said.

'It's a plane,' Guy said, puzzled.

'We know that,' James said. 'But what kind?'

'A fighter,' Guy answered, looking down as if he'd only just noticed his feet were soaked.

'A Spitfire?' Kate asked, naming the only wartime plane she could remember.

'I don't think so, no.'

'A Hurricane?' James offered.

'No,' Guy said, impatiently. 'I need to review the footage. The tail markings are long gone but the shape of it leads me to believe it is in fact, something else entirely.'

'Such as?' Kate prompted.

'A Messerschmitt to be precise. It's not British at all. It's German.'

CHAPTER 40

1940

Constance stood still and stared at Matthew. There were a few seconds of silence as she tried to understand what he'd just told her. 'You're *German*?' she asked, stepping back a few paces. 'No. You can't be. Your accent . . . you're English.'

'I'm not. Not completely,' he said softly.

'I don't understand,' Constance replied. 'I watched you crash. I watched you crash your Spitfire.'

He shook his head. 'No. I'd love to have flown a Spitfire,' he said wistfully. 'So much faster than our 109s.'

Constance's mouth dropped again. 'But . . . I . . .' Thoughts spun around in her head and jumbled together. 'You can't be German. Why do you sound English?'

'My father,' Matthew said, 'is German. My mother was from Cambridge. They met in Cambridge, married and had me. We lived in England for the best part of my childhood. Then my mother died when I was young and my father took me home to Germany. He said there was nothing for him here, especially after the way Germany had been destroyed at the Treaty of Versailles. Father hated what had happened; hated the part the Kaiser played in the last war, hated what Germany had *done* in the last war, but the financial punishments meted out to Germany made my father hate England, hate the country he'd called home for so long. We moved back to Germany.' He paused and looked at Constance uncertainly.

'I was born and raised here, Constance,' he said pleadingly. 'I spoke English to my mother and German to my father. I feel English. But I feel German too. I was a child when I left England. I came back to Cambridge to go to university. I missed England when I was in Germany and then when I was in England, I missed Germany. I didn't really know where home was anymore. But at university in England I found myself. I joined the Air Cadets and I really felt I'd found my calling. It looked likely there was going to be a war and I'm ashamed to say I was excited. I was going to fly, for a purpose. But I have a German father, a German last name and having been through the first war, my father knew life for me wouldn't be safe here. I might have been interned at best, mobbed at worst. Father summoned me back to Germany. Convinced me it wouldn't be safe for me in Britain, convinced me to join the Luftwaffe. There was no time to stop and think about picking sides. I'm a pilot, not a soldier. Everything I said about not wanting to fight is true. Everything I said about not wanting to kill, about shooting my fellow man from the skies is true. Every time I shot a bomber or a fighter down, I prayed to God the men inside reached safety. Men my age, men who I might have sat next to in lectures at Cambridge, men I might have played cricket with on the green, men I might have trained with before I went home to Germany.' He swallowed hard and then spoke quietly, 'Men I might have flown alongside if things had been different.'

Constance looked at the man she'd fallen in love with. She looked at his kind green eyes, at his pained expression. Her heart hurt more than she ever thought it would again, but she couldn't help the words that came out of her mouth next.

'I don't know you.'

'Please,' he begged her, 'say anything but that. You do know me. Everything I told you is true. I've never lied to you, Constance. Not once. I want no part of this war, which I suspect the Nazis will win.'

Constance gasped. 'Don't say that.'

'I'd rather be locked away for the duration of the war than fly for Hitler.'

Constance moved away from him and her legs gave way as she sat in the armchair.

'I should have left a long time ago,' he told her. 'I should have handed myself in to the British, instead of waiting for my commanding officer to behave so badly he forced my hand. But I was scared of the repercussions, Constance. I'm going to go to prison, and all my fellow inmates will see is a traitor. If they don't beat me to death, it will be a miracle.'

He watched her, waiting for her to say something. But she couldn't.

'I shouldn't have stayed here and brought you down with me,' he said. 'I should have gone before now, but I didn't. I was scared. And then there was you. It was selfish of me, but I fell in love with you and everything that you and this cottage represented. And now, if that man tells all and sundry about us, there will be unthinkable consequences for you. You have no idea how much I hate myself for this, Constance. And how much I love you.'

Constance blinked tears out of her eyes. The shock of Matthew's true identity meant she could not force herself from the chair and into his arms. She was torn. She loved him. But he had kept the truth from her, allowing her to go on believing something that wasn't true.

'Why didn't you tell me before now?' Her voice was barely audible.

He hung his head. 'I didn't want you to ever look at me the way that you are right now.'

'You deceived me,' Constance said. 'All this time, you've lied.'

'No,' he said emphatically as he looked up at her. 'I never lied to you, Constance. I hid the truth but I never lied.'

'That story about your commanding officer,' she choked out, 'was it even true?'

'Yes. My God, yes. Everything I've told you was the truth. I am scared to death of what will happen to me now, but none of that matters if . . .'

'If what?' she asked, her gaze finally meeting his.

'None of it matters if I don't have you anymore. If losing you is the punishment for hiding the truth from you, then it's nothing less than I deserve.'

Constance looked down to where her fingers were dug tightly into the fabric of the armchair. Shock was getting the better of her.

'Say something. Constance, please,' Matthew begged.

Slowly, shakily, she stood and moved towards the door. Her mouth was open but no words came out.

Matthew closed his eyes as Constance moved past him. 'I love you and I've lost you,' he muttered. 'I'm so sorry.'

Constance couldn't reply. The lump that had formed in her throat threatened to suffocate her.

'Goodbye, Constance,' Matthew said. Tears clouded his green eyes.

'I don't know what to say. I don't know what to think. I loved you.' She looked in the direction of the loch, shielded from view by the darkness of the night and the forest. 'I'm going to stop Henry,' she said eventually. 'He'll rouse the house. He won't explain it properly. I need to . . .' She trailed off and then started afresh as she aimed for a pragmatism she didn't quite feel. 'I need to explain your side of things, with what little time I have.'

'Are you . . . are you going to tell them I'm German?'

'You're partly English,' Constance deflected. 'They—'

'They'll make an example of me,' he said, clenching his jaw. 'I might be partly English, but in this war, I'm German. I left England to shoot British men out of the sky. That man Henry, and any officers in the house the Luftwaffe have helped put there – if they get their hands on me, they'll kill me.'

'I don't think Douglas will see it like that,' Constance said. 'He'll help, not condemn. He's the voice of reason, especially when it comes to Mother and Father. They worship him. They'll listen to him.' She didn't wait for his reply, before breaking into a run.

'Constance,' he called after her. 'Constance, come back. Wait.'

But she was gone, speeding through the darkened woods. The time for hiding in the tree line was gone and she made her way down towards the loch. Barely a flicker of light shone from the windows of Invermoray House, shrouded as they were by the blackout blinds within.

She emerged minutes later, breathing fast as the moonlight shone on the loch on the clearest night she'd seen in a long time. Two men were standing on the jetty and it took her a moment to realise one was Henry, almost shouting at the other man. Constance saw it was Douglas from the sling he was wearing. She felt a renewed sense of hope. Douglas would know what to do.

'What's this?' Douglas asked as she ran up to them. 'Has Henry lost his mind? He says you've got a pilot hidden in the cottage. Is this true, Constance?'

Henry stood to one side, shock and disappointment on his face as he watched Constance.

'Douglas,' she said, steadying her nerve. 'He crashed. He was unwell and needed my help. The way that farmer's wife helped you. He was shot down weeks ago. He's going to hand himself in now.'

'You should have told me, Constance. But no matter,' Douglas said, reaching out with his good arm to place a hand on hers. 'It's all right, we'll sort it.'

'There's nothing to sort,' Henry said. 'The man's a coward. We need to report him.'

'Bit strong, Henry. We'll give him the chance to do it himself first,' Douglas said. 'The very least we can do is talk to him.'

Douglas looked behind Constance as Matthew emerged from the tree line. When he saw them he stopped running and began walking. A flicker of forgiveness emanated within Constance. She loved Matthew, but she felt betrayed. And it was too late to know how she truly felt about him now. But despite everything, she needed to seal Matthew's fate for the better; prohibit Henry from doing anything rash. What might a spurned man do? Henry could rouse any able officers into a rabble to confront Matthew, believing him to be a coward. If they knew his true nature it would be unthinkable.

'Right,' Douglas said, taking charge. 'I hear you've been shot down and want to hand yourself in, is that right?'

'Yes,' Matthew said. He looked out of his depth and ready for Douglas to take the lead. He eyed Henry warily and Henry returned the look with a trace of hatred in his eyes.

'All right, come back to the house with us and we'll tell Mother and Father and then we'll telephone . . .' But Douglas had stopped speaking, his eyes narrowed as he looked at Matthew. He rubbed his jaw and then said, 'I know you. I do, don't I?'

CHAPTER 41

2020

'A German fighter plane? What happened to the pilot then?' Kate asked as they went inside. It had been growing cold and James had gallantly lent her his jacket. It smelled of his aftershave and smoke from the fire in the hall where his jacket usually hung.

'Parachuted out?' James asked.

'Perhaps,' Guy said.

Kate shuddered. 'You don't think he went down with the plane, do you? You don't think this is the pilot who drowned?' Kate asked James.

'We'll have to search records to see when he was picked up, if he was still alive,' Guy said.

'There will be a list of confirmed shootings. The RAF were pretty hot on that kind of thing. They loved a list of planes they'd downed, chalking it up on the board afterwards. I may be able to do some digging, cross-reference that to the location here if you can't find anything, but I suspect with a look in the local archives you'll easily find a story as juicy as an enemy pilot being captured.'

Kate nodded. She was finding this all very strange. By filming in the loch, they'd only wanted to add some flavour to their story about the monster. Instead they were now discussing missing Luftwaffe planes and downed pilots.

'I need a drink,' Kate said, standing up and pouring herself a gin and tonic. It was warm but she didn't care.

James looked at Kate curiously and as she gestured to the decanters, offering him one, he shook his head. Guy was looking at his phone and suddenly sprang to his feet.

'Oh Christ,' he said, the most flustered Kate had seen since she met him. 'I have to go.' He looked around as if a car might suddenly appear in the sitting room ready to whisk him away.

'What's happened?' James asked.

'It's Melissa,' Guy said. 'She's at the hospital. She's gone into labour. I have to go. She's going to kill me.'

'She'll be a bit busy for that, mate,' James said. 'You start booking a flight on your phone; I'll drive you to the airport. Assume your crew are occupied packing up?'

Ever polite, Guy turned to say goodbye to Kate and she laughed. 'Go. Just go, and quickly.'

'Yes, right, yes,' he replied and the two men ran from the room.

Kate was in the estate office when Angus popped his head around the door.

'You're back,' she exclaimed. 'That was fast.'

'Aye,' he said. 'That flight's a godsend. Full o' businessmen. And me,' he said with a wink. 'Back from the big smoke, seeing m' girlfriend.'

Kate could tell he was trying the word out for size even though he and Jenny had only been seeing each other a matter of days. 'How is she today?'

'Better. Her mum's staying for a bit. I had to sort out a few things up here and Morven's giving me hell for leaving her in charge of the pub for so long. I told her, "*What would you do if I suddenly dropped down dead?*" She'd be running the whole shebang then. But I got an earful for that so thought it best to come back for a wee while.'

Kate smiled.

'I just met Liz heading towards the cottage. I hear it's been a hive of excitement while I was gone. German planes and *no* monsters.' He wiggled his eyebrows. 'Might still be something in there y'know; something that shouldn't be. All the stories over the years of monsters carting sheep away cannae be for nothing.'

'Oh, Angus,' Kate said with a laugh. 'I couldn't care less about a monster now. What trouble it's brought us.' She shook her head.

'Oh I dunno,' Angus said. 'I'd not say trouble, exactly. Just a mystery finally solved.'

'How's that?' Kate asked. 'We none of us knew the plane was there.'

'The drowned airman, the pilot,' Angus said with a frown. 'That was him surely.'

'I wondered about that,' Kate said slowly. 'But if your grandfather knew about it, knew the man had drowned, he didn't say it was alongside a hulking great plane.'

'No,' Angus said. 'No, he didn't. He was too young to join the war and was up at the house as a gardener's boy. But he's got dementia now and it's unlikely he'll remember any of that this long after. He told us that story when we were knee high to a grasshopper. Maybe it wasn't true. Maybe it was just to keep us wee ones outta the loch.'

'Maybe not,' Kate replied uncertainly. 'There is a plane in the loch after all.'

James would be back from the airport soon and Liz was settling the Canadian guests into the ghillie's cottage.

'I'll be back soon,' Kate muttered, looking at her watch. 'There's something I want to look at.'

A few minutes later Kate was inside the house, looking at the picture of Constance on the stairs. Now she knew the rip was there, along her silver-grey dress, it was all Kate could see. She grabbed her car keys from the hallstand and headed outside.

*

The village was busier than usual and Kate watched a steady stream of coach tourists heading towards the Invermoray Arms. She smiled to herself. She could see why Morven was giving Angus hell if she'd been handling that lot on her own. Kate and James still hadn't quite got themselves together when it came to the tearoom – they'd been so busy sorting the accommodation side of things. But it was one more thing they'd have to do; or perhaps with the accommodation side taking up most of Kate's time, it was one thing Kate would have to leave Liz and James to iron out. She would, in all probability, be leaving in a couple of months. She wasn't sure how she felt about that but put it from her mind as she parked in the square and strode purposefully towards the library.

Kirsty was chatting animatedly about the wonders of books to film to a woman who was clutching a copy of a bestseller. Kate waited patiently and when the woman left, Kirsty turned to her and said excitedly, 'We're doing it. We're going rogue. Our book-to-film book club is go.' Her eyes were wide and her smile even wider as she looked expectantly at Kate. 'I'm no' saying we ditch saintly Brenda's group entirely, more that we may just keep our new one a wee bit of a secret. We start next month. You'll join, won't you?'

'I can probably come to the first couple,' Kate said. 'But then I think I'll be moving on.'

'Ach, surely not? Why?'

Kate muttered something about end of contract and then tried to steer the conversation into less choppy waters. 'Kirsty,' she started, 'a while ago you told me that you had a lot more resources at your fingers than just that lot in the local history section.'

Kirsty puffed up proudly. 'I do. What is it you need?'

'Can you find me some local newspapers from September 1940?'

Kate glanced over at the huge leather-bound newspaper archives in the corner of the library and hoped Kirsty wasn't just going to send her over there and tell her to fend for herself. She hadn't had enough coffee for that kind of activity.

'Sure,' Kirsty said. 'Any specific date?'

Kate thought. The date on the grave had been indiscernible. And both Constance and Douglas had been alive in September according to the photograph of them on the lawn. 'Can we start in the last week of September and work our way back?' she suggested.

Kirsty started clicking the mouse and typing a few words.

'What are you looking at?' Kate asked.

Kirsty spun the little, out-of-date computer round so Kate could see the screen.

'British Newspaper Archive,' she said as if Kate was stupid. 'It's mostly online these days. What are you looking for?'

'I'm looking for a German fighter plane that crashed. And I'm looking for reports of someone drowning,' she said. 'Ideally I want to know if the two events happened at the same time.'

Kirsty was silent for a moment and there was a lot of clicking as she ticked boxes to show different local newspapers, as well as the larger Scottish ones. A few headlines came up for articles and photographs that had been catalogued. Kirsty looked at Kate with a satisfied expression on her face.

'Oh wow,' Kate said as she read the selection of headlines. 'That one first,' she said, pointing.

MIDNIGHT ARREST AT INVERMORAY HOUSE.

CHAPTER 42

1940

'I know you,' Douglas said, louder now. 'And you know me. I can see you do. Tell me why.'

Matthew closed his eyes and sighed. 'University,' he said. 'We were at university together. I thought I recognised your name when Constance mentioned you. Only, I didn't know it until I saw you.'

'Yes. I remember now. The University Air Squadron.' Douglas was overjoyed with the familiarity of recognition. 'So you joined up too, obviously.'

Henry coughed as if the conversation had turned in the wrong direction.

'Yes,' Matthew said, his gaze flicking to Constance.

'I seem to remember you went home,' Douglas continued. 'There was a hue and cry when we found out because it was just before the war started and we all thought, given where you were going, that you must have known something we didn't. Oh . . .' Douglas frowned, coming to his senses. 'Berlin. You went home to Berlin.' Realisation danced slowly across his face as he remembered.

'What?' Henry chimed in. 'What?' he repeated, louder now.

'Hamburg,' Matthew said quietly. 'I went home to Hamburg.'

'And then you came back here?' Douglas questioned uncertainly. 'To fight for us?'

Matthew closed his eyes for a moment and shook his head. Constance could see he could no longer carry on the charade. 'No. I joined the Luftwaffe.'

Douglas gasped and then: 'Bloody hell.'

Beside him, Henry's eyes widened and he opened his mouth to speak but Constance got there first. 'Douglas, he needs our help. He's handing himself in and . . .'

'You're a bloody Nazi,' Henry shouted, finding his voice.

'I'm not a Nazi,' Matthew said solemnly.

'He's been shooting us out of the skies and we let him live? We hand him in?' Henry continued. 'I think not. This Nazi has been with your sister!' Henry lunged forward, fist raised. Constance flew in front of Matthew to shield him but Henry dodged her deftly, instead knocking her sideways so that she fell against one of the jetty posts. She cried out as it hit her stomach and turned to grab the post to steady herself. But she mistimed it. As she watched Henry launch through the air and push Matthew to the ground, Constance – pained and winded – fell into the water.

She splashed and flailed in the cold water and tried to put her feet down. But she was deeper than she thought and, finding no traction, she sank under for a moment. As her head came up, above her on the jetty she could hear only scuffling and shouting as the men fought. She feared her rib was broken as agony rippled through her. She screamed out to Matthew, but instead gulped down water as the pain forced her to halt treading water and she sank underneath again. She wanted to shout at Matthew, to tell him to run. She wished she'd helped Matthew leave the very moment Henry had left the cottage. She knew she should have helped him leave days ago.

Constance resurfaced into the dark night air to see Henry landing blow after blow on Matthew's face. Douglas lurched forward, using his only free arm to try to pull Henry off the man she loved. She grabbed the edge of the jetty and tried to pull herself up, to help Matthew. But her grip wasn't strong enough.

The three men were locked in a fight. Matthew's head had lolled back under the force of Henry's punches and briefly, her gaze connected with his. But she couldn't help. Henry raised his fist to land a strong blow, and as he swung back he caught Douglas in the face. Her brother, tangled with Henry and Matthew, staggered at the end of the jetty. Constance was forced under the water as the three men, locked tightly together, fell on top of her.

She spluttered, sucking water into her lungs. It burnt as it went down her throat and she screamed a voiceless sound as the freezing, dark water surrounded her. She grappled with nothing, her hands flying wildly through the water. The men were gone and she was on her own, deep in the water, her nostrils burning as the loch water punished her for everything she'd ever done, for the advances she'd spurned and for the promise she'd kept.

And then she felt a pair of hands grab at her dress. The water blurred her vision and she didn't know where the surface of the loch was, only that she was being pulled towards it. The water broke above her and she coughed and coughed as she felt herself being dragged towards the shore. Water poured out of her mouth and down her face until she was dizzier than she'd ever been before. Constance was lifted, clumsily, and then she was on her front, someone thumping her back as she threw up the contents of her stomach alongside the remaining loch water she'd swallowed. Her lungs burned afresh and she rolled over and laid her head on the hard pebbles, unable to think and barely able to breathe.

Matthew was slumped beside her, his face a mess. Blood ran from his forehead, from the corner of his eye and from his lower lip.

She touched his face. 'Matthew?' she said, although her throat scraped with pain.

He moaned and coughed, spitting blood over the ground. He pulled her towards him and embraced her as they sat, both dripping wet. 'You're safe now. I've got you.'

They held each other tightly for a while, as they regained their breath.

'Where's Henry?' she asked after a few moments.

'Gone,' he said, kissing her head, his breath rasping. 'Gone to the house. It's too late. It's over.'

She moved in a frenzy, turning to face him. She grabbed the collar of his shirt in desperation. 'Run,' she commanded. 'You can still run.'

Over Matthew's shoulder, she could see a line of people running through the arch that divided the formal garden from the path to the loch.

'I can't,' he said, hanging his head. 'It's too late. But it's all right, Constance. It'll be all right.'

'Why didn't you run?' she asked as tears streamed down her face. 'You had all that time, why didn't you run?'

'Ssh,' he placated and stroked her hair. 'I had to get you out of the water. I lost you down there for so long I was sure you were dead. But I had to get to you.'

She shook him by his shirt collar. 'Oh, Matthew. Run. Please run.'

'No,' he said as voices sounded closer now. 'We don't have long.'

She fell gently against him, one last time, feeling his lips on her wet hair; and she closed her eyes tightly, waiting, knowing within minutes, seconds, he would be gone.

'They're going to take me,' he said. 'But I will come back,' he mumbled into her hair. 'However long it takes, I will come back here for you.'

'I'll wait for you,' she cried.

Suddenly he stiffened. 'Oh good God.' Constance moved with him as he climbed to his feet.

'What is it?' she asked.

Matthew's hand gripped her wrist and his eyes widened as he watched the crowd descending on them, led by Henry. And then he looked into the dark and foreboding loch before asking, 'Where's your brother?'

CHAPTER 43

2020

Kirsty and Kate had been staring at the same passage on the screen for so long that a screensaver of swirly psychedelic images appeared, making them both jump.

'Bloody hell,' Kate said, coming to her senses.

'Sorry,' Kirsty said, wiggling the mouse to restart the screen. 'What do you think this all means?' she asked.

Kate shook her head. 'I rather hoped it wasn't like this but I think,' she said, working it through in her head as she spoke, 'that Douglas McLay drowned the same night the German pilot was arrested.'

Next to her Kirsty shivered. 'Och, it was as if a ghost just walked over my grave. You think the two events are related?'

'Same loch. Same night. I'd be surprised if the two events *weren't* related. I suppose we'll never quite know how he drowned now.'

'Doesn't make it any less tragic though,' Kirsty said.

'No. It doesn't.'

Kate walked back to her car. There was still something bothering her. The German pilot had been arrested, and Douglas had died in the most tragic of circumstances. Drowning was not an easy way to die. Kate wondered about this man, this good-looking, young RAF officer whose portrait hung on the staircase of Invermoray House and whose body lay in the churchyard. He hadn't been disinherited as James and Liz had assumed. He'd died. And so what of Constance? Constance whose portrait had been slashed; Constance whose name had been so forcibly scrubbed out in the family Bible? What had been her fate?

Kate had half a mind to go back into the library and look Constance up in the newspaper archive, but Kirsty was switching the lights off one by one as the working day came to a close. Kirsty left and locked the door and spotting Kate in the car, gave her a grin, pointing to the novel she was holding with a smile as if to remind her to read it for the new book club. Kate smiled back and gave her a half-hearted wave. She wanted to know about Constance so much that she could barely think about anything else.

CHAPTER 44

1940

Matthew had been wrenched from her and marched forcibly towards the house. When he'd tried to beg for help to swim into the loch and find Douglas, his cries had been ignored; the porters and the relatively able-bodied officers refusing to let go of the opportunity to strong-arm a Luftwaffe pilot. In the formal garden, in the dark shadow of the main house Matthew had been beaten and then, head lolling back, he had been dumped on the floor of the housekeeper's room and locked in to await his fate.

Douglas's body washed up on the far side of the loch hours later, as the sun rose. He was carried home, his body limp, his broken arm free of its sling – lost to the depths below. The wail that emanated from Mrs McLay had been audible throughout the house and Constance, locked in her room, fell to the floor and wept with grief. Douglas's dripping-wet body was laid out on his bed.

At the funeral, Constance sat and stared towards the front of the church, wide-eyed in disbelief, waiting for it all to be over. Matthew had been arrested and she had no idea if she'd ever see him again. And her beloved brother was dead. This time, not missing, presumed dead, but actually gone forever.

Keeping Matthew hidden had led to Douglas's death. She knew

it was her fault. She would never forgive herself. And equally she would never forgive Henry for the part he had played. Douglas had gone into the water because he had been caught in the fight, trying to prevent Henry from killing Matthew.

As the parishioners shuffled in their seats to the sombre organ music, Constance and her mother broke down in tears. Constance reached for her mother's hand, but it was snatched away. She grieved for the brother she had lost and for her parents, who had not spoken a word to her since Douglas's body was found.

Constance herself had barely spoken since Matthew had been wrenched from her arms. At Henry's insistence that Constance was a traitor, she found herself being roughly hauled towards the house alongside Matthew. She had been unable to help in the search for Douglas, and had stared bleakly back towards the loch as her father and some of the nurses began combing the shore for him.

Constance couldn't fathom that Douglas was in a coffin at the front of the church, that he would never call her 'Smidge' again, or encourage her to make something of herself in this war.

The mourners who attended the small gathering at the house whispered about why a healthy young man would end his own life in the loch. She wanted to scream at them, to tell them her brother would never have done such a thing. Her parents didn't know how to address the rumour. Which was worse? The idea that Douglas committed suicide or the fact he'd drowned because their only daughter had harboured a German she had fallen in love with?

When the small crowd departed, Constance closed the heavy front door, placing her palms against it as if by doing so she could shut out the world. But the world had closed in.

Climbing the stairs to her bedroom she was summoned by her father. 'Come here,' he commanded and Constance dared not refuse. She walked in to his study, the grim expression she always seemed to wear fixed firmly on her face.

Her mother stood behind her father's desk, hands splayed over the polished mahogany. Her father sat stiffly on the settee. The portrait of Constance, resplendent in her silver-grey dress, was propped on an easel to one side of the room, waiting for someone to hang it. Constance looked at the girl in the picture and barely recognised her. It had been a few short weeks but she felt she'd been reborn when Matthew had crashed – and then had died the very moment Douglas was dragged from the loch.

'We agreed you would say it,' her mother said to her father when no one had spoken for at least ten seconds.

Constance waited, her gaze moving between the pair.

Her father sighed. 'You can't stay here anymore.'

'What?' Constance asked, her voice laced with shock. 'What do you mean? Where will I go?'

'It's not our concern,' he said in a clipped voice. 'You have ruined this family. You are no longer considered a part of it.'

The speech sounded rehearsed and Constance blinked as she tried to make sense of it.

'How long for?' she asked quietly.

'Forever,' her father said.

Her mother remained resolutely silent, her expression fixed, almost menacing.

'Mother?' Constance questioned.

'Don't speak to her,' her father said. 'She has vowed never to speak to you again.' His voice wavered. 'Do you know the hurt you've caused? Your brother is dead,' he wailed.

He collected himself and Constance replied, 'I'm so sorry. Douglas was trying to help and—'

'Don't you *dare* say his name,' her father shouted. He stood. 'Go. Just collect your things and go.'

Constance stood. 'Now?' she asked meekly. 'You want me to go now?'

Her father looked to her mother for confirmation. Behind the desk, Mrs McLay gave the faintest nod.

'Yes,' her father confirmed.

'But, Father—'

'Don't,' he said. 'You are not my daughter anymore. I no longer have any children.'

Constance moved towards the door, shaking with distress.

'Constance,' her father called.

'Yes?' she asked hopefully, turning back.

Pained, he looked at her for a second or two and then said, 'Don't ever come back.'

In the hallway, Constance shook with fear and disbelief. As she slumped onto the staircase, clutching the ornate mahogany spindles with one hand, the fingers of her other hand worried at the hem of her black dress until the hem came loose. If she waited long enough, perhaps her father would emerge from his study. Perhaps he would have talked her mother down – she had always been the stronger of the two but maybe when he realised the severity of her punishment, her banishment, he would speak up – and they would agree to Constance staying at Invermoray.

But the longer she sat there, the more she realised no one was coming for her; and that she didn't want to stay anymore. They would never forgive her. And she would never forgive herself. But she knew, deep within, that she had done the right thing, shielding Matthew from harm. But the consequences . . . oh, had she but known what they would be.

From inside the study, Constance heard a cry. 'She's killed my son,' Mrs McLay wailed. 'My Douglas.'

'Put the knife down, Augusta,' Constance heard her father shout. The slice the knife made as it ripped through the portrait was audible from behind the closed study door.

Constance stood, waiting for her mother to spring forth. There was cowardice hiding somewhere deep inside Constance and she did not wait to see what would happen. But there was bravery within her, too. Constance's dream of leaving Invermoray had been realised, albeit violently. She thought of the loch and as she did she felt calmed, closer to Douglas, closer to Matthew, although both were so far away now. She just needed a few moments there and then she might know what to do. Without a backward glance or stopping to collect her things, Constance opened the door and ran.

CHAPTER 45

2020

Back at the estate office, Kate collapsed into her swivel chair. She wanted to tell James what she'd just found out. And she wanted to share her theories about what had happened to Constance, even though she knew James was far more interested in the news about the German plane than he would be in Kate's theorising about a young woman who lived here many years ago.

It just seemed too coincidental that a German pilot would be arrested the same night Constance's brother perished in the loch and that sometime afterwards Constance would be disinherited. Or, like Douglas, had she died? If not, what had she done that was so bad? As she wondered, Kate looked down and saw the welcome hamper.

She slapped her hand against her forehead. It was supposed to be in the cottage, not at her feet in the office, Whisky sniffing the fresh biscuits and oatcakes with excitement. Kate would have to take it round. It wasn't heavy, just awkward, and as she struggled to open the estate office door, she saw James walking across the courtyard, jangling his Land Rover keys in his hand.

He gave her a wide smile. 'Guy got off all right,' he said. 'Mad to think in a few hours' time he's going to be a father. It's so . . . grown up.'

'It is,' Kate said as she wrestled to lock the estate office door. 'I only hope his girlfriend doesn't give birth while he's on his way.'

'Missing the birth of his own baby won't earn him any brownie points, will it? Ah I do love kids, don't you?' he said with a smile.

'Yeah,' Kate turned to him. 'Then they turn into children, and then teenagers and then they go off the rails and do things that get them disinherited,' she said knowingly.

'Hmm,' James said. 'I've been wondering about that. What's that?' he asked, changing the subject suddenly.

'Welcome hamper. Needs to go up to the cottage. Want to come and say hi to our first ever paying guests?'

'Absolutely,' he said.

The new table lamps in the cottage were casting a hazy glow onto the front garden. It looked more homely than Kate had seen it before, nestled as it was in the woods. Liz had worked wonders on the garden and James had installed a picket fence that set the cottage apart from the wilderness in which it sat.

As James had driven them the few minutes round to the cottage Kate told him what she and Kirsty had discovered at the library.

'Bloody hell,' he said. 'So you think this German chap being here somehow resulted in Douglas's death?'

Kate nodded, an uncertain expression on her face. 'I think so. It's too coincidental for the two events to have nothing to do with each other.'

James nodded and they looked past the small rental car that obviously belonged to the Canadians, and towards the light streaming through the window. 'Cottage looks nice,' he said. 'Even if I do say so myself.'

'You did really well.'

He reached over and touched her hand. '*We* did really well.'

There was suddenly so much Kate wanted to say and so much she didn't. 'We—'

'Yeah?' he asked, his hand still on hers.

'We should go in,' Kate said, pulling her hand gently away and hating herself for it. If anything was going to happen with James, she reasoned, it would have happened, properly, before now. Either way, it seemed their destiny to sabotage whatever might have been possible.

They knocked on the cottage door and were surprised to see Liz still there. She let them in and the Canadian woman and her husband, who was sitting on the settee, both greeted them warmly. Kate remembered he had a disability and walked over to shake his hand and say hello to them both.

'We brought your welcome hamper,' Kate said.

'You're our first proper guests,' Liz said enthusiastically and James and Kate both shot her a look. They'd already forgotten the welcome hamper; they didn't want to exude much more in the way of amateurism.

'I guessed as much,' the Canadian lady said kindly. She was in her late sixties, slim, with greying hair and rectangular glasses. 'I'm Marianne. And this is my husband Nicholas.'

James and Kate introduced themselves and then James asked, 'How did you know you were our first guests?'

'Ah,' Marianne said. 'I've been keeping a little eye on the house from afar, checking in from time to time on the internet to see what the latest was.'

'Really?' Kate asked. 'Why?'

Marianne didn't reply immediately. Instead she said, 'Little bottle of whisky in here,' gesturing to the welcome hamper. 'Might I suggest a tot all round? I think you may need it.'

James and Kate looked at each other and then nodded.

'OK,' James said uncertainly.

Kate volunteered to fetch glasses and Liz came with her to help carry them over from the other side of the open-plan room. The kitchen section was now very well stocked and clever James had even installed a Nespresso machine and a selection of capsules. Kate was impressed.

'What's this about?' she whispered to Liz. 'Do you know?'

'Vaguely,' Liz said. 'The woman, Marianne, was just starting to tell me why she's here and then in burst you two.'

They joined the others in the large open-plan sitting space and opened the whisky. James was expertly starting a fire in the grate after Marianne said it might be a bit beyond her and her husband.

'I'll pop back each evening, if you like, and fix this for you?' James nodded towards the fire.

'Oh that would be lovely, thank you,' Marianne said warmly. 'Your mother told me how you ended up running Invermoray House after your father passed away. Quite a challenge, this house, from what I gather.'

James gave Liz a stern look that she seemed oblivious to.

'Well, you know, it's grown on me, shall we say.' He looked over at Kate. 'Wouldn't be anywhere else now.'

'That's lovely to hear. I'm glad to hear it went down the family line to someone who values it, someone who loves it, rather than hates it. This house has seen too much hate.'

Kate stopped breathing. Marianne sounded very knowing. She wasn't sure how to phrase her question without sounding rude but she voiced it regardless as she handed round the whisky glasses. 'How do you know that?'

'Don't run a mile when I tell you this,' Marianne said. 'But this house would have been mine, eventually.'

Silence descended on the room and then James broke it with, 'What?'

'Oh don't worry,' Marianne said. 'I don't want it and without even looking into it, I know I've got no legal right to it. The will clearly stated it was your father who inherited it and I'm glad, seeing how wonderfully you've treated it. I wouldn't have wanted the upkeep and, of course, I'll bet it costs a king's ransom to keep the roof on and the house warm.'

Kate looked at James but he was looking at Marianne. 'Who are you?' he asked, somewhat rudely.

'Oh I'm so sorry,' she said. 'I'm your second cousin once removed, I think, although I've not got as far as working that bit out yet I'm afraid. I'm Constance's daughter.'

'Oh my God,' Kate spluttered, amazed and then overjoyed, realising that she would find out what had happened to Constance. 'Really?'

'What?' James simply said again. 'How can that be? I've never heard of you.'

Kate could see James was about to engage in open hostility. 'It's all right,' Kate said, putting her hand on his arm. 'She says she's not here to take the house from you and Liz.'

Marianne laughed. 'No,' she said soothingly. 'I'm really not. And I wondered for a long time if I should telephone or write or, well, something. But I didn't. I daren't, while my mother was still alive. It was very raw for her for a long time and so I dallied and I missed the opportunity of knowing your father. I felt disloyal to my mother, you see. But she passed a while ago and until then I didn't feel able to really acknowledge the Scottish side of our family. And so, it's only now, in my twilight years that I felt I should come, see the house that brought my mother so much love, and then so much heartache. And I rather hoped, in doing so, I could close that chapter of our history and move on, having met my family at least once before I returned home.'

'Bloody hell,' James said, sinking into the armchair. 'I need that drink.'

Kate handed James a tumbler of whisky and he drank. She sat on the arm of the chair and asked in disbelief, 'You're Constance's daughter?'

Marianne nodded and sipped her whisky as her husband spoke. 'We've been in Scotland a little while, touring the Highlands, visiting Edinburgh. We're making a real road trip of it. Having the time of our lives. Our friends think we're crazy. They're all about Florida these days but we just had to come. It might be the only time we make it. We're not spring chickens. I can still get about pretty well but long-haul travel is complicated when wheelchairs are involved.'

Marianne held Nicholas's hand lovingly and looked around. 'We were intending to simply drive here one day, just take a peek at Invermoray, a little look at the cottage, and then, if I had enough courage, I was going to knock at the door of the big house where my mother once lived and introduce myself. Everything that happened here was so long ago that I thought we might all get along like a house on fire and that it wouldn't really make a dent in your day.'

James opened his mouth like a codfish and then closed it again. Liz smiled as if she wasn't *quite* sure what was going on and Kate sipped her whisky as the fire finally got going in the fireplace. No one knew what to say next.

'It looks different to how I'd imagined,' Marianne said in the hushed silence.

'What does?' Kate asked kindly.

'The cottage. It's just how my mother described it, but then of course everything looks different in real life, doesn't it?'

'Yes,' Kate said, wondering why Constance had been describing an out-of-the-way ghillie's cottage from so long ago to her daughter. And then the penny dropped. 'Your mum was here, wasn't she?'

'Yes.' Marianne nodded.

'With the pilot?' Kate ventured slowly. 'The German pilot?'

'Wait? What?' James coughed on his whisky. 'Really?'

Marianne smiled sadly. 'Yes. She had promised she'd keep him safe and she kept her word, to the detriment of all else as it turned out. And then he was arrested anyway. That night changed everything. For everyone.'

'What happened?' Kate asked.

'She was thrown out,' Marianne said simply. 'They blamed her for her brother's death. Although it was an accident. A fight broke out between some young cad called Henry who'd been trying it on with her and then took umbrage against the fact she'd found happiness, although fleetingly, with another man. Douglas went into the water during a quarrel between them and he never came back out.'

'How horrible,' Liz said.

'Douglas's body is in the churchyard,' Kate said. 'I found his grave.'

Marianne mused. 'I shall go tomorrow and lay some flowers. My mother would be pleased I'd done that, I think. They loved each other deeply. They were the best of friends as well as siblings, she said. A crying shame it ended the awful way it did.'

'But, your mum,' Kate prompted, thinking of the pretty girl in the silver-grey dress, her name scrubbed from the family Bible. 'What happened to Constance in the end? I'm desperate to know. And what happened to the German pilot after he was arrested?'

CHAPTER 46

Gloucestershire, January 1948

Matthew sat on the rackety train, clutching his papers. He had been one of the last PoWs to be released that month. He marvelled at the British administration system that could legitimately keep hold of a German PoW three years after the war had ended. All who had encountered him had treated him with near animosity. His fellow German officers looked on him as an oddity and his incarceration alongside them had done nothing to dampen their resolve to dislike a German officer with a staunchly English accent, no matter how often he spoke their language or talked of Hamburg. Someone would always give him away as being *not one of us* and he'd be shunned. The prison guards had been kinder to his fellow prisoners than they had been to him. His English accent had been his undoing. And instead of beating him black and blue, which is what he'd assumed would happen, the guards treated him as if he was a spy who had been given far too lenient a punishment. Loneliness threatened to engulf him until he thought he would run mad.

He had watched prisoners come and go from the camp as the war years wore on, obtaining jobs on farms and falling in love, helping with harvests and being treated with kindness by their employers before they would be escorted back to the camp to sleep. Some even went to the pub and mixed with the locals after a day in the fields. As a German with an impeccable English accent, he had not been allowed such privileges. They thought he could escape undetected and never be seen again. And secretly, he agreed. Given half the chance he would have absconded, made his way back to Scotland, back to Invermoray. But Constance probably hated every fibre of his being. He had been the cause of her brother's death. He had been allowed to write letters but he assumed none would filter through to Invermoray House and so he decided not to write, wondering if he would do more harm to Constance than good.

So instead, he listened to the inmates' stories from his bunk at the end of the day, jealously hearing tales of the outside world. And he would think of Constance every day, until the pain of missing her hurt more than he thought it would, and he would fall asleep, desperate and lonely, and await the next day to begin in much the same way as the previous one.

And then the day had come when the prisoners were told the camp was disbanding. That they could no longer be held here or be considered prisoners of war, but alien citizens, allowed to live and work here, to marry if they so wished. They were invited to stay on, to help with the harvest, to settle here permanently. As the majority of the men around him thanked God that Britain wanted to rehome men who had once been considered the enemy, Matthew acquired the relevant documents and, eight years after he had last seen Constance, he made his way to Scotland to find the woman he loved.

Glasgow, February 1948

Constance folded the newspaper over and left it on the side table of the nurses' room for one of her friends to read next. Ten thousand German PoWs, almost but not quite the last lot to be released, had chosen to settle in England, she read. She could not believe it had taken so long to repatriate those who wanted to go, and process those who wanted to stay. They now had the right to live, work, and marry here. It had been such a long time since she had seen Matthew and she felt like an entirely different woman now.

She didn't know if Matthew was one of those who was still being held or if he had gone back to Hamburg, to his father and to put his short-lived affair with Constance from his mind. Would they even recognise each other, were they to meet now? She was almost thirty and if she carried on as diligently as she had been, she would be promoted to Matron soon. She thought of the Matron at Invermoray, who had caught Constance running out of the house the day she'd been banished, and had hastily written on a scrap of newspaper where she could enrol as a trainee nurse. Constance would have dearly liked to have known her name and to be able to send her a letter to thank her for an action that had undoubtedly saved her.

She had changed so much since those last days at Invermoray. Knowing Matthew had made her stronger, being removed from her family home had made her stronger. But still her heart hurt for the only man she had ever loved. She wondered if it had all been a dream. But he had told her he loved her and that after the war he would try to find her. She didn't know how he would do that now she wasn't at Invermoray, though, or even if he still wanted to find her.

Still, she thought, smoothing down her starchy uniform and adjusting her nurse's cap, she was a better person here than she'd ever been at Invermoray. But her heart had not changed. As the nurses around her fell madly in love with various doctors who came and went from the hospital, Constance knew it was Matthew who still claimed her heart; Matthew who she would never stop loving.

'You've got a nerve,' the elderly gardener said as Matthew stood in the rose garden and looked up at the house. He had walked from the village. The house looked changed, as if neglect had started to take hold almost the moment he'd been arrested, dragged away.

'I'm looking for—'

'I can guess who you're looking for,' he said with a wry smile. 'That floozy.'

Matthew's mouth dropped open. He couldn't be speaking about Constance so disrespectfully, surely.

'She's nae here,' the gardener continued. 'No one's here. Not anymore. Not really. They come and go. But for the most part they're at the London house. But her though, that strumpet, long gone. And not wi' them.'

Matthew gritted his teeth. 'Where is she?'

The gardener looked him up and down. 'She went to Glasgow to be a nurse. That's what I heard the medical staff whispering about here all those years back. But that was a long time ago. I don't know what happened to her after that.'

'And if you did, you wouldn't tell me?' Matthew guessed.

The gardener took his gloves off and wiped his brow with the back of his hand, looking at Matthew properly for the first time. 'Aye, I'd tell ye,' he said. 'It's nae your fault your pa was German.'

Matthew was shocked.

'Aye, we heard all about that,' the gardener said. 'Nae your fault you picked the losing side either,' he said. 'Not all you Germans are a bad lot, I'm sure. Still, I doubt I'd be saying that if you'd won.' He picked up his gloves and turned his back on Matthew to resume his work. 'Try your luck in Glasgow, pal. And if I were you, I wouldnae come back here again.'

Constance helped a mother and her newborn baby down the steps of the maternity hospital. The father was pushing a perambulator but the mother insisted on holding the baby. Constance had grown attached to the young woman, who had been in hospital with her baby for weeks after a tricky birth. But it was time for them to go home and Constance was pleased of the opportunity to say goodbye and send them into their new life as a family.

After the hell of watching Clydebank burn she had been only too happy to take up a midwifery position. She had seen enough death. It was new life that Constance focused on now. She had been offered transfer to a new mother and baby hospital but something had forced Constance to stay in Glasgow. She had moved only once in the time she'd left Invermoray.

She waved the mother and baby off and stood for a few moments, inhaling the fresh air. Her shift was almost at an end and then she might take herself off with the other nurses to see what was on at the pictures. She was sure Ralph Richardson was in something at the moment. But before that, she would write yet another letter to the Red Cross to enquire where Matthew was and hope this time she received a more positive reply than the one that had taken months to arrive last time. She had to find him, to know he had survived prison camp, if he had returned to Germany, and to ask him directly how he felt about her.

As the new mother and father turned the street corner, behind them a man, clutching a map and looking completely lost, squinted around him before turning back the way he had come. Constance's breath caught in her throat. For a fraction of a second she had seen him. Matthew. She paused. Was she going mad? She walked after him and then her pace quickened into a run. People began staring at the nurse who was sprinting along the street. Her hairpins came loose and her little cap fell but she didn't care; she carried on running until she reached the street corner.

The man, too, had sped up as a bus pulled into the bus stop ahead of him. He looked at the map in his hand and then up at the bus in confusion. He was going to board it, she was sure. Was it Matthew? It had looked like him; for the small amount of time she had seen him; older certainly, but him.

He put his foot on the back step of the bus and reached out

to the pole to swing himself in. There was nothing for it. He would be gone in seconds. At the top of her voice Constance shouted his name and the man turned his head, a frown on his face. He took his foot off the step. Constance gasped as she saw him fully. The emotion that she had been holding in for eight long years broke forth and she burst into tears. But even through the tears and the pedestrians winding round her on the busy street she could see him, she could see Matthew, after all these years, running towards her.

Her legs gave way and she reached out to steady herself against a brick wall, her palm chilled against the ice-cold brick. Tears streamed down her face, clouding her vision, and she raised her hand to wipe them with the cuff of her uniformed sleeve. But Matthew was in front of her in seconds, wiping her tears of joy with the sleeve of his frayed overcoat. He enveloped her as people bustled past them, paying them scant attention on the busy street.

'You came back.' She remembered the last time she'd seen Matthew. After he'd been wrenched from her on the shoreline, she had been locked into her bedroom and from the window she had seen him handcuffed, hours later, and taken away. His eyes had searched desperately for her but he never saw her, standing at her window as he was led towards the motorcar.

'I didn't think I was going to see you ever again,' she said.

'I know,' he said soothingly. 'I know.' Above her, he kissed the top of her head the way he used to. 'I've had to wait so long to find you but I'm here now.' He pulled back and looked into her eyes before she held him tightly again and murmured his name into his chest. 'I swear that nothing will force us apart again.'

EPILOGUE

2020

If Constance hadn't been thrown out, James's father wouldn't have inherited Invermoray. Kate would never have met James; and Marianne, Constance's daughter, would be running the house all those years later. One decision, one promise, could impinge on generations for decades; forcing people apart and bringing others together so many years later.

Marianne fell under the spell of the house and Liz's enthusiastic tour. She paused in front of the portrait of Constance at twenty-one and touched it delicately, tracing the line where the deliberate cut had been fixed as if she knew exactly what she was looking for. Liz offered to take it down, to give it to Marianne, but the Canadian had refused. 'It belongs here, alongside Douglas,' she said as she looked at the portrait of her uncle, the RAF officer who had died so suddenly, the night her mother and father had been ripped apart at the height of war and not reunited for almost a decade. 'I have pictures enough of my mother but if there's any photographs of Uncle Douglas knocking about, would you send them on to me?'

Liz agreed she would. 'And I have some of your grandparents,' she mentioned, but Marianne shook her head.

'No, thank you. My mother forgave them in the end. But I don't think I can. I'll let you keep those photographs.'

Liz touched Marianne's arm gently and Kate could see the two women forging the beginning of a friendship. Marianne didn't want the house; she was clear about that. She listened to her cousin James accidentally-on-purpose admit the roof had cost him £50,000. He'd been oddly specific about how much that was in Canadian dollars and Kate suspected he'd looked it up on their return to the house just to bring his point home. Kate laughed at Marianne's expression of horror. In some things James remained a complete mystery; and in others he could be so utterly transparent.

As the day drew to a close Kate could see him on the jetty, looking directly at the house where usually he looked down, concerned, into the water. His head was higher and he looked more at ease with himself and with his responsibilities than she'd seen him previously.

It was Kate's turn to bring wine. They'd forged a kind of evening ritual, while the weather had held, but the season had changed, and with it, them. If Kate left, she would miss it all. She would miss Angus and their yoga classes. She'd miss cosy dinners with Liz where she pretended to eat what Kate cooked. She'd miss the book clubs in their various factions with Morven and Kirsty. And she'd miss Jenny, because madly she was moving to Invermoray to be with Angus, to help him run the pub so Morven could spend more time with her children who she barely saw.

Only a few months ago Kate had wanted to be nomadic. But now she knew what she wanted. She thought of Constance, her life only truly beginning once she'd left Invermoray, and Kate's only just starting the moment she arrived. She wanted to be settled. She wanted to be here, and she wanted to be with James, only she knew she was going to have to be the brave one and open the discussion. He knew the reasons she'd left her last job and Jenny had said it was clear James liked Kate and yet, he'd said nothing at all to her about any of it. She clutched the bottle of wine tightly, nervously as if it was a shield.

'What do I have to do to convince you to stay?' he asked without turning round, the moment Kate's foot touched the wooden jetty. Kate smiled.

'We can afford you now,' he continued. 'The house is finally starting to make money. Have you seen the bookings diary? I'm struggling to keep up. I think I've double-booked some people. And I think we've priced Christmas week way too cheap because when I opened those days up they went within hours. You have to stay, if only to stop me messing up the admin. And have you seen the office? It's got even more paperwork on the floor than ever before.'

'You just want me here to keep an eye on your terrible filing system?' she asked with mock offence, sitting down next to him.

'No,' he said, taking the wine with a smile and starting to open it. But he changed his mind and put the wine down. 'No,' he said, raising his hands to hold her face gently and looking into her eyes as if he was examining them, seeing how she'd respond. 'I want you here because I want you here. I want you here because I don't want you anywhere else. I couldn't bear to think of you leaving. It may have escaped your notice – I thought the way I felt about you was pretty clear. But obviously not.

'Jenny told me what happened in your last job,' he continued. 'Why you left. And I don't want to be like that guy. I don't want to make your life hard or embarrass you or make you uncomfortable by hitting on you if you don't feel the same way. I'd hate myself if I made another move on you and it wasn't reciprocated. So I'm just going to ask you this once and then I'll never mention it again. Even if you don't feel how I feel, if you don't like me the way I like you, please don't leave. Please stay and continue working with me and Mum. And I promise it won't change anything. I promise I won't embarrass you and mention how I feel about you ever again.' He paused and then: 'Now is probably a good time to tell me how you feel. Now is probably the time to stop me making a complete and utter fool of my—'

Kate didn't wait for him to finish. Instead she leant forward and kissed him, folding into him as he wrapped his arms around her. In the heat of the moment he knocked the bottle of wine into the loch, but neither of them noticed. When they pulled apart he kissed her softly again and his face broke into a smile before he chuckled to himself in disbelief. 'Oh thank, God,' he murmured happily.

Somewhere down in the depths of the loch, there wasn't a monster. Instead, there was a German fighter plane. On the jetty above, James and Kate sat with their fingers entwined; their bodies curled into each other as they talked, interspersed with kisses until the sun disappeared behind the mountains. It cast a faint light over them as the moon began its ascent in the sky. Eventually they stood, James pulling her to her feet. Kate carried the unused wine glasses and James put his arm around her, holding her close as the air turned chilly. They walked around the shore towards the house, pausing at the entrance to the parterre.

James moved through the narrow arch first, but just before Kate followed she glanced back at the loch. What was it Angus had said? If there had been a monster, those who saw it were destined for a lifetime of happiness. Perhaps the fighter plane in the water did represent the same message of hope as a prehistoric creature. It had brought a forbidden love and eventual happiness where it was never supposed to have been found. Kate paused, watching the water. Out of the corner of her eye she thought she saw something large move just under the surface of the loch, before disappearing quietly into the depths below. *A lifetime of happiness.* Kate looked up at James as he exhaled audibly, his eyes fixed on the loch. He had seen it too. He looked down at her and smiled, before taking her hand in his as they walked towards the house.

Acknowledgements

I was lucky to have not one but two heroic editors for *The Forbidden Promise*. To the wonderful Rachel Faulkner-Willcocks, thank you for trusting me and taking me up on my offer to submit this, a completely different 'book 2' months after the agreed deadline. Thank you for your enthusiasm and for the outstanding work you did getting my debut *The Forgotten Village* into the Amazon Number 1 bestseller slot! For two weeks! And in the Top 100 for over four months. Unbelievable. You are a star.

To Tilda McDonald, aka the cavalry, thank you for attacking this manuscript with gusto and making all the characters feel just that little bit more likeable. Under your guidance I feel I've really grown as a writer and learnt so much in such a small amount of time. For that and for being super lovely: honestly, I can't thank you enough.

My fab agent Becky Ritchie is a wonderful champion for me and my work in Britain and beyond and I'm so chuffed she's in the background doing all the scary stuff I don't know how to do. Thank you for the big things, the little things and everything in between. Likewise, big thanks to Alexandra McNicoll and her brill team for finding overseas homes for my work.

My long-suffering husband Stephen, my parents and in-laws need the biggest of thanks as I regularly thrust the children and the pooch upon them so I can travel for work, write, or sit in the sunshine reading endless research books. I promise you all . . . I really am working.

To my gorgeous, clever, funny daughters, Emily and Alice:

thank you for being the shining lights you are, and taking it very much on the chin when Mummy has worked herself into a dopey stupor and reads bedtime stories a little bit wonkily because her eyes don't work at the end of the day!

To super PR Sabah and the entire Avon team, thanks for the continual support and huge thanks to Helena Newton whose forensic copyediting abilities are the icing on the bookish cake.

Thank you to my writing group, aka Write Club. Tea, sympathy and cake once a month is just the ticket.

As I write this, in September 2019, I am reeling in shock at having just won the Romantic Novelists' Association (RNA) Joan Hessayon Award for new writers for my debut novel *The Forgotten Village*. I've been on such a whirlwind journey since I started writing and it is with all the thanks in the world to the RNA and to Alison May, its Chair and reader of the original manuscript, for helping get my debut out into the world and then once it was there, believing in it enough to bestow upon it such an amazing accolade.

But it is you, the reader, who I need to give such, unending, appreciative thanks. Thank you for picking up *The Forbidden Promise* and buying it. I do so hope you enjoyed it! And if you are one of the many that pre-ordered *The Forbidden Promise* on the back of reading my debut, you have no idea how much you spurred me on while I wrote, edited and panicked over this novel.

If you enjoyed *The Forbidden Promise*, may I encourage you to leave a review on Amazon and/or Goodreads. Reviews are 'it', and go such a long way in helping an author's career and to introduce new readers to our work.

Come and find me online and say hello. I love hearing from readers and try to reply to everyone. Find me at:

www.lornacookauthor.com
Facebook: /LornaCookWriter
Instagram: /LornaCookAuthor
Twitter: @LornaCookAuthor

Don't miss Lorna Cook's #1 bestselling debut

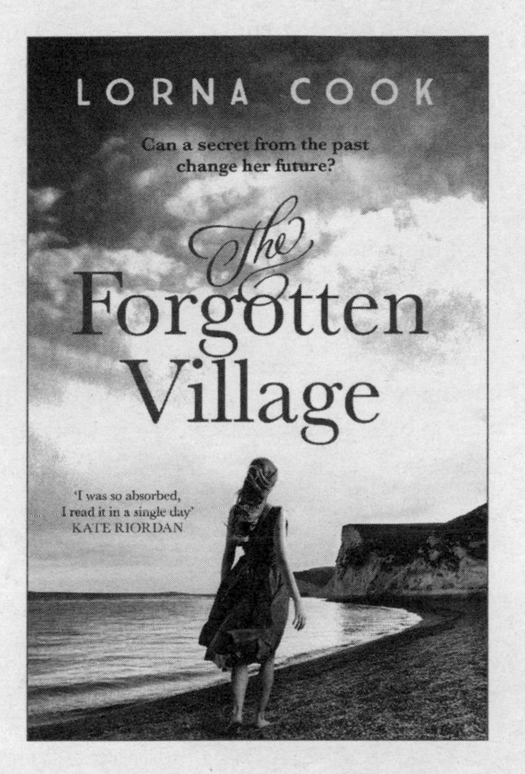

1943. The world is at war, and the villagers of Tyneham must leave their homes behind.

2018. A wartime photograph prompts a visitor to Tyneham to unravel the terrible truth behind one woman's disappearance . . .

Available now

Published in Canada as *The Forgotten Wife*